I0891615

Corvus Warchives

Death Song

By Gabriel Miller

7MNK

Corvus Warchives: Death Song
By Gabriel Miller

Zmok Books is an imprint of
Winged Hussar Publishing, LLC, 1525 Hulse Road, Unit 1, Point Pleasant, NJ 08742

PB ISBN 978-1-958872-86-4
EB ISBN 978-1-958872-88-8
Library of Congess 2025946486

Bibliographical references and index
1. Science Fiction 2. Space Opera 3. Action & Adventure

For more information on Winged Hussar Publishing, LLC, visit us at:
https://www.WHPSupplyroom.com
Instagram: WingedHussarPublishing
Facebook: Winged Hussar Publishing LLC

Death Song

By Gabriel Miller

Chronicles of the Human Sphere & Infinity Timeline:

N1

N2

Campaign Paradiso

N3

Uprising

- *Outrage*

Third Offensive

- *Downfall*
- *Team Zed*
- *By Fire and Sword*

Daedalus' Fall

- *Defiance*

N4

- *Betrayal*
- *Basilisk*

Raveneye

- *Aftermath*
- *Airaghardt*

Endsong

- *Death Song*

N5

Until we return,
I walk this road knowingly
singing the end, death.

Takeshi 'Neko' Oyama, 74 NC

i.

The chaos of conflict was no stranger to Takeshi Oyama. He let it wash over him like the storm that bombarded his power armor; eyes remaining locked on his sole opponent. He thought they looked like an iconic faceoff in a Maya film as they recovered their breath on the lonely, rain-slicked wharf. The downpour came so densely that he couldn't see beyond his immediate surroundings, slain comrades, and the masked warrior before him. The datasphere roared utter chaos while far-away hackers and technicians fought for control of the digital landscape. Takeshi's lens glitched as enemy hackers shut down tactical feeds from headquarters, causing the figure's silhouette—outlined in red—to briefly disappear into a curtain of torrential rain. His comms bled static, and coordination had long ago broken down. With the network spotty at best, Takeshi found himself isolated and alone in a world of violence and blood.

The pair stood, chests heaving in exertion. Takeshi Oyama, the noble Japanese warrior in bone white power armor, felt his chest heave in exertion as he faced his orange and black clad assailant. The markings on his foe's plate told Takeshi his desperate last stand was against an Imperial Agent.

Briefly taking stock of his surroundings, Takeshi's eyes caught his slain team and etched their names upon his soul. There was no victory here, despite having destroyed the drone launch and control facilities that were the objective of this mission. Perhaps a success, yes, but pyrrhic at best. A distracted memory tugged at the edge of his awareness as the words of Takeshi's mentor came unbidden.

One cut at a time, Takeshi-san: one fight, one strike, one mind.

He shook the rain from his face and the thoughts from his weary mind.

Focus.

A deep inhale brought the warrior back to the present once again, and the two warriors launched themselves at one another in their fifth exchange. Blades flashed in the early dawn gloom, a dozen moves flowed flawlessly from each warrior's mind to his heart to his blade as they met amidst the thunder. Each strike was punctuated by the whipcrack Double-Action discharge of his opponent's sword against his own razor sharp, teseum-edged blade before they parted once again.

Fighting to slow his breath—locking his eyes with his assailant—Takeshi's face set into a grim mask. Clearly a master at his craft, the impassively armored warrior stood a sword's reach away. With helmet destroyed and long gone, Takeshi struggled to keep both rain and his own brown hair from his eyes as the two circled once more.

The emotionless orange faceplate that stared back was cracked, chin to left ear. A near kill. The trickle of blood from beneath a compromised gorget told Takeshi he had struck true, if only off by millimeters. In the prolonged duel, it was the only blow he had landed. Meanwhile, Takeshi felt a searing pain in his right shoulder and thigh, despite his armor's attempts to heal them. His opposite had the luxury of arriving from the now destroyed armory fresh for the fight, even if hastily armored and skipping his robes of office in the process.

Taking stock of his own bloody injuries and compromised armor, a silent resignation washed over Takeshi, followed by a grim smile that crept slowly across his weary face. Newly developed drones had delivered Takeshi's team, sealed in their suits of armor, from a nearby submersible. Gripping the drone would have exhausted the Japanese warriors if not for their armor's magnetic locks. Even so, after the arduous undersea travel, the strain of this stealthy approach had worn him down before the fighting had even begun.

Welcoming death as a bitter old friend, he quickly activated the waiting detonation command in his comlog. On the far side of the island, a dozen submersible drones imploded beneath the surf. There was no going home now.

The pause in combat hung like an unearthly silence as more Yujingyu soldiers rushed to surround the wharf. With an unspoken consent, the two combatants collided once more and surrendered themselves to the blade song. Strike after strike they battled, searching for an advantage.

Seeing a fatal opening in the warrior's guard, Takeshi issued forth a perfect killing strike. Left foot forward, balanced across both hips, blade extended to meet the horizon. A flawless rising cut. Perfection. A lifetime of precision, practice, and skill arced his blade at his opponent's neck—but he was not there.

Impossibly fast, his opponent had sidestepped the strike, and Takeshi had only a desperate second to see the long dueling blade darting for his wrist. Weak between the plates, the armor of his sword arm parted like water beneath the oncoming blade. The double crack of kinetic energy was barely audible over the roar of blood in his ears. No amount of stims or narcotics pumped into his system by his armor could dull the pain. Losing his blade, vision white from pain, Takeshi clutched his nearly severed wrist to his chest as he stumbled forward. Will alone kept him on his feet.

His pain-blurred vision cleared as his armor's automated stim kit kept him standing, and Takeshi drew his second blade in his offhand.

He turned back to see his foe standing over the fallen katana, looking back and forth between Takeshi and the blade, until he settled on the samurai.

"Traitor."

The only word spoken in the entire exchange. Disgust and contempt rode a voice comfortable with authority as it rumbled through the face plate's damaged emitters. An orange boot rose and fell with the force of a power armored comet. Takeshi could only watch in horror as his blade snapped.

Takeshi charged, framed in the flare of lightning striking a nearby boat. If not for the thunder, both warriors might have heard the incoming ordnance.

ii.

Shattered glass formed a carpet of glittering crystals on the tiled floor, and the spiced scent of nutty liquor was carried away on the breeze. Unphased by the sultan's outburst, Yasbir studied the fallen pieces from behind his wrapped shemagh.

"My son. They took my son! Are you even listening?"

"Yes, Your Majesty. I am listening," Yasbir replied calmly while the sultan fumed. What he truly wanted to say was, '*Your son is not worth the death you would impulsively unleash, Your Majesty, but there are greater prizes to be had.'*

The sultan was not a patient man. He was among the more ruthless on Bourak. Yasbir knew if he hadn't been here, now, orders would already have been given: soldiers sent and fleets dispatched. Patience and planning would yield sweeter fruit, yet patience mattered especially little in the measure of one's own family.

Fortunately, Yasbir knew patience intimately.

Sultan Kerim Bey stood straight by the balcony, even in his rage and grief he was a rigid man, upright and solid. Long smart-silk robes draped his body. Beneath his short cropped hair, the sultan's eyes were impossible to ignore. Pale blue-silver irises ringed with hard black—like collapsing galaxies caught death.

Yasbir's order, the Hassassin Barham, was always seeking the pattern of things. Mankind was governed by their own patterns. No matter how advanced civilization had become in this spacefaring age, he already knew the shape of the pattern that unfolded before him.

No matter the man, no matter the offense. It was the same. Yasbir knew the pattern well.

Retribution. Retaliation. Revenge.

These would be the sultan's next demands—unfailingly—and he would have had them if not for Yasbir's timely arrival. The destructive urge to call for vengeance would cause a rift that would derail too much, and destroy much more. He could easily predict the conflict that would ensue—they could not allow such a thing to pass.

The sultan would get his son back—probably. But first, he would need to calm himself. Rage and wrath were blinders in the endless game of empires. Blinders that hid his true desire.

Rescue.

As ever, the volatile leader of the Funduq Sultanate must be guided, and at this moment, Yasbir was best suited to do it. He had subtly shepherded Sultan Bey for years, curbing the worst of his impulses.

Hot wind cut through the balcony, bearing the smells of the city to their rooftop—rich spices mingled a salty sea breeze. Yasbir waited. To no surprise, and no small amount of pride for the man who slowly guided from the shadows, the sultan took a moment and collected himself.

"My apologies, my friend. I forget myself."

"You are bereaved, Majesty. No amount of honeyed words will console a father at such news." Gesturing to the table, Yasbir continued as he rose, collecting his robes about his form. Simple robes that concealed an armored bodysuit beneath, bearing the instruments of his art. "The Consulate may speak words of unity and peace, but his gift can be taken as only one thing. It is a slight, Majesty, an offense. To a father, it is nothing short of outrage. To the powers within the StateEmpire, our Prince is a bargaining chip—not a person."

"The *nadhl* barely had the courage to deliver it himself. The ambassador claimed to have rescued Hasib. They know he is my only son. Keeping him safe—bah! A hostage. My son is a hostage. The survivors from his own guard swore it was the Yujingyu that took him and the thrice-damned, Silk-cursed worm denied it to my face!" Temper rising, the sultan took to bracing himself on the balcony. A sprawling metropolis stretched before him beneath Bourak's clear sky lit by a skyline of neon quantronic images dancing above the rooftops; a veritable paradise thanks to terraforming, the Silk trade, shrewd politics, and a bit of good geography.

Yasbir looked past all this and waited. His ever-seeking eyes moved beyond the raging father and tracked a small Hassassin drone that glided stealthily through the air, floating around the palace. It continued out of sight, following the pattern he had programmed minutes before he arrived at the sultan's side.

Silence hung as the sultan took the time he needed to control his grief. Giving him space, Yasbir returned to the table where the lacquered box sat alone.

The message was clear, yet never spoken. The precious box bore a gold leafed Imperial Seal of the Yu Jing StateEmpire. It was made with rare huanghuali wood and had been lacquered by hand. All this and more overlaid across his vision as his geist, the operating intelligence within his personal network, constantly analyzed his surroundings through hidden sensors embedded in his armor. The box bore such exquisite detail and craftsmanship that it was unlikely this operation came from anywhere but the highest echelons of Yu Jing leadership. He knew this already, the box merely confirmed his suspicions. Within, Prince Hasib's ring sat undisturbed on a bed of jade silk.

"Your Majesty, I have spoken at length with the few survivors of Hasib's guard. Their reports are consistent with what little uncorrupted footage we could scrape from the Circular's data banks. The prince was returning to us from his *holiday* on Aconticimento." It was more likely yet another hedonistic binge, Yasbir thought. "His route took him through Yujingyu space, and there, Imperial Agents stormed his suites. Only those Odalisques fortunate enough to be guarding his yacht were spared the slaughter, though their own fight was dire.

"As quickly as they arrived, they vanished. Security forces were entirely too slow to amount to any assistance. My master has contacted the clans loyal to Yu Jing to ascertain their involvement. There can be no other way, to my mind, that the assault on the prince's suite and the security system blackout happened so perfectly simultaneously and remained undetected.

"There are still some within their organizations that still hold deep respect for The Old Man and we of the Mountain—those who remember the price of war between us." Data from his own investigation scrolled across Yasbir's vision as his geist recalled the information almost instinctively. "The pattern fits."

"Yes, yes, patterns. Your precious patterns, with respect to you and your order, do not return my son to me."

"On the contrary, patterns are just the thing that shall return the prince into your embrace. You could well go to war with Yu Jing over this. It is a pattern—a nudge in the wrong direction." He paused to let the thought linger. Such a thing would be devastating to both sides, and both men knew it. "No one wishes such a thing. Someone in the StateEmpire ordered this offense, someone who knew the value of such a prisoner…

"So listen to me once more as a student to a teacher, Your Majesty, and let us speak of patterns. Let us speak of the Uprising." Yasbir watched the sultan's grief-stricken eyes focus. "Let us speak of the Japanese."

iii.

"Will they answer when called upon?" The Emperor asked aloud.

///Unknown. It is a risk, Tennō Heika*.///*

He pondered the response as it played across his lens. The tiny implant displayed the response privately for his vision alone. "My advisors deem it an unwise risk."

///They wisely see the danger. Danger to your great domain and to their own interests, Dono*.///*

The Emperor of Greater Independent Japan pondered that as he looked out over the Tokyo skyline. He knew the wiles of *his* court, and the limitations of his own power. "And what of you, my faithful friend? What do your eyes see?"

///Risk, Dono*—but also reward. There is much to be gained by such a visit to Kuraimori, and something precious to be protected. The honorable representative from Bourak knows only of the prince, but there is a greater bounty to reap, should you will it. The support he offers would be invaluable. The* kuge *know this also. Your subjects trapped on Shentang would bear the brunt of the StateEmpire's wrath.///*

A cold wind crept through the palace gardens where the Emperor of Japan knelt alone in his private gardens. He wore a beautifully embroidered silk kimono made of state-of-the-art materials that kept his thin frame warm in the breeze—in addition to the protections it offered against blades and small arms fire. His black hair was pulled high into a top knot, one of the many reborn traditions of his newly independent nation. He embodied their culture, the past preserved into the future. *He* was Japan.

"And the risks?"

///Some of may die, Tennō Heika*. They suffer under a jade boot, masked as peace and prosperity.///*

Soft green eyes set in a hard face contemplated a shrine before him, dedicated to fallen *bushi* and framed by juniper *bonsai* trees cultivated by his open hand. Before the beautiful stonework scrolled the names of the lost, hovering in the digital space before the cleverly concealed emitter. He was not ungrateful to those noble warriors who gave their lives to save him from the clutches of the StateEmpire. It was their duty to their Emperor, but such was the divine duty of all loyal Nipponese to their lord.

No matter how much power the wealthy *kuge* wielded in matters of law and finance, no one commanded the hearts and minds of his subjects as the Emperor did. That held its own power. One that could not be kept from him. A subtle smile crept across his face as he pondered the labyrinth of power.

"See it done."

///To do such a thing would require the use and possible loss of many resources. One must also consider the use of—and therefore exposure of—our precious hidden assets on Kuraimori well. The Mountain of Bourak has pledged its aid in such an action as well. Unusual for the Hassassin order, but such aid will speed us on our way to success. When it does succeed, the rewards may be great indeed. Should you will it, it will be done, Tennō Heika.*///*

"Show me."

Data scrolled across his augmented reality, visible in his lens. The Emperor smiled. This was sensitive information that many would kill for, friends and foes alike. It was information that many thought lost, buried, or destroyed. The *kuge* may keep much from him, but his loyal friend shared more than they could dream of in these silent moments. Much to gain indeed, and much to protect. It took him some time to parse through it all in the silence.

"See it through, as quietly as possible. Whatever you need, it is done." Stirring from his solitude, the Emperor barely noted the painstakingly detailed data had already begun removing itself from his personal network. Such was the way of his loyal servant. No footprints left in the sand. "Thank you, my faithful friend."

///Your will, Tennō Heika.*///* The connection ended.

His aides watched from the garden's entrance while the Emperor rose from his solitude and strolled contemplatively through his private sanctum. Traditional palace architecture rose up from the roots of a modern bastion below him. It was an impressive feat of contemporary engineering, but here on this rooftop retreat, Mount Fuji commanded his view. As they often did, the miracles of modernity paled in comparison to its snow-capped wonder.

The Emperor of Japan scanned his private garden. He saw no one—not that he expected to. As it had been for generations, this garden was kept and cultivated by the shadows he kept close. He left, trusting his word would be carried out. His faithful shadow had much to do.

1.

The docks of Sakuramachi were no place for the lone woman standing there in the pre-dawn hours. The once beautiful city, the heart of Nipponese culture in the Human Sphere, hardly looked like the place Mizu had known as a child. Signs of failed rebellion were wiped away after years of intense occupation, giving way to a neon skyline. Architectural wonders, rich with Japanese culture, were gone; and in their place, Yujingyu propaganda had molded the skyline into something modern, yet foreign. In Mizu's opinion, reconstruction had done the once splendid city no favors.

It felt wrong—alien. The city's revival was never meant for its own children. Its new face smiled only for the StateEmpire, a mask worn for their pride alone—a stage for their power, not a home for the Japanese who endured it.

Here, pinned against the unforgiving sea, the docks were still a place for the rough or the soon to be disappeared.

Salt air whispered through Mizu's fading blue hair as she stood in the open, arms crossed. The cold cut straight through the thin sweater she wore over a sleeveless shirt and a Boarding Pistol tucked in the waistband of her synth-leather pants. She briefly looked down at the old combat boots, visible in the neon glow of the city. They were in desperate need of replacement, but she couldn't quite bring herself to do it yet.

Loud, slurring laughter brought her attention back to the bars a few blocks away, and voices getting closer. Yujingyu occupation initially chose to leave many operating near labor centers: factories, docks, agricultural fields. A drunken population was a more pliable population—and at this hour, it was a common sight, like the duo of laborers that staggered out from a nearby access road.

The pair stumbled down the pier, not bothering to go home after a long shift and the solace of drink. Long work shifts were encouraged. Ever present propaganda twisted concepts of duty and honor into useful tools to the StateEmpire. Gone were the days of getting rounded up in labor gangs and shipped off to some unnamed camp, but the specter of it remained: a lingering fear in a society's subconscious. She shuddered at the thought.

The staggering pair noticed Mizu, and the cat calls began. "Hey p-pretty lady. What are you doing out here?"

"I think she is waiting fer us." Grins crossed both of their faces when she appeared to pay them no mind. Emboldened by spirits that they clearly over-imbibed, the strangers advanced.

The smell of cheap liquor beat them to her, and she could sympathize with that at least. The need to escape. The need to forget. Screams of memories—still raw—roared in the back of her mind. Some of the screams were her own.

Twenty meters, her geist pinged—counting down the distance.

Deep inside her, the shake hungered. It scratched at its cage, itching to be fed.

"I think you should move on." Mizu kept her voice flat, and ice-cold.

Her glitchy old combat geist began to bounce gleefully in the corner of her vision as it plotted out killing vectors, routes of escape, and every other detail that would give her an advantage. In their state, she wouldn't need any of that. Every movement of the men was telegraphed.

The shorter bald one favored his right leg, while the taller of the two held an arm close, as if nursing a recent injury. Information scrolled across Mizu's vision while she waited. Each had a utility knife, outlined in red by her geist, on their belts; not a combat weapon per se, but deadly enough in a brawl. If either reached for their cutter, this could get messy fast. Thankfully, neither seemed aware enough to even ponder it yet. Regardless, the shake crawled in her gut.

"Oh… She's a fresh one, Benji. You know I like them feisty!" Ten meters.

///I don't know, Hando.///

Her geist read through Benji's muttered response and displayed it across her lens. Augmented reality certainly had its perks…

"Not tonight, boys. I'm meeting someone. You should listen to Benji, Hando."

"You know her, Benji?"

///No.///

Five meters.

At this point, Mizu knew everything that she needed. Her scan showed neither man had much of a quantronic presence on them, beyond the usual mandatory identification halo and personal comlog. Hando would be the biggest threat, she decided—broad framed, a head taller than her, and his exposed arms suggested he was easily twice as strong as her.

Dealing with low-tech combatants was always more difficult, ruling out a quick hack and incapacitation. What she would give for a proper non-lethal weapon for times like these; her Boarding Pistol wouldn't do. Weapons of any kind were hard to come by when you lived under the heel of the StateEmpire. Her options limited, Mizu needed to choose between her preciously low ammunition or fists.

"Come here, sweetheart. Don't you wanna have a good time?"

///I don't like this, we should go, Hando./// Still muttering, Benji held back.

One meter.

Slagg it.

"I like your hair. Blue is my favorite—"

Before Hando's hand connected with her short cropped hair, Mizu exploded into action. Right hand batting away the unwelcome grope, she twisted inside his reach to land the heel of her left palm into the man's nose. Before he was done recoiling from the broken nose, Mizu was behind him and kicked his leg out. She didn't have the leverage to break it, but her boot connected with enough force to drop the man and eliminate his height advantage. A swift elbow to the temple staggered him.

Benji lunged in protectively as his friend fell and was rewarded for it with a reinforced boot to the knee he had been favoring just moments before. The audible crack of the impact was only partially that of her boot, and Benji's screaming face bounced off the pier as he collapsed.

Hando staggered to his feet, going for his blade as he put some distance between himself and the woman a full head shorter than him. Despite his best effort and the adrenaline, he was still unsteady on his feet.

"Kuso," Mizu muttered to herself as the shake ground in her gut. This needed to end quickly. The shake disagreed.

"I warned you. I told you to move on." Mizu's voice was practically a growl.

Stepping over a whimpering Benji, Mizu made a show of angrily pulling off her sweater and tossing it to the ground. A quick glance at the Boarding Pistol tucked into her belt and the subtly moving dragon tattoos on her arms was all the drunken idiot needed to come to his senses. Adrenaline and fear carried him limping into the night, abandoning his friend.

"Going so soon?!" She knew it was a pointless taunt, but it felt good. Mizu looked down at Benji. "You need better friends."

Benji clutched his shattered knee, still whimpering, while blood poured from his nose. Mizu squatted down next to him, lowering her voice to a threatening whisper.

"No screaming, Benji-boy."

A vigorous nod showed his senses were still mostly intact.

"I've got some business to do. You don't want me to miss my appointment, do you?" Mizu collected her sweater.

More nods.

"Good boy. Stay put. I'll be right back."

* * * * *

"It's a good day to be alive, isn't it?" The voice came from behind a crate as she waited near the pier's end. One lonely fishing boat sat docked in the quiet industrial yard. Slowly, a figure emerged from the pre-dawn gloom.

"I don't think I'll die today." Mizu's nerves were still frayed from the fight or the shake. It was likely both. She waited. Her hand hovered close to where her gun was hidden at her waist.

This was the most dangerous moment of any exchange. She never let anyone in her crew carry this risk for her. If the voice in the darkness was not the man she meant to meet, it could spell a long night in an interrogation cell—or worse.

"Perhaps not today, then. Thank you, Mizu, my love." Tanto approached her and extended his right hand to shake, leaving the left in his pocket. "As professional as ever, and as entrancing as moonlight. You will make me fall in love all over again if you don't take care."

"It's hard to feel the love when I know the hand in your pocket is holding a gun, Tanto." Mizu waited firmly in place until he threw his hands up in mock surrender.

Tanto, as she knew him, was a short man of the usual mixed heritage found throughout the Human Sphere. Heavy brows knitted together, giving his dark skinned face the sense of a perpetual scowl that Mizu found amusing in its direct contrast to the rest of his joyful features. A thin attempt at a beard did nothing to hide his rounded face that matched his slightly wider mid-line.

The coded call and response had been her idea in the early days of this business, a left over habit from the war. After the Yujingyu army staked its flag into the heart of Kuraimori for having the audacity to want to chart their own future, trust was thin, even with those who had helped each other through it all. Quantronic clearances and codes were more efficient, more secure, but not everyone she did business with had a secure comlog.

"Is everything okay back there?" Clearly Tanto had seen the fight.

"Yeah, nothing I can't handle." She changed the subject. "Are you ever going to shave that ridiculous beard, Tanto?"

"It is my best feature! You wound me, Mizu." His odd accent, unplaceable and wandering, became even thicker with feigned hurt before a grin took over, transforming into the cherubic face she was used to. "Alas, it was never meant to be between us, Mizu. I would only break your heart. My first love is the sea, always and forever."

The two continued to banter as they approached Tanto's boat. It was an unmarked fishing vessel that should never survive the rough seas of Shentang, let alone pass unnoticed by the drone-net that surrounded the isolated island. Yet for as long as Mizu had been making this run, Tanto always arrived in his simple fishing boat, always with fresh catch piled as high as it could be in the hold. Trolling nets bundled haphazardly across the deck made her wonder, not for the first time, how he managed to accomplish anything without breaking his neck on the rough seas. It also reminded her of a rumor.

Mizu's network was limited these days, but she still heard things. The Kempeitai once operated an extensive clandestine network throughout the planet. In the years since the failed rebellion, cells had been eliminated by Yujingyu forces or simply gone dark. With backing from Greater Independent Japan, the subversive agents had prosecuted their war of vengeance in the shadows, partnering with anyone with a grudge against the Yu Jing Empire, Mizu and her crew included. With support from PanOceania, it was easy days when the Uprising began. Supplies and able bodies had been plentiful back then. Mizu had participated in more than her fair share, along with the rest of the Third Hand, and Tanto had been present since the beginning, bending between the world of the criminal and the clandestine. These days, his shipments included fewer weapons and catered more to the needs of the underworld. But once, she had heard they had included people.

"I heard a rumor recently." She paused to see his reaction.

"Oh?"

"Have you ever met the Emperor?"

"Mizu, my love to-never-be, I simply cannot say." The sly smile that crept into the man's face took Mizu off guard. Had this silly man actually met the Emperor? In his flight from Kuraimori, it was rumored the Emperor had been smuggled off the island, and if what she had heard was true, she wondered if Tanto had been the one to do it.

The thought of fleeing the island crossed everyone's mind from time to time. Staring out at the open sea as dawn crept in, her own shame rose as she dared to think of abandoning everyone herself. Shaking her head, she focused on the business at hand. As long as her crew was here, she would be too.

"What have you got for me?"

"Why, everything you asked for, my lady in the dawn. Always and forever."

An idea began to form. "Do you happen to have a MediKit? A personal favor."

After a puzzling look turned to understanding, Tanto grinned once again. "For you, my sunlight, anything."

Mizu looked toward the cargo hatch of the small vessel, and a grin spread across her face. "Actually, Tanto, I have an even better idea."

Working quickly, the pair offloaded several crates of 'fish,' that would get them both arrested or killed if more than a cursory inspection was done, onto a rolling pallet also provided by the smuggler. Tanto followed along as she journeyed back up the pier.

Benji was right where she had left him. Whether it was from the alcohol or the pain of his injuries, he was snoring in a fetal position, still clutching his injured leg. Her geist popped its silly little avatar back up, laughing at the man.

A quick scan revealed a very familiar story. The StateEmpire mandated certain details be visible in one's personal network. The 'halo' was a quick means of identification to anyone that scanned them. Failure to comply was swiftly punished—publicly. The Nipponese citizenry were laid bare, an open book for agents of the Imperial Service to read at their whims… or a particularly resourceful criminal like Mizu.

Mizu read off Benji's quantronic aura, and it was an all too common tale of woe.

///Benjiro Tanigawa. Conscript, labor, manual, Sakuramachi, Suda Industrial Co. Skills: cargo vehicle operator, manual labor. Work permit: 74839217(A). Next of kin: Yui Tanigawa (Relation: Grandmother. Location: Nogoyu).///

"What do you think? Can you use him?"

"I could always use a hand for hauling in the catch, if I'm honest, but new hands on the boat are always risky. Some don't make it." Tanto's half-truths were probably the most honest shot the unconscious man had.

"I'm willing to accept that."

"Is he?"

"Let's find out. I brought something for you, Benji-boy." Not bothering to wait for a response, Mizu knelt directly on the man's chest and jammed the injector Tanto had given her in the drunkard's neck.

Benji's eyes shot open as tiny needles punctured his skin and flooded his system with Silk-laced meds and the best medical nanotech in the Human Sphere. He shuddered wildly, feeling more wealth flood his veins than he would ever see. Serum hypercharged his immune system and purged his veins of more than just the night's booze while the nanites knitted back injuries he had long thought beyond hope.

Mizu shifted the man's broken nose back into place with the second audible crack of the night, lest it heal itself into that position for good. Benji might think she was ruthless, but she wouldn't let him think she was heartless.

Benji stammered, but before he could get a sound out, Mizu shoved a rag in his mouth. Despite the muffle, the scream was still impressive.

"He has some lungs on him." Tanto chuckled while Mizu held Benji down.

"*Kuso*, shut up! That, Benji-boy, was a mil-grade Serum injection. You can thank him." She thumbed toward Tanto. "You are gonna feel like a billion Yuan, but the shakedown is frankly gonna suck."

She took her knee off Benji's chest, giving the man room to move. He tested out his leg, then rose with a nimbleness she was willing to bet he hadn't seen since a long lost youth. He moved to remove the rag from his mouth but stopped, waiting for permission.

"Go ahead, I'm sure it tastes terrible. Sun's coming up, Benji-boy, but I'm afraid you won't be making your shift. Can't have you spreading tales of a beautiful, yet mysterious woman on the docks. Consider yourself reassigned." She would have to track down and deal with Hando sooner than later, before his fear abated and he started to spread tales of the very same beautiful, yet mysterious woman.

Just another body in the bay, another weight on her soul.

A shroud of fear fell across Benji's face once again. He removed the rag. "What? I wouldn't…"

"I'd like you to meet my friend." Mizu cut him off. With an offered hand, Mizu helped Benji up and stepped aside so that Tanto could be clearly visible. Somehow, in the dawn light, Tanto managed to make a friendly smile seem threatening. "Lots of water today, and don't forget, you owe me two."

"Two? I don't understand." As his voice failed him, Mizu watched something between regret, confusion, and amazement war for control of Benji's face as he tested his weight on his healed knee.

"One for the patch up. One for letting you keep your hand." Deadpan and dead serious, Mizu pulled her sweater on once more.

"*Kuso*." Benji's senses had returned enough to recognize the change of fortune the marks on her skin meant for him. He chose wisely and bowed deeply, awkward and unpracticed.

"Language, Benji."

"Yes, ma'am. What do I call you?"

Mizu considered as she walked back to the cart Tanto had given her. "'Boss' will do just fine, but don't worry, you won't be calling me. Benji-boy, meet Tanto. Tanto, Benji."

Without a second glance at Benji-boy, Mizu pushed her cargo pallet toward the waking city as Tanto took Benji by the shoulders.

"You don't get seasick do you?"

2.

The pause in combat hung like an unearthly silence as more Yujingyu soldiers rushed to surround the wharf. With an unspoken consent, the two combatants collided once more and surrendered themselves to the blade song. Strike after strike they battled. Two masters, each searching for an advantage.

Seeing a fatal opening in the warrior's guard, Takeshi issued forth a perfect killing strike. Left foot forward, balanced across both hips, blade extended to meet the horizon. A flawless rising cut. Perfection. A lifetime of precision, practice, and skill arced his blade at his opponent's neck—but he was not there.

His opponent had sidestepped the strike, and Takeshi had only a desperate second to see the long dueling blade darting for his wrist. Weak between the plates, the armor of his sword arm parted like water beneath the oncoming blade. The double crack of kinetic energy was barely audible over the roar of blood in his ears. No amount of stims or narcotics pumped into his system by his armor could dull the pain. Losing his blade, vision white from pain, Takeshi clutched his nearly severed wrist to his chest as he stumbled forward. Will alone kept him on his feet.

His pain-blurred vision cleared as his armor's automated stim kit kept him standing, and Takeshi drew his second blade in his offhand.

He turned back to see the Imperial Agent standing over his fallen katana, looking at the blade. The warrior looked back and forth between Takeshi and the blade.

"Traitor."

The only word spoken in the entire exchange. Disgust and contempt rode a voice comfortable with authority as it rumbled through the face plate's damaged emitters. An orange boot rose and fell with the force of a power armored comet. Takeshi could only watch in horror as his blade snapped.

Takeshi charged, framed in the flare of lightning striking a nearby boat. If not for the thunder, both warriors might have heard the incoming ordnance.

"Stop."

Frozen in time, the splintered pier hung motionless, caught in the act of destruction. The explosive force was a visible wave rippling mere feet away from the combatants. Takeshi Oyama moved through the projection, dressed in the traditionally styled training garb of the sword school. He stood, brown hair untouched by the hanging droplets of rain or flying shrapnel. His left hand rested on the solitary, surviving blade at his hip. He worked his sharp jaw in contemplation and ran a hand through his styled but shaggy brown hair.

"Play back, one quarter speed."

The projection was a composite of satellite imagery, hacked cams, and quantronic sensors. His own armor's records added to the realism, copying the tactical data he saw into his implanted lens. The scene moved forward at a crawl, and Takeshi watched the reconstructed recording as his opponent was consumed by fire and wrath. A victory, but there was no satisfaction for the neo-*bushi.*

"Damn."

///Command: /Damn/ - Error. Command not recognized, would you like a list of available commands?///

"No. Rewind to marker seven. Replay." His geist's command prompt dismissed from his lens's display as Takeshi watched as the scene rewind.

"Traitor." Disgust and contempt rode the authoritative voice as it rumbled through the face plate's emitters. An orange boot rose and fell with the force of a power armored meteor…

"Stop. Replay marker seven."

"Traitor." Disgust and contempt rode the authoritative voice as it rumbled through the face plate's emitters. The boot rose and fell with the force of a…

"Stop." Stepping closer to the projected holo recording to study his foe, Takeshi absorbed every detail.

The near perfect projected reality showed the Yujingyu warrior in achingly fine detail. No identifying markings beyond the make and signs of care on the armor. Skipping the ceremonial portions of armor was common for those rapidly responding to lightning raids such as this. The element of surprise prevented most from armoring at all, though this one had chosen to take the time to don his heavier armor, opting for protection over speed of engagement. Intelligence had not revealed the presence of heavy armor assets on the island.

"End playback." The soft voice echoed from the back of the training holosuite Takeshi had thought empty. "Lights."

The frozen scene fell away, dissolving to the floor, falling away like so much digital sand to reveal a figure he had most certainly not expected.

"*Kensei*!" Takeshi turned to face his mentor and dropped into a deep bow, as was befitting his honored master. "I was not aware you had returned."

A seemingly unremarkable older man in a simple black kimono and grey hakama strode to the center of the room. As he had many times before, he returned Takeshi's bow with far more respect than the younger warrior felt he deserved. The improved human baseline of the new century made the pains of aging a thing of the past for most humans, yet here he stood. Though, only a fool would think him weaker with age; many students had learned that lesson over the decades. Subtle hints of age had been cleverly sculpted across his master's frame. Flawless smart fabric, sewn into Edo period inspired garb, draped across his taught frame. A pair of masterwrought blades rested on his hip. Beneath a wiry gray topknot, a face that seemed both young and old regarded Takeshi.

Everything about *Kensei* Minato Hayachi was artistry at work. His movements, his bladework, even his appearance was seemingly torn from a twentieth century samurai film: deliberately chosen, designed to look older, wiser. Many had fallen for the deception over the years, both friend and foe. To assume Minato-sama was lesser or enfeebled in any way was to have already lost. A general in his earlier career, and now one of the most legendary swordsmen of his era, he was named 'Sword Saint' by the Emperor himself.

The title of *kensei* was not bestowed often, or lightly. Not since Chiba Shūsaku, in the 1900s had the honor been given. The Aleph recreation of *Kensei* Miyamoto Mushashi—for entertainment in Aristeia! fighting circuits no less—had caused no small amount of stir.

A living *kensei* and a recreated one, the two sword saints had met blades only once. It was a private affair, with only the Emperor in attendance. Rumors swirled as to who won, arguing who was truly the better swordsman. Neither would say.

It was hard to believe the man Takeshi knew as *kensei* could be defeated by the AI recreation. Few had even struck Miyamoto-san in practice bouts. Takeshi could claim that honor only once in the decades he had known the man. He had never laid a blade upon his own mentor—he had never even come close.

With the projectors off, both warriors rose in unison. Takeshi noted that they two looked like a scene pulled from an antique film. Tatami mats and traditional wood-paneled walls surrounded them. They merely hid the trappings of modernity throughout the space while the two warriors stood in the center of the room.

"You are recovering well, Takeshi-san."

"*Hai*. I am fortunate."

The older warrior waited patiently for his student to continue.

"Our intelligence was horribly wrong—again. I become frustrated with the StateEmpire moving to thwart our every move."

"Indeed. I grieve for the loss of your team, Takeshi-san. I was briefed on my return flight. At this moment, I am more concerned with your recovery, and grateful that it has been better than expected. I am told it was a very near thing to have kept your hand. While it could be replaced, the blade knows the hand that wields it. It would seem your luck holds, Neko."

A grimace came unbidden to Takeshi's face at his mentor's last word. He had heard the nickname circulating for several years. He hated it. Fate may have spared him the embrace of death, but making light of the loss of life that came with each one of his miraculous survivals always sat ill with him. So many died, yet he kept living.

"*Hai*, Master." Distaste visibly crossed his face.

"The name still sits ill with you, then."

"It does."

"Takeshi-san, *bushi* to your core and leader amongst your comrades, no less. A commander as much as a combatant. Your legend is already outstriping you, already growing faster than you have risen through the ranks. Most can only aspire to become legends in death, yet death seems to have no want of you. You must live with your legend. I can promise it is a heavy burden, but one that continues to inspire others as you continue on this path." The old master's brow furrowed in memory and contemplation.

"Shall we train, Master?" Takeshi, wanting to do anything other than talk about his own fame, gestured to the waiting rack of wooden training weapons he himself had not dared touch since his return.

"Walk with me, Takeshi-san. Let us enjoy what remains of the day given to us. We will train tomorrow."

"As you say, Master."

The *kensei* led the way to the entrance where traditionally fashioned *shoji* doors slid into the walls on their own. Their hyperlight synthetic materials, brought about by the technological revolutions of the era, barely made a sound as they retracted on their own.

Takeshi fell in behind his mentor as he had many times before. Exiting the building brought them both back into the cooler autumn air. Perfectly cultivated trees, painted in vibrant autumn reds and oranges, greeted them as they left the training hall. Like the interior of the building behind them, each and every visible architecture could be taken from an ancient painting; each one painstakingly recreated with all the trappings of modernity present, but carefully hidden.

With a glance across the space, Takeshi's lens recorded his view and archived it to sort through later. Whenever he was deployed, he took great comfort in using these images to remind him of home.

Nearby, the shouts of instructors were echoed in chorus by their students. Without looking, Takeshi Oyama knew the scene by heart. Behind the trees would be a packed clay training area. Within, the students would be standing precisely two meters apart, wielding training blades. They would be repeating the instructor word for word and mirroring his movements as he moved through form four. A high guard, effective for quick and powerful downward strikes, but it exposed the legs.

Takeshi smiled at the sights and sounds of his chosen home.

Mount Gassan towering to the north and Tsukiyama Lake to the south, the training complex was situated in a picturesque, if less populous, area of central Japan. While most of the technology was cleverly hidden, to keep from distracting students from their rigorous training, his eyes were drawn to a transport craft being guided in by holographic lights to land at nearby hanger facilities. It was a jarring contradiction, but it served as a simple and subtle reminder of the day and age they lived in.

Takeshi kept his silence along the trail, as was their habit on these walks. *Kensei* Hayachi was many things to many people: mentor, teacher, advisor, friend, even an idol to some. One thing he was not, was willing to repeat or explain himself to his students. Even ones as close as Takeshi had become.

On these walks, one remained silent. Without fail, a walk with the legendary swordmaster would mean a lesson at its end. Listening for words from his master, while enjoying the peace and serenity of the grounds, one could almost forget that here, men and women trained for the grist mill of war. Those very same warriors gawked in awe of the pair walking by before being corralled by their instructors.

To Takeshi's surprise, their leisurely stroll through the gardens and training yards brought them to an isolated building at the edge of the grounds. Worshipped long ago, several ancient shrines to the mountain spirits were preserved inside. Some had been painstakingly restored while others wholly recreated in an effort to preserve the cultural identity of the region. Each and every student was expected to memorize the layout of the entire grounds complex, so it was not unknown to Takeshi, but he had certainly not spent much time inside.

"I have enjoyed our walk, Takeshi-san, but here I must leave you. Inside you will find someone I would like you to meet."

"I... *Hai*." Takeshi's faith in his mentor was absolute, despite his surprise.

"He is a friend, and I trust you will treat him as such."

"Of course, Master."

With a bow, knowing better than to ask further questions, Takeshi turned his attention to the isolated shrine building. Removing his sandals after only a moment's hesitation—an old custom still held on these grounds—he boldly stepped in. It was a dark space, with air that hung thick with incense. Rich wood and earth smells cut through the incense spice, bringing Takeshi back to earlier days spent in contemplation of war before harsh instructors.

A double clap of a prayer's end brought Takeshi's focus sharply to the only soul sharing the sanctum. Rising from his knees with the grace of a lifetime of practice, a man carrying wooden prayer beads clasped in one hand turned to face him with a smile. An unremarkable face sat above a thin frame clad in simple, unremarkable robes of blue, rough spun wool.

"It is an honor to meet you, Takeshi-sama. I am called Nakama." The voice, soft as silk, was quiet but nonetheless assured. The monk bowed his shorn head as Takeshi bowed in kind. "Minato-sama speaks highly of you. It is not often he speaks so singularly of one pupil."

"The *kensei* is most generous in his opinion of me, Nakama-sama."

The monk held up a palm in objection. "Just Nakama, please."

"As you say."

Ordinarily, a digital handshake between their personal networks would have already occurred. Especially within the military hierarchy, it would give Takeshi a wealth of information about his conversation partner. The top left window displayed in his lens remained empty, giving only blank boxes where a picture and biographical information should be. It seemed to Takeshi that Nakama had paused, knowing Takeshi would be processing this… absence before replying. He wasn't sure what unsettled him more.

"The trappings of duty. You understand."

"As you say." Takeshi's absolute trust of his teacher and mentor warred with an odd confusion of the peculiar man before him. Utterly forgettable and, well… bland was the only description that Takeshi could summon to mind. The man bore no scars or identifying markers to set him apart. Nakama's face presented the most ordinary features of an ethnically Nipponese citizen. It was unnerving how easily the man's soft demeanor disarmed Takeshi.

The fatherly smile on Nakama's unremarkable face never faltered or belied any alternate agenda beyond genuine interest in the warrior before him. "I am told you are fit for duty again."

"I have been released for duty, *hai*. May I ask how you are aware of such things?"

"The trappings of responsibility, Takeshi-sama."

The obtuse answer bothered Takeshi at a visceral level. He pressed the issue. "Do you hold a military rank, Nakama? Or will you simply reply, 'the trappings of duty' again?"

"My apologies, Takeshi-sama. I mean you no insult, I assure you." Hands up in a peaceful gesture, the unfaltering smile remained. "I bear no ill intent. I am a curious soul. I hear of you and I wonder… What does this man who has faced his own death so many times look like? What art does he create? What songs does he sing? I simply wished to meet the man I have heard so much about. Your master has been kind enough to indulge me in this."

"I do not feel my near scrapes with death and the loss of my comrades are things to be lauded."

"Lauded? No, that is for scholars, historians, and maybe even artists, Takeshi-sama. For a man so surrounded by death such as you, it is a thing to be respected, honored, and feared."

"Feared." A deep sigh of escaping truth left Takeshi's lips. The strange monk waited patiently for him to continue. In a courtly world of stoicism and hidden meanings, something about Nakama's forthrightness compelled Takeshi to answer before he knew it.

Unbidden, Takeshi continued. "It is certainly a thing to be feared. I seem to bring death upon those who fight beside me. No matter how I try to save them, the end is the same, and I feel the weight of every loss." Struggling through the admission, a world of weight rested on his shoulders. "I—"

The words caught in his throat. Why was he being so open with this man? A quick digital check of his own vitals showed no abnormalities. No traces of intoxicants detected, or anything else untoward for that matter.

"Please, speak freely, Takeshi-sama."

Trusting in the *kensei's* intent, Takeshi did just that.

"I do not think I am fit for duty, no matter the doctor's assessment. All I see are ghosts. I hear their screams and wonder why I live when so many do not. My blade has been broken, and so my honor with it—No." Frustration finally broke through the unexpected forthrightness. "I do not wish to continue this conversation, Nakama. I dishonor the fallen and myself."

With that, he turned to leave as Nakama's heavy sigh broke the silence.

"Your burden is real, Domaru Takeshi Oyama," his words stopped Takeshi in his tracks, "but you cannot hide from it. Fate has marked you to live, and so you live. We all play our part in the tales they will one day tell. The ancient Norse called it writing one's own saga—such a true thing, the name saga. It fits. In those sagas, not everyone survives to the ending of things, but some do, and must learn to live again.

"I offer you this truth as a gift, Takeshi-sama. One learned from many lifetimes of witnessing the worst of the struggles in the hearts of men. As warriors, we all sing a song of death, a saga, in our own way as we fight for our people and their freedom. Our only duty to death is to sing of it with a smile on our lips. We must not fear death, but embrace it. Welcome it as an old friend. To die with light and laughter on your lips is the greatest victory. No foe can take that from you, no matter how hard they try. Embracing death is a warrior's way, not just when it finds us, but especially when it eludes us. When you do find it, die with a smile on your lips."

His words hung thicker than the incense in the air between the two men.

"You will receive an—" Nakama lingered, considering his words. "—opportunity soon. I encourage you to give it serious consideration. I thank you for your time, Takeshi-sama."

Caught off guard by Nakama's sudden pronouncement, Takeshi turned to respond quickly as the monk began to leave.

"You claim no rank yet speak as a warrior. I have not seen you in the training circle here, nor at another school, war room, or field of battle."

Takeshi watched as the monk paused for an eternal moment and responded over his shoulder. "I will pray for you Takeshi-sama."

With that, Nakama was gone, and Takeshi found himself alone within the shrine with his long hidden guilt and faces of the lost as his only company.

* * * * *

Takeshi stood in the gardens outside the small shrine, frozen in contemplation, as night crept in. Minato-sama had departed during his conversation with Nakama, of whom there was no sign upon Takeshi's own exit but moments later. Talking to the strange monk had brought unbidden thoughts and fears Takeshi dared to entertain only in the darkest corners of his mind, and he mentally chastised himself for spewing such secrets out in the open.

Now, his solitude in the cool evening air only served to amplify the pain of his admission. Years of honor-bound tradition and training warred against the truth in his heart. War was his craft. It was his honor to serve on the frontline as he did. Yet the weight of survival when so many others had fallen serving with or under him… Takeshi could not shake the image of Atlas, carrying the world upon his shoulders, but the face was his own; the world made of slain friends, comrades. Now he carried the same of his blade being sundered as well.

The neon glow of holographic landing lights that lanced up hundreds of feet from the transportation depot served only as a gleeful, mocking contrast to his dour mood. The darkness of the garden suited him more than the lights of the military complex. A few quick gestures and Takeshi's personal network went dormant, shutting out the quantronic landing markers, leaving him truly alone in the small garden.

After aimlessly wandering, Takeshi found himself astride a rock outcropping looking down on the cultivated garden of the central space. In white sand, the sun-shaped seal of his nation, Great Japan, sat in its center. Stones, carefully cultivated bushes, and more pure white sand sculpted the mosaic of the Human Sphere. It artfully highlighted the scattered Nipponese colonies. Some stood strong, some were lost, but all were represented. Together they lovingly illustrated the interwoven story of far flung colonies. It was the heart and soul of the Japanese people, crafted in sand.

Takeshi knew personally the hardships faced on several of those planets by the Japanese, having served on several of them. His eyes strayed to the outline of Shentang and the island of Kuraimori. Once the jewel of Japanese society now conquered, now occupied by the Yu Jing army. The black sand of its shape felt appropriate with the number of lives lost and dreams destroyed there.

Takeshi walked away from the mosaic and into the growing shadows. Darkness enfolded him as the night sky overtook the horizon, leaving him to his equally dark thoughts.

3.

Mornings in Sakuramachi were beautiful once. The city was the jewel of the Nipponese peoples, if not a little cramped for Mizu's tastes. The city *was* an architectural marvel. Efficiency was built into every facet of the metropolis, from the sprawling landscape of skyscraping buildings at its core, to the suburbs that fed its workforce. Public transit allowed anyone to go anywhere, with ease.

That was before. Now that it was rebuilt in Yu Jing's image, it felt foreign. Mizu could barely remember it as she led Jon, Kairi, and Goro through the *Hanabira* ward.

It had been a mercantile district before the war, famous for its fashion and artisan goods. The StateEmpire had no need to attack the neighborhood, but did so regardless of the lack of military targets—as if tearing away the identity and pride of the remaining population was the entire point of the war.

Leveled and rebuilt, the district was bustling with life once again. Yujingyu companies flocked in during the reconstruction. StateEmpire-owned corporations took the place of master craftsmen and artisans.

"Checkpoint ahead." Jon moved up next to Mizu.

Jon was an attractive man by anyone's standards. His striking green eyes were weapons of mass distraction. Clean shaven and well kept, he took pride in his appearance. Mizu thought he looked like old pictures of the Emperor, from what she could remember anyway. In any other time and place, he would be an interplanetary supermodel. In Sakuramachi, he wore plain work clothes and old boots. With a pack on his back, he looked like a vagrant—albeit a very handsome one.

The pair moved past a sleek new building housing a StateEmpire-controlled banking firm. Looking at the building filled her vision with quantronic messages promising fair wages for honest work or great returns for investing your wages back into the StateEmpire. Mizu could remember its prior life as a counterculture fashion headquarters and then a food distribution center in the early post-war days. It disgusted her to see it now.

"I see the damn thing, Jon." Mizu's mood was sour enough, but the sight ahead didn't help matters. Even a few blocks away, the Yujingyu checkpoint was easily visible. They wanted it to be, of course.

Floating holographic signs warned citizens to have their halos on and be prepared to stop. Identification information floated around heads waiting in line to pass between the black armored trucks lining the street further ahead. Overhead, propaganda floated in the augmented vision of all below.

///Loyalty is its own reward.
Work and reclaim your honor.
We are all one Yu Jing.///

To anyone left who had a spine, it was just another visible sign of a boot on the neck of the Nipponese people stuck here. They were a far cry from blatant military occupation, though checkpoints like these were far from uncommon. The StateEmpire had moved on from black bags and disappearances to vying for the hearts and minds of the Kuraimori citizenry.

In the years since their defeat, the citizens of Kuraimori still felt the oppression of occupation, despite a sense of twisted normalcy that had returned to the city of Sakuramachi.

Mizu knew they couldn't afford to get inspected. Each of them carried a fortune's worth of contraband in their packs. "Slagg it. Plan B. Go dark."

Audible double-click replies came over comms as her team signed off, one by one. This was nothing new for her crew. Imperial Service hackers no doubt cast a wide net around the checkpoint. No matter their skill, one simple truth always beat the best digital warrior. You can't detect something that isn't there. Mandatory halos were all that they absolutely had to have.

A few short gestures at her wrist-worn comlog, and Mizu's digital presence shrunk to near silence as she moved through the crowd and ducked into a narrow alley. She couldn't risk a full holographic window above her arm being spotted, so she had preprogramed the bracelet-like device to read a few subtle gestures. Going completely silent wasn't an option, given the mandatory ident-halo orbiting each person like a digital fingerprint. Dropping that would draw almost as much attention as an active hacking device, and the order of the day was stealth.

The sudden appearance of the checkpoint wasn't unheard of, even if they were rarer in recent days, but it still came as a surprise and fueled her shake. Jon's intel had been solid to this point, but the district practically buzzed with the nervous anxiety of a prey beast trapped by the hunter. A surprise checkpoint in the ironically named Flower Petal District was inconveniently very much their problem. Mizu could still see the burned flower beds and leveled gardens when she closed her eyes.

Paired off, Goro and Kairi would find their own way while she and Jon went another, but these alleys were their home. Years of barreling through the city on tricked out motorcycles gave them a good, instinctual lay of the land.

Those very bikes would be a liability these days; not quite outlawed by the StateEmpire, they brought more scrutiny than she needed. The *bōsōzoku* crews were once a normal sight throughout Sakuramachi. Now no one dared ride in groups, if they were brave enough to ride at all. Some 'fearless' gang they were—not the first bitter thought that crossed Mizu's mind today.

Leading her crew on daring raids and assaults during the Uprising had been the greatest joy she had known: the blistering speeds, insane maneuvers, the roar of the torqued out ride beneath her. The shake rumbled like a caged beast within her at the thought. Not that they had access to enough working bikes to make such daring runs anymore.

Shortly after the Uprising, one particularly angry Yu Jing commander had hunted down every last bike shop, garage, and wrench jockey he could find over the course of a few months. They probably gave the bastard a medal.

As they hurried through the streets, Mizu reminisced that it was painfully slow compared to the thrill of her bike. Thoughts of better days came unbidden to her mind. A glance at Jon caused the memory of when he built his first ride to intrude in her thoughts. Back then, he was the natural leader, being the oldest of their close-knit group. But when the bombs started falling, the fear of being unable to protect everyone paralyzed him, and Mizu had to step up.

She shook her head to clear her thoughts. War changes everyone, after all.

"Mizu." Jon quietly drifted up beside her as they moved into a small crowd a few blocks over from their original route. "Something's wrong."

Following his gaze, Mizu scanned the way ahead more thoroughly. A small squad of Yujingyu troops created a perimeter in the narrow street. Several civilians were pulled into their cordon and searched. As she looked more closely, it was impossible to miss… they were spending more time scanning the crowd than inspecting each person.

They were looking for someone.

"Slagg me… That's Agent Hsu, I think." Jon trailed off.

Mizu followed Jon's gaze and spotted the lithe armored form in orange armor questioning a freighted woman. A visceral fear came over her. Hsu was a Zhànying Imperial Agent. His jade duster swayed gently behind him as he carried himself with a haughty presence; he would have been picturesque if not for the threat of violence Mizu knew he possessed. As the bald-headed man turned to look at the crowd, Mizu felt a chill as the agent's jade green eyes swept over their surroundings.

"*Kuso*, they..." Mizu trailed off as she watched the officer point down the street toward them. Jon's contacts at the local garrison were how they knew which routes to avoid—usually. It also meant he was a known quantity, recognizable.

That was her only warning before six Combi Rifles rose as one. The shake screamed to get out.

Like a flock of birds sensing danger, the crowded street erupted into motion. Mizu and Jon tried to move with the scattering masses, but the street was clearing too quickly. It was impossible to tell if they were the target or another in the crowd. Either way, they were no longer two invisible specks in a sea of moving people, but trapped in the open. Facing arrest—or worse—Mizu and Jon did the only sensible thing left to them. Run.

Screaming voices echoed after them. That's when the shooting started.

* * * * *

"What the hell just happened, Jon? No checkpoints or raids today? Your guy was slagg'n wrong!" Short of breath, Mizu gasped as they both crouched near a dumpster in a trash-strewn alley.

"They just started shooting! They don't *do* that anymore. I—*chikusho.*" Jon trailed off in shock, looking at his pistol as if he didn't know why he was holding it.

Mizu took a few deep breaths and tried to compose herself. "They pointed right at us. Put that slagg'n thing away!"

She knew it was the shake talking, but Jon's heavy revolver was as much a flag waving for attention as it was a weapon.

"Right." Loyal to a fault, Jon hid his weapon once more, shaking off the shock and awkwardly throwing a piece of garbage in frustration. "How many do you think?"

"How many got shot? Four or five maybe? They just opened fire! They knew exactly what they… *Kuso*, are *we* on IS's radar?!" The implications rolled through Mizu like a tidal surge, overwhelming. "Might not be us, but we need to move. We don't have long till they figure out where we—"

Almost prophetically, two orange-clad soldiers blitzed around the corner with weapons raised and firing. Bullets cascaded across the wall behind Mizu as she lunged for the cover of the dumpster alongside Jon, suddenly wishing she hadn't told Jon to put the gun away. Both leaned against its metal side, scrambling to arm themselves once more.

"On me." Not waiting for his confirmation, Mizu launched into a dead sprint in the only direction she had available to her. While the shake raged quietly in her gut, urging her on, Mizu screamed; she pushed her body to its limit and charged directly into the hail of bullets as her Boarding Pistol screamed with her. A burst of superheated shrapnel sprayed from the pistol's muzzle—a cone of metal projectiles filling the air—in contrast to the Combi rounds flying back at her. At this range, it would be little more than a nuisance, even to the lightly armored soldiers, but it would make them think twice.

The unmistakable bark of Jon's heavy revolver echoed through the tight space twice, and just in time. The click-beep of her weapon running dry was lost in the torrent as one soldier was kicked off his feet.

She threw the empty weapon at her attackers as a distraction. Mizu launched herself at the surviving trooper as he sidestepped the flying pistol. The projectile had done its job, and the Yujingyu was off-footed as Mizu barreled—shoulder first—into his stomach, knocking the wind out of him. He instinctively brought the butt of his rifle against her back and bludgeoned her free as both tumbled to the ground.

On sheer reflex and determination, Mizu fought through the pain and was the first to rise, a small knife in hand. Dancing left, she struck. One, two, three lightning quick strikes to the weakest spots between the armor. With a scream of pain, he kicked out, clipping Mizu's lighter frame and throwing her to the ground.

She tumbled but managed to roll onto her back, desperately gripping her blade to keep from stabbing herself. Mizu looked helplessly up at the unwavering barrel of a rifle.

An eternity stretched as Mizu held her breath before the muzzle slowly lowered. The soldier's shoulder dropped, rifle clattering to the ground as he toppled forward in a spreading pool of crimson.

In a flash, Jon was beside her again. She recovered her empty Boarding Pistol and they ran.

* * * * *

Perched on a small balcony overlooking an empty alley junction, Mizu and Jon silently scanned the streets below for their friends. Hours had passed since their desperate encounter, and Mizu's mind was left to wander impatiently.

This job came to them on short notice, and the checkpoint tugged at something in Mizu's subconscious. Why today? It had been weeks since they had come through the cramped streets of Sakuramachi's lower wards. Each of her crew carried a fortune's worth of merchandise on them, and any one of them getting snagged would be a problem for everyone who touched this tangled web. No one wanted to lose their head, or a finger for that matter.

Feeling confident that they had lost their pursuers long enough, Mizu took a calculated risk and looked deeper into the digital world as her comlog rebooted, automatically reactivating the lens in her right eye. Her vision flooded with arrest bulletins, state propaganda, work notices, a particularly bouncy avatar, and more.

Curiously, a small glyph flashed into her vision. An origami sparrow floated before her as the faintest focus spurred her geist to force it front and center in her vision. Her combat-tooled geist was a fickle thing; getting a legitimate update was difficult on Kuraimori, and that only left her with checking in the underworld markets. She would deal with her glitchy programming over a spyware-laden black market option.

The unmistakable thundering bark of another heavy revolver knifed through her attention, cutting off any thought of looking further into the odd symbol. Mizu instinctively ducked for the cover of a long empty planter. Low-tech Ariadnan gear was easier to come by these days than more modern weapons like her precious Boarding Pistol that now sat empty in her pack. It was contraband of the death-on-sight type, and she knew for a fact Jon wasn't the only one with one.

If Goro was out there and had drawn his gun, stealth was not an option at this stage.

Mizu kicked on her comms, hoping the others would do the same. "Who's up?"

"G." Struggle rang through Goro's voice. He was in trouble.

"K, up." A burst of automatic weapons fire pierced the air.

"J is with me." A quick gesture at her wrist sent her location to their comlogs. "Situation?"

"We're foxed. At least three." Kairi's data burst shared her lens's field of view in a small window of Mizu's vision. Goro fought, knife in hand, with a Kănrén operative in full kit while another lay dead on the ground. His pack was torn open, and their precious cargo of meds was scattered across the road. Some had already been crushed in the melee.

"*Kuso*..."

Mizu's network cycled up and pinged her lens with even more data, extending her effective range. A predictive algorithm pulsed through the scene as a green wireframe. Just in time, too, as the program highlighted a silhouette behind cover, buzzing with digital lethality—a hacker. Her avatar reappeared and bounced on the silhouette's head.

///WARNING: Spotlight///

Data scrolled through Mizu's vision as the Kănrén hacker tried to target lock her. She fired from muscle memory even as the warning flashed.

The holographic control projected above her wrist blinked green as a triple vectored program launched through her personal network, through the repeater, and hammered through the Kănrén's own quantronic assault. The menacing shape of the enemy hacker convulsed as her attack struck home, burning through his firewall—and his skull. The soldier seized violently before falling dead, brain fried from the feedback as her geist filled in the silhouette with ominous red. Her glitchy avatar reasserted itself as a tiny laughing monkey.

///Trinity successful: Target Neutralized.///

Goro quickly dispatched the remaining trooper, collected what he could of the fallen merchandise, and was once again running.

"Let's move!" Mizu vaulted the balcony—Jon followed close behind, swearing. Mizu ran as fast as her legs would allow, racing against their pursuers and the shake within her.

4.

Neoterra was the crown jewel of the PanOceancian hyperpower. Its soaring skyscrapers and verdant landscapes were shielded by the might of the largest navy in the entire Human Sphere, a prodigious military complex, and the stalwart guardians of the NeoVatican Military Orders. Across its continents, most citizens were afforded the best medicine, education, and opportunities money could buy… most. The disparity between the haves and the have nots were stark. Many initiatives had been proposed to uplift those left behind. Most were rife with corruption, incompetence, and bureaucratic ineptitude.

It took a human lifetime to learn all the complexities of PanO bureaucracy. It was a common joke amongst the press that the amount of red tape one had to cut through for a new civil initiative could giftwrap a starcruiser. Most civic initiatives never got moving past a splashy announcement and fanfare, especially those that dealt with the underprivileged—chiefly the Ateks, citizens without Cubes, whose lack of digital immortality and deep-system integration left them a permanent underclass in the eyes of Neoterra's elite.

Few cities had made as much progress as Santiago De Neoterra. Clinics and schools had sprung up in barrios by the dozen in recent years, thanks to funding freed up by automating many public services with fleets of drones developed by the many corporations with research divisions in the region.

It was a fascinating humanitarian story, and a total fluff piece, that any reporter worth their credentials would devour in a few days and be on to the next assignment. Yet Bianca Chen's own words simply taunted her as she lay on the floor of her highrise hotel suite, paid for by a boring politician who of course wanted credit in the piece. At least he was honest and actually wanted to be involved in the project, unlike most other politicians she had worked with over her storied career.

As her work stared back—suspended on a holographic screen above her—Bianca hated them. She didn't hate the story exactly, it was a good piece—straightforward. But Bianca Chen was a news stringer used to the thunder of frontline coverage, the thrill of running for her life, or digging into the seedy underbelly of darker subjects. There was no danger on the streets of Santiago de Neoterra, at least not when it came to the Atek clinics. There wasn't even a worthwhile corruption story beyond a low ranking bureaucrat only sending business to corporations that his family held interests in. That itself was not an uncommon occurrence anywhere in the Sphere and wouldn't capture the sort of attention a war story could.

Freelance journalists were a dime a dozen, but Bianca Chen was a known quantity. She was now a two time recipient of the prestigious Hildy Johnson Award and member of the War Correspondent Hall of Fame for her in-your-face coverage of the conflicts on both Paradiso and Concilium.

And now she was doing fluff pieces as far from the frontline as possible. Her agent called it a well-deserved break, but he was just trying to protect her—probably from herself.

After her body had been found, tied up and murdered on the planet Concilium, he had been exceptionally protective. To Bianca, it felt like purgatory—an apt description considering she had passed through death and was resurrected into a rather expensive new body—a Lhost. Her original Cube—the tiny implant that stored her memories—was destroyed by her attacker, leaving her with a week's old backup and no memory of what happened. There was still something odd about living in the new body. It looked the same in every detail: long limbs, tan skin, lean muscles. It was her, down to the dark eyes and grey streak in her hair. There was nothing wrong with it in the slightest, but still—

///Receiving call: Edwardo Mecatis./// A small picture of the politician appeared, shattering her reverie.

"Deny. Mute all calls." Dismissing the text from her augmented vision, Bianca wandered to the suite's well-stocked minibar. Mecatis might have been the main subject of her piece, but she certainly didn't want to speak with him again if she could manage it. Bianca gave herself a generous pour of whiskey, the amber liquid catching the light just so. A discreet ping from her geist—and a flickering holo-banner in the corner of her vision—reminded her it cost almost as much as her hotel suite. She laughed under her breath. At least this assignment had its perks.

"No more fake smiles for today. Playback interviews two and five." Viewscreens popped up in her field of view as she wandered outside to sit on the plush balcony.

Sitting in the late afternoon sun, Bianca half watched the recordings and tried to enjoy the picturesque horizon, and her whiskey, as she waited for the sun to set.

At least it was a purgatory with a view.

* * * * *

Two more days of work saw a passable article transmitted to her agent. Bianca was grateful to be done with the assignment. It wouldn't make much of a splash by any means, but Mr. Mecatis looked like a saint. Her agent had already forwarded several options for her next assignment, none of them interesting in the slightest. She didn't have much to pack, but her hotel was booked through the week, so she had options. Bianca was in no rush to leave.

Sitting at a cafe, she sipped her latte as the headlines droned past her vision. Since the armistice on Concillium, things had quieted down. The alien Combined Army had staked their flag into the governing headquarters of the Human Sphere, then immediately sued for peace. An odd twist, given the history of enmity between humans and the mix of alien races that made up the Ur Hegemony. They still held a portion of the planet under their direct control. The tension was thick.

Here on Neoterra, the war was a thing to see on the news. It was so very far away. Its effects were barely felt. Most residents would never leave the planet, making places like Concillium and Paradiso exotic, near fictional places. Bianca conceded that the disconnect was partly due to the near constant war coverage by Warcors like herself. The action-packed footage and valiant heroics she and her colleagues sent from the frontlines blurred the lines between propaganda, news coverage, and entertainment.

It was a dangerous job most days, but Bianca wouldn't trade it for all the tea in Yu Jing.

The day turned into another beautiful night in Santiago de Neoterra, and the nightlife district was alive with energy. Done with her assignment, Bianca found herself looking for an excuse to wear the sleek blue dress she bought the week prior and took it. It felt good to feel good in her clothing. Even if it did show a lot more skin than she was used to.

She paused by a mirrored wall outside the club and appreciated the irony. Suits made her uncomfortable, and the last two weeks had been entirely too corporate for her tastes. It had taken an hour to tame her mane of hair into something resembling respectable, and looking in the mirror, it was worth it.

The Refuge had a reputation as one of the premier nightclubs on Neoterra—so much so that it was recreated in countless Maya films. Everyone who was anyone in the Human Sphere knew it was one of those places you went to be seen, like a pilgrimage for the social elite. It had taken some string pulling to get a reservation. As the brick wall of a bouncer waved her through, she could see why. The transition from outside to inside was made by a long hallway with its own slow build of light and noise; entering the club proper was a riot of color. Quantronic lightshows projected directly via a patron's lens could be trimmed and tailored to each user. Scantily clad servers moved about the space with dance-like grace. A few, no doubt handsomely paid, exotic catgirls and chrome-skinned adonis-like men prowled amongst the patrons.

Bianca found a seat at the bar.

"How may I be of service?" The bartender was terrifyingly handsome—no doubt sculpted that way.

"Can you make a Blood and Sand?" Bianca's favorite drink was also her favorite test of any bartender. It was beyond an old drink by anyone's standards. She doubted he could make it, but would the pretty boy look it up?

"Don't know that one I'm afraid."

Pretty but disappointing.

"Equal parts blood orange juice, sweet vermouth, cherry liquor, and whiskey." The unexpected voice beside her was rich with baritoned accent. "If you would like to impress the lady, chill the glass, grab that bottle of MacArthur twelve-year, and garnish with an orange peel and three cherries."

A chill ran down her spine, not out of fear but worry. She knew that voice all too well. Why was *he* here?

Against her better judgment, she turned to greet him. He moved with a fluid grace as he slid into the seat next to her. His hair—longer than one would expect from a covert operative and graying at the temples—was perfectly groomed in the latest Neoterran fad, and his smart-silk suit would have been right at home on a mannequin in the chicest boutique. A warm smile crossed a neatly goateed, tanned face while intelligent green eyes bored into her.

"Hello, Yasbir."

"Good evening, Miss Chen."

* * * * *

"As flattered as I am by the social call, what really brings you to Neoterra?"

"Am I that transparent?" Yasbir checked the rooms twice before ever meeting Bianca at the bar, but instinct and habit had him checking the concealed sensors once again as they arrived back at her hotel. They were alone.

"Yes." Bianca's laugh was friendly and warm as she made her way to the balcony.

Yasbir smiled back. "Can I get you anything, Miss Chen?"

"Water, please."

In the corner of Yasbir's vision, he checked the video feed from a spy drone he had orbiting outside. Satisfied they were as secure as possible, he joined Bianca, water in hand.

"Hasib has been kidnapped."

"Shit." Bianca's face sunk. "Is he okay? Do you know—"

Yasbir held up a hand to forestall any further questions. "He is alive and in the care of the StateEmpire."

"Double shit."

"Indeed." Yasbir watched Bianca's face roll through fear, outrage, and settle on strength. He admired her for that. Bianca had as much—if not more—fortitude as most soldiers he had encountered. "I would like you to help us get him back."

"Why?"

"Why not?" Yasbir kept his tone playful as he sat across from her.

"No, why would they take him?" Bianca's instincts were as sharp as ever.

Yasbir smiled, genuinely. Even now, Bianca managed to surprise him. "Sultan Bey dotes upon his son. With him, they have leverage over the Silk trade."

"Not what I mean, Yasbir."

"Enlighten me, Miss Chen." Yasbir playfully feigned ignorance.

Bianca's sigh was as melodramatic as her eye roll. "I like the kid—yes, I know he's not a kid anymore—but he is kind of a lost cause precisely *because* his father has given him anything and everything.

There is a reason I haven't gone back to visit him after my last assignment on Bourak.

"Sultan Bey will never let him rise to power. Between medical treatments and resurrection—which we both know is practically free for him since you can't do it without Silk, and he basically controls it *all*—Bey could well live forever. He may love his son, but he doesn't trust him."

"As shrewd as ever, Miss Chen."

"Didn't you threaten to kill him once?"

"Twice, actually." Yasbir kept his face neutral, perfectly matter of fact.

"What is this *really* about, Yasbir?"

Yasbir smiled broadly and pondered how much to tell her. He wouldn't be here if the Loom had not predicted Bianca's impact on the future—she had already shaped the future with her reporting more than once. She understood the importance of discretion, but Yasbir did find himself caring for her safety and hoped he would never be sent to shatter it.

Such hopes would not keep him from his duty.

"Hasib is but one goal."

5.

The morning sun beat down on Takeshi as he ran. The eight kilometer long loop wandered through the training grounds and into the foothills of Mount Gassan. Takeshi loped easily along the trail—clad in fitness gear rather than his usual training garb. He nimbly dodged roots and other obstacles as his mind worked. A floating green line, visible in his lens, guided him along the pre-mapped route, but he knew these trails well and could have gone without it.

Thankfully, his dour mood had warded off the sparring invitations that usually dominated his liberty and training time. Meeting the strange monk, and confessing something locked deep inside, gripped the warrior in a dysthymic haze following the odd encounter. All he wanted to do was escape the burning shame inside.

Takeshi's thoughts wandered. His mother was a caring woman, duty-bound and loyal, but not unloving. She raised him more than anyone. The beautiful garden of his childhood home was a testament to the care and craft she brought to that which she loved. Takeshi missed that garden. His mind moved unbidden to his father, and darker clouds began to form in his mind once more. He pushed them aside along with the thoughts he wished not to dwell on.

One cut. Focus.

His mind moved back to the recent mission. The destruction of his blade was a crushing blow to Takeshi. Initially, it had clouded his thoughts with personal failure. Even as exercise brought clarity, he felt the shame of failure still, but something new emerged from the murky places of his mind—uncertainty.

Takeshi's legs worked to drive him onward, outpacing the thoughts that chased him. So on and on he ran. The mountainous terrain reminded Takeshi of home. It was comforting. The simplicity of exercise helped him push through the cloud hanging over his mind. Endorphins pressed back the gloom and allowed his thoughts to float freely, wandering aimlessly.

Sword in hand, Takeshi Oyama had forged his path forward for years. Now that sword was gone. His family commissioned the set of blades on his induction to the Domaru Butai. His chest ached to see the sword rack half empty in his quarters.

Leaning into his ascent, Takeshi roared his defiance. He would *not* let this failure define him. His pulse pounded in his ears as birds took flight from trees nearby, fleeing his angry cry.

Takeshi crested the final hill and accelerated. He tore through the descent to the valley floor, as if pushing for a speed record. Letting gravity, his legs, and pure will to succeed drive him faster and faster. Pushing aside thoughts of doubt and loss, Takeshi raced to the end of the trail.

His comlog chirped, and a new record time flashed across his lens along with his heart rate. Takeshi slowed to a stop and began to cool down. Moving through katas and stretches brought him back to a calm center. Takeshi felt a tiny bit grounded for the first time in days, despite the rumblings of his subconscious.

///Join me in the training circle, Takeshi-san.///

* * * * *

The mid-day sun was bright and pitiless, baking the training circle until the clay ground shimmered faintly with heat. Two sakura trees framed the clearing like ancient sentries while pink buds littered their branches, waiting for their moment to bloom. There were many such circles on the grounds, but the sword saint's personal favorite was on a small rise in the center of the grounds, visible to all.

"Begin."

Takeshi shifted his stance, bokken steady in his hands. Across from him, the *kensei* stood like a statue from an older age—not quite weathered—composed, his expression unreadable.

Leaning against the trunk of the left-most sakura tree, a silent Kempeitai that Takeshi's geist identified as Officer Ryōki Kano watched with arms crossed and a relaxed face, as if observing a midday sparring match between two legendary swordsmen held no more importance than a cup of tea. The hood of his long grey-white coat was pulled back, revealing a bald head and neutral expression. He was a broad man—a warrior. The ease in his posture was disconcerting—*too* casual, too practiced, like a blade resting in its sheath, not forgotten but waiting. Beside him, a holographic screen projecting the image of a face cloaked in shadow. Whoever it was said nothing, but the hollow gaze behind that silhouette felt colder than the warriors that clashed in the ring.

Takeshi didn't know why he was here. Only that he was meant to be watched.

Then—movement.

Hayachi came forward, no warning, no breath drawn. His first strike was sharp, testing. Takeshi met it with a solid parry, the crack of wood echoing through the courtyard. Their blades separated like magnets repelled.

Takeshi pressed forward—high slash, pivot, thrust low. Clean, disciplined, no wasted motion. The old master slipped free, but only just.

Another pass. Steel on steel—or it might as well have been. The bokken in their hands sounded like warhammers as they struck, parried, turned each other's balance against the other. Takeshi wasn't overpowered. He held ground.

Then came the riposte—faster. A diagonal cut toward Takeshi's collarbone. He twisted, barely slipping aside. The bokken hissed past his face. The wind of its passage kissing his cheek.

They reset.

Takeshi's heart pounded in rhythm with the breath in his lungs. A drop of sweat cut down his cheek like a blade. His eyes never left the *kensei's*.

They clashed again. For the first time in years, the *kensei* took two steps back. His eyes narrowed slightly.

Takeshi struck low and rose into a spin, his blade arcing for the master's ribs—deflected. He reversed grip, dragged the bokken up and around in a half-circle and nearly tagged him. The *kensei's* blade intercepted at the last moment. The collision shuddered through both arms.

They locked, neither yielding.

Takeshi gritted his teeth and pushed. For all his strength, it became like trying to move a mountain. Their weapons ground together, sweat falling like rain between them. Then—release. They separated. Both breathing hard now.

"Again." The *kensei's* face was stone.

"*Hai*." Takeshi nodded, already moving.

This time, the master attacked before Takeshi could strike—three quick slashes in a rising rhythm. Takeshi matched each one, letting instinct take over. His movements were less polished but more alive. Fluid, adaptive. He struck with precision and purpose. He was not following anymore.

He was challenging.

A final exchange, lightning-fast—strike, block, feint, counter—and they froze. Each with a bokken at each other's throats, Takeshi's only slightly further from his target than the sword saint's.

Stillness. No breath dared intrude.

Then both slowly stepped back.

The *kensei* gave a nod, respectful and unforced.

Behind them, the Kempeitai stepped forward, his voice flat. "He'll probably die."

Takeshi blinked—confused, chest still heaving. He turned slightly, caught the faint edge of meaning in the master's eyes.

The bout had never been just for them. It was a test.

Somehow, in the heat and rhythm of battle, he had passed.

"He may." The *kensei* looked to the Kempeitai. "That is his choice."

The sun blazed overhead.

Takeshi bowed to his master—slow and deep—keeping his eyes on the stranger, uncertain what was unfolding before him.

The Kempeitai looked to the holoplane—as if conferring in private—and for the first time, the Kempeitai gave the faintest of nods. "Very well."

Takeshi watched silently as he departed without another word, discomfort rumbling beneath the elation of the fight. *Kensei* Hayachi waited to speak until the Kempeitai was far out of earshot.

"You are a warrior, Takeshi. Brooding does not suit you." He turned to face Takeshi, his face a mask of stone.

The words were soft, but Takeshi felt the sting of them as if he was being struck with the bokken in his mentor's hand.

"*Hai, Kensei.*" He replied quietly.

"You are forged in the fire of battle, Takeshi-san. You will not be reforged by sitting here."

"*Kensei*, I am—"

"Uncertain."

"Yes." It took all of Takeshi's will to keep his eyes up and locked on his mentor.

"I know how you feel. There was a time long ago when I lost my resolve. Warriors who live long enough will all encounter such times.

What matters now is what you choose to do. How *you* chose to reclaim your honor, to reforge yourself into the Emperor's blade."

The sword saint's admission surprised Takeshi. *Kensei* Hayachi was a figure of myth to him. To hear him speak of uncertainty in any form made him more real—more human.

"*Kensei*, Nakama spoke of an opportunity."

"Yes. There is a mission—a dangerous one." The *kensei*'s voice lowered to hush conspiratorially. "Our Emperor commands it be done, and so it shall. You, however, must choose to accept this task. Others will go regardless of your choice, but your presence would help ensure its success, and their survival."

Takeshi's pulse quickened.

To be chosen for a mission under the Emperor's command was a high honor indeed—but it was an honor that was rarely without blood.

In that moment, Takeshi understood the true purpose of the *Kensei's* words—it was not just a mission being offered, but a chance to prove himself worthy again. Whatever dangers lay ahead, he would meet them blade-first.

6.

Leaning low on her bike, Mizu plowed into the storm, riding the shake as much as her machine. The barrage of rain and wind on her helmet made keeping her head forward a feat in itself. Surrounded, on her left and right rode her lifetime companions, her trusted friends—her bōsōzoku.

Once the Third Hand Gang—now the newly constituted Third Kuraimori Guard Platoon of Aragoto Senkenbutai—they had blitzed through Yu Jing supply lines and communications hubs for weeks. Spirits were high even as the platoon rarely slowed their relentless pace; stopping only to sleep, rearm, and refuel both body and machine. This was what each and every one of them had been born to do.

Her comlog chirped an alert in her ear. Opening a newly received data packet, information flashed across her visor as the kilometers of open countryside flew by.

"Eyes up, Hands! Retasking. Yujingyu rally point spotted at new marker A-Seven." A quick verbal command shot the data to her crew. She suppressed the urge to sit up and release the controls: no need to go hands-free and use her comlog just to show off, especially in the rain. "Let's show them who's home this is, and let's let them know we are coming while we are at it. Loud and proud, Hands. On me!"

The sudden and deafening roar of twenty tricked out war machines pretending to be motorcycles blasted through the sleepy rural highways, sound dampeners disengaged. With the reins cut loose, the full capabilities of their machines could be brought to bear. Whoops of joy and excitement cut through the comms as the rebellious bōsōzoku-*turned-militia fell in behind her accelerating form. Dares, bets, good natured insults, and encouragement filtered through comms soon after. The shake rattled in its cage.*

"No sheath for this blade, eh, Mizu?" Despite the incredible technology in their bikes amplifying their voices, she could barely hear Henzo's private channel over the roar of twenty-seven steeds at full throttle while the world blasted by. Slick roads only made the thrill of the run more intense. One wrong move and any one of them would discover what two hundred kilometers per hour did to the human body.

"Getting cold feet, banchō*?"*

"Not a chance, babe. No way, no how. I ride where you ride, and you know it."

"Loud and proud?"

They looked at each other as they rode side by side.

"Loud and—" Henzo's scream was lost in the explosion that disintegrated his bike.

Training and adrenaline were all that kept Mizu together as she saw her right hand, her lieutenant, sometimes lover, and best friend's last moments. The serenity of the ride shattered as more and more missiles streaked in. The shake started to scream.

"Ambush, ambush, ambush! Blow through and scatter four! Rendezvous at..."

Something solid hit Mizu's bike—heat, a flash of light and pain—and Mizu found herself launched through the air as her bike immolated behind her. She collided with Goro, knocking him from his ride too and sending them both tumbling away from their mounts.

* * * * *

"Wake up, he's here." Goro's gentle nudge to her booted foot ripped Mizu out of the past and flung her recklessly into the present. The shake dragged her adrenaline and fear screaming right out of the dream along with her. The nightmares always came back after being shot at—after killing.

He had probably drawn straws to wake her by the sheepish look across the big man's leathery face. Tracking his eyes, it took all not to gasp at her outstretched hand and the weapon pointed at Goro. She didn't remember drawing her gun. She dropped her arm and ran her other hand through her hair.

"*Chikusho*, Goro. I'm sorry."

"No need, Boss, but you gotta get up. He's here, and you know he will only deal with the *sukeban*."

"*Sukeban*." That word always itched at her conscience. "Some leader I am. Goro, you gotta stop calling me that. We don't even have enough working bikes for the four of us, let alone everyone else."

Despite the mix of frustration and sarcasm in her voice, half a heartbeat was all it took for that ridiculous smile she had known all her life to creep under that disorderly scruff the big man called a beard.

"Whatever you say, Boss."

"Slagg me. Gimme a minute. I'll be right down. "

Goro was one of the most fearless men she knew, but Mizu couldn't help but note her friend chose to stand just close enough to nudge her booted foot with his own, but not close enough to be stabbed.

Kuso.

The shame of drawing a gun on one of her closest friends nearly crushed her. Mizu knew better than to lie to herself and pretend it was the first time.

"Wait… He?" Mizu's words fell on an empty doorway. Their delivery was most certainly not to a *he*.

The two story flop house held little in the way of luxury for those who passed through, but it had running water and beds that seemed clean enough that one might forget what else went on in places like this. Holographic advertisements bloomed unbidden in the corner of Mizu's vision—half-clad escorts, miracle tonics, discount augments—each jostling for attention with enough color and motion to make the eyes ache. She dismissed them from her lens, rubbing her eyes to clear the intrusive after-images.

Here in the neon-draped pleasure wards of Sakuramachi, one could lose themselves in just about anything.

They were here, precisely for that very reason. Laying low for two days while holding contraband was one thing, but having recently killed a total of five Yujingyu soldiers, it was even more important to keep a low profile.

They couldn't go straight home. Hiding, like smuggling, was easier to do where things got lost. It didn't hurt that the client also operated here as well.

Once a beautifully gardened district, the StateEmpire had forbidden its restoration. On its bones, the new urban neighborhood was constructed. Tonight, the streets bore no trace of the old gardens—only the hum of late-night commerce and the quiet, watchful glances of those who preferred their business remain unseen.

The spot was already paid for, and the owner was nowhere to be seen, but at least their biometrics let them into the place's back door. Pretty normal operating procedure for jobs like this. They rarely used the same drop site twice in a row, but at least the clients had some sort of standards, and the beds were always clean.

Splashing water across her face from the washroom sink, Mizu took a good hard look at herself.

Years of hard riding and a rough life wore on the skin of anyone, no matter how much they cared for their bodies. Mizu had given up on applying makeup years ago and just had it tattooed on around her pale brown eyes. The number three sat above her left eye, '*san*' made out in red ink. It was the sole other visible body mod she allowed herself; the others, she kept as hidden as possible. Three for the Third Hand. Three for the Third Platoon. Three to remind her of those she lost. Three to remind her of those left that she was responsible for: Goro, Jon, Kairi, and the rest waiting back at their hideout.

The blue dye of her hair was fading again. She could get that fixed with programmable body modifications, but that meant visiting a clinic. Mizu did her best not to leave a trail for the StateEmpire to follow.

Since the StateEmpire had reclaimed Kuraimori and squashed their rebellion like an annoying insect hive, those who lived in such opulence and luxury were friends of the StateEmpire. Japanese villas, Imperial residences, and manor homes were all now home to the occupiers and overlords—or traitors who cozied up to them. A few streets away, she could get lost in a haze of forgetfulness and bliss if she was inclined. It was still tempting to taste the Bite, even after all this time.

No.

To her shame, Mizu had often been found in places just like this after they lost the war. Goro had carried her limp body home. Kairi had bathed her and nursed her through the shakes. Jon had hidden her from the rest of the crew and ruthlessly put down any opposition to her leadership. All this and more when Mizu just wanted to let go, to forget what little she could remember.

When she saw her *san* in the mirror, it kept her wire-taught body moving. The memory, though blurred as it was, of what her friends had done for her and of those she had lost kept her going, even now.

Show time.

Waiting in the cramped common space below, Mizu found her friends were not alone. Five black suits covered what she knew to be four heavily tattooed bodies carrying plenty of weapons. Waiting at the table was not the person she was expecting, but someone else indeed.

"*Chikusho.*" She immediately regretted her language.

Yoshihiro Shubitsu. His own *irezumi* tattoos showed at the neck of an impeccable black smart fabric suit that rippled faint greens with each movement. Modern takes on the ancient designs, dragons and demons moved slowly across his skin, locked in an eternal struggle—traditions immediately recognizable by Nipponese and Yujingyu alike. Jewel-inlaid teseum cufflinks, worth a fortune no doubt, brought the eye to Yoshihiro's tattooed wrists and hands as well. Cufflinks that he proudly displayed, despite the occupation, were the clearest of messages to the Nipponese of Kuraimori: we are still here and we are strong.

"*Oji-san*! I was not expecting you, Uncle, you honor us." Crossing the room briskly past the guards, Mizu bowed deeply to her guest as if it were his own palace. Obediently, Mizu waited for permission to rise, mind racing and stomach knotted with shake and worry. She was expecting the fixer, a middle man… not the boss himself.

"Hello, Mizoku." When Yoshihiro Shubitsu spoke, he was used to being heeded. He spoke slowly and deliberately in the most unnerving of ways. Any who took the aging boss's slow speech and small frame as weakness came to quickly regret it, from all she had heard. Not that they did… her Hands knew better. "Rise. How does your little family fare? I understand the Third Hand is not quite what it used to be."

"I… I do not understand." Despite the insult, Mizu's mind rushed to understand what was happening with the weight of four armed killers at her back. "Have we displeased you, Uncle?"

"You've lost weight," he said, ignoring the question and beckoning Kairi from the stairs. "Kairi-chan, I trust you will ensure she is eating well and not losing herself again."

"*Hai*, Uncle. No concern there." She bowed.

Before her frustration at being coddled and being reminded of her own shameful past—or the shake—tore her apart, Mizu dove into business. Keeping her temper in check was a herculean effort.

"You will see your merchandise is here, save for a small damaged lot, Uncle. Premium Haqqislamite medical nanotech as ordered: serum, medikit autoinjectors, and narcotic cleansers, detox shots. Untraceable, the—"

The heavily tattooed crime boss stared with ice blue eyes, no doubt bioengineered to cut straight through her soul, silencing Mizu as a dread hung over the room.

He knew.

The air stilled. Silence roared in Mizu's ears.

"Mizu, I have nothing but faith that you have delivered—as best you could." His words cut through the silence like a precision-guided munition, the insult undisguised. "That is not why I am here. There was an incident near the old *Hanabira* ward this afternoon. Five soldiers are dead, Mizoku-san." The pause was excruciating. "Someone will have to smooth things over with the garrison commander."

He let it hang. His slow way of speaking taunted the shake as it rattled its cage.

"Do you know, child, who this might have been?"

Of all the absolute truths Mizu was certain of, three were indelibly clear in that moment. The yakuza boss already knew who did it, and the smoothing had already happened. All that was left was to pay the price.

"*Hai, Oji-san.* I do."

Yoshihiro sat silent, waiting.

"Sir, if I may..." Jon tried to step in, but Goro physically stopped him while Mizu silenced him with a glare. Yoshihiro ignored Jon completely. His eyes burned through Mizu's soul.

She looked to her friends and thought of the others waiting at their small shelter. This was her responsibility. Protecting them was the only thing she had left. All the euphoria of surviving the chase was stripped away from Mizu as she told Yoshihiro what happened. She had answered questions as he asked them and left nothing out.

When it was done, Mizu knelt before the yakuza boss and placed her left pinky on a small box provided by one of his men. She took the offered blade and swallowed the pain. One swift cut and it was done. On her knees, Mizu offered Yoshihiro her finger.

* * * * *

The day stretched on in silence as the four friends carefully picked their way home. Her three companions hung protectively close to her as they slowly worked their way back to their small garage in the northern outskirts. The streets were crowded with weary faces, eyes fixed on the ground, drifting past in a haze.

Once-proud factories loomed overhead, feeding the StateEmpire's endless appetite. Their gates spilled workers back into the city like water from a cracked, neon lit cistern.

Children darted through pools of shifting neon, their laughter oddly out of place against the drone of mag-rail cargo haulers and the low thrum of industry. Overhead, animated holograms painted the streets in flickering colors, projecting grinning hosts and patriotic slogans that no one seemed to notice anymore. It was all treated as the unremarkable rhythm of daily life—ordinary to everyone but her. To Mizu, the saturation of light and sound felt like a fever dream laid over a city that had once breathed freely.

A glare from Goro was enough to discourage any further questions from the others hanging around the small, decommissioned garage they called home. Silently, Mizu found her way to the room in the upper level of the abandoned mechanic's shop. It was a modest space, but one took what they could get—it was hard enough to feed and house her crew together while keeping a low profile from the ever-present eyes of the StateEmpire. More space meant a bigger target on their back, so the remaining members of the crew-turned-family took pride in their humble abode.

Hanging her pack and stowing her kit next to a worn red riding jacket stripped of its patches, Mizu finally gave in and let the shock of the day wash over her once again. She caught herself staring at the medikit—and its painkillers—in the corner.

Mizu prayed for sleep to quickly claim her before the shake could.

7.

Dressed in his service uniform, Takeshi inspected every detail in the two meter tall mirror. Focusing his wandering mind was more difficult than ever this morning. The light gray, band-collared coat was perfectly tailored to him. Smart fabrics kept it impeccably clean, fitted perfectly, and eliminated the need for pressing.

Takeshi could not keep from constantly adjusting it. His rank stood paired with the spiral of the Domaru and adorned both collars, while numerous marks of merit and valor were visible on his sleeves with his service stripes. Wide legged, black trousers—reminiscent of his training hakama—and black shoes completed the uniform.

Over it all, Takeshi had donned a sleeveless red haori. Far more ornate than the armor-cloth garment he wore into battle, this beautiful hand-woven silk garment was a sign of station, of family. Gifted by his mother upon achieving his induction into the Domaru Butai, it was embroidered with the crest of the Oyama family, and the mountains of their family estates. Wearing such a garment was traditional amongst the *bushi* warriors of the Domaru Butai that hailed from noble lines; a modern day incarnation of the samurai of old. Takeshi was blessed by a lifetime of training, education, and a cultured life. Despite it all, Takeshi couldn't help but feel absurdly out of place.

Though noble, the Oyama family was of modest station, and he felt more comfortable in the field than in formal attire.

The single lonely katana sat uncomfortably at his hip, missing the weight of its longer twin. It was his right to bear two blades, as the *bushi* tradition dictated. 'Traitor' echoed through his mind as he gripped the solitary hilt. He felt the hate in the warrior's words even now. It punctuated the shame he felt for losing his primary blade.

The waiting room was sparsely furnished, but that did nothing to hide its importance. Deep within the palace complex, there were subtle reminders everywhere: the Imperial Seal above the mirror, the handcrafted table and chairs, the beautiful hand-woven rug beneath his feet. Everywhere he looked, the not-so-subtle trappings of power surrounded Takeshi in a most uncomfortable way.

He had been picked up before dawn in an unadorned craft, whisked away skyward before the sun threatened the horizon. The lights of Tokyo were the only warning of his destination. The auto-pilot geist that flew the craft was silent other than simple instructions to don the dampening cuff that waited for him when he boarded, sharing nothing otherwise. Takeshi had worked with hundreds of virtual intelligence programs over the years, but this one was by far the least helpful.

With his personal network blocked by the cuff, Takeshi had little to go on other than the horizon beyond his window; but as the city loomed, the shuttle craft went dark. The passenger compartment plunged into utter darkness as armor panels rose over its windows. Once landed, he was met by a stuffy aide and two silent, power armored Hatamoto warriors. Their armor was unique—exclusive to the Emperor's personal guard—and absolutely exquisite. Crafted in the image of samurai of old, their crested *kabuto* helms sealed the warriors' faces behind emotionless armor.

At the opposite side of the hangar, two Mechazoid Sokorentai, Tactical Armored Gears, rested in their launch cradles. The elegant lines of the warmachines stood nearly three and a half meters at full height. Clearly designed with nods to ancient samurai illustrations married to sleek, modern technology, he had seen them fight with an unbelievable amount of grace for a hulking machine that size. Both the oversized Heavy Machine Guns on their backs and the dual katanas—as long as he was tall—were paintbrushed in the hands of the artists that piloted them.

The Mechazoids sat in alert configuration, fully armed and loaded, ready to deploy at a moment's notice. The TAG pilots looked up from the game of *shogi* set between them and watched him disembark.

Usually his personal network would have tapped into the datasphere, but the cuff kept him blocked. His armored escorts and the pair of TAGs had spoken volumes as to where he stood—few places warranted this level of security. After escorting him there, the helmed warriors slightly inclined their heads before departing. Whether out of respect or pity, Takeshi was unsure, but their marks of station and service gave no doubt as to his location. He was deep within the Imperial Palace.

Returning to the present, he turned away from the mirror. His eyes widened as he noticed a blank envelope of parchment that waited for him on the table. Its wax seal—plain and unadorned—fit its surroundings while being utterly out of place at the same time. In this hyper-digital age, who used paper notes? How he had missed its presence over the last hour wracked his brain, until settling on the belief that it was not there—the table was clear when he entered. And that did nothing for the subtle unease building in his mind. He crossed the room and picked up the envelope, feeling the subtle textures of exquisite craftsmanship, then broke its seal.

What song will you sing at the end?
–Nakama

The beautifully brushed calligraphy stared back at Takeshi, jumping off the rough parchment. The brush work, exquisite in its form, spoke of a lifetime of practice and patience. Patience. Sighing deeply, he felt once again confounded by the strange old monk.

Takeshi cut quite the pose when he glanced at the mirror once more; a modern, noble warrior holding a parchment missive straight out of the Edo period. He thought it was an odd, if elegant, juxtaposition.

Any further contemplation of his strange journey to this moment was cut short by the door retracting into the wall. Sliding the note into his coat, Takeshi turned to greet the newcomer, only to be stunned by who stood before him. General Daichi Takeda stood in the simple unadorned duty uniform of the Hatomoto with a wide, warm smile on his noble face.

"*Oji-san*… General!" Takeshi corrected himself, snapping to attention and bowing. Daichi Takeda had been Takeshi's role model for most of his life, however General Takeda grossly outranked him and was due the respect of his rank.

By the Emperor's side as a member of his personal guard throughout the rebellion, he had taken more than one blade meant for the Emperor and escorted him safely, in secret, back to Earth from Kuraimori. He never spoke of how they escaped the embattled island several systems away. Most believed it was nothing short of a miraculous feat—Takeshi included.

A peerless swordsman, infinitely fierce in battle, he had swiftly risen to command the Hatamoto Imperial Guard in the aftermath of the Uprising. The pale white synthetic replacement sitting where his left eye had once been was the only telltale sign of what may have happened on that harrowing journey. He bore the mismatched replacement proudly. Rumor held that the Emperor personally asked him to keep it white, but on that subject, 'Uncle' Daichi was silent as well.

General Takeda was not Takeshi's uncle by birth, but the noble warrior's family held close ties to his own. Takeshi learned the blade at Daichi's feet—rather than his own father's—and had him to thank for many of the opportunities he was given early in his career.

The general's swords, a pair publicly gifted to him by the Emperor, were stunning. Works of the finest bladesmiths in the Sphere, each marked with the Yoshihara family crest, the blades were undisputed masterpieces, crafted hands that served the Emperor of Japan exclusively. Black lacquered scabbards, etched with golden cranes in flight, kept their lethal edges hidden from view.

"Be at ease, Takeshi-san. It is good to see you." His voice was a deep rumble, like a thunderstorm on the horizon.

"Yes, sir."

"I said at ease."

Takeshi hadn't realized he remained locked in the rigid military pose and slowly did as he was commanded, looking once again upon the smiling man he called uncle.

"That is better. It is good to see you. I am sorry to have been away for so long, but it does me well to see you now. I have meant to visit over the years. Duty does not allow me much liberty in these times."

It had been long indeed. Uncle Daichi had never married, and many privately considered him practically wed to the throne. Marshaling his will to be at ease as the general commanded, Takeshi leapt straight to the heart of it.

"It is good to see you too, sir, but… why am I here? Actually, *where* am I?"

"Ever into the fray, I see. Sit, Takeshi-san." Both men went to the table and sat side by side. "I have reviewed the reports from your most recent engagement. You performed admirably."

Surprising even himself, Takeshi snapped back. "Every soldier under my command died. I call that an absolute disaster." Takeshi stunned himself into silence at his own outburst while the general sat impassively and waited while he brought his temper under control. "Forgive me, *Oji-san*."

"There is nothing to forgive, Takeshi-san. I read your personal report and reviewed your logs. You did well. Losses in battle are inevitable. That does not mean we have to like it. You honor yourself and your comrades that you hold such losses as unacceptable." Daichi's eyes wandered. The act itself was slightly unsettling as his artificially pale eye seemed unfocused. "We all grapple with the loss of those we lead. The day we stop is the day we become the very monsters we fight. Do not ever forget that."

"*Hai*," Takeshi quietly replied.

"Now, to answer your question, you are in the Imperial Palace. You entered through a private hangar and are now deep within the complex, but you had already surmised that. As to why, that is more complicated. There is an opportunity at hand." He paused, patiently waiting.

"Nakama said as much, as did *Kensei* Hayachi. Who exactly *is* Nakama?"

"Unfortunately, that is not something I can easily answer." Disappointment clear across Takeshi's face, the older warrior continued. "In full honesty, I do not completely know myself. He knows many things and moves about quietly. The man we call Nakama lives behind the scenes with the full blessing of our Emperor. That is all I need to know, and that will have to satisfy you as well."

It took Takeshi a moment to wrap his brain around the deep implications of this. With the full support of the Emperor. That could mean anything.

"Why me?"

The Hatamoto's smiling visage seemed to crackle as he furrowed his brows.

"That is even more complicated. To answer that, we must speak of your family." He sighed heavily. "Your father was like a brother to me. I miss him dearly. I know you do not speak of him often, but now we must."

The whiplash of recent days seemed paltry in comparison to the mention of his father. Kōichi Oyama was a brave warrior, fond of the arts, and one of the smartest men Takeshi had ever known. His mother swore they looked just alike, and she wept openly the one time he had considered shaving his face. He told himself that keeping his facial hair was to make his mother smile, having nothing to do with styling it in the same manner as his father.

The distance between them had begun when Takeshi had voiced his intentions to follow his father into the Domaru Butai. Kōichi had transferred from line duty into research and development in the First Home Guard. The one thought that dominated Takeshi's memory of his father was how completely obsessed with his work he was. He was rarely home when Takeshi was on liberty. They rarely spoke. There had been light-years between them by the time of Uprising and—to Takeshi's eternal shame—he would never be able to mend those bonds. Japanese family holdings were all brutally attacked and destroyed across the Sphere. The Oyamas' were no exception. It nearly ruined the family at the time. He had been told his father died defending one such facility, but the details of which were classified.

"I see it written across your face and know that pain as well, Takeshi. His death was a blow to us all." He paused, breathing deep as if processing a deep anguish. Daichi had been closer to his father than any man alive. "Today, we must look past the man and look to his work." With a wave of Daichi's hand over the table, a small holographic image rose from it via hidden projectors. Takeshi immediately recognized the sweeping foothills of the Hansei Valley—home.

"It must be understood that this conversation is considered confidential and highly classified from here on in. Am I clear?"

Takeshi immediately took the gravity of Daichi tone to heart and returned to his military bearing as well. "*Hai.* Understood, General."

"Good. Now, there is an increased Yujingyu presence in Hansei Valley of late. Their forces are concentrated here." He gestured to the map.

Takeshi hadn't realized he had avoided looking at his family estate until it lit up as a StateEmpire stronghold.

"We have reliable intelligence that suggests they are either unable to locate the datavaults or are unaware that such a valuable asset resides so close to their feet. Either way, an opportunity has arisen to return to Hansei and recover some of your father's precious work in the process."

"Datavaults? What precisely was he working on, sir? We—" Mixed feelings floated through Takeshi's mind. "We did not speak often."

"I know. Your father did not have the vocabulary to express how the distance between you two pained him."

"On that we agree."

Daichi stopped and turned from the projection, locking eyes with Takeshi. "Your father loved you, Takeshi, but he was broken by war and did not want you to feel the same. He did not know how to speak his heart. Your mother knew this as well. War changes us all in the end, but you must choose how it will change you. Kōichi let it choose for him. He closed himself off. His own ties to the military industrial complex gave him the only tools he understood to keep you safe. The weapons of war."

"He was there in the beginning, *Oji-san.* He took pride in my studies and training. For most of my childhood he was there. I wanted to be just like him." Takeshi spoke from the heart. A vice of unspoken pain cranked on his chest.

"You are more alike than you know, Takeshi-san."

"But then he was—gone."

Takeshi watched the struggle on the older warrior's face. Takeshi's first sword lesson was at Uncle Daichi's feet as his father looked on.

Both warriors sat in silence. Pride and tradition struggled against the need to speak, to share their minds and hearts.

The briefing lasted several hours. Takeshi and his adoptive uncle had sifted through holographic data projections by the dozen as they rose from the elegantly carved wooden table. Hundreds of weapons schematics, vehicle designs, cybernetic augmentation prototypes, and more floated in the air like wireframe mannequins of light. The ins and outs of weapons development were far beyond Takeshi's area of expertise. He was a warrior. He trusted the JSA armorers with his life every time he went into battle—blades and blood he knew. The enormity of the task had driven Taskeshi to pacing as the general watched on.

"It is on Shentang. We would have to fight through both Yutang and Shentang planetary defense grids—the entire State Empire navy. Then there is the Imperial Service and Invincible Army to deal with. It cannot be done." The sheer impossibility of what he was hearing had driven Takeshi into his outburst. Remembering himself, he added, "Sir."

"I agree, Takeshi-san. Which is why you will not be fighting your way through." A smile crept across the older warrior's face.

"I do not follow, General." Takeshi was beyond confused.

"Fighting our way through the combined naval and ground forces of Yu Jing would be a death sentence for Greater Independent Japan. We simply do not have the forces to achieve such a thing. Such an action would ruin our fragile nation, not to mention the repercussions from Concilium would cripple us further. It simply cannot be done—at this time. So you will not fight your way in, Takeshi-san." Mischief took hold of the general's face. A look Takeshi had never seen before. "You will walk in with a smile on your face."

8.

Mizu shot upright, the phantom throbbing of her missing finger blending with nightmares of gunfire to wrench her from a restless sleep. Blinking against the haze, she struggled to focus on the window—her mind slow to register that midday had long passed. A low groan escaped her lips. Even with the Silk-laced meds from their dwindling stash, losing a pinky still scrambled her nerves. Phantom pain sparked along her arm, flickering all the way up to her skull. With trembling hands, she reached for an injector nearby and pressed it hard into her thigh. Another followed quickly, a desperate attempt to drown the ache. She told herself it was just to kill the pain. Shaking her head, she stumbled to the sink, her hands unsteady as she splashed cold water on her face. Gradually, the tremors eased, but the dull ache lingered beneath the surface.

She was numbly poking at the stump where her left pinky had been just this morning when a knock on her door brought reality crashing back in along with a surprisingly fierce headache. Scrambling through the wreckage of her bunk for a shirt to throw over her ink-covered form, Mizu dressed in something at least manageably clean.

"What?!" She shouted at the door.

"It's Kairi. Heard you up and moving."

"Yeah, come in." The door retracted into the wall, and Kairi stopped just inside, leaning against a locker while Mizu sat back down on her cot, and caught a whiff of herself. Damn, she stank. "Sorry for the smell. Slagg, I'm filthy. You weren't waiting long, were you?"

"Oh, I can tell; and no, don't flatter yourself." Kairi chuckled. "Though, I wouldn't be volunteering to ride behind you, for what it's worth." A quick wink and a smile from her friend brought the absurdity of the moment into clarity, and Mizu smiled back.

Silence stretched and smiles faded. It still amazed Mizu that her friend had only been fifteen when they took up arms against Yu Jing. Barely into her twenties now, Kairi's face showed far more lines of wear and wisdom than it should beneath her short, spiked hair.

"You know I'm gonna ask, right?" Mizu stared at the floor, refusing to look at her friend when she spoke.

"Yep. Let's get it over with."

"Have you been feeding information back to Yoshihiro?" Fierce determination met Mizu's eyes as the two friends locked their gaze on the other.

"No."

"Do we have a rat?"

"Probably."

"Yeah, you are probably right. *Kuso*, one more thing." Shame washed over her for doubting her friend in equal time to the relief she felt. Trust was invaluable in this life, and rarer still. "That's all I needed to hear." Mizu trailed off, unsure what to say next to one of her dearest friends. Thankfully, Kairi broke the following silence.

"He could have called on any of us in the moment. He knew it would create division. Slagg it, Mizu, you know him better than most. The shake's got you jumping at shadows now?"

"My head is pounding, and we have enough on our plate without this shit. *Kuso.* I'm sorry for doubting you, even for a nanosecond." Mizu held her hands up in surrender.

"It's okay, Mizu, seriously." A pause. "We may have another problem though…"

"Of course we do. What is it this time?" Frustration written across her features turned to surprise as Mizu realized her friend was carrying a small black box. How had she missed that?

"Emil and Foks found this sitting on the chow table. It wasn't there, then it just… was. Jon and I both checked the place over twice, and checked the box. No trace of intruders, no trace of where the box came from—nothing. We aren't exactly secure here, but nothing appears to have been tampered with. Nothing in the cam feed."

"What's in it?" She took the box cautiously from her friend. It fit in the palm of her hand.

"See for yourself. I don't get it, but you might."

Opening the black lacquered box gingerly, Mizu dropped its contents into a waiting, four-fingered hand.

Kairi continued. "We were hoping you knew. No prints. No trace. Like a slagg'n ghost dropped it."

"The hell—" they both stared at the crisply folded origami sparrow in Mizu's hand. Made of flawless linen paper, such things were unheard of in modern times. Relics for a museum more than anything. "No trace of who left it? Nothing at all?" She asked as she turned it over in her hand.

Mizu flipped on her comlog and ran a scan over the box and its contents. Holo-light filtered over the small objects, and her vision filled with information about the small paper bird. Before she could search for the strange message, forgotten in yesterday's chaos, her geist made the connection for her. A digital mirror of the sparrow appeared once again, front and center. She shared the projection with Kairi as it began to unfold itself in their overlaid vision. The digital image dissolved into a self gibberish of revolving letters and numbers.

Kairi's muted gasp broke the silence.

"Wait. No?" Frantically, Kairi worked her own wrist-mounted comlog, spinning through her holographic dial of commands.

"What are you thinking, Kairi?"

"Do you still have your old protocols?" Trailing off, Kairi laid her left hand across her mouth in a knifing gesture then tapped her right shoulder. Mizu's geist automatically translated the hand signals as it fell into long dormant combat programming, targeting Kairi before moving on to scan the small room as if in an actual combat scenario. *Silence. Command.*

The Aragoto Senkenbutai had developed their own hand sign—a mix of combat signals and *bōsōzoku* slang gestures—during the Uprising. They used simple gestures that could be spotted from the back of a bike, at speed.

Activating a long archived protocol, Mizu watched as the constantly changing symbols began to lock in place. Letter by letter, Mizu's chest clenched tighter and tighter. Her avatar bounced cheerily across the numbers as her gut flipped in knots.

Years of waiting for this moment had passed by in a haze of fight-or-flight survival. Open war gave way to guerrilla hit and run operations which itself gave way to a desperate flight, running and hiding for their very survival.

The Third Platoon slowly dwindled back into the Third Hand. A *bōsōzoku* gang in tradition only, now relegated to petty drug running for their yakuza protectors. Mixed feelings flooded through Mizu, and she and Kairi read the decoded message.

///The Divine Sun does not forget the MIDNIGHT RIDER. Rise and ride once again.///

Time and location data followed the message before both were deleted, slowly dissolved from their vision like falling sand by some hidden algorithm in the data. Mizu and Kairi both stared into the empty quantronic space before them in dumbfound silence. Two days. They only had two days.

The paper bird in her hand was an atlas stone of grief, obligation, pride—and anger. Before either of them could speak, Mizu quickly unfolded the paper bird in her hand. Inside, a handwritten strike order for this evening was scrawled in more elegant penmanship than either woman had ever seen.

Mizu's missing finger throbbed like a pulse of fire, the Silk-laced painkillers still fogging her mind and twisting her nerves. She forced herself to focus on Kairi's calm voice, but every word felt like it slid through a haze of suspicion.

"A strike order." Kairi's voice was soft.

"*Chikusho*. Forget someone leaking to the yakuza," Mizu muttered, voice tight—willing it to not be true. "It's Yu Jing—on our slagg'n doorstep."

Her eyes flicked toward Kairi, searching for a hint of uncertainty—betrayal—but found nothing. Still, the doubt gnawed at her, sharper than any pain.

"Slagg me." Mizu's heart sank, and the shake burned in her soul. She looked around her small room, memorizing every detail. "I need a drink."

"*Kuso*, me too." Kairi grabbed Mizu's jacket from its hanger and tossed it at her before departing. Mizu held her jacket, frozen—daunted. It was heavy with brutal meaning and memory. Mizu grabbed her pack and was stuffing supplies in when Kairi returned with her own matching red jacket. With a nod between friends, the pair silently exited her bunk.

Fingers to her lips, Kairi let out a shrill whistle, bringing the eyes of each and every Hand present up to the pair. "I need a drink."

Wide eyes looked back at Mizu. They knew what the code meant. They knew what the jacket meant. Fear and anxiety permeated the air.

"Midnight Rider." The stunned silence that followed Mizu's words hung, frozen in time. Her Hands processed what their *sukeban* had just said. Veterans of the Uprising, or orphaned by it, each and every one was pulled into the gravity of Mizu's announcement, falling into the blackhole of suspense.

In the quiet, Kairi's left hand flashed once more. *Danger. Exit.*

"When?" Goro was the first to speak, his deep voice carried all the tension of thunder in the night sky. For an instant, Mizu didn't see her friend staring back at her through determined eyes, but a soldier. Her soldier. Her responsibility.

"Now." Mizu's face wore the only mask it possibly could to cover her own conflicting thoughts, the mask of command, as her hands flashed. *Destroy. Retreat.*

The moment stretched impossibly long. This was their home...

Goro once again shattered the silence, a soldier once more. "You heard your *sukeban*, Hands! Get your slagg'n feet moving!"

* * * * *

Neon banners buzzed and flickered over cracked pavement, casting fractured colors on windows across the district. The once-proud neighborhood lingered in an uneasy twilight between decay and forced renewal, where flickering holo-ads battled the ghosts of a nearly forgotten district. From her shadowed vantage point down a narrow side street, Mizu's eyes fixed on the target building. It was just another nondescript garage fading into the monotonous line of identical buildings. The simple holo-sign above the door cast a weak, steady glow—enough to mark its presence, but never enough to draw attention. It was their home.

Above, the harsh roar of Fēiquán jet bikes shattered the silence. Neon trails carving ribbons of electric blue and green across the sky marked their passing. The squadron surged forward with brutal efficiency, converging on the garage like a pack closing in for the kill. Holographic warnings flickered to life around the building's perimeter, casting a ghostly light across the block. Lines of Yujingyu soldiers advanced on the entrances.

Leading the assault was a figure wrapped in armor sharp enough to cut through the neon haze—a sleek, authoritarian suit of burnt orange plating, polished to a merciless gleam. Severe black hair sat chin length, framing intense eyes that seemed to bore through the building, hunting the occupants within. She moved with deliberate calm, every motion precise, commanding the squad with silent authority. There was something unnatural in her presence—an almost palpable chill that seeped into the air, as if the city itself recoiled beneath her gaze.

Then, the moment broke.

Heavy metal doors burst inward under ruthless kicks, triggering simultaneous charges that detonated at the building's interior. The garage exploded in a furious bloom of flame and debris. Shards of concrete and steel were thrown violently outward. Soldiers were hurled from their feet. Quantronic signs overhead sputtered and flickered wildly in the shockwave, as if the light itself shuddered—sympathetic to the destruction.

Mizu sucked in a breath, the blast illuminating the night sky—a jagged wound ripped through the heart of their world. Around her, the ragged remnants of the Third Hand Gang stood frozen, swallowed by a silence heavier than the explosion. Each carried a hollow ache inside, a wound no amount of resolve could mend.

Mizu and Goro had activated the charges themselves after filling the hollowed out motorcycle engines with anything that might further fuel the blast. Years of safe harbor in a semi-gutted garage were gone in a trio of fiery blasts. No home, no resources, the Third Hand was truly in the wind.

Mizu's eyes flicked back one last time, her breath catching as she searched the dancing shadows. There—the faint glint of polished armor caught in the billowing flames and neon haze. The Imperial Agent who led the raid stood motionless, an unyielding silhouette against the glowing cityscape. That cold, unreadable expression felt like a weight settling deep in Mizu's gut, twisting with dread.

"What now, Boss?" Jon posed the question on everyone's minds as Mizu turned to face her crew.

"I don't know." She wouldn't lie to them. "What happens next is anyone's guess. Look, if you don't want to take this ride, I don't blame you. They came to our home and took it from us. I intend to find out why. Pair up and stay out of sight for a few days. No data trail, stay dark, and wait for Goro or Kairi to make the rounds and update you. I'll get more info in the meantime. Jon, you're with me."

Jon's hand flashed *Affirmative*.

"Stay safe, Hands, move out."

Mizu and Jon waited for the rest to vanish into the night before starting their own journey to the coast.

///Get moving, Rider.///

The text scrolled across Mizu's vision as she turned to leave, stealing the solemnity of the moment and bringing reality crashing back in.

9.

Across the Human Sphere, each of the hyperpowers maintained their own territories, some encompassing whole planets. These independent empires, frequently at odds and often in conflict, were interconnected nonetheless. The connective threads between them were maintained by O-12, the governmental body that kept the peace as best they could. Massive space faring vessels—Circulars—connected the planets. It was one of many ways O-12 maintained some semblance of balance in the chaos. Stabilized wormholes could be transited by these vessels thanks to incredibly costly specialized engines.

The fragile balance hung at a knife's edge, poised to fall into madness. After the recent invasion of Concillium, O-12's seat of power, and the destruction of an entire Circular during the fighting, resources were stretched to the breaking point. Nowhere was the strain more evident to those disconnected from the fighting than on one of the remaining Circulars.

Bianca had to admit traveling with a press badge had its perks. Digital fast lanes for her Maya connection, priority seating options, and private areas reserved for VIPs were some of the many perks she enjoyed on the weeks-long journeys through space. The ship was large enough to berth short range freighters within its long frame; it was the fastest way to travel between planets, unless you happened to have your own capital class starship lying around. Small populations lived and died on these craft, never setting foot on real soil. Circulars had all the comforts of a small city packed within their hulls.

She could have caught a direct route to the Yu Jing system but opted for the tickets Yasbir had provided her that routed through Sol. He was a mystery to her, even after all these years, but had her trust all the same. From their first introduction almost six years ago, he always found his way back into her life in one of two moments: before a major event or, more pointedly, when she was running for her life. Bianca had long since given up trying to make any sense of it. When she asked the Hassassin about his appearances, he always replied enigmatically by referencing the Old Man of the Mountain—the rumored leader of his order—or the Quest for Knowledge, a core tenant of Haqqislam.

She had heard it so many times that she had given up asking. Despite having her trust, he still unnerved her some times.

The ticket Yasbir provided Bianca was a middle class seat on the massive spacecraft. It was not an uncomfortable area by any standard, but her preferred VIP section was full, so she accepted his ticket begrudgingly. Each passenger had a small sleeping berth with private refreshers along a series of hallways that led to a common area with sitting areas that doubled as crash seats. As far as Circular travel went, it was certainly not even close to the worst option.

After a morning walk down the spine causeway of the craft and an indulgent long shower, Bianca spent most days wandering the public areas of the craft. Here in the commons, she could catch news and rumors from across the Sphere. From her current seat at an open air cafe, Bianca felt like she was plugged directly into a news stream.

"—no, no. Sell off our shares of Broska, they are going to get caught soon enough—"

"—Listen man, I don't care how much money they have. I don't want to get in bed with Minescorp. There are too many bodies in those closets—"

"—Oh, I'm so sorry dear! I know he was a soldier but I thought the fighting was over—"

"—Varuna, no I've never been—"

Bianca sat back and sipped her latte as the noise of the crowd washed over her. Her geist was set to maximum sensitivity and recorded it all to parse through at a later date. Just another day between jobs.

Her agent had taken some convincing that her source was real enough to risk the trip. She couldn't directly disclose Yasbir's involvement. Officially, she was heading to the twin plants of Yutang and Shentang to cover an upcoming spring ceremony. If her experience told her anything, it would be unlikely she would see the ceremony at all.

Thankfully, the StateEmpire had quietly lifted her travel ban after more than a little bribery by her agent. It was originally put in place for her revealing the callus and offensive remarks regarding dead Japanese soldiers by Yu Jing high command. Publicly, it was that very coverage which sparked an open rebellion. However, the speed with which the Uprising came together made her think the seeds had already been sewn.

Regardless of the past, the ban being lifted would make getting planetside easier, but Bianca expected scrutiny regardless. Behind the scenes, she had no doubt Bianca Chen was persona-non-grata, regardless of official stance.

Bianca summoned a floating holopane and scrolled through her personal archives. Like most in her profession, she jealously kept her sources secret. Their safety, and hers for that matter, depended on it, as well as the desire to keep lines of communication open and trust strong. Her source in the StateEmpire had been secretive to the extreme. She had never even met them in the flesh, and they had used a different encryption for every message sent. She had tried to contact them post Uprising, to check in on their safety, but had received no response. Curiosity compelled her to try again nonetheless. After all, she was going to be in the galactic neighborhood anyway.

Accessing an old message database, she found their last message. Bianca took a moment to refresh herself on the phrasing and coded language, then clicked reply.

///Hey! I know it's been a while, but hope you are well. Let's catch up sometime. How have you been?///

It was a flimsy excuse for coded language. She didn't really have much to go on, since her contact had always reached out to her first in the past. It would have to do.

Tapping the floating send button hovering above her wrist, Bianca leaned back and smiled as she brushed a stray lock of hair from her eyes. Just beginning to dip her toes back into the dark pond of the clandestine brought a smile to her face. There was no telling if she would hear back from them, but if she did, it was never disappointing.

* * * * *

///Are you sure the reporter is necessary?///

Yasbir pondered his reply as the words hung in his lens. "Not necessary—helpful."

///Very well.///

Yasbir patiently waited for the sultan's reply. The lag was small but noticeable when transmissions were still limited to the speed of light.

///I will pray for your succ—///

The transmission cut abruptly, leaving Yasbir alone in the gloom. The subtle vibrational shift beneath his feet indicated the Circular had entered the jumpgate. Transmissions were impossible through wormholes, only increasing the value of the Circulars that traveled through them.

Yasbir inspected the last piece of his gear before he donned it. The helm's sleek green visor stared back. It was the last thing many had seen before their deaths. Sealed inside his armor, Yasbir's mission began.

10.

The trip was bumpy; breaking orbit in any craft was never as smooth as one of the megalithic space elevators that dotted the planet's equator. Dressed in simple, unadorned fatigues, Takeshi was just another one of the dozens of military personnel along for the ride.

He generally thought it best to not focus too hard on the impending, existential dread waiting just on the other side of the uncomfortably thin hull. It could be meters thick, and space would still win if something went awry. Tutors had drilled physics into him from a young age, but all the logic in the universe could not shake the sense of vastness underpinned by dread every time Takeshi found himself in space. The more precise gravity plates sported on larger ships and stations could almost make one forget—almost.

Amongst the ballet of ships moving about low Earth orbit was *Tengoku Five*, the station was the pride of the Japanese Navy—the new independent anchorage for the small nation that boasted the absolute best in modern technology, from what they said on Maya newscasts.

From where Takeshi sat, it looked more fragile than mighty. Docking rings spun about a central column. The station looked like a half finished, insane jigsaw puzzle. The immense mobile construction yard looked like a madman's mind unleashed. Considering the Nomad Nations were hard at work building it, that was not too far from the truth. How anyone accomplished anything at all in the chaos was beyond him. ALEPH could have made short work of the chaos. With sweeping, algorithmic efficiency, the omnipresent AI was a fact of daily life for most, but wholly rejected by the spacefaring Nomads.

The station itself was ahead of schedule—according to briefings he had received—but enough sectors were functioning for Takeshi to not need to wear an EV suit.

Takeshi really still felt blind on his assignment. The meeting with General Daichi had focused on the past more than the future. After entrusting his remaining blade to his uncle and changing into the unadorned uniform provided at the palace, he was whisked away to shuttle launch facilities and blasted into orbit.

Too fast.

The whole day was simply going too fast for Takeshi to fully process. Up before the sun, it was mid-afternoon planetside, and now he was hurtling through orbit. Operations take time to plan, iterate, brief, and rehearse. Was he really expected to leap into enemy territory with a team he'd never met?

///Approaching station, Tengoku Five. *Please remain seated and secure during final approach and docking procedures.///*

* * * * *

A sudden loss of gravity had sent Takeshi tumbling through a corridor to be roughly returned to upright when it was restored—painfully. A soft chuckle from Kempeitai Kano—who surprised him at the shuttle—was his only indication of the regular nature of such things. "You get used to it. Techs haven't quite worked out all the bugs."

The man wore a similarly unadorned, black uniform. Euro-ethnic features and a shaved head made him feel more like a bar bouncer than a Nipponese political officer.

Takeshi found little choice but to follow. He was at a loss for who or what his guide could be in the military structure he was used to. Takeshi had undertaken secret missions before, but they rarely sat well with him—his strict code of honor clashing with the shadowy nature of such work. The cold, empty weight of this assignment felt especially at odds with the warrior values he cherished.

Passing through a security checkpoint they were both—to his surprise—Cube scanned. An unusual and incredibly costly measure, Cube scans were rare outside the most secure locations in the sphere. Yujingyu territories being the exception. Cube scans were simply a means of control for the StateEmpire over its twin planets and other territories. There was much one could do to disguise their identity, but a Cube would never lie, to Takeshi's knowledge. The tiny implant recorded your entire life, saved for the hope of an eventual resurrection in a Lhost artificial body. The exorbitant cost and mountains of restrictive permits for such a procedure baffled the mind.

The Cube scan was quickly forgotten as he entered the adjoining chamber.

"Back here!" boomed across the room. Beyond the data banks and holo screens, past the techs in similarly blank uniforms, a woman stood up from a console she was working on and waved them over. She was tall with short, cropped black hair. Her smiling friendly face was a welcome change from his curious escort and suspicious surroundings. She crossed the chamber, past technicians glued to their console, to greet him.

"You must be Major Motoko," Takeshi said as he bowed courteously, not taking his eyes off of her. "Sergeant First Class Oyama."

"No need to stand on formality. From here on in, it will only get you killed." A lethality flashed across her smiling face. Takeshi wondered if this is what a mouse saw when looking at a cat. "Follow me, please."

"Yes, ma'am," he responded reflexively. Rising awkwardly from the unreturned bow, Takeshi followed the major into a glass walled room, his smiling Kempeitai escort trailing behind.

"Once you enter our wing, the rank and courtly manners are useless, so knock it off. You are no longer a sergeant. I am no longer a major. My callsign is Song, and that will do from now on, understood?" Song did not bother to wait for a reply. "Welcome to the Watchtower, *Tengoku Five*'s dirty little secret. This wing is officially labeled as a redundant maintenance depot, but as you can see, we are fully operational here, even if the rest of the station is a heap of *kuso*.

"This is the growing heart of our operations throughout the Sphere—primarily small, independent units like Ryūken or Kaizoku, but we dabble in everything. In coordination, of course, with a few loyal clans and Kempeitai, like Mr. Cuddles here."

Takeshi was aghast at the informality, let alone that Song had just called a political officer 'Mr. Cuddles,' despite the man's short chuckle at the name. Song's smile grew into a sly grin, and Takeshi struggled to keep his mouth from hanging open.

A Kempeitai's authority was extrajudicial—on a good day. It would seem the rumors that their clandestine roots were never truly abandoned proved true. Not that he could share a single word about what he was seeing. Not that anyone would believe him.

"Taka. His callsign is Taka." Song's laughter cut Takeshi's confusion into a thousand pieces of embarrassment. "Let's get started."

Following Song's instructions, Takeshi and Taka gathered around a familiar looking briefing table. With a wave of her hand, Song summoned several holopanes from her comlog and inputted a series of commands into the interface dials floating above her forearm. Darkness fell as the glass walls shifted to an opaque black.

A peculiar sense of pressure settled over Takeshi. His lens told him that he was now cut off from Maya, meaning the room was secured from the outside net. Light returned in the form of holographic projections manifested throughout the room. Black silhouettes surrounded Takeshi, like shadows holding court. He felt absurdly out of his depth in the lair of secrets.

"Let's get the unpleasant part out of the way." She turned to face him directly, brown eyes boring through his soul. "None of us were excited when you were called in. You are a known quantity, and therefore a liability. We live and die in the shadows, Mr. Oyama. Do you understand?"

Takeshi nodded silently. Song continued.

"From our perspective, you might as well be a Maya celebrity, and there is no avoiding that. Bringing you along is an unfathomable risk to our operators and, frankly, the biggest operational liability known to human history…"

Warring between the desire to be anywhere else or to defend his honor, Takeshi chose to remain silent. He was no stranger to being dressed down by a superior. His actions being questioned was one thing, but it was never this… personal. This was a completely different experience.

"Ma'am, I…"

"Song. You address me as an officer again, and I'll shove you out the nearest slagg'n airlock, am I clear?"

"Trust me, she will." Taka's voice made Takeshi feel like a mouse being toyed with by the hawk he was named for.

Song's use of PanOceanian slang reminded Takeshi of cross-training with the Svarlheima Winter Force. The phrase was ubiquitous throughout the military now, but he rarely heard such language amongst the Domaru Butai.

"Yes, Ma'a… Understood, Song."

Behind him, Taka stifled a laugh.

"Better. Now, your clearance is woefully inadequate for the rest of this discussion. Taka, go find Hiro and tell him to get his useless backside in here."

Taka stepped out with a nod.

Song tapped out a series of commands into a newly manifested holographic console above the table, prompting a notice that scrolled across Takeshi's vision as his lens informed him of a new security clearance escalation.

///Temporary Security Clearance Authorization: Level – Ryu Seven.///

With a wave of Song's hand, Takeshi vaulted into the stratosphere of intelligence availability. Secrets he couldn't fathom were at his fingertips as his geist adjusted to the overwhelming change. Song, seeing his wide eyes, smiled wickedly.

"Welcome to the big leagues, Mr. Oyama. Now, stop gawking and tap your comlog on the table."

Following instructions, Takeshi's lens flooded with new, highly classified information projected across the room. Several of the silhouettes filled in with unfamiliar faces as well as their names and locations, scattered across the Human Sphere.

The presence of the Hassassin Yasbir did not surprise him. The holographic figure nodded to Takeshi.

"I am pleased you have joined us."

Takeshi met Yasbir once before, but the man's infamy preceded him regardless. He always appeared at pivotal moments in the Sphere.

Of all the faces projecting in the digital space around him, the one that least surprised Takeshi was the familiar-yet-half-forgotten face of Nakama.

"Hello again, student-of-my-friend. I am pleased to see you have joined us for this undertaking. I have taken the liberty of asking the *kensei* to assign your callsign. Your mentor had no hesitation in his choice. Trust you will appreciate it in time."

The message piped directly into his datasphere, for his eyes only.

///Name: Takeshi Oyama, Sergeant First Class: ~~Unit of Origin: 5th Domaru Butai, 1st Company:~~ Assignment—REDACTED: Callsign: NEKO///

Takeshi watched his personnel tag scroll across his lens in dismay—Neko.

"Thank you, Nakama," Song continued before Takeshi could even think to react. Taka returned with another in tow. Taller than everyone in the room, Hiro moved with the grace of a leopard. As the gray-haired man entered, it seemed he prowled more than walked. "'Bout time."

"You know me. Fashionable entrance." Hiro smirked as if he had been caught doing something underhanded and simply did not care. The man's every move spoke of a quiet, lethal confidence that bordered on insubordination. A far cry from the disciplined ranks Takeshi called home.

"Hiro, this is Neko."

Takeshi nodded politely, unsure when to speak.

"Hiro has been my partner since before the Uprising. Taka you've met. Now, ladies and gentleman, let's get to the heart of this operation. Any operations on Shentang are a calculated risk. We have avoided this particular op up to this point. We simply didn't have the assets to pull it off."

Takeshi struggled to hide the shock from his face.

"Oh, don't look so surprised. Driving into the heart of Yujingyu territory is a nightmare of a logistical endeavor. Thankfully, our friends from Bourak have a vested interest in our success. So, let's go rescue a spoiled prince."

11.

The seaside path they walked was once a beautiful, winding park, filled with life and laughter. Years prior, Yujingyu commanders had burned the cherry trees that lined the avenue, brought all the way from Earth, in a public display while executing supposed dissidents. Plum trees were planted in their place. Tonight it felt haunted to Mizu.

Societal scars still kept many from the park even to this day, and few ventured out at night for fear of disappearing into infamous—if long gone—work gangs, or worse. Those days may be past them, but no one truly forgot. Crews like hers made a living between the cracks of their fractured society, so the places others avoided became their stomping grounds.

"There is no way you are entertaining this." Jon's frustration was palpable. Mizu was honest enough to agree he had every right to be. This whole thing was insane.

"I hear you, Jon—"

"No, you don't. We owe them nothing! They slagg'n left us. Abandoned. Gone. Dead to rights. Look how life has been since! *Kuso,* how many did we lose when it all went south, Mizu? It's like you've just forgotten them!" She hadn't, and Jon knew this. As her steadfast second, he had every right to give it to her straight, even now—even when it hurt.

The message had been cryptic at best. A time, location, and an old passphrase the Thirds used during the war, 'Midnight Rider.' It all felt so sudden, but the encryption was legitimate as far as they knew. That left Mizu with only one choice, but she wouldn't force the others to ride with her.

"You remember what 'Midnight Rider' was for, Jon? Eminent danger, high risk, high priority. It was *the* call, Jon. The call we waited for when we went to ground. So many other cells got clipped by the IS, but not us. It's been years, *chikusho*. Maybe we weren't forgotten after all!" The realization shocked Mizu. Forgotten. All these years, the buried pain of being left behind bubbled once again.

They all knew the moment the war fell apart for the Hands. Sounds of explosions and death preceded months of panic: command structures vanished, outposts were overrun, and friends were lost. A platoon of thirty was reduced to less than a dozen in short order as one by one they were picked off—or picked up.

"You talk like we were slagg'n special. We have no guardian spirit, Mizu. No one was watching over us but us! We survived because *we* survived." The anger in Jon's heart was creeping into his voice.

"I get it, Jon. Then this…" Mizu held out the little wooden box the note was delivered in.

"Boss, I hear you. We ride where you ride, but I just slagg'n can't keep my mouth shut on this one. You kept most of us alive in the aftermath, but how many more will we risk?"

This clenching pain in Mizu's chest was instant and nearly as blinding as her rage. Most of us. The hitch in Jon's step said he sure as hell knew he'd gone too far.

"Mizu… I…"

"Shut. Up." The barely contained fury in her voice stopped Jon dead in his tracks, recoiling. She saw something on his face between hurt and fear. Fists clenching in anger caused the nerves to fire up her left arm, reminding Mizu once again of the most recent price she had paid: her pain, her penance.

A cold sea breeze cut through the silence like a knife. Mizu couldn't tell if the chill down her spine was cold, fury, or nerves. They were both dressed in warm layers against the night's chill. Their tattered, old riding jackets were proof against the worst of it, but still it bit. She turned, and the walk continued on in tense silence, only punctuated by the crashing waves and occasional nocturnal hunter taking wing.

Target. Overwatch. As Mizu's hand flashed, the shift into a hand sign anchored the silence and ended the possibility of further discussion for now. Jon might have been one of her closest friends, but he knew when his word was welcome and when it was time for business. *Dark.*

"Roger," was his only response.

Mizu shut down her personal network, and Jon drifted off the path into the shadows; nominally there to back her up, though his presence had lost some of its comfort at this point. With Goro and Kairi on standby, close at hand, they were as prepared for disaster as time had allowed. Despite her frustration with Jon, she wasn't going to hit this meet alone, and trust was hard to come by when folks disappeared into the not-so-loving hands of the Imperial Service.

Taking up a seat on the lonely, stone bench, Mizu took a moment to breathe the night air and appreciate the beauty before her. A coastline, rich with life, stretched in both directions. Shentang's twin planet Yutang hung in the night sky, like a megalithic moon. It truly was breathtaking. Mizu might have thought it was peaceful.

Right up until she remembered that Yu Jing was headquartered there in sprawling, beautiful cities. Yu Jing citizens lived their lives in ignorance at best, and contempt more likely, of those they trampled on. The propaganda preached 'one people, one Yu Jing' from every screen and loudspeaker, but the Nipponese knew better. One people, over the ethnicities they deemed lesser. It had been the case for hundreds of years, only now the boot was hidden behind silks and honeyed words.

Lost in her thoughts for only a second, Mizu jumped to notice an older woman standing a few feet away. The graying woman stood with the ramrod straight stature that spoke to a lifetime of labor strengthening her body. Her simple worker's coveralls were one in a billion here on Shentang.

"Apologies, *Oba-san*. I didn't hear you."

"Be at ease, noble warrior. May you walk among friends." Straight into passphrases and betraying no emotion on her weathered, wrinkled face, the old woman waited patiently, gnarled hands visible and empty. Everything about the stranger fit Mizu's idea of a factory worker perfectly, down to the dirt under the nails—everything except the unwavering focus of the woman's brown eyes.

"Friends who ask for but a token of favor," Mizu continued in code, wary.

"One the spirits will surely give. Thank you, Captain."

"It's just 'boss' these days." Mizu didn't enjoy being referred to by her military rank. Silence stretched for too many heartbeats. "*Sukeban* if you want to be fancy."

"As you say, Boss. I transmitted my clearance to you before I arrived. Have you forgotten your standard procedures?"

"I received it, but a lot has changed, *Oba-san*."

"You may call me, Sparrow. You and your riders are called to service once more."

The shake spoke for Mizu. "I don't care who you are. A lot has still changed."

"Of this, I am keenly aware. Your Third Platoon is gone—a shadow of its former self. Some who flocked to your banner never fought in the war. Yet despite all adversity, you are strong, tight knit, and an effective outfit at your core. I have need of you. Your Emperor has need of…"

Mizu spat on the ground, cutting off Sparrow mid-sentence. "Need us?! After being abandoned!" Even in her quieter tones, the emphasis in Mizu's voice was unmistakably laced with anger, her conversation with Jon bleeding through her thoughts. Taking a deep breath, Mizu looked back to the sea.

"Your wrath is understandable, justified. Much was sacrificed to keep our peoples alive; and like a phoenix, the sun will rise on a nation reborn. The fear and anger of your found family is justified. Not all who fought for it have seen its beauty. You are called to serve nonetheless. I have selected you, Captain Mizu Oniko, because you have kept your family together. You have kept them safe. You have kept them functioning as a team and heroically serving your people. Smuggling medicine is no open battlefield, but it is still heroic." Sparrow's intel was good and caught Mizu off guard, surprise written across her features. "You serve your family nobly and protect them at all costs," she said, gesturing at Mizu's recent disfigurement.

"How…?" Mizu looked down at her gloved left hand. A hasty alteration had removed a finger from the glove to match Mizu's hand and stitched it back up; red thread against the black leather riding glove.

"There is little I do not know, Mizu. It is in my service to our Emperor that I persevere in this benighted land. While I am alone, you have the fire of an Aragoto Senkenbutai squad behind you. There are things I simply cannot accomplish alone. You, however…"

"I will not commit my people—" She stared daggers at the old woman.

Sparrow waved the argument away. "Yes, the rules of a *bōsōzoku*. You must have a quorum. You carry your own customs, your own path of honor. I am aware, but as their leader, their *sukeban*, you hold the power. All must follow where you ride."

"You seem to know our ways well enough." These thoughts were already racing through Mizu's head. Sparrow somehow gave voice to her inner dialog. "So you must already know my answer."

"I do. You have two days to bring as many around as will decide to join you. Things are in motion, and you will be needed before the month is out, noble knight. You will receive a data packet shortly with further details. Rally your family. Rally your soldiers and ride again."

"No." Mizu looked to the sea for a moment and took a deep breath. This was all happening too fast. She thought of her younger charges, those not yet burdened with nightmares of bloody hands and dead faces. "Just four, four and the rest get out unharmed. This or nothing."

"Very well." Sparrow's voice was a whisper in the wind.

"I..." Mizu turned back to find herself alone in the night. "*Chikusho*."

* * * * *

Once the gangers departed, Sparrow peeled herself from the shadows. Things were progressing quickly now and could not be slowed. The bikers would need to be on board to fulfill the bargain that was made.

The appearance of an old woman faded away in the shadows. In her place stood a young woman, simply garbed—one of thousands.

Sparrow scanned her surroundings from the sea to Sakuramachi. The StateEmpire's fingerprint was everywhere. Holographic banners waved in a digital wind—taller than the rebuilt city—extoled the virtues of Yujingyu society. Slogans, myths, propaganda, and heroes in orange armor flew across a neon skyline. Years ago, glorious white and red symbols of Nipponese pride flew where now orange and jade propaganda fought for the hearts and minds of the Japanese left behind on Kuraimori.

Sparrow sighed. The night was short.

They all were.

12.

"Agent, are you reading me?"

"Yes, doctor, I can hear you." Takeshi nodded as much as the harness would allow. The doctors had strapped him in just on the firm side of comfort.

"Good. As we discussed, the first procedure should be familiar to you for the most part. A small probe will be pressed against your Cube and take a new backup. You've been through this before, so it should be no problem.

"I'm going to talk you through the rest of the process, step by step. You received all of this information in the briefing, but it tends to help patients to hear each bit, step by step. Minor appearance alterations are not particularly difficult, and painless. Do you understand the procedures?"

"I understand them, yes."

"Do I have your consent to proceed?"

Why did he agree to this? Trepidation swept over Takeshi for what felt like the millionth time.

Following the briefing, he had been given a brief period to process the whole assignment, his role, and the limited intelligence he had been given. Operational compartmentalization, Song had said, meant he would be mostly flying on blind trust. Trust in his fellow soldiers was always built on training, time, and shared experience.

Here, Takeshi had nothing but the word of strangers who operated in the shadows… Lies and deceit were the hallmark of those who lived and died behind the scenes. The rules of society and the veil of civility were convenient masks to be discarded as necessary. A lifetime of noble upbringing railed against it all. General Daichi had warned him this would happen. Living in the Emperor's direct service, he had experienced enough to provide that cryptic warning.

"All bushi *do what is necessary, Takeshi-san, for the glory of our beloved Emperor and the benefit of our people. We are the sword that fights so that they don't have to, the shield that guards them against a harsh universe, and the example of courage to inspire others to rise in our place when we fall. But there are those who fight and die in silence. Their sacrifice is no less noble, their example no less inspiring."*

"How can we put our faith in someone who would kill in the dark? Someone who would strike from behind... without honor?"

"You think they are without honor, Takeshi-san?" Takeshi had hesitated at that. Honor was a personal thing to each warrior. While all *bushi* followed the same basic code, it was meaningful to each warrior in different ways.

"I do, General."

"Then I must insist you seriously consider this mission. Honor takes many forms, Takeshi-san. Learn to see that, for you fight for them all."

It had felt like a rebuke that stung even now, suspended like in a low gravity operating suite surrounded by surgical robotics.

"Do I have your consent to proceed, Agent?"

The probe hovering next to his neck was not nearly as daunting as the nano injector, just out of eyesight—waiting to overwrite Takeshi Oyama and hide him beneath a fiction.

As much of a boon as a Cube was, on Shentang it was also a liability. If he was scanned by a moderately attentive soldier with the right gear, Takeshi would find out exactly what the bowels of the imperial dungeons looked like… in all their horror.

But if it was overwritten, edited? Even if only as a shield to cover his true self beneath…

Takeshi was about to find out exactly how good Japanese hackers really were.

The PanO NeoVatican called it your soul; the Haqqislamites, your *sheut*. No matter the belief, it was indelibly the 'who' of what made a person who they are.

"Cubes are a one way street, in most circumstances. The exception is when one is implanted into a grown Lhost. Even that is only once, Neko."

Song had been quite clear on this delineation. Yet there were stories, rumors…

"Do I have your consent to proceed?"

Hair and skin editing didn't bother Takeshi in the slightest. He had indulged in minor alterations before. Human hair was not quite so naturally perfect as his, after all.

"Agent? Do I have your consent to proceed?" The doctor's voice practically dripped with impatience.

Takeshi released the breath he didn't know he had been holding.

"Proceed."

* * * * *

Despite his imagination playing merry havoc on his nerves, the procedure was not some excruciating thing. Takeshi chided himself for doubting. In fact, he felt nothing throughout. Medical advancements in the quantronic age meant the subtle sculpting of his body was done by Silk-infused nanites, painlessly, entirely while conscious. Post op protocol was a day's rest, mostly for observation; a hold over from ages past and not necessary in the slightest.

During his brief reprieve, Takeshi had been given spare fitness clothing and taken to a sparring suite; moving through his sword forms for the first time in weeks was a comfort. He inwardly admonished himself for having dodged something that was so very important and grounding in his life.

Finishing in a sweat, Takeshi returned the training bokken before kneeling in the center of the room. A training implement was a poor replacement for the blade he had lost, but it felt good. One that had been by his side since his first days of service, back when Japan served the Jade Throne… served Yu Jing. He found an uncomfortable symmetry in his weapon being broken by that Yu Jing warrior, he thought. Broken bonds and broken promises around it.

The bare metal walls of the station bore no resemblance to the painstakingly crafted historic recreations he was used to, but it served well enough. Silence washed over Takeshi as he struggled to ground his mind. Nakama, the mission, the Yu Jing warrior, Uncle Daichi… Try as he might, he found no peace, his mind racing. As the sweat dried on his body, Takeshi's mind surged forward. The sensation was so unsettling that he actually welcomed the interruption as the door chimed and slid open, revealing the unsmiling form of Taka.

"How are you feeling today, Neko?"

"I have recovered, thank you."

"Glad to hear it." Taka entered and stood before him. His causal posture was utterly out of place to his rank and position. "We have all been through it a time or two. The doctors just want to be nearby out of habit, I think. Makes them feel in control."

"I trust they know their craft. How can I be of service?"

"You can't." His words came out laced with venom. He sighed. "Frankly, we all argued against your inclusion on this mission. But here we are. Everything about who you are is a liability. Your family…"

As the political officer spoke, each word felt purposefully chosen to provoke the growing anger in Takeshi. It worked.

"Excuse you!" His anger winning over, Takeshi rose, half kneeling instinctually: a warrior's pose. "You may question my suitability for an underhanded, clandestine mission. You may question my qualifications for such dishonorable deeds. You may also remind yourself who they are and never speak of my family in such a manner again."

Dark brown eyes bore into his very soul as Taka stared back. Slowly, a smile crept across his face, and Takeshi knew he had been baited.

"There it is; the fire, the pride. That's why, 'Takeshi-san.'" His name was spoken somewhere between playfully and distastefully. "That is why you are unsuitable and grossly unqualified, as you said yourself. That didn't take as long as I had thought it would, to be honest. You are raw. You are too used to the world of honor and ceremony. If you want to survive this, leave Takeshi Oyama behind. Now stand up."

"I understand." Takeshi cut in, doing as he was told. He mothered his outrage with implacable, ice cold discipline. Even still he felt it under the surface, barely held in check. He knew he was just proving Taka's point by diligently obeying. The command did come from a political officer after all, it was instinctual.

"No, you don't. Spar with me."

Takeshi paused, thoughtfully. Striking a political officer was both career and social suicide. "Will the doctors object?"

"I don't care, and I don't think you do either."

Taka struck out with an open hand flat into Takeshi's chest. Takeshi took the blow stoically and stood his ground. "Is this wise?"

"Does it matter?" Taka kicked at Takeshi's feet. Takeshi moved only enough to avoid the blow. "What does the scion of the Oyama clan do when attacked? Turn the other cheek, it seems."

Takeshi held his tongue.

The next attack came swiftly and without warning. Taka exploded into motion, catching Takeshi across the jaw with a right hook. Takeshi stepped back and pivoted with the punch, absorbing the blow and gaining distance between them. As he kept his hands at his side, unthreatening, Takeshi stared back. The ice was burning through his veins.

"And here I thought the Domaru Butai never retreated? Come on. Show me what you've got."

Takeshi kept his gaze focused on Taka as the man danced on his feet. "I do not think this is wise, Kempeitai." He hoped that mentioning Taka's rank would deliberately defuse the situation.

Taka stilled and flicked open his comlog. "I hereby give Agent Neko permission to strike me. He will face no recourse for his action."

Takeshi saw the recording pop up in his lens, shared as an official record. He had no idea what the goal was here, but Taka wouldn't let it go. "Very well."

Takeshi saw the punch coming. He leaned back just a fraction as the blow moved past his face, not connecting. He turned with the attack, translating his movement into a spinning kick that connected with Taka's chest. His assailant flew backward with the force of the blow but managed to land on his feet. Takeshi stepped forward into a guarded stance. "Is this what you wanted?!"

Takeshi watched as Taka grinned maniacally and launched forward, fists up in a boxer's guard. His left jab preceded a series of attacks that Takeshi blocked one by one, letting instinct lead him. He saw each coming before they were launched and moved to counter in kind: hooks, jabs, uppercuts, knees, kicks. Nothing touched him. Takeshi felt the rhythm of combat pull him into its song. He had held back at first, unsure of what was happening, but the pull of violence was strong. Takeshi wrapped himself in its warm embrace for just a moment.

He side stepped to avoid Taka's next attack—leaving Taka extended—and chopped down on his opponent's exposed neck. As Taka reeled, he pushed in close, landing a swift elbow to the face of his already staggered opponent.

He struck one, two, three, four times in rapid succession; closed fists into the sternum. He pressed forward with each staggering attempt Taka made to retreat. Takeshi gave him no respite, continuing to strike the exact same spot. Taka threw a wild haymaker in a desperate attempt to gain some breathing room.

Takeshi stepped aside, the fist whizzing a breath away from his face. His hands moved without conscious thought as he grabbed the wrist of his opponent and flung him in a hip toss. He felt Taka reciprocate the tight grip on his forearm and tried to twist Takeshi as he fell, but the *bushi* used the momentum to flip over his opponent.

Wrist still locked, Takeshi rolled backward, bringing Taka with him, and planted both of his feet into his chest. The force of the kick broke his opponent's grip and sent him flying.

Taka crashed into the wall, upside down. He crumpled to the ground before righting himself. He sat against the wall, chest heaving, with something new in his hands. Too late, Takeshi recognized the handheld Flash Pulse pointed at him as the trigger was pulled.

Blinding light swallowed his senses. His lens overloaded, shutting off. Takeshi staggered back—blinded and stunned, but on guard.

By the time Takeshi's vision cleared, Taka was sitting casually, one knee propped up, resting his arm on it—the arm holding the weapon. His posture had eased, but the pistol shaped Flash Pulse remained a threat.

"Take your time, Neko."

"What is wrong with you?" Takeshi slurred angrily, still shaking the stun. Flash Pulses were useful tools. Multispectrum light and extremely high frequency datawaves were focused with laser precision to stun the target. Non-lethal, but getting hit with one still hurt like hell. It felt like a burning needle to the brain, right behind the eyes.

"Lesson number one: honor will get you nowhere. When you have to fight, fight to win." Taka kept his voice level.

"I know that." Takeshi's anger was waning, frustration remained.

"No, you don't." Taka paused, letting his words hang like a lingering blade, waiting to strike. "You'll get there though. You are *bushi*, a soldier—"

"You would be correct."

"Let me finish." Taka paused, waiting for another interruption that never came before continuing. "You are an exceptional warrior, but for now, I need you to do things my way. If you don't, you will die. Song and Hiro are the best operators there are. I've never met a better hacker than Song, and there is nothing Hiro can't blow up in spectacular fashion. They have been all over the Sphere and back again."

His remarks left Takeshi off-footed—mentally.

"Frankly, you are the liability here. If you can't adjust, people will die."

"And you? What is your role in this?"

"I get Neko into Kuraimori and make sure he gets home alive." Taka paused. "You and I will work together until we arrive in-system.

Takeshi couldn't do this. But with a little work, Neko just might."

"You have my gratitude." Takeshi felt deflated.

"Not needed, but appreciated. Lesson number two starts tomorrow morning. Get some sleep so the docs feel better, will you?" With a wink, he rose to leave.

Takeshi spotted the limp, no matter how hard Taka tried to hide it.

"I will do my best. You are right. I have been a soldier all my life. Honor and duty have been my waystones, and you read me like a book, didn't you?"

"I did. That's what I do. I get in close." Taka grinned. It was predatory and cruel.

Taka paused by the door, leaning against the wall for support. Answering a call, he lingered, turning his gaze back to Takeshi.

"He's an incredible warrior. I couldn't even touch him once he started trying. In a straight up fight, he's invaluable."

The one-sided conversation paused, boring through Takeshi's mind—feeding his uncertainty.

"I know." Pause. "I said I know, Song! He's not what we need him to be." Taka pushed himself off the wall and limped out the door continuing his conversation. "Not yet anyway."

13.

Days ticked by as the C1-Circular made its ponderous trek across the stars. Seemingly endless tracts of empty space within each system needed to be crossed to get from jump gate to another. As the system slowly crept by, smaller ships would move in and dock with the craft as it made its way.

Once again, Bianca watched a series of craft make their way to and from the Circular from a cafe in a portside observation dome that Yasbir had insisted she visit every day. She likened it to a ballet in motion, each craft playing its own part in the slow moving performance.

Public announcements shared via Maya told her they were nearing the next jump gate. In two days' time, she would be through the next wormhole and back into StateEmpire territory. A few days later, she was scheduled to disembark. As soon as she stepped off the Circular, it was anyone's guess how things would play out.

"—let the shipment go. The Coalition—"

"—It'll be fine mom, Bourak has the best doctors money can buy—"

Bianca half watched the feed in the corner of her vision as her geist absorbed her surroundings. It was a familiar buzz at this point in the journey.

"—Corregidor?! Why in hell would you make your mother cry like—"

"—One cut at a time—"

"—You are seriously going to be a Knight? Like the Mendoza flicks?"

Finishing her coffee, Bianca rose to leave. Despite the Circular's immense size, space was still at a premium on any spacefaring craft, and the cafe seating was no exception. Sliding out of her small booth, Bianca pulled her small backpack with her, noticing too late as the bag knocked her empty mug from the table. She lunged to catch it but never made it.

From the table behind her, a man caught it, moving so swiftly she barely saw the motion. Turning to face her, he presented her mug back with a polite smile.

"I believe this belongs to you."

He was tall with short, dark brown hair, worn wild, but it was his eyes—twin wells of honey-brown—that entranced her. They had an intensity that was threatening, but their depths were laced with what Bianca could only describe as 'pain.'

"Yes, thanks!" Suddenly uncertain of herself, Bianca took the cup and turned to leave, but something nagged at her mind, stopping her from departing. She had been at ease here on the Circular, but as a war correspondent, she was no stranger to sudden shifts in fortune. She was also no stranger to the look in someone's eyes who had seen too much death. "Great reflexes, by the way."

"It must be luck." A shadow of discomfort betrayed his casual smile. Good instincts were a vital part of staying alive as a reporter. Good stories often meant rough actors who rarely told the truth. Bianca would have bet an entire moon on the hunch that he had just lied. He was not lucky, he was just that good.

"I'm Bianca." She locked in a charming smile and extended a hand as an introduction.

"I am Tak…" He hesitated. "Gi-ung." It was subtle, but Bianca caught the stumble.

"Bianca Chen." Bianca's smile turned sly as she played along. "Nice to meet you, Tak Gi-ung."

"And you, Bianca."

* * * * *

Yasbir moved like a breath between shadows. The maintenance corridor was narrow, tucked behind the primary drive stacks of the Circular, a place so boring and lifeless it was only checked when the need arose. Which made it perfect.

He slowed when he saw them—Taka and Neko—outlined in the fractured spill of utility lights. Taka had his back to the bulkhead, arms crossed, one boot casually pressed against the wall. Neko stood before him like a student trying not to fidget.

Yasbir sank into the shadows behind an open panel, watching through the slats of a loosened vent cover. A perfect angle. He exhaled silently.

Taka flicked his fingers once. Startled, Neko flinched—catching something.

"Too slow," he said.

"What is this?" Neko muttered aloud, examining the object. A sliver of shaped metal. Almost invisible. Yasbir knew it on sight and had used something similar on Paradiso.

"Quantronic dataspike," Taka replied. "Single use. Since just about every firearm is keyed to the user, it won't work for anyone else, and it won't shoot a friendly."

"I know this."

"Well, this burns out a weapon's Friend/Foe system and replaces it with a new one."

Takeshi scowled. "How does this help me? This isn't teaching."

"No," Taka said. "This is teaching."

He stepped forward, quick and quiet. Takeshi tensed—but not enough. In a blink, Taka placed one palm on his chest, leaned in close enough to whisper almost intimately, and deftly lifted Takeshi's comlog.

Yasbir saw the spark of frustration in the warrior's shoulders, the flare of ego dented just enough to leave a bruise. But he also saw something else—focus. Neko bit down on the reaction, studied the sleight-of-hand like it mattered.

"Again."

Taka obliged.

"I watched you fight a man who is arguably one of the best swordsmen in the entire Human Sphere to a draw," Taka murmured, pressing the comlog back into Neko's hand. "But that kind of strength gets you killed in our work. Above all, you have to learn *not* to fight, Neko. If you do, you will get us all killed. There will come a time for blades."

"Then what doesn't get me killed?"

He tilted his head. "Knowing when you're being watched."

Takeshi stiffened, eyes flicking down the corridor.

Yasbir didn't move. He could feel the pulse in his temple, steady as breath. If either of them had true sixth sense, they might've noticed. But they weren't ready yet. Not for him.

Maybe Taka, Yasbir conceded.

Taka smiled and turned, heading back down the hall—away from Yasbir. Takeshi lingered a moment, as if trying to sense something just beyond perception. Then he followed.

Only when the sound of their steps had vanished into the faint thrum of the ship did Yasbir step out from the shadows, folding his arms. He looked after them with a rare softness around the eyes.

"He'll do," he murmured.

Then he vanished the way he came—soundless, scentless, unseen.

14.

Mizu watched silently as Jon, Kairi, and Goro each read the files provided by Sparrow with as much incredulity as she had. There were so many moving pieces to this operation that she didn't even know where to begin. What mattered most was her crew. The four of them were all the most competent of the lot, experienced and battle tested, but each and every life was precious to her. As was tradition, the vote came down to a drink. In better times, it would have been saké, placed in front of each of them. Now saké was invaluable, outlawed alongside many other Nipponese traditions. Each had a thimble of cheap whiskey to bind their choice.

She could have overruled them all, but Mizu refused to place that tile on the board. Make that play too often and respect would crumble. Mizu's gaze swept over their faces, each marked by the same mix of doubt and determination she felt inside. Her voice was low, steady, but carried the weight of everything they'd survived together.

"We don't get many chances like this—choices that matter. There are bigger things bind us beyond the scars and battles. You know I won't ask you to follow blindly." She lifted her glass slightly, eyes meeting theirs one by one.

"We're with you, Boss." Goro gave a nod.

Kairi and Jon echoed their support.

"But when we decide, we decide as one. No regrets. No turning back. Just the four of us, like old times." She tossed back her shot and placed the glass upside down—a challenge and a promise. Leading the way as *sukeban*, her vote was cast. "Ride, die, ride forever. Loud and proud."

"Loud and proud." Goro, Kairi, and even Jon raised their toast and joined her. Four glasses sat upside down on the table. After, they parted ways.

Mizu reached out, as planned, and made her offer. Sparrow agreed. Every single member of the Hands would be smuggled off world. Her Hands would be free. Now the four of them just had to live up to their end of the bargain.

The first few days of hiding felt like the war's end all over again. Moving from place to place, staying off the grid… Terrified. Despite herself, Mizu was constantly jumping at shadows as the shake ate at her calm. Isolation always brought its comrades: paranoia and fear.

Stealth and subterfuge had become necessary skills for the Hands long before they entered a life of crime after the war. Skills they all needed now, Mizu thought, as she had laid low in one ruin or another for two weeks. Each day, she slowly made her way north; and each day, the shake whispered in her ear.

Mizu only risked only a few quick looks onto the network to look for updates and data bursts from her crew. Nothing came in from off-planet that wasn't *heavily* curated—censored—by the StateEmpire, so she had no operational contact beyond the mysterious Sparrow. Despite the risk, she spun up her comlog each day. When she was content that no flags had gone up, Mizu shut her network down and kept moving. Every time she did, the shake would tell her to give up.

The shake always started the same. Adrenaline junkies to the last, *bōsōzoku* who came before her had named it. The gut-wrenching adrenaline addiction, coupled with bare-knuckle anxiety of living on the razor's edge of life and death. It always caught up with you if you lived long enough. Mizu knew she wasn't the only one it had consumed, nor would she be the last. Once the war had ended, she turned to darker paths to silence the shake…

"No." She shook her head to try and dispel the memories. Focus, Mizu. Focus on the now. She had places to be and better, more bitter memories to indulge in.

* * * * *

The Steel Saké was more than just another cheap dive in the furthest suburbs that could be reasonably accessed without a vehicle. It was also a piece of *bōsōzoku* history. Bikers from all across Kurayami rallied here to celebrate the new year, settle inter-gang disputes, and show off their skills at blistering speeds on the rolling hillside roads leading north toward Kume. Legends were made here. J-Punk bands once blared at reckless volumes that could be heard outside. A good thing, too, as the tiny little dive was entirely too small for the sheer numbers that rolled in.

A sad smile crept across her face as Mizu remembered the day the Third Hand gang rolled into the lot for the first time; Henzo, Jon, Goro, and Mizu. The founding four were swarmed by enforcers from the other crews. A riot of colorful vests and coats surrounded the small group before they even parked their bikes, bombarding them with questions, insults, and testing boundaries. Goro squared up to a man from the NRC Riders who pulled a knife on him. They were all lucky it hadn't gone further. She knew now it was a test, but it wasn't clear back then. They all thought they were going to die that night.

Goro and Henzo had been the first to be accepted into the bar. The abstract vetting process was never really codified from what she knew, but against all odds, the owner let Mizu in, then finally Jon. Inside was more chaotic than the riotous party outside. The who's who of *bōsōzoku* life could be found in the Steel Saké. Colors from the NRC Riders, Blue Rose, Bandit Brothers, U-Ladies, Killtriku, and so many more were an ever-present icon of everything the Hands wanted to become. Legends.

Then the war came.

Tonight the bar was a sad reminder of everything that was lost. Flashing holograms and projected vids of idiotic feats of prowess on the back of a bike were gone, replaced by memorials and StateEmpire propaganda.

An empty lot sat where hundreds of motorcycles had once been. While some of the memorabilia was still on the walls, the banners of the crews that called this place special were gone. Rumor was Yujingyu soldiers had collected and burned them, but Mizu didn't have the heart to ask. So many of the *bōsōzoku* gangs had ridden in the Aragoto regiments that it made sense why this place had been targeted. The first crews to emerge after the failed Uprising were executed publicly against the front wall of this very building. Shortly after that, they started trashing bikes. It was a small wonder that they didn't tear the place down.

Like in every crew, the Hands each had a role to play. Goro was the guardian, unfailingly keeping them all safe. When Kairi joined, she was undoubtedly their soul, ever caring and uplifting. Kairi gave them all hope. Jon had always been her naysmith. Someone to keep her balanced and focused. She was going to need that now more than ever. They had agreed to wait out a day and think things over before they had committed. Mizu was glad for it. It felt like forever ago already.

Sipping her cheap whiskey to numb the shake, Mizu's mind warred quietly. The argument with Jon still bothered her, even now. He was right. Across the board, point by point, he was right. The Hands didn't owe anyone but each other. Any greater loyalty to Japan was forfeit when they were abandoned. Instructions to go to ground were all they received from command, then chaos. Years of waiting with no word had sapped the resolve of many along the way. The Killtriku had turned themselves in to spare their families, only to be forced to watch them be executed anyway. An explosive collar was strapped to each and every one of their necks before they were shipped off to war once again as suicide troops.

Her reverie was rudely broken by headlights playing across the walls—through the few, thin windows—as a heavy cargo truck rumbled into the lot. Mizu's eyes locked on the entrance as vehicle doors opened and shut outside. Nerves wire taught, her hand slowly drifted below the bar toward her hidden Boarding Pistol. Cargo drivers weren't viewed favorably by her fellow veterans—seen as bowing to their oppressors in hopes of less brutal accommodations. They were traitors and turncoats in the eyes of many, Mizu included.

The door swung open, revealing a total surprise. Mizu gave a small smile as the cherubic face of Tanto entered the bar. Mizu released the breath she hadn't realized she was holding. Eyes catching one another, a simple nod was all that passed between the two as he looked around to find a booth.

Behind him, the startled form of Benji in a courier's uniform nearly tripped over Tanto. When his eyes found Mizu's, his face went white with fear.

"Come along, Benji-boy," Tanto chided, leading him onward. Mizu was glad to see the pair. Benji would have been just another corpse in the bay if Tanto had judged him a liability. At least this way he had a fighting chance to do something meaningful instead of slaving away under Yujingyu shift masters.

The door swung open once more, revealing a slighter frame than the two men. A thin woman entered the bar with wonder written on as much of her face as could be seen past the small, snug-fitting breather mask. Clad in work boots, heavy trousers, hands in a black jacket's pockets, and an old camouflage field cap, the masked woman looked about in wonder.

The stranger's gaze lingered on Mizu for a moment, and she felt like prey being appraised by a hunter. Dark eyes that spoke of darker deeds sent chills down Mizu's spine before moving past her and across the rest of the bar. Mizu scanned for an ident halo and was surprised when her lens slid right over the newcomer, unable to lock onto her.

///That one is with me. On the job, Mizu my love, no time for pleasantries.///

The quick message was accompanied by her geist as a cute little cartoon of Tanto drove a truck around the edges of her vision. Mizu turned back to her drink as she pinged back a quick confirmation and rebooted her rampant geist.

In the mirror behind the bar, Mizu watched as the newcomer wandered the room, searching over the memorabilia slowly. Stopping in front of a photo-covered wall, the woman reached a gloved hand up and tenderly straightened a photo of the U-Ladies, a long ago wiped out *bōsōzoku* crew from distant Kofuku, before continuing on.

Mizu knew the feeling all too well. Just another ghost, remembering those they lost. It had taken her years to come back to the Steel Saké after the Uprising. Not that there had been much time for sightseeing in those years. Then there was too much time. Staring into her whiskey glass, Mizu remembered all too well the early nights of drinking herself into oblivion. They would all have been dead if it wasn't for the others carrying her weight on their shoulders too. Eventually, booze wasn't strong enough to help her forget... Her Hands had emerged from hiding eventually as just more street trash dodging work gangs.

"What'll you have?" The barkeeper had flagged down the newcomer while Mizu's mind wandered. When she approached the bar, Mizu could just make out a tangle of red hair tucked into the stranger's cap in the low light as she removed her mask.

"Shakeout."

"*Chikusho*, haven't made one in a long time. Let me see what I can manage."

"Thanks." The newcomer's voice hovered between smooth and synthesized. Mizu's geist still couldn't lock onto the woman, despite being a scant two meters away, but it easily analyzed the vocals. It was not purely her natural voice, but she wasn't intentionally masking it.

"Been a long time since anyone's had a reason to have a Shakeout," Mizu stated, equal parts curious and on guard. An act of will kept both hands firmly in view, despite the impulse to move toward her weapon.

"No. Doubt there are many sworn in these days." The stranger leaned forward, elbows on the bar.

"Slagg, no. I'll join you." Mizu motioned for the bartender with her left hand, drawing a stare from the stranger toward her missing finger. "Drinking for the living or for the dead?"

Shakeouts were a legendary drink for *bōsōzoku* culture, one reserved for celebrations and funerals. The actual recipe varied greatly from town to town, but the basics never changed: hard as teseum, like swallowing razors, and a taste like the gut-wrenching rattle of the shake.

"The lost and the damned." The woman, pale as a ghost, turned and faced Mizu.

Mizu had served alongside the coldest of killers during the Uprising, and she put down her fair share too. Nothing had ever turned her veins to ice quite like the soulless rage in the newcomer's eyes. The moment stretched until the bartender dropped two glasses in front of them, startling Mizu.

"For the living. For the Third Hand." Hoping she covered her discomfort enough to not be noticed, Mizu reached for her glass. The blue-black liquor swirled like an oil slick. The bartender produced a caseless bullet from somewhere below the bar—it was death-on-sight contraband—and snapped off the propellant and dissolved half in each glass.

Mizu's geist hadn't stopped scanning and slipped through the stranger's quantronic shield for just a moment as she raised her glass to toast. Neither Mizu or her geist could make sense of the insane readings they were seeing. Before it was shut out, her geist registered extensive cybernetic augmentation replacing much of the woman's body. The avatar, a mouse this time, ran scared across her vision.

"Ride, die, ride forever. Loud and proud." The stranger caught Mizu off guard once more, giving the toast of the Aragoto Senkenbutai, the mounted regiments of the Japanese Successionist Army. One Mizu had not heard from anyone other than her Hands in years.

"Loud and proud." Mizu tossed back her drink in time with the stranger before slamming the glasses down in unison. "You rode in the regiment?"

The stranger paused, as if considering what to say before looking toward Tanto. They locked eyes and she turned to the door, leaving Mizu's question hanging in the air.

Tanto and Benji left behind the strange woman with nothing but a nod. Mizu moved to the door and glanced outside. Their large freight truck powered up as Benji climbed into the driver's seat. Her eyes caught the faint outline of a concealed weapon strapped beneath Tanto's jacket. Did he always carry a weapon and she hadn't noticed? Perhaps he really was more dangerous than she'd given him credit. She turned back inside, signaling the bartender for another whiskey.

15.

Sweat poured down Takeshi's body, rapidly cooling in the recycled air and fighting with his body's own heat. He told Taka it was the strict regime he was used to. If he was honest, Takeshi would have admitted it was a comfort. He was strictly, and repeatedly to be more precise, instructed not to practice any form of combat. The fictional Tak Gi-ung he was pretending to be would have no reason to. It made perfect, logical sense, but Takeshi longed for a bokken in his hand and to step through kata to find an inner quiet. For now, he would have to settle for a good sweat.

Traveling the C1 Circular was nothing new, he had done it many times, but always as Takeshi Oyama. Now, Gi-ung rode the Circular for the first time. It was an unwelcome experience.

Bumping into Bianca Chen was an equally disquieting piece of the journey. He had successfully avoided close proximity to her since their meeting, but he caught her watching him twice over the following day. She was good, he nearly missed her both times. He still couldn't share the feeling of being watched constantly.

Very few Nipponese didn't know who Bianca Chen was. Her reporting on the indifference shown to his slain comrades—whose heroism saved hundreds of lives—lit the fuse of rebellion. It was the spark that unleashed outrage and cries for vengeance against the Yu Jing StateEmpire. A spark that followed with wholesale destruction. He knew exactly who she was when he shook her hand. Now days into his first truly clandestine operation, inserting behind enemy lines under an alias, he had one of the most famous Warcors to worry about. At least the odds of her being there planetside were slim to none. It was a big universe after all.

The exercise deck of the monstrous spacecraft was long and narrow, running along the central corridor, before sticking out over the main plaza. Over the railing, he could see hundreds milling about the metroplex hall. Like a giant hollow in the craft, the hall was a multistory living space. Vendors, officials from every nation, news agencies, and entertainment venues all sat along various levels of the hollow space as travelers wandered from one floor to another via skywalks, like the one he was currently lingering on. The C1 Circulars, being so incredibly large, hosted a small population of permanent residents, and nowhere was this more evident.

Takeshi leaned against the railing as he began to stretch. From his vantage point, he watched a young family three levels down from him as they sat for lunch, oblivious to the dangers of the universe… It had been so long since he had even considered a family that the idea felt foreign to Takeshi. He moved through a short stretching routine as he contemplated what their life might be like. Were they business people? Athletes? Celebrities? Dozens of possibilities cycled through his wandering mind as he stretched. Whatever it was, it was a life he couldn't fathom.

Service had consumed Takeshi. Life in the Domaru Butai was grueling and without much hope for the stability it took to hope for a family. Constant deployments and dancing with death saw to that.

"Focus." Shaking himself out of his reverie, Takeshi repeated the mantra to center himself. "Focus. One cut at a time."

* * * * *

"Focus. One cut at a time."

The voice played back through Bianca's comlog as she cycled through security footage. She managed to tap a favor, and owe a few more, amongst the security staff on the Circular to get the footage, but it was wholly worth it in hindsight. While sending up her camera drone would have been infinitely easier, flying unauthorized drones on the Circular was a quick way into a private conversation with the very same security officials in a much more official capacity. Her press credentials would only get her so far in a more official interview.

"Focus. One cut at a time."

Her run in with Gi-ung had sparked her curiosity. Enough for her to owe an entire case of Neoterran wine to the Circular's security chief. It would be waiting for him by the time the C1 made its way through the next wormhole and back to Neoterra. It was paid for by Mr. Mercatis for the fluff piece she had written, but he didn't need to know where it would wind up in the end. It felt like closing a loop, poetic.

Her geist made quick work of sorting the footage, cross-referencing it with her own recordings to isolate any snippets of Gi-ung.

A few quick calculations, and Bianca had a rough physical mockup of the man. She had subtly scanned his public halo when he boarded a shuttle to the Consulate. Beyond that, she couldn't find any publicly available information other than a distant juvenile record.

She knew it was a distraction, but she had the time to kill while she waited for her shuttle. Odds of running into him again were probably slim to none.

"Focus. One cut at a time."

The phrase repeated itself throughout her captured audio as well as the security footage. Various, small alterations occurred, but he seemed to repeat the phrase often enough. Inspired, Bianca quickly tasked her geist with creating a voice print. That was something she could use. Cross-checking it with the physical stats she was able to build from her pilfered footage, her geist got to work.

///Query compiled. Searching local Maya relays.///

She had been in Yu Jing space for days now, and any hope of information from Sol would take some time. The Circular had slowed as it passed by the twin planets. A public notice across the craft warned of the impending acceleration as it made its way out-system.

///Incoming Call. Unknown Caller.///

Bianca flicked her hand over her waiting comlog to accept the call and then tapped the hovering record icon above her wrist. "This is B."

"Miss Chen. Events are in motion." Yasbir's voice soothed the anxiety Bianca didn't know was gnawing at her. Bianca impatiently waited for her next instructions, and her mystery man in the cafe kept her mind focused.

"You certainly know how to keep a girl waiting. I—"

"My apologies, Miss Chen. Please collect your things and prepare to move. You must follow my instructions precisely. You have four minutes." The friendly demeanor left Yasbir's voice in the span of a few words.

"Wilco. Company?" Bianca knew what go time sounded like.

"Yes. Kill your halo." Yasbir's voice was tense.

Bianca's calm began to erode as fight or flight instincts raced through her thoughts. She deactivated her public network and quickly packed her things. An active halo would have been as good as shouting 'I'm Bianca Chen' down the corridor.

Her drone case took up most of the backpack, with only a sparse few personal supplies to keep her comfortable. Of course, with the newest model Flash Pulse hidden in her coat, she felt a bit more prepared. The room scrubbed, she opened the line again. "Ready."

"Exit left."

Bianca moved, exiting the room and turning left, walking as calmly as she could. Adrenaline warred within her. Moving through the suites, the other passengers paid her no mind. That was a good sign. Ahead, the exit loomed closer.

"Exit left again."

"Roger." Bianca swiped her hand past the sensor, and the door opened. The promenade was a crush of people moving about their lives, and Bianca became one of them.

After a few moments of walking, Yasbir's voice cut back in. "Enter the next shop and tie your boots."

Heart racing even faster, Bianca did precisely as she was told as a small apparel shop loomed around the bend. She hoped she appeared to all as if she simply stepped out to the thoroughfare to be courteous.

From her kneeling vantage point, she could see the crowd slow and part as orange armored boots moved through the corridor. Jade robes brushed the floor two meters from her position. Bianca's hands began to shake.

"Wait, Miss Chen." Yasbir's voice was comforting despite its stern tone.

The boots and robes gone, the crowd began to mill about once again.

"Exit and continue."

Bianca couldn't help but glance over her shoulder. The backs of armored heads were still visible in the distance. O-12 nominally had jurisdiction over the Circulars as a whole, but the blue uniform clad escort trailing the Yujingyu warriors certainly couldn't stop them from detaining someone in Yu Jing territory.

It was then that Bianca noticed a team of orange clad warriors in an armor style she didn't recognize watching from the next level, and they were looking right at her.

"Eyes front, Miss Chen."

Heart racing, Bianca's pace quickened. So much for lifting her travel ban!

Unprompted by her, Bianca's halo lit back up and flashed brightly, Spotlighting her amongst the crowd. Her hacked comlog began broadcasting location data on all frequencies. "Shit!"

"Run." Yasbir remained unshakable, calm.

How the hell he could be calm in a time like this was beyond her, but he certainly didn't have to tell her twice. Bianca leaned into a run. Legs pumping, heart racing, she tore down the corridor. Shouts rose behind her.

"Reset!" She shouted the command between breaths, unable to do it manually. Her top-of-the-line geist immediately responded, and Bianca's augmented vision vanished. Her lens shut down with the rest of her personal electronics as the hasty command left her with nothing but one old fashioned MK1 eyeball.

Heart pounding, Bianca raced down the corridor. There was no doubt her pursuers would catch her at this rate. If even one was wearing powered armor, she was as good as dead. The shouting behind her was getting louder.

"—left!" Yasbir's voice cut through the noise.

Her comlog rebooted, bringing the rest of her personal quantronic net online. She didn't catch the entire transmission, but a looming maintenance port on the left whirred open on its own. Trusting in both fate and Yasbir, Bianca plunged into the in-between spaces of the Circular.

16.

The Báijīng Orbital Consulate facility looked much like Takeshi remembered from years gone by. His own travels, before the Uprising, often filtered through this very orbital station, albeit mostly through the military wing on the opposite side of the facility. Now that same wing would be full of orange clad warriors of the Imperial Service and Invincible Army with not a single piece of the pearl white armor he would have worn in sight. Without a blade in hand, Takeshi felt more grateful than ever for the dozens of bulkheads between him and his enemies.

It had all started here. The massacred warriors that inspired millions to rise up were washed away with so much propaganda and cleaner. But the warriors of the Japanese Secessionist Army would never forget the memories of those horrific losses and the casual contempt with which Yujingyu commanders had dismissed their lives.

"Next!"

Takeshi stilled his racing mind and unclenched his hands as the line shuffled forward toward the waiting Yujingyu checkpoint. He silently repeated centering mantras as he reflected on the last few weeks and waited for his turn.

Focus. One cut at a time.

Each step of his journey had been smooth thus far. Transit had been simple if not a bit cramped. Takeshi was thankful he was able to meet with Taka along the journey and continue his training, no matter how abridged. Still, he itched for the certainty of blades over sneaking around.

Such a vast distance between stars would have been impossible without the Circulars. Passing through a wormhole required a vast amount of power fed through a specialized Minotaur motor and permanent jump gates to stabilize the wormholes. Sub-light, it would have taken centuries. A little over two weeks, and he was here. Standing a few meters from what was supposed to be the first real test. Dodging Bianca Chen had been a bonus, as Taka had put it.

The jade-robed consulate official ahead of him inspected travelers waiting to descend to Shentang's surface with an air of boredom, no doubt weeks on end of mundane duties wearing at his discipline. Just another day for the Yujingyu and his Celestial Guard detachment, but the first real test for Takeshi… for Neko, nonetheless.

"Next!"

Unarmed and unarmored, Takeshi shuffled obediently forward. A lifetime of experience told him to trust the plan and follow his orders. The clandestine nature of the operation was pulling at the edge of his nerves regardless. If they were caught, they would be disavowed—there would be no rescue. He was well and truly on his own.

Ahead in the line, Taka, dressed in a business suit not quite nice enough to draw attention and yet clearly well-fitted enough to be slightly distracting, stepped up to the waiting official.

"State your name, port of origin, and business on Shentang." All of this was readily available at the man's fingertips. He had probably already read it, Takeshi mused. Such intimidation plays were commonplace for Yujingyu officials. The StateEmpire knew everything about its citizens and travelers at all times. Forcing travelers to repeat their information was yet another tool of oppression.

"Bolormaa Oyune from Mars. Heading to Sufbaatar to inspect ki-rin herds…"

The official's guard focused on the space around Taka as he scanned the big man's digital aura. Throughout it all, Taka kept talking, smiling as the Yujingyu official listened to him chat.

As the guard behind Taka scanned his Cube, Takeshi watched with painful anticipation—hoping the thin fiction it told would pass scrutiny. With a signal from the guard, Taka was waved through with a forced smile plastered across the official's face.

"Safe travels, and welcome back to Shentang. Next!"

Releasing the breath he didn't know he held, Takeshi shuffled forward. Taka, being a Kemaitai, would be a priority target for Imperial Agents if caught. If he made it through without trouble, Takeshi could too. Song and Hiro had arrived two full days ahead and were, with a bit of luck, waiting on the planet below. Two more travelers passed through the port of entry without incident. Now or never.

"Next! State your name, port of origin, and business on Shentang."

Heart racing, Takeshi lied.

"Tak Gi-ung. Earth. Migrating to Shentang." A practiced line, repeated a few hundred times to feel slightly more natural, but a lie nonetheless. Takeshi spoke in neutral, efficient tones of someone used to delivering their information to authorities respectfully, wasting no time. He took some comfort in helping craft this part of his backstory, leaning on his military training before Greater Independent Japan charted its own path once again.

Every detail was believable with his cover story, but it ached to lie nonetheless. Despite the practice and the necessity, it still left a sour taste as it slid effortlessly from his tongue.

The digital aura around Takeshi reflected a hard life in youth, but someone who turned things around to become a productive member of society. Tak Gi-ung was a menial laborer, one of millions. Nothing remarkable in his life's story—nothing memorable.

"Migrating?" The official's curiosity piqued; not unexpected, but not ideal.

"Yes, sir. Attempting to leave behind the, ah… rash choices of youth that still haunt me, and begin anew."

"I see your record includes time in a juvenile rehabilitation facility. The StateEmpire commends you on turning your life around. I see you have lodging arranged in Yián Xiáng, but no appointments or work lined up yet."

Takeshi kept his breathing calm while he screamed inside.

One cut.

"No, sir. I am meeting a family friend in hopes of work." This part was not rehearsed. The man's sincere smile was a nightmare come true.

"Oh, no. That won't do, hopes don't fill a belly. I am sending your information for worker placement planetside. Be sure to check in with the local magistrate's office within two days. If it doesn't work out, the clerk is a friend of mine and will help get you settled." The Yujingyu made a few deft notations in the holopane before him and quickly glanced past Takeshi before waving him on.

Takeshi let out the breath he did not realize he was holding. The lie in his Cube had held up—one challenge down.

"May the Jade Throne bless your new life, welcome to Shentang. Next!"

* * * * *

"That went well, all told." Taka's reflection showed a smile as he activated a dampener program. Takeshi stared out of the viewport as their car descended the space elevator. How Taka had gotten them onto a descent in a private car was beyond him at this point. As the blue sphere of Shentang rapidly approached, Takeshi waited for the telltale flicker of his lens display before responding.

Takeshi raged against the man's calm demeanor, struggling to keep his voice down. "I've been flagged. You know Yu Jing well enough to know that's a death sentence for the operation."

"Nothing we can do about that right now. Trying to break into the planetary network to pull that notice out of the system on our timeline will alert the Imperial Service immediately. Do you think any of us would have survived this long if we didn't know how to adapt? Stop worrying about the next problem and *think*, Neko." The Kempeitai's words paralleled those of *Kensei* Hayachi and sent a chill down Takeshi's spine.

One cut at a time. Focus.

Taka's smile never faltered as Takeshi stared back. "You are used to military actions, what happens when they go wrong?"

Takeshi drew a deep, centering breath. "Right, we adapt. Just the same as you do."

"Exactly. So what happens now?"

"Once we make planetfall, we will split up. I will get something to eat on my way to the designated hotel, taking my time. Tomorrow, we will head to the airfield separately and catch the night flight to Sakuramachi as laborers." Takeshi could not help but feel more focused as he recited the process despite the horrific danger each and every step presented. Not since his first foray into the jungles of Paradiso had he felt so out of his depth. But just like then, repeating his next steps moved his mind from worry to action.

Focus.

How Song and the others lived like this day in and day out, Takeshi could not fathom. Thrust into a world of shadows and subterfuge, he longed for the certainty of open combat—blade in hand, warrior to warrior.

"You've got it. Just a few anonymous faces in the crowd of those with nothing to lose." Taka sighed as his fingers hovered over his comlog. "I'm going to drop the shroud so we do not draw any more attention. Continue as planned, Neko."

With that, the veil was lifted and the two rode the orbital elevator down in silence, despite having the car to themselves.

17.

Bianca crouched in the low light, behind a structural beam, weapon in hand, hidden in the bowels of Circular. She felt more like a victim in a horror vid than a hero. Fading adrenaline dragged at limbs the longer she waited.

She could hear something else in the space with her. No, she couldn't hear anything more than her own labored breathing and the pounding pulse in her ears. She could feel *it*. She wasn't sure what exactly 'it' was, but Bianca was willing to bet her precious Hildy Johnson trophy that she was not alone.

The faint tick of some unknown mechanism of the ship kept time with her pulse. Yasbir hadn't made contact since the promenade, and Bianca didn't want to risk diverting her attention for the few precious moments it would take to send him a message. Bianca slowly scanned the gloom for an exit, her pursuers, anything she could use to her advantage. A hunt was on, and she was the prey. Spotting an exit, she prepared to move. As if hearing her thoughts, a voice split the darkness.

"Bianca Chen! You are under arrest for crimes against the StateEmpire." The voice echoed off the metal walls disorientingly. "Come out with your hands up, and you will not be harmed."

Gripping her Flash Pulse tighter, Bianca crept toward salvation. She heard the shot before she ever saw her attacker, and she dove for cover. From somewhere to her left, the sharp, charged sound of an electromagnetic carbine sliced through the air with an almost surgical quality: crisp, clean, lethal. It missed her by millimeters.

Their surprise attack ruined, her attacker advanced toward her into the light. Their armor was cast in Yujingyu orange, with a black cloth over their shoulders and face. A wide-brimmed hat sat on their head, reminiscent of the ancient Japanese style. The curious mix of cultures was quickly forgotten as the stealthy soldier brought their rifle to bear once more.

"Bianca Chen, in the name of the Jade Emperor, I sentence you to…"

The soldier's face exploded, spraying her with blood and brain matter. As the body fell to its knees, Bianca saw Yasbir's expressionless helmet materialize in a crawling cascade of hexagonal energy. Yasbir's pistol was smoking in his outstretched hand. To her credit, Bianca managed not to scream.

"My apologies, Miss Chen. Time is not on our side."

The rest of the flight through the bowels of the Circular was a blur of hide and seek. Yasbir would occasionally leave her in a hiding place before returning a few moments later, appearing out of thin air. Bianca was so very tempted to send her drone after him, but she knew it would be a futile attempt to track the Hassassin. After an hour of cautiously moving through the Circular, they arrived at a small, private hangar containing a single, completely unadorned shuttlecraft. Bianca habitually tried to scan the vessel, but her geist was unable to get a reading of any kind. Yasbir led her inside, and she found a pair of menacing combat machines sitting dormant. She squeezed past their bipedal frames and found herself a bench to strap into as Yasbir climbed into the pilot seat and started up the craft.

She watched the Circular disappear from the windowless shuttle's viewscreen. Immediately the share of reentry began to pull at her as gravity welcomed the craft into its embrace. As the planet Shentang rose up to meet them, Bianca's comlog pinged.

Search results were in. Grateful she had remembered to update her geist with the latest search and research tools, Bianca sorted through them. These were not from Sol, but the information had been scraped from the Yujingyu Maya relays. That in itself was intriguing. It was a ninety-five percent match. Footage from a Yu Jing high command ceremony played in her lens. The recording began as the Japanese Army, then still a part of the StateEmpire, marched in rigid parade formation. Bianca watched the video three times just to make sure her eyes had not betrayed her.

As she closed out her comlog dials, a notification blinked in her vision. Opening her messages, a rotating origami sparrow hovered before her. Bianca shouted triumphantly. Yasbir said nothing from his pilot seat as she laughed aloud.

///Great to hear from you. I look forward to seeing you very soon. -S///

Despite the adrenaline dump exhausting her, Bianca felt more alive than she had in months.

* * * * *

In the dark hours of the early morning, Mizu rose to her comlog's alert. She had laid in hiding, waiting. Now was the time. She rose from the store room cot she called a bed for the night. The Steel Saké was empty and locked up. The owner knew she was there but never said a word when she walked in and set up. A veteran of the Uprising and many other wars to boot, he often offered safe harbor to those in need.

After a quick wash in the sink, Mizu was on the move again. Hidden amongst the scarce supplies and plentiful garbage, she pushed on a dirty wall tile behind the water filter. With a click, the wall panel dropped out of socket enough to begin pushing her way through. Shielded and shut for years, the small safe room remained undisturbed. Barely big enough to lie down in, the claustrophobic space was one of dozens scattered throughout the city. Her crew would be rousing from similar spaces and moving to the rendezvous.

The cot was little more than a board stacked on boxes, but the scratches on the walls told of the space being home to many like her over the years. The Imperial Service made hiding a difficult proposition on a good day, and the days hadn't been good for a while. If a chance patrol had scanned her sleeping in the bar, Mizu would have been another vagabond or homeless Nipponese amongst millions. If they had clocked her behind a wall... She shuddered to think of it.

Beneath the cot lay a loose floor panel. Popping it open, Mizu rummaged around and removed a box of field rations, long since expired, and a shielded lockbox. With a grin on her face, Mizu popped the lock and found its contents undisturbed: a spare Boarding Pistol, enough ammunition to share, four custom quantronic emitters—no bigger than her palm—that Henzo designed before his death, and a bundle of synthleather that had once been a red sleeve. It was all gear salvaged off her bike before they ditched it.

Reverently, Mizu placed the bundle on the cot and knelt. The shake torqued through her as she reached out with unsteady hands. In a lacquered wooden scabbard, covered in painstakingly intricate gang graffiti, was her blade. She had been gifted it by her commander during the war. It was not some fabled katana of a legendary warrior, but it was hers.

Henzo named it '*Akai Te*.' In her rage and grief, it truly was her 'red hand.' All of the blood that she shed over the years of throwing herself recklessly into battle after battle, some leaving permanent stains and scars on the blade and scabbard, gave proof to that.

It had been five years since she had stashed it here for safe keeping. For five years it slumbered while she fought for scraps. Taking her blade in hand, Mizu steeled herself. Armored in her jacket and armed with her red hand, it was time to fight for more than just scraps again.

Her Hands had spread these out across the city. With any luck, the others had found their gear undisturbed also. Even the new members kept stashes hidden as a precaution. They had all gone to ground more than once. But now the others would be getting the same alert she did. They would begin moving through the sewers and back ways of Sakuramachi toward various link ups. Goro would be meeting her shortly as Jon and Kairi rounded up everyone else and gave them their instructions.

Mizu stashed her kit in a bag and prepared to move. Pistol in hand and blade on her back, she keyed another false panel in the floor, revealing a ladder leading down into darkness. She counted the number of rungs as she descended into the underworld, and the shake screamed against any calm she tried to will herself.

* * * * *

The airfields were once a thing of beauty. Hailed as an architectural wonder, architects had blended its many terminals, civilian and industrial alike, with an absolutely stunning landscape. Placed atop a cliff overlooking the sea, it had once set the scene for anyone arriving to one of the most beautiful cities in the entire Human Sphere… and Takeshi did not even recognize it.

The airfield had seen some of the fiercest fighting in the region. Takeshi was on Earth during the brief war, defending every inch of soil with his whole heart, but he knew many who had been stationed at this very field.

The hills were quiet now, their scars wiped away by time and wind. The airfield had been rebuilt thoroughly—deliberately. Gone were the familiar lines of timbered eaves and stone walkways. In their place rose structures of poured concrete and brushed steel, angular and austere, trimmed in lacquered jade. The fluorescent glow of holographic signs and directional markers illuminated the sprawling complex in the light of a neon day. The roofs curled slightly at the corners in the style favored by the StateEmpire, a subtle flourish that only made the place feel more alien. Elegant architecture intertwined with wide courtyards had been paved over, and garden paths replaced with rigid corridors and functional plazas. To Takeshi, it no longer felt like coming home. It felt like stepping into someone else's idea of order. It was precise, disciplined, and foreign—uninviting.

Landing in the dark of night, Takeshi and his fellow passengers were lined up in the rain and scanned through a checkpoint like the one on the consulate station, but with decidedly more guns visible. Eleven civilians, each as equally hopeful as fearful, joined them on their flight. The crew was busy unloading pallets of industrial material before they had finished disembarking.

Soaked, they were moved to an outdoor holding area and made to wait for an hour before being lined up and questioned one at a time by a Bào Trooper. The late hours of the night no doubt amplified the Bào's rough manners. His compatriot roughly grabbed a passenger from behind to hold a small device up to their neck, a Cube scan. Takeshi had been briefed that this could happen.

It wasn't supposed to happen tonight.

Random searches were more common for late night industrial transports, even if those were the easiest to take on short notice. To Takeshi, it was just more control tactics by the StateEmpire.

All the survival training in his career and preparation for the mission had not prepared him enough to be here, now. If the Cube edit was not perfect, this mission was about to fall apart—if their local operatives were compromised—if—if—*if*.

Bào Troops were not unfamiliar to Takeshi. Their stylized helmets were designed for intimidation but were nothing compared to their reputation. Fanatical was the kindest light they could be painted in. The segmented armored plating that covered their torsos held in no kindness, no mercy, within their hearts.

Having served alongside them only once, Takeshi considered them to be reckless zealots who did not care what lines they crossed in the pursuit of their mission. Where there was one Bào, there was always—

Takeshi spotted a slim Imperial Agent slide through the darkness beyond the Bào who questioned his fellow passenger. She prowled through the gathering, like an apex hunting beast, keeping her pack in line. Clad in orange armor—with jade robes of office hanging about her like skirts—her swaying sensor tail hung like a mechanical braid from the back of her helmet. If the Invincible Army was the right hand of the StateEmpire, the Imperial Service was its left hand. Answering directly to the Jade Throne, encountering Imperial Agents was never a good thing. They were barely less ruthless than the Bào they kept on a leash and notorious for making people disappear.

"Who are you and why are you here?" The harsh impersonal voice that emitted from the speaker grill—beneath ominously glowing eyes—on the soldier's faceplate brought Takeshi back to the more immediate concern. The soldier was shorter than Takeshi and much less broadly built. He noted that the large weapon held in the Bào's hands would be more than enough to even the odds.

"Tak Gi-ung, from Earth, sir. Looking for work." The three other times he had told the lie had done nothing to ease the distaste of it. The night sky rumbled, threatening the storm's wrath.

"Why Kuraimori?" The question came from behind him, and as Takeshi began to turn to answer, an unseen hand grabbed the back of his neck. Takeshi tensed—unable to control the reflexive conditioning—and was rewarded with a boot to the back of his knee. Before he knew it, he was kneeling and staring down the business end of a Boarding Shotgun. The hardly restrained aggression startled the woman next in line.

Violence called to him.

"He asked you a question!" The voice boomed from behind him at maximum volume.

Everything stopped.

Every single pair of eyes was on the confrontation. Takeshi willed his body still, keeping his hands at his sides, clearly visible.

One cut at a time.

"Good work is hard to find when you have a criminal record." The excuse was rushed, Takeshi hoped it sounded fear-filled and powerless—rather than the cold rage building inside him.

"What kind of record?" The muzzle pressed up under Takeshi's chin, steady and unrelenting. One wrong twitch and there would be no recovery from that wound.

"I was a stupid kid, sir."

"You're still stupid." Takeshi felt the grip on his neck release, the barrel withdrew, and the pair moved on to the startled woman.

Takeshi tried to focus anywhere but the Bào, lest his wrath be visible.

She was still there, watching him. Staring directly at him. His eyes scanned her armor's markings—Pheasant Rank. She was ten meters away, arms crossed contemptuously over her orange armored torso. Rifle and sword locked to her back, the agent's jade robes were midnight black in the rain and low light. As they stared at one another, Takeshi felt like her impassive mask bore through his disguise with ease.

He felt exposed, laid bare.

She tilted her head to the side and brought up her wrist—cycling through her comlog. Eventually she shut it down with a self-assured nod, finding whatever she was looking for. Drawing her pistol, she walked toward Takeshi.

Panic threatened to grip him. Was he caught? To act now would remove all doubt, but he was incapable of doing nothing. Sweat poured in sheets, mixing with the rain. Decades of combat, training, and a martial life pushed him to do something—anything. The Imperial Agent stared on, daring him as thunder broke the night sky, taunting him.

Shouting brought his attention beyond the agent to the Bào Troopers interrogating his fellow passengers; the one next to Taka was on his knees, hands up, being aggressively interrogated. The two troopers were rapid fire questioning the poor soul with a very familiar shotgun pointed at his face. Takeshi was ashamed to feel relief when the Pheasant Agent turned toward the commotion as well.

His relief was short lived as the night air was split by the thunderous roar of the Boarding Shotgun. The rest of the passengers screamed in terror and dropped to the ground, cowering. Time slowed for Takeshi. He stood staring at the headless corpse of a stranger, listening to the wail of the terrified and powerless.

He saw Taka in the darkness, prone with the rest, staring at the still standing Takeshi. He felt his guide willing him to drop down, to cower. He felt the pull to follow his instructions—to be no one.

The shotgun Bào moved to another cowering civilian and pulled the trigger contemptuously. Another life was snuffed out—for sport. As the shot registered, Takeshi's jaw clenched. There was no warning, only laughter emitting from the faceplate of the Bào.

Takeshi realized he was moving but couldn't—or rather wouldn't—stop himself. His rational mind cried out as instinct and honor took hold of his motor functions. Taka's eyes implored him. The Bào Troopers screamed at him. All in vain.

All came to stillness inside Takeshi.

One cut. One fight.

Time caught up.

Focus.

His awareness focused on the laughing murderer, and razor sharp tunnel vision shut out the rest of the scene. The trooper must have sensed him coming and pivoted, bringing the shotgun to bear. Takeshi stepped forward quickly, taking away the only advantage the Bào had, room to move. Takeshi gripped the shotgun with both hands and slammed a shoulder into its wielder. The Bào let go of the weapon as he tripped over the corpse of his first victim.

Takeshi stepped forward and, in his frenzy, discarded the shotgun—it wouldn't fire for him anyway. His fists clenched. A detached part of his mind wondered what the man saw as death stared down at him.

The ground buckled violently, sending waves of earth and water surging through the scene. In a sudden moment of awareness, something inside took hold of him and screamed a warning.

"Down!"

The world tore itself apart.

The ground beneath his feet heaved in violent protest, throwing up waves of mud and water that splattered and coated everything. The force didn't just knock him down—it ripped him off his feet, as if gravity had momentarily failed.

A brilliant flash of light—brighter than the lightning above or the neon glow—engulfed the ruined terminal yard. The shockwave hit like a hammer, throwing everyone like ragdolls. Takeshi hit the ground hard, his body skidding across the slick mud until he slammed into the remains of a lamp post. The impact stole his breath, leaving him dazed and choking on rainwater.

The storm seemed to pause, as if in awe of the explosion. Then came the aftermath. An eerie silence broken only by the patter of rain and the hiss of steam rising from the scorched earth.

Thunder roared above, as if to mock the cries of the injured. Armored as they were, the soldiers were up and moving far before their charges, weapons bared and scanning for threats. Within moments, the scene was swarming with more soldiers screaming and indiscriminately shooting some of the remaining civilians.

Head still ringing, Takeshi rose to his hands and knees. He found himself staring at the Pheasant Agent's Combi Rifle. Its underslung E/Mitter blasted him in the face. The force of the point-blank non-lethal shot bowled him over, stunned and unable to move. He received the swift application of an armored boot to the head, and he crumpled to the ground. In his dazed state, Takeshi could barely register the manacles latching shut around his wrists while the world went black.

18.

"No."

It was a single word from the Hassassin, but it startled Bianca to stillness inside the shuttle. The small recording drone she started to take out fell limply from her fingers, back into her pack. She sat up straight and exhaled slowly from her nose.

"No?"

"You are not to record any of this infiltration." The Hassasin spoke from his seat without turning to look at her, and there was a finality in his voice that she didn't question. Okay, so no drone. She could still—

"Please do not betray my trust."

"Of course," Bianca said, pursing her lips. "I'm not stupid enough to jeopardize our friendship."

Yasbir nodded but did not reply. She wasn't really sure if they were *actually* friends. Even though she had known Yasbir for years, it was hard to make friends in her line of work. She suspected a 'friend' had been the cause of her recent untimely demise and resurrection. She didn't have proof, just a reporter's hunch. Bianca turned to stare out the window of the craft as they began landing, and her lens told her that they were at a tiny inlet off the southernmost tip of the Furuitsue Peninsula. She stood up to leave, but she paused when Yasbir did not join her.

"There is a spot by the rocks, just outside where we've landed," Yasbir said as he turned his icy gaze on her. "Wait there for me."

"By myself?" Bianca cocked an eyebrow, fighting back a scoff. "I'm an amazing reporter, not a trained fighter or assassin."

"You will have support." Yasbir lit up his comlog and pressed a few holographic buttons. There was the sound of maglocks releasing, and the two combat machines rose and moved to stand on either side of Bianca.

She felt her eyebrow rise higher instinctively. Yasbir called the bots Sunny-Duck-Butts or something close, but she hadn't quite caught the name. Had she still been connected to the greater Maya network—rather than the highly filtered version available in Yu Jing space—it would have been an easy thing to check.

As it was, she didn't need Yasbir to explain their purpose. Bianca wasn't sure if they were her gaolers or her guardians. Judging by their armaments, they were definitely made to kill. There was a quality to them she couldn't describe, like they could fold or transform into a smaller shape. They were menacing, boxy, raptor-like machines with smaller manipulator arms folded under the central frame. At full height, they stood a head taller than her.

"They're no Hassassins," she said, giving Yasbir a sly smile, "but you must value my life to bring these. What will you be doing?"

"Hiding the shuttle."

"Right, makes sense." Bianca adjusted her bag, giving the combat remotes another quick glance before turning back to Yasbir. "See you in a bit."

Yasbir lowered the loading ramp and turned his attention to the holomap appearing in the space before him.

Bianca took a few steps forward, and the remotes matched her pace, staying alongside her. Content that their shoulder-mounted launchers, underslung rifles, and mine racks seemed primed and ready as they scanned with every step, she hurried outside into the oppressive dark and followed the waypoint on her lens to the outcropping.

The shuttle took back off, and she watched it until it disappeared. Silence reigned, broken only by the crashing of the waves. The remotes made no sound as they meticulously scanned the area for any threats. The reality of the situation weighed on her, and for some reason, the waves started sounding louder. She shook the paranoia from her mind and exhaled deeply.

How long had she waited for Yasbir? She checked her comlog and grit her teeth; time seemed to be passing so slowly. She started chattering from the cold and willed her teeth to stillness.

Her heart sank as the remotes turned their weapons toward the sea in unison, and she drew her Flash Pulse. Her lens identified the armored shape emerging from the surf as Yasbir, and she sighed heavily, holstering the weapon.

"Where the hell did you hide the shuttle?"

"Somewhere safe." He beckoned her toward him, not breaking his stride. "Come, we must hurry."

Bianca hurriedly fell in beside Yasbir and the twin remotes followed.

"I will need to take this." Yasbir reached for the pack containing her drone.

"I need that!" Bianca recoiled.

"You will need to trust me."

There was an earnest tone to his voice that gave her pause. Yasbir had never given her reason to doubt him. She was told the Hassassins had found her slain corpse after her disappearance. She shuddered at the thought and relented.

"I want that back."

"I give you my word. It will be returned to you."

"Okay, okay." Her teeth chattered in the wind. "Slagg, I'm cold."

* * * * *

A shadow sliced through the winding mountain valleys with the precision of a predator. Its sleek, matte-black hull absorbed the faint light of the approaching dawn, rendering it a phantom against the jagged silhouette of the peaks.

Inside the cockpit, Su-Yeong's vision flickered with real-time overlays of the terrain directly to her lens, potential threats marked in red. Her fingers danced over holographic controls, adjusting the prototype craft's trajectory as it wove through the mountain labyrinth. Sensors swept the surroundings, mapping every crevice, every tree, every sudden outcropping, ensuring its path remained undetected.

Noiseless to all but the most sensitive ears, the transport employed state of the art stealth technology, its engines emitting a low thrumming vibration that blended seamlessly with the wind's whispers over the forest-covered ravine below. Mountain ridges loomed like teeth on either side, their snow-dusted edges glinting faintly in the pale glow of the rising sun just beginning to brush the eastern horizon.

Agent Lin Su-Yeong hugged the valley walls, maneuvering the craft with uncanny grace. Cutting edge fusion jets pulsed softly at its rear, their glow masked by an adaptive shield that mimicked the hues of the sky and earth around it. To the naked eye, it would be little more than a shimmer of motion; an afterimage lingering too briefly to confirm.

Below, the valley floor was a patchwork of shadow and fog. Rivers glinted like molten silver in the dim light, their currents hidden beneath a shroud of mist. Occasionally, the craft would ascend slightly, cresting over a ridge before diving back into the shelter of another gorge, always one with the landscape, always unseen.

At the helm, Su-Yeong took visceral pleasure in moments like these. It made the day to day of her recent assignment more worth it. Prowling amongst the shadows was her preferred position in life. The unseen threat. The hidden blade.

The resources that went into constructing each craft like hers strained the mind. The StateEmpire, of course, had resources to spare for its Imperial Service. For operatives such as she, it was an indulgence to be cherished. Many others in her shoes preferred assault craft, bristling with weaponry. Su-Yeong preferred a subtler approach to her comings and goings, as unseen as the breeze.

Behind the pilot compartment, a shackled prisoner sat strapped to a reinforced combat harness. His manacles were wired through to a bolt in the floor, forcing him to hunch uncomfortably forward as the harness pulled him back. The dim interior glow barely revealed the bag over his head. A blinking collar sealed the bag to the neck and indicated the bomb within was functioning correctly. Two of her Celestial Guard detachment watched the prisoner as the weight of their presence filled the cabin. The prisoner shifted uncomfortably against the unyielding restraints, breath visible through the bag in the cold, cabin air.

"Where are you taking me?" The prisoner's rasping voice was pained but defiant.

The guards didn't answer, remaining impassive as the aircraft banked sharply to avoid an outcropping. The movement jerked the prisoner against their restraints, eliciting a sharp grunt of pain.

Su-Yeong locked in a level flight path and gave herself a moment to take stock of her injuries, minor though they were. The explosions that rocked the airfield had left the garrison reeling. She made silent thanks to a lifetime of training and conditioning that she hadn't been seriously injured. The garrison commander would lose his post for this outrage. If he was lucky, that would be all he lost. As an Imperial Agent, it was well within her authority to have simply done him a favor and shot the coddled idiot herself. While faster, it wouldn't have provided any answers, and the unrelenting state apparatus would have the commander occupied for at least a month.

The embarrassment of the impending thinly veiled interrogations made Su-Yeong smile. All the rank and title of his family couldn't shield him from what was coming. They wouldn't find anything of value, making it worse for the feckless commander in the end. To add to his troubles, she had left her Bào detachment there to keep an eye over his operations. Let him sweat. She wasn't usually a cruel person, but sometimes—

"I know you can hear me," the prisoner shouted, straining against the cuffs. His voice cut like a blade made of anger, but Su-Yeong detected the unmistakable tinge of fear. It was clear he was saving his strength, wisely storing it for the days to come.

"You'll know soon enough," one of the guards finally replied, tone as cold and unyielding as the mountains outside. Their comrade chuckled to himself as the prisoner's shoulders slumped.

Outside, the valley outside was a blur of shadow and motion, the world rushing past too quickly to discern.

///Incoming transmission: Urgent: Lieutenant Da.///

"Yes, Lieutenant?"

"Ma'am, message from Yutang. Control is requesting an update on the airfield attack."

Lieutenant Da's portrait hovered in her upper field of vision as she kept her eyes locked on the flight path. "You can say 'demands,' Lieutenant. Control *demands* an update."

"Yes, ma'am."

Su-Yeong cut the line and left Da to wonder—to worry—what her next move would be. Far ahead, nestled deep in the mountains, their destination loomed. She smiled grimly as the Hansei province rushed in like the dawn.

* * * * *

"Thank you again for the tea." Yasbir savored the last sip. A quiet moment in the dark of night and a drink with a friend was a rare luxury in his line of work.

"It is always a pleasure to see you, friend-of-mine. It is the least I can do to honor the occasion."

"How many years has it been? How many planets and how many operations? Yet each and every time we meet, you prepare tea. Even when we meet at crossed purposes."

"Perhaps I simply enjoy your company. It is a rare gift. You are kept fairly busy and far afield."

"True, but this is important, and thus I am here, having tea."

The pair sipped in silence. Bitter leaves mixed with real honey-laced Silk—a rare and priceless gift from Yasbir years prior—his friend never failed to blend the flavors to perfection. Yasbir couldn't deny it was an indulgence he looked forward to. When the opportunity arose, of course. "Hasib held so much promise once. So much more than his father ever could."

"Why have you taken an interest in this prince? Of all those who lord over Bourak, why this one?"

"He wears the only role his father allows him. Were he not yet jaded by power and influence, Hasib could have truly made the Sphere a better place, given half a chance." Yasbir spoke honestly—another luxury rarely afforded to the Hassassin.

"Could have?"

"Trust that the Old Man has taken an interest in his survival. In events yet to unfold, the prince will play his own part."

"You cannot blame me for asking, friend-of-mine." He smiled from behind his tea cup.

"I don't." Yasbir offered a sincere smile as the two sat in a moment of silence. A warm breeze cut through the forest, filling the air with the hollow rattle of bamboo and pine. Plants so ingrained into the culture of Japan that they were among the first things bioengineered to survive here on Shentang. "Do you miss this place?"

"In truth, I spent little time on the island itself. The trappings of duty, you understand. It does hold its own unique beauty though. I am grateful for the chance to return. As I am grateful you sought our help."

"It brings me joy to hear you say it." In truth, Yasbir had known the prize his friend truly sought long before the events unfolding had begun—the vault. Hasib was the excuse they needed to seek it out, much like he had been the excuse Yasbir needed to pursue his true prize.

With one conversation, the sultan had been but the pebble to start an unstoppable avalanche. With the prize dangled before them, the Japanese began their inexorable movement toward this point. This was true power. Quietly guiding the Sphere from the shadows. Yasbir—alongside his brothers and sisters of the Hassassin Bahram—shaped the future. That said, there was a much greater chance of success for the prince's safe return this way, and Yasbir truly was glad for the help.

"I am glad as well. You, of course, know why the Emperor so eagerly agreed." His friend sat quietly, a knowing smirk on his forgettably plain face.

Yasbir's jaw hung slightly agape for a moment before a throaty chuckle came unbidden to him. After a long lifetime spent in a world of secrets wrapped in half-truths, few kept him on his toes quite like Nakama.

Silence returned as the pair watched the dark, quiet valley below—equal parts enjoying the peace of it and scanning with a tactician's mind. Their cliffside perch overlooked the length of the Hansei Valley. Bioengineered bamboo and pine forests stretched behind them, as well as the valley below. It was peaceful in the pre-dawn hours. Here, Yasbir mused, two clandestine warriors meeting atop a cliff face to share tea in secret—it was the stuff of Maya films.

The mountains of Kuraimori were certainly not without their dangers. Indigenous predators may roam its wilds, but the ever-present surveillance drones were the largest threat. They were no danger to the companions sharing tea, but certainly more so to the less subtle instruments of wrath and redemption approaching.

"Time is precious, my friend. To business then?" Yasbir held a hand out, palm down expectantly.

"As you wish."

With a tap on an upturned palm, Yasbir's geist shared an encrypted file. "Everything was delivered, as requested."

Strike plans filtered through synched lenses as the unlikely duo reviewed the plans together. Small icons lit across the valley in a wireframe overlaying their vision. At the center of it all, the once Oyama residence sat.

"And of the drones?" Nakama asked, gesturing toward the east, where the nearest air base sat a mere ten kilometers away. "They remain a threat."

"At your signal, they will be dealt with. Do not concern yourself, my friend. It will be done." The finality with which Yasbir spoke left no room for discussion. "But for now, we must be careful." Disconnecting the datalink, both rose to depart.

Both warriors paused at the subtle shift in the air. As if by some unspoken command, they looked south. They silently watched a sleek black stealth craft come tearing into the valley. Its swept wings and tight lines were more aquatic than avian.

"That is a thing of beauty." Yasbir grinned, admiring the craft.

"Indeed it is."

"Be safe." Shirking the simple traveler's robes, Yasbir's chameleonic armor began immediately blending into the surroundings.

"You as well, friend-of-mine."

Without a second look, Yasbir turned and departed. With a silent command, his helmet unfolded and sealed his face from sight. The subtle shift of digitized camouflage patterns moved across his armored frame as Yasbir faded from view.

"The woman we brought in. What role does she play?"

"I will tell you when you tell me why you brought Miss Chen." Nakama's voice was light and playful across the link.

"Very well." He heard Nakama chuckle in the distance. He had known the answer before he had posed the question. A smile on his face, he began the long trek down the mountain. "I will see you soon."

19.

The room was a bare, utilitarian space; its walls painted a peeling dull gray that seemed to absorb the dim light from the fixture above. A single desk separated Takeshi from the empty chair on the opposite side, its surface plain except for the signs of wear and neglect—and dried blood—as if the destruction and decay was the point.

The air was tinged with the faint scent of antiseptic and something metallic, a subtle reminder of the room's new purpose. Outside, muffled voices and distant footsteps hinted at activity, but within these four walls, time felt frozen.

Takeshi had only his imagination to keep him company as he sat, bound, manacles maglocked to the table. There was no ticking clock like old Maya films portrayed. There was no digital noise; the constant buzz of information was gone. His comlog had been taken, leaving his lens with nothing to display. It surprised Takeshi how used to his augmented reality he truly was. To be stripped of it was akin to losing a primary sense, like hearing or sight.

A stiff metal collar was locked around his neck, blinking an occasional green light at the edge of his vision. He had seen what collars such as these could do when Japan had lived within the iron grasp of Yu Jing. Little better than brainwashed prisoners with nothing to lose, Kuang Shi units had much bigger devices locked around their necks when they went into battle. Their mindless charge was near enough to the zombies they were named after. Takeshi had seen the results. Kuang Shi were armed and lightly armored, but their options were a swift victory or an explosive defeat. The device on his neck was much smaller, but no less threatening.

He shifted uncomfortably, the hard chair offering no respite. His clothes, still damp and muddy from the night's upheaval, clung to his skin. The side of his head ached, and dried blood had glued his eyelashes together. All of it was a constant reminder of his ill-fated attempt to rise after the bombing. The pain in his ribs and beyond was proof enough that the kick to the head wasn't the only one he had received.

He studied the room with wary eyes, searching for weaknesses, anything that might offer leverage. There was a single surveillance camera in the corner, its eye locked on him, silent and ominous. Takeshi kept his gaze impassive and faced the door.

It was a heavy, reinforced affair with no window, just a narrow slot at the bottom where food could be slid through. Takeshi wasn't sure how long he had been here. Even his rigid sense of time was distorted within the windowless space, which was made only worse from not knowing how long he had been unconscious. Takeshi felt himself longing for the grounding of time itself.

He hated waiting. It gave the mind too much time to spiral, to imagine what nightmare was coming for him.

One cut at a time. Focus.

The last he had seen of Taka was with the Bào Troopers. They swarmed him before the explosion. Where had that come from? Was this a part of the plan he wasn't briefed on? Since accepting this assignment, Takeshi felt increasingly out of depth, day by day. Taking it in stride was difficult after so much. Takeshi longed for the certainty of combat. Opponent in front and blade in hand.

The sound of footsteps approaching the door made Takeshi straighten in his seat, body tense and breath held. The footsteps paused. For a moment, he thought whoever it was might pass by, but then the lock clicked, and the door swung open.

A long sleeveless green coat was worn over a broad torso bearing light orange armor. The warrior appeared unarmed but no less dangerous than a cornered viper. His bald head, dark skin, and deep brown eyes projected an ominous air in the pale, overhead light. He entered the room, and the door closed them both in. Takeshi heard the lock click into place and swallowed a dry mouth of air.

Much lower rank than the agent he had seen at the airfield, this man's armor and coat marked him as a member of the Imperial Service nonetheless, a Zhànying. Risen into the StateEmpire Imperial Service by merit alone, Zhànying had little chance of rising higher without the patronage of a greater house. They had to impress unimpressable lords. That alone made them a threat to not be taken lightly.

"Tak Gi-ung?" the Yujingyu demanded.

"Yes, sir." Takeshi answered obediently, allowing himself a modicum of relief. He hoped blindly that his cover was still intact.

The interrogating Zhànying brought up his comlog as his fingers played through the air. Takeshi long ago had lens optics implanted directly into his retina, yet he saw nothing. He saw none of the holographic projection above the man's arm.

"You are wondering why your lens isn't working." The Zhànying spotted his brief confusion. Amusement flickered in his eyes, the kind a mouse sees in the eyes of the cat who has it trapped. He tapped his neck, indicating Takeshi's heavy metal collar. "It helps keep you here. You belong here, and here I make the rules… Why did you board the transport last night?"

"I am looking for work. I was told that opportunities to rise quickly over the local population were a good option for someone with my background, sir." Pretending to be morally bankrupt enough to step on his imprisoned countrymen made Takeshi sick to his stomach.

"Who told you that? Where will I find this person to verify your story?" The agent's impassive face betrayed nothing. This man was as cold as stone in winter.

"Yes, sir. The officer responsible for my parole and rehabilitation program." Takeshi hurriedly shared the fictitious parole officer portion of his tale-of-lies. Such programs followed juvenile delinquents for up to fifty years after their release, ever suspicious. Most who were in such programs failed its exacting standards miserably. "What happened at the airfield, sir? Is everyone okay?"

Feigning deference was an easy lie, but a lie nonetheless, and it still troubled him that the falsehood came so easily. Still, Takeshi was reaching the end of his scripted information on this track and would be venturing uncharted paths soon.

His concern was genuine, at least. He had no idea what happened to Taka after the explosion.

"No, no they are not." A wicked smile crossed the Zhànying's face but never touched his eyes. "Your accent is unusual, Tak Gi-ung from Earth." The agent began to pace around behind Takeshi. A warrior to the bones, having a threat behind him made him on edge. A cold hard object was placed against Takeshi's neck. "I will have the truth from you. One way or another."

Takeshi was certain his Cube was being scanned yet again, but the additional sharp prick and hiss of an auto-injector caught him off guard.

"Sir, what is—" Takeshi stopped as his interrogator sat on the table in front of him, holding an empty injector. The room began to swim as a euphoric fire spread from his neck, racing throughout his body.

The Yujingyu rested his hand on the table and drummed his fingers softly. Takeshi was not afraid of a lone opponent. In this case, however, he was powerless. If he moved against the man, his collar would explode. The room became suffocatingly quiet, save for the drumming of his interrogator's fingers, which started echoing impossibly loud, tickling his senses. Takeshi sat shackled to the chair, trying to keep his breathing steady as the toxin rushed through his veins. He willed his eyes to remained locked on the interrogator; focused but non-threatening. He was trained to resist interrogation long before his journey to the Watchtower and into the dark embrace of espionage.

It was not enough. A numb smile spread across Takeshi's face.

The interrogator, calm and composed, leaned in slightly, his voice smooth yet laced with quiet menace that seemed to pulse through Takeshi's skull. "You are not Tak Gi-ung."

"I am?" Takeshi's slurred speech betrayed him.

"No, you are not." The drumming stopped, and the Zhànying's other fist rose to strike him. Takeshi saw the blow coming, horribly telegraphed and not nearly fast enough. A rattle of his manacles was his only reward for the instinctual, but horrendously slow, pivot and block he tried to throw up. The fist connected with Takeshi's skull with the weight of a meteor moments before, then his skull bounced off the table. His body betrayed him, and it stopped responding to his will.

"Who planted the bombs?!" The flash of steel was almost imperceptible—quick, brutal, and precise. Takeshi bit back a scream as a long thin dagger suddenly pinned his hand to the table before he had recovered from the first strike.

"You know," his tormentor continued conversationally, "this can all end with one answer. Who planted the bombs? You knew they were coming. You shouted a warning!" The Imperial Agent leaned in as he screamed in Takeshi's face, hauling back his right arm and striking him yet again.

Takeshi's head still rang with the force of the first blow as the room doubled upon itself. Agony seized through his body, pain coursing up through his arm. His brain had a hard time wrapping around what his eyes were seeing, but it finally dawned on him that the blade was still in his hand as he was rocked by the punch.

Takeshi screamed.

* * * * *

The walls were not made of stone or steel but of time—vast, unrelenting, and crushing. Takeshi sat on the floor in the corner, his cuffed hands—one still poorly bandaged—limp in his lap, staring at the floor like it held answers to questions he could no longer articulate. Had they dimmed the light? It flickered overhead, bathing the space in a jaundiced glow, making the shadowy corners of his confinement stretch like mocking specters.

How long has it been? Day and night no longer held meaning. The beatings continued. It was always the same agent who came, the bald Zhànying. Sometimes he would bring others to join in, but it was always him who did the talking. Takeshi would be beaten, sometimes stabbed, and hit with a medikit laced with something that kept his head swimming and put him to sleep. How many times has it been now… ten, twelve?

The mission had hardly begun, and he was already trapped. The operation had been doomed from the start. No better than a whispered secret shouted into a typhoon. There was no backup, no extraction team to breach the night to carry him home. His cover had burned to ash the moment he confronted the Bào, and the enemy did not need words to make him understand his new reality. This room, with its dark walls and floor that felt unsteady, was reality on Kuraimori.

They had opened the doors for him once. Attempting an escape was rewarded with the worst beating of all. He was stabbed several times, shot once. Laughter. The guards laughed at him as they delighted in his torture, healing him before beginning again.

Stale air pressed down on him, heavy and suffocating. Each breath felt like a concession, a reluctant admission that he was still alive when a part of him begged to give up. His chest ached—not from any physical wound, but from the gnawing weight of hopelessness sinking its teeth into him.

His mind turned inward, retracing the steps that had led him here. He had told them he was not ready, hadn't he? His voice—faint, uncertain—still echoed in his head, swallowed by the stern stares of General Daichi, Song, and the others. You'll rise to the occasion, they had said, their words gilded with false confidence. But he hadn't risen; he didn't even have the chance.

The silence of his failure screamed. It was nearly as loud as the loss of his katana. It felt like a wound he could never heal now—honor he could never restore.

Takeshi leaned forward, pressing his forehead against his hands. The cold steel cuffs around his wrists bit into his skin, a cruel reminder of how tightly the world held him now. The bomb around his neck cheerily blinked green, an ever-present condemnation. He couldn't tell where the mission ended and his punishment began. All those impossible victories… his survival when others died… he knew the scales always come back to balance.

His mind drifted, sliding further into its dark recesses.

A faint sound reached him—the creak of a door and clicking steps somewhere far away. It could have been a guard, or it could have been his mind playing tricks on him again. It didn't matter. He no longer strained to listen for the sounds of rescue. Hope was a fire long extinguished, leaving him with only the cold, suffocating dark.

There was no way out.

* * * * *

"I still do not understand where I fit, General. Gene-coded or not, the vault can be opened by the right hacker."

"Yes, it can." General Daichi's voice was stern. "But with your presence, two problems are solved. First, the vault will unlock for you, saving precious time. Your father ensured this was the case against the chance he met an untimely end. Second, you are a warrior with few peers, Takeshi. Your presence provides a bulwark for those you will be working with."

He paused. Takeshi sensed the hesitation.

"You were also specifically asked for."

"By whom?" Takeshi asked.

"Yasbir."

"The Hassassin*?"*

"Yes. They move in odd ways, always at pivotal moments in history. They intervene at seemingly random, only to have saved someone who later prevents a major catastrophe.'"

Takeshi's mind ran with possibilities.

"Bianca Chen would not have lived to tell her story of what happened on the Báijīng Orbital if not for Yasbir. She lit the spark that ignited the flame of our freedom. If not for Yasbir, she would have died

in a jade cell, if she had made it that far. I do not claim to know his motives. I do trust that, at least in this, thus far Yasbir has been a friend of Greater Independent Japan."

"I am bushi. *I am not some faithless knife in the shadows."*

"You are what your Emperor commands you to be, Takeshi-san." Impatience had worked its way into the older warrior's voice.

General Daichi was as dutiful as ever. Takeshi could not help but wonder how many deeds done in the name of duty weighed on his soul.

"The transport departs in one hour. If you are on it or not." 'Uncle' Daichi had spoken his peace, and now the general gave his orders.

Takeshi already knew his answer. Honor, duty—they both demanded he go. Beyond that, Takeshi wanted—no, needed*—to dive back into the fray.*

"I will answer the call, General."

20.

The walls pulsed faintly, alive, like a beast breathing in its sleep. His breathing quickened, though he fought to steady it. The honor of a warrior demanded calm in the face of the unknown. Yet fear, like a whisper in the dark, curled around his thoughts. Fear was a thing to be honed, controlled. It ran rampant through Takeshi.

His mind lingered in an unceasing fog of uncertainty. It was not the pain he dreaded—he had endured torture before. It was the *not knowing*. The slow blinking light of his collar taunted him, red and menacing. Takeshi couldn't remember if it had always been red. He thought it was green, but color, much like time, seemed to blur.

Takeshi's hand twitched instinctively, searching for the comfort of his katana. It wasn't there, of course. His blade had not yet been replaced when he was spirited into a world of shadows. Without it, he felt hollow, as if a piece of his identity had been ripped away and discarded like so much debris.

The room's only light flared suddenly, casting jagged shadows across the walls. Or was he hallucinating again? The sound of approaching footsteps echoed down the corridor. Each step seemed to grow louder, more oppressive. Each one echoing like the beating of a war drum heralding his doom.

Takeshi clenched his jaw, but his heart betrayed him, pounding a frantic rhythm against his ribs. He thought of all his teachers, his uncle, and his father. He thought of the code that had defined his life. Was this how it ended, kneeling and powerless in a StateEmpire prison? Was this how Takeshi Oyama died?

The door to his cell opened with a screech, revealing his tormentor silhouetted by the low glow of the corridor. His gaoler's face seemed to loom, changed by the narcotics or his imagination, Takeshi could not decide. He stood there for a moment, silent, as though savoring his fear; mocking.

Takeshi summoned the warrior deep within him and lifted his chin, forcing defiance into his gaze. But the fear remained, buried just beneath the surface. Fear of what he could not see, of what he could not fight. Fear of the unknown that stretched out before him, vast and merciless as the void between the stars.

The Zhànying entered the room and leaned casually against the table, arms folded across his chest. Takeshi stirred, uncertain under their watchful gaze. The hard floor in the corner of the room had done him no favors. Everything hurt, he wasn't able to tell the difference between the beatings and the pains of sleeping on the floor. The room still spun.

"How long have you been here?" The voice was different somehow… less contemptuous despite the lethality radiating from the Yujingyu. They had played this trick before. Takeshi's head still swam with the narcotics in his veins. His wounds weren't quite healed from the last beating he had taken. Half full med-injectors had given him just enough to survive, but not quite enough to fully regain his strength and never enough to recover his faculties.

"I asked you a question."

"I do not know." It was the truth.

"Really worked you over, huh? Get up."

"What?" Takeshi struggled to reconcile the reality he was experiencing. Was it disdain he was hearing? The room kept swimming despite his failing attempts to rise.

"I said get up." His tormentor pushed off the table quickly, moving with all the grace and menace of a predator. Bringing his comlog up, the agent worked through a few holo-dials before finding the prompt he wanted.

Somewhere in Takeshi's mind, he questioned why he could see the holograms.

Closing the short distance, the Zhànying dropped to a knee, eye level with Takeshi. "Wow, you stink. It's time to move, Mr. Tak."

Takeshi recoiled, fear rising to the surface once more as he stared at the outstretched hand before him. It looked like a claw. His movements were lethargic and slow. He had been offered a hand once before. How long had he been here? The agent patiently waited, hand extended.

Doubt.

Takeshi was afraid, he was honest enough to admit that to himself, but doubt… The haze of confusion was slowly lifting, but the latest round of narcotics must have broken something inside him. He wanted to go with the agent. He wanted to join all those souls he owed his life to. He wanted it to end. Why should he keep living when so many others had not? His gaze drifted down to his hands. These hands had seen so much war. These hands had caused so much suffering.

"You don't have time for that, Neko."

"What?"

"And just who are you?!" Neither of them had heard the door open again. The bald Zhànying stood in the doorway, eyes full of fury. Takeshi felt his grasp on reality slipping as suddenly there were two of him.

The bald Zhànying kneeling in front of Takeshi stood with his back to his twin, identical in every way. A frown creased the figure's dark features as he frowned."*Kuso*."

The man in front of Takeshi exploded into motion before his twin. A katana appeared in his hand as if pulled from thin air, and a holoplane flipped open and blinked a command Takeshi couldn't quite make out as the Yujingyu lunged toward the newcomer. Takeshi struggled to make sense of what he was seeing. Identical to the last detail, the Imperial Agent, mirrored, stretched his sanity.

The structure shook beneath him with a muted boom, and the room plunged into darkness as the identical agents collided. To his credit, the newcomer was barely a microsecond behind. As the darkness took the room, Takeshi saw the glint of cold steel as blades lashed out. The air was thick with tension, vibrating like a taut string, as Takeshi scrambled as far into the corner as physics would allow, disoriented but keenly aware of every minute sound. The faint scrape of boots against concrete echoed—sharp and jarring—as two figures moved in a deadly dance taunted him. Each breath they took, heavy with exertion, felt like an ominous prelude to the clash of steel. There were two distinct voices.

Suddenly, a low grunt pierced the silence, followed by the sharp clink of metal kissing armor. The attackers' bodies shifted in the dark, a rhythm of anticipation and aggression. Takeshi strained to focus on the space around him. If he was wearing his comlog, or his armor, the onboard programing would have adjusted the optics of his lens, revealing the space in low gray light and highlighting the combatants. As it was, in this prison of darkness, his other senses sharpened and his heart began to race. He imagined tasting their adrenaline in the air…

"Come on!" An unfamiliar voice, laced with fury, challenged. The struggle was closer now. Takeshi could picture the razor's edge of a blade slicing through the shadows to cut him.

A feint, quick and reckless, followed by a sharp inhale. The metallic taste of blood began to hang in the air. Takeshi couldn't see, but he could hear the urgency, the desperation of their movements. The shuffle of feet as they aimed for the other. Grunts and labored breaths mixed with the rasp of blades.

Then—

A cry erupted from the darkness, the kind that stemmed not just from pain but from a premature awareness of mortality. The world fell silent for a heartbeat.

Then the swift, agonizing sound of steel slipping from flesh combined with the wet thud of a body hitting the ground. A thump echoed, reverberating in Takeshi's drug-addled mind, followed by a morbid stillness. A heavy, shuddering breath came next, a sign of defeat.

"Why couldn't you just die?" came the unfamiliar voice of the victor, trembling and laced with madness. "*Chikusho*."

Somewhere in his mind, Takeshi recognized the adrenaline grip of violence in the voice. More rustling followed as one figure rose to their feet and stumbled against the wall.

The sound of shoes dragging imperceptibly through blood and remnants of the fight was tormenting. Takeshi could only imagine the wildness in their eyes and the reckless triumph that coursed through the victor.

In that moment of ephemeral silence, a finality fell over Takeshi. One attacker would not rise again. A pool of rapidly cooling fluid slowly crawled across the floor to touch Takeshi's bare feet. In the suffocating darkness, he was left with the weight of the unknown and death.

"Slagg me." Anger and pain threaded through the unfamiliar voice. Takeshi braced himself in the darkness, waiting for his end.

Emergency power routed through the building, and light flooded the space, blinding and sudden. As Takeshi's eyes adjusted, they revealed the aftermath of the lethal clash. The bald agent lay sprawled face down in a pool of his own life blood, red and oily. Three horrific wounds visible across his torso told Takeshi he died badly. The Zhànying's own small stabbing knife was lodged in his neck.

Just beyond him, the woman who stood against the wall for support was not untouched by the battle. Her padded, form-fitting pants were slashed across the right hip. The red leather coat she wore would have been proof against a grazing strike, but her left arm clutched her abdomen, holding back the tide of blood as best she could. Beneath the coat, her shirt was cut open and failed to hide her heavily tattooed torso. Takeshi thought he recognized the stylized art inked into her skin, but the lingering narcotics in his system made chasing the memory like swimming against an avalanche. Her eyes were full of rage. They bore into Takeshi like lasers from beneath bright blue hair.

"You had better slagg'n be worth it!" She spat at Taekshi. From within her coat, she produced an auto-injector and slammed it into her thigh. Takeshi recognized the Serum injection through his haze as he watched her wounds begin to heal.

The newcomer brought her comlog up and flicked a pair of commands before speaking. "I've got him, but it got messy. Plan B." A pause. "Understood."

How could he see her comlog dials? His head was reeling. Darkness began to creep at the edge of his vision. Takeshi shook his head, trying to clear the fog as the woman knelt before him, clearly unconcerned for how much over her shirt had been cut open. Her torso was threaded with lean muscle.

"Hey, Neko. Don't you slagg'n lose it on me! I don't know what they hit you with and I don't have time to figure it out, we gotta move." She reached into a thigh pocket and produced a second a-doc and unceremoniously slammed it into his chest.

Takeshi screamed in surprise as the injection did its work. It was like cold lightning racing through his body as his wounds knit back together. Takeshi recovered enough of his wits to form a complete sentence. "Who… wait, Neko?"

"Yeah, that's right, you slagg'n idiot."

"How?"

She laughed in his face, blue hair dark in the low light. "A little bird sent me. Now how to pop those…" She trailed off in thought looking at his restraints.

Takeshi watched her shift over to the dead Zhànying and search him quickly before removing his comlog. Holding it up next to hers, Takeshi watched her form a sprawling set of holographic rings over them both as she searched.

"Got it!" Her exclamation was punctuated by the double click of Takeshi's manacles unlocking before clattering to the ground.

"How can I see your holos? And why are the walls still… swimming?"

The woman smirked. "I jailbroke your collar before I walked in the room. Didn't want it to blow us both up. It's pretty standard for them to have dampeners in them. As to the walls, that injection wasn't a mil-grade medikit, so it won't purge everything. I'm pretty sure I know what they hit you with." She reached around Takeshi's neck and removed the collar. The proximity to another human that wasn't actively harming him was jarring. "Now, get up already, we need to move!"

Punctuating her worlds, the building began to tremble beneath him.

* * * * *

Sparrow's silhouette melded seamlessly with the jagged edge of the rooftop. Her eyes, sharp and cold, scanned the neon-lit cityscape below with vision overlaid by tactical readouts. Cloaked in shadows yet illuminated by the soft glow of distant holo-ads, she was a ghost—unseen, unheard, and deadly.

"Begin."

At her signal, Hiro's surprise attack rocked the Yujingyu building. The hidden Imperial Service facility was concealed amongst a dozen buildings just like it, but she knew just where to strike. To their credit, hidden Yujingyu sentry posts immediately returned fire, revealing their positions.

"Song. Your turn."

Automatic fire spoke from three directions, converging on Yujingyu responders with precision. Sparrow crouched in rooftop shadows, hidden from the fray. Her work was already done.

"Decoy team, are you in position?"

* * * * *

Ten minutes. Mizu's heart raced as they burst through the doorway at a stagger more than a run. Struggling to maintain her balance, she half-carried Neko over one shoulder, his weight bearing her down as he struggled to maintain balance. His face was pale and sweaty as he fought through the lingering drugs in his system. She had stolen an injector from the dead agent's body before they left it behind. Hopefully they could make sense of it later and get him moving under his own two feet for good. *Kuso*, he was heavy.

The municipal building, turned into a torturer's playground, screamed around them. Alarms blared across the facility, broken by the thunder of heavy weapons fire and explosions. The plan went sideways the second the Zhànying she was impersonating entered the room. She tagged his location in another wing of the building when she made her move, but luck was against her. Sparrow coordinated from the shadows, ensuring her there were reinforcements in the area and her Hands wouldn't do any heavy lifting. She had no idea who the guards were shooting at at this point, but there was an intense firefight on the western face of the building. As if to punctuate her thought, explosions could be heard as rockets pummeled the building.

Five minutes. The structure around them groaned under the strain of chaos. Walls crumbled, and debris fell like rain, but she couldn't stop; there was no time. Each step was a battle against gravity and the terror all around her. Gunfire echoed through the hall, punctuated by cries of a building not designed for this sort of punishment.

She tightened her grip on Neko, her other hand brandishing a Boarding Pistol, ready to fight off anyone who dared bar her path. Mizu thought about grabbing another weapon from the dead, but hacking the Friend/Foe identifier would waste precious time.

The weight of fear mingled with the instinct to survive, propelling her forward through the haze of dust and smoke. Every shadow felt like a threat. She turned abruptly, dropping Neko, at the sounds of running soldiers behind them. Her aim was wild in the turmoil as she sprayed an entire magazine in burst mode. The staccato clack-clack-clack of metal shrapnel pelting the walls and floor punctuated the chaos.

For a split second, she felt invincible, and the shake screamed in joy.

Then the world closed in again, the urgency of escape outweighing the pain of her muscles screaming for relief. Two soldiers stumbled blindly into her fire, tumbling over each other in a mad scramble to seek cover. Neither of them made it. When no further soldiers came behind them, Mizu reached for Neko.

"I can walk now, I think." Neko tested his own weight, one hand on the wall. He was unsteady, but mobile. That would make this much easier.

"*Kuso*, finally."

The corridor lit up with gunfire as the ambush sprung.

Neko staggered and fell, eyes glassy. Toxins must still be pulsing through his system like syrup.

"I—" he slurred.

Mizu was already moving. "Stay down!"

She screamed as she charged, not out of fear, but joy—raw, violent joy. The shake took her sword in hand as Mizu laughed. The first soldier barely got his rifle up before her katana split the weapon in half and took two fingers with it. Blood sprayed, metal shrieked, and Mizu shoved him into the wall with her shoulder, blade dragging sparks in its wake.

Another fired at her. She ducked too late—felt the round graze her thigh—but kept going, heedless. She grabbed his barrel with her off hand, yanked him close, and slammed her forehead into his helmetless face then slashed his throat. He went down.

She spun—off-balance but moving—and laughed maniacally. She held her katana more like a bat than a weapon of finesse.

"Is that all you slagg'n got?!"

The last one came at her, knife drawn—too close for guns. She let him close then pivoted off the wall and drove the katana straight through his side—not cleanly, not like a swordsman. She had to twist, wrench, kick him off the blade. It tore free with a wet sound.

Neko climbed to his feet once more, swaying. Mizu hurried back, panting, grinning, covered in blood. She wiped the blade on her sleeve. "Let's go."

"Who are you?" Neko's eyes focused on Mizu as he appraised her more clearly.

"We don't have time for this song and dance. Slagg'n follow or die." She sharpened her tone to invite no argument. "Those are your options."

Two minutes. She cursed under her breath.

Neko smiled at her and mumbled something encouraging. She could tell he was trying to be anything but helpless, but his limbs fought him every step of the way. Almost there. Mizu sheathed *Akai Te*, drew her pistol, and forged forward.

They stumbled into the garage, nearly tripping over two slain soldiers. Both lay crumpled with long cuts across their throats, deep… to the bone. The blood sprayed across the wall started from head height. They had still been standing when they died, neither had drawn a weapon. They didn't even have time. Curious.

"Blade work. A sword." Neko stared at the two dead bodies, clarity peeking through briefly. "Attacker was standing right in front of them."

Equally curious was the armored truck waiting, doors open. Taking it on blind faith, Mizu bodily shoved Neko into the back seat and climbed into the front. She hated cars. Four wheels and four walls was a cage to the *bōsōzoku.*

The engine fired up on the first try. No security locks or IFF stood in her way. Reaching to disable the beacon and remote override, Mizu found them already disabled.

"What the…"

Unexpected, but not unwelcome, Mizu closed her door and activated the HUD. A myriad of data appeared in her lens as the truck's systems linked with her comlog.

Gunning it down the ramp, five metric tons of armored assault truck rammed through the retractable barricade and onto the street. Mizu swerved to the right, toward the sea, slamming on the horn as she did.

Heartbeats later, the car bomb Goro had planted went off behind her, filling the night sky with fire.

Barely a block away, Mizu pulled over and idled. She didn't come to a complete stop as Goro ran out of the shadows, pistol held low, and jumped in. Mizu slid to the other seat, and Goro slammed the pedal to the floor and blasted into the night. The shake chased her the whole way.

"Decoys away—look." Goro pointed at a pair of trucks peeling away from the scene just before they took different turns, one after another.

Neko moaned uncomfortably in the back seat where she had unceremoniously dumped him. The potent drugs coursing through his veins were slowly fighting back against the injection she had given him. She felt sorry for him, she knew what he was going through. So did Goro.

"Are you sure about this? He looks like *kuso.*" Goro glanced back at their passenger, reading his symptoms like a book in seconds.

"No, do you have a better idea?" Mizu was still full of fire and wrath.

"Will Yoshihiro even take us in after all this noise—take *him* in?"

"No idea, but that's what we are slagg'n doing. " She threw a finger in the big man's face as he chuckled. "Don't say it!"

"Whatever you say, Boss." Goro chuckled to himself despite the life-or-death moment.

"Slagghead." Mizu had already tuned him out and focused on the road ahead—and fighting the shake rattling in her chest—but she found herself grinning nonetheless. "You think he can swim?"

21.

Su-Yeong stalked through the wreckage, a blade of stillness. Her boots crunched glass with a rhythm too calm for someone surrounded by devastation. The tail of her robes hissed behind her like a shadow not quite her own, swaying with unnatural precision. A single gloved finger traced a line across the blasted wall—lingering, slow, intimate.

The sun had yet to rise on the wreckage.

Then she stopped. "What *happened* here?"

Each word fell like a blade.

Corporal Ming—the surviving member of any rank from this detachment—stood rigid, trembling. "W-we believe it was a coordinated strike, ma'am. The team on site reported a dozen or more assailants—"

"I know what it wasn't," she snapped, voice sharp—like a railgun cutting down the inept trooper. "It wasn't supposed to be possible. This facility is *ours*. That means something. Or it did—before last night."

A strand of hair, lacquer-black and pinned with surgical precision, had come loose. That detail—that one detail—seemed to infuriate her more than the bodies. She turned to face the crumpled remains of a corpse at her feet—shredded beyond recognition by close range fire.

"I told him." Her voice was quiet now. "I told Hsu what would happen if security was lax. Do you remember that, Da?"

"I do, ma'am." Lieutenant Da answered from behind the trembling corporal. Da loomed over the terrified trooper's shoulder—a specter of death.

Ming opened his mouth—and closed it. Wisely, he said nothing.

The gurney bearing Agent Hsu's corpse floated toward her down the hall.

Su-Yeong's hand trembled. Not with fear, but with rage barely bottled. Then, with a sudden, animalistic growl, she drove it into the wall like a dagger. Her gauntlet groaned in protest.

"I want names! Every soul who accessed this building in the last seventy-two hours. Every call, every delivery, every custodian. I want faces. I want proof. I want it *all*."

"Ma'am, that could take—"

She turned.

He didn't finish the sentence and wisely bowed instead.

"I am not angry," she said, stepping past him, "I am *disappointed.* And disappointment leads to consequences."

Da dismissed the warrior before he drew her ire further. His attention quickly shifted to a holoplane that appeared above his wrist. "Ma'am. We have identified one of the drivers. A local informant. Would you like the details?"

"Handle it." She waved a hand to dismiss him.

Da lingered.

"What now?" Su-Yeong's wrath drifted into annoyance.

"We have lost contact with two more listening posts in the last few hours, Ma'am."

* * * * *

Mizu leaned against the wall, alone with her thoughts finally. The transport's engine ticked softly, cooling under the moonlight, its hum fading into the echoes of the distant cityscape. The scent of saltwater still clung to her leather jacket—from where they drove the Yujingyu truck off a pier—mingling with the faint waft of spring blossoms carried by the wind. Tanto had given her the van after he fished them out of the bay. Yet another favor owed.

She had not come to this quiet stretch of road, far from the chaos and concrete, just to think. The highway was a liminal space, an empty artery of Sakuramachi's pulsing heart. A place to wait as well as think.

Mizu exhaled slowly, the cool night air twisting her breath like the threads of her soul. Unwinding the shake piece by piece, her mind was ill at ease.

On one hand, the family she had fought to protect. Her brothers and sisters were everything to her, their loyalty forged in asphalt, adrenaline, and blood. And yet, behind that loyalty lay the specter of the yakuza—the real power in their world once the war fell apart. Yoshihiro Shubitsu's words replayed in her mind.

"We will protect your bōsōzoku*, Mizoku-san. Your strength is our strength."*

A veiled threat cloaked in the veneer of respect. She knew what it meant: the gang was free only so long as it served the family's interests. How would he react when he knew she was about to drop a war on him?

She thought of Japan. The land of her ancestors, the country whose traditions had once been interwoven into the fabric of society. Her grandmother had always spoken of *giri*, duty, as the highest virtue. But where was *giri* now, in this tangled web of modernity and war? *Giri* had gotten her parents killed long before the Uprising.

Was she even still loyal to Japan? She glanced at the distant city lights with the weight of her choices pressed on her chest; heavier than the jacket she wore, heavier than the pistol in her belt or the blade sitting on the hood of the truck. It was heavier than the shake.

If the Imperial Service didn't know something was happening beneath their noses before, they did now. Two additional trucks—parked waiting for them by the mysterious Sparrow—made for decoys. That meant three trucks had blasted through Sakuramachi at breakneck speeds. All the other Hands had to do was drive. Kairi had checked in and was heading to round up the rest of the non-combatant Hands.

No word from Jon yet. His vehicle was found with no sign of him, but there was also nothing indicating an unwelcome fate. He was the most cautious of them. He would turn up.

Yu Tang hung low and full in the night sky. The planet was a silent observer of her quiet rebellion, her unspoken doubts; it judged her choices, the decisions that brought her to this moment.

"He's waking up." Goro walked up, tapping his comlog. He had been monitoring Neko's vitals. For being a monster of a man, Goro was also their platoon medic in the war and had a knack for it. Years of nursing her through the shakedown had only honed his skills.

Mizu nodded, voice low and clipped—full of memory. "His ride is just beginning."

* * * * *

Takeshi couldn't remember the last time he felt this depleted, this beaten. The dive off a pier had been a harrowing experience that he could barely remember. Sleep had claimed him as soon as his shivering body was hauled from the endless abyss of the bay and onto the shore. He only vaguely remembered being carried through tunnels. The stolen hours since were blank.

Taking stock of his mind and body, Takeshi closed his eyes. One breath and then the next. In and out, each breath bringing oxygen and awareness into his body—bringing clarity and focus. Centering himself was less of a fight, thanks to the Serum-empowered narcotic suppressant his rescuers must have injected him with. In and out, balance.

His body felt as if it had been thrown from orbit without a chute. Even when a building had dropped on him in the frontiers of Paradiso, he hadn't felt so abused. But his body and mind were his once again. A lifetime of training and discipline had warred against the wild swings of reality his mind experienced in the not-so-gentle hands of his captors.

Takeshi slowly tensed and relaxed, one muscle at a time, as he took stock of his frame. He shook gently, as if feverish. A burning, aching… need… tore at his mind. He wanted it all to go away, to sleep again. He wanted to forget.

He still had no idea how much time had passed in captivity, but he did not feel weaker for it. The improved baseline of the human body, laced with Silk networks and reinforced by modern science, was a resilient thing. It would take months of captivity and deprivation for his body to atrophy considerably. Even so, he felt… weaker, unsteady.

A voice brought Takeshi back to full awareness, and he opened his eyes.

"He's waking up."

Takeshi found himself in the back of a small cargo vehicle. A crude cot of blankets padded him from the colder metal shell. His breath was visible in the low, ambient light of a bright night sky filtering inside.

Instinctively looking for his absent blade, a slowly blinking of a green light caused a burst of panic. Hands darting to his neck, Takeshi found nothing. Bringing his arms up showed a small medical monitor, no bigger than the palm of his hand, was adhered to his forearm. Its slow green blink indicated no alerts to be immediately concerned about. It took a moment to bring his nerves back into check.

Untangling himself from the blankets, Takeshi removed the thin silicone pad laced with circuitry and held it up as the light went out. Recognizing it as Haqqislamite tech, Takeshi discarded the device and gingerly exited the vehicle.

The night was cool and crisp, a pleasant spring evening, all things considered. The smell of earth and pine mingled with faint traces of salt drifting in from the sea. He gave himself leave to embrace the moment as he steadied himself against the truck. His feet were betraying him, and the world didn't seem quite so steady. Still, the smell of it… it felt like home.

A moment of peace passed as he found his balance, listening to the wind, before the crunch of footsteps put him back on guard. He caught his first real glimpse of the woman that saved his life.

She was fairly average height but a thin sort of muscular, all things considered. He could imagine a craftsman had sculpted her while not wasting time on the softer curves. Faded blue hair and brown eyes set a pretty, if hard, face that stared back at him with hardly concealed sympathy. Her stance spoke of combat training, though Takeshi had seen firsthand how dangerous she could really be. Wrapped in that same red jacket against the night air, she held a cup in each hand, but he could not miss the unmistakable bulge of a pistol at her hip. Her wakizashi sat on the hood of the vehicle, within easy arms reach. She saw that it caught his attention as well.

Her companion was taller built and broader set. His blunt features looked like they would win a contest of wills with a planet if given a chance. He wore a similar red leather jacket and hung back a few feet behind his companion, on guard despite their isolation. Despite the dark, Takeshi spied a heavy shotgun hanging from him by a sling.

"Look who's finally awake. I know how the shakedown feels, so we can skip that part. Tea?"

Takeshi accepted the self-heating cup from his rescuer in silence and sat down, worrying his legs would betray him again. His whole body shook. What was this 'shakedown' he wondered? Popping the seal, the cup began to steam. The comforting smell of field ration tea sent his stomach growling.

Despite being a meter away from him, both of them were cold and distant as the silence stretched.

The woman turned to her companion. "Goro, mind taking another sweep for me?"

"Whatever you say, Boss."

Takeshi watched him turn and leave without another word, trudging down the hill. Goro was a mountain of a man. Takeshi did not want to be on the receiving end of those fists.

They both watched him leave, neither looking to the other to start the conversation.

"So… Neko, huh?"

"Yes." Keeping his tone as neutral as possible, Takeshi kept his guard up. This woman may have rescued him, but she was still a stranger, and he was still trapped behind enemy lines.

"Hell of a callsign to pick."

"I did not pick it."

Her low chuckle caught him by surprise. "Slagg, someone must hate you."

"I am beginning to think you are not wrong." The world started spinning once again.

She laughed aloud. It was a pleasant thing, carefree and wild. "I rarely am."

The world slowly rolled under Takeshi's feet. "What did they inject me with?"

"'Bite,' unless I miss my mark." Takeshi's blank expression prompted her to continue. "It popped up shortly after the war. The side effects are… unfortunate." She furrowed her brows, concern written across her face as Takeshi's world started to fade. "You aren't through the woods yet."

"I… I do not…" Nausea and vertigo sliced through Takeshi's awareness.

"We have to get you a detox, and fast. For now, just drink the tea. It'll help you get back to sleep." She reached out her hand to help bring the cup up to his lips, which was suddenly much further than he thought. He obediently drank. Takeshi noted the missing finger on her left hand and frowned. His rescuer saw his reaction.

"Get used to it." A gentle contempt took hold in her voice. "You're going to see a lot of that where we are going."

22.

The crisp, clean mountain air was, perhaps, the best part of this assignment for Su-Yeong. In a lifetime of service, she knew her loyalty was not to herself, but the throne which she served. In that, Su-Yeong was at peace. A tranquility known by few of her colleagues scattered throughout the Human Sphere. She was often dispatched to the darkest places humanity could offer, moving in the shadows. Exercising in the full dawn light atop a mountain was a small peace to be grateful for. Armor and ceremonial robes left behind at the estate, she bound up the trail at a steady pace, clad in only workout pants and a cropped top.

The bombings in the outer ward and the airport had pushed Control into a frenzy. Usually she was left to her own devices—and liked it that way. As the violence rose to levels not seen since the early days after the Uprising, a new level of oversight was brought to bear. Su-Yeong felt it was onerous. Hours spent in briefings and reports were hours wasted. For now, she forged up the mountain, letting the clearer air clear her mind.

Her guard contingent was clearly ill at ease with her choice to exercise so far from them. They held their concerns knowing the futility. Kuraimori's mountains were never truly tamed, evidenced by the fighting knife on Su-Yeong's hip.

Overprotective guards were certainly the least of her concerns, so she bore them no mind as she sprinted the last one hundred meters to the cliff's edge. Heart rate steady, she brought the workout to a close, moving into tai chi forms to cool down.

She wondered what the drone operator thought of her, balanced in a standing vertical split. It was picturesque, no doubt, overlooking the Hansei Valley. Nothing but bioengineered bamboo and pine forests mixed with native flora stretched in all directions. The controller would see a lone woman, gracefully flowing through martial forms atop a cliffside clearing; one rather fit, rather attractive woman. Su-Yeong worked hard on her fitness and was fully aware of her natural beauty. It was the stuff of Maya films.

She knew the surveillance drone was there of course. She was no fool. Her first day here she had dropped her own multipronged worm program into the surveillance net. Her hydra highlighted everything in the valley in her personal network. No one and nothing moved in the Hansei Valley without her knowledge.

Isolated from the nearest city by rock-strewn foothills, yet not quite in the more dense mountainous tracts, the location couldn't have been more perfect. She had handpicked Hansei for her assignment, moving the pieces into place. Small research and development facilities dotted the valley. She had seen them stripped for anything valuable and cordoned off.

The nearby airfield was a bit of a nuisance, but not overbearing on her day-to-day. The whining turbines of drones and Feìquán patrol craft were baffled by a mountain, providing her small facility even more sense of isolation.

Looking down the valley, Su-Yoeng could just make out the estate amongst the small city's buildings. It took her breath away, as it always did. Walled gardens surrounded several buildings cast in quintessentially Japanese architectural style. Despite the protests of her guard, Su-Yeong had insisted they remain and hired a gardener to maintain them.

Their tranquility brought her peace, or perhaps nostalgia… Regardless of her reasoning, as an agent of the Imperial Service, no one pushed against her word. Many of her colleagues would have been far more harsh to the local populace, especially since the Japanese rebellion. Memories were long, and Su-Yeong found a gentler hand made for a calm and quiet populace, which this particular assignment certainly called for.

The catastrophe at the air base was the talk of her detachment. Her soldiers shared rumors and speculation when they thought she couldn't hear. Her plans were in motion, even now, to bring it all to a swift conclusion. It had taken a bit longer than intended, she admitted, but these things happened.

The serenity of Su-Yeong's morning was ended, per usual, by a chime in her comlog. She silenced the alert and finished her cooldown before answering. The holographic form of an impatient Lieutenant Da appeared in her lens, as if hovering before her. When he realized she was not completely clothed, his figure turned slightly. Blushing, he looked away from her sweat-covered form. He was a career soldier, going grey from long years of service, and looked every bit the part. His troopers wouldn't let him live this one down.

"Ma'am."

"Yes, Lieutenant?" There was only one reason for the officer to be calling her, but the pantomime made him feel more in control, so Su-Yeong continued to indulge it.

"We are receiving reinforcements and a second agent. They should be here by midday."

"Did Control provide a reason for the reinforcements?" She had certainly not requested them.

"No, ma'am. Control did not mention the additional forces, only that they have identified the hostiles involved in Agent Hsu's murder."

Su-Yeong snorted. "Murder is being too kind, Lieutenant. He was killed because he was an overconfident idiot." She had walked the halls herself and seen to it that what little footage survived the raid was contained. "Say it again."

Despite the discomfort of the command, Lieutenant Da was a soldier through and through; orders were orders.

"Control has identified the hostiles who dispatched Agent Hsu."

"Close enough. Send it to me." She noticed the soldier's hesitation. "Yes?"

"One more thing, ma'am. The woman involved matches the description of the smuggler we have been pursuing. She seems to be something more."

"Thank you for the conjecture, Lieutenant." Su-Yeong applied just the right amount of contempt to her tone to invite no further curiosity from her subordinate. In the Imperial Service, knowing too much could end someone's career abruptly, and violently.

"My apologies, ma'am."

As the data packet came through her comlog, Su-Yeong cut the line, letting her subordinate stew on her displeasure. It was good for him. Filtering through the data, she flicked two fingers through the floating holopane and projected a pair of silhouettes where Lieutenant Da was moments before.

"Shit."

* * * * *

Bianca walked the simple streets of Nogoyu with her guide. Benji was a softer soul than Yasbir—who vanished along with his machines after making introductions. Where Yasbir was composed and controlled, Benji seemed haunted. He didn't talk much but had been overly kind to her from the moment she boarded the old fishing boat with him.

The sea, however, had not been kind to her. The contents of her stomach rebelled more than once. Each time, Benji went out of his way to tend to her while the boat captain—a man named Tanto—stayed at the wheel.

Benji wore a simple coverall and a heavy jacket against the wind. As they coasted into the small, local docks, he had given Bianca clothes to fit in more closely with the locals, and she was grateful for it as the wind bit through her sodden clothing.

The village was home to barely a hundred souls—once it had clearly been more—but other than those working the fishing docks, little noise was heard. The life of the place was muted, or even wholly absent in some neighborhoods. A full half of the buildings were empty. Some were still riddled with small caliber bullet holes, left unrepaired so far from larger population centers.

Bianca was in awe of the deluge of propaganda that started appearing in her vision whenever she activated her personal network for a brief moment. She recorded it all. Across the Human Sphere, the noise of the modern age was an ever-present hum of information. A constant stream of information scrolled through the datasphere at all times, visualized by a lens or an implanted device like her eye: advertisements, directions, friend requests, banking information, *Aristeia!* Hexadrome footage, war propaganda, and so much more. Since she set foot on Kuraimori, it had been different—altered. The StateEmpire controlled everything these people saw. She couldn't even search for her own name.

As they walked, Benji stopped at a small house. Built simply, the structure wouldn't have been out of place back in a lower, middle class neighborhood back in Santiago de Neoterra. Somehow it felt diminished. It, like every house around her, was painfully quiet.

"Why is it so—" She trailed off, throwing her hands up in exasperation. "There is no life here."

It felt like an eternity before Benji replied. He didn't take his eyes off the home in front of him.

"You see that?" He pointed to a small wooden plank by the door, no bigger than her forearm. Written in black dye, the plank noted a date two years prior.

"What is it?" Bianca began to notice similar plaques set by the entrances of most houses. They all felt funerary—final.

"They tell you the date someone who lived here went missing." Benji was solemn as he explained. "It was a labor conscription in this case. He served during the Uprising, supply and logistics corps. Nothing frontline, but that didn't matter. He fought back when they came for him. No one ever wants to go, of course. Some of them were snapped up by the StateEmpire to serve in the Kuang Shi. Some just vanish."

Bianca knew of the unit. Prisoners with bombs around their necks and a gun.

"Some were simply shot as an example, or for boredom… some just vanish. Eventually they ran out of veterans and just started choosing people at random. Not so much these days, but no one forgets." Benji's face was haunted.

Overhead, a single holographic banner blew in its own, digital wind. The words flared to life across her lens as she neared the near the edge of the fishing village. Bianca wasn't fluent in the complexities of kanji—some of the symbols escaped her—thankfully her comlog autotranslated.

///The Jade Throne forgives you.
The StateEmpire cares for you.
We are all one Yu Jing.
Through work, you reclaim your honor.
Loyalty is its own reward.///

It made her stomach turn. Not because the words were aggressive—quite the opposite. They were serene, calculated, and soothing. But beneath them, Bianca could feel the pressure of control. This wasn't the uplift of a people. It was a lullaby sung over shackles.

She took in the rest of the street. Weathered awnings drooped under years of sea air, paint peeled from low stucco buildings, and the smell of brine and fish oil lingered in the breeze. There were no soldiers in sight. No checkpoints. No visible damage. Just quiet.

Too quiet.

People peeked out from behind screens and curtains as they passed. No one greeted them. No one smiled. Fear still lingered in the fringes.

Benji walked beside her, head down. He said nothing as they moved past narrow alleyways and stacked homes that clung to the shoreline like barnacles. He placed a small flower—plastic, clearly handmade—on a windowsill and moved on without explanation.

Bianca followed, the weight of the silence heavier than the sea air.

When they reached the edge of the village, a transport truck waited. Its simple, drab paint had faded to gray. Though not actively rusted, its seams and bolts showed age. It was a military vehicle—just old enough to be forgotten. Long past active service but not quite derelict—suspended in time.

"How do you know what each one means—the planks?" Bianca asked. "All I see are dates."

"I don't know most of them," Benji said softly. "Some, yes. Others were after my time."

Bianca blinked, realization dawning. "That was your home."

He paused, looking back toward the village. "Long ago. A different life."

"Why didn't you stop in?"

"*Obā-chan* thinks I'm dead. It's safer that way."

Bianca felt her chest tighten. She didn't press further. The grief was his to carry.

"I'm sorry."

"Don't be," he said, climbing into the truck. "When I met Miz—Boss—I was given a choice. For the first time in years, my life is my own again. I could *do* something."

The engine coughed to life, and they pulled away from the village on a narrow gravel road that wound through low pine forests. The trees grew in stubborn clusters, their roots cracking through the neglected roadbed. Mist clung low across the earth.

"I can finally do something," Benji said again, his voice low but steady. "I can fight back."

Benji wasn't interested in talking after that, so Bianca leaned against the window, watching the island move past. Kuraimori was still beautiful in its own, haunted way. The land hadn't forgotten its soul, even if the people had been taught to.

They passed crumbled guardhouses half-swallowed by moss. Bunkers with overgrown antennas. Cement towers with trees growing from their hollowed hearts. The signs of war were still present here, but weathered, muted—blurred like an old bruise.

They crested a rise where a twisted metal structure still pointed blankly at the sky. "Old anti-air," Benji muttered as he slowed the truck. "Used to be a whole grid along this stretch."

They stopped, and Bianca stepped out to walk a little. The wind carried the scent of pine and the ghost of old war smoke—now just memory. Twisted metal jutted from the ground like half-buried bones, wrapped in creeping ivy. No blood. No bodies. Just decay. The kind that took years to settle in.

She imagined what it must've looked like before. Lights blinking. Crews shouting. Then silence.

She didn't linger long. She let the ghosts rest.

Back in the truck, the road sloped inland. Soon, they passed under a weather stained overpass—Route One.

"They kept the factories running," Benji said, almost absently. "After the Uprising. Since we were still using StateEmpire tech back then, there wasn't much to retool. Munitions, armor, drones. The machines never stopped."

"They made you build weapons?" she asked, her voice soft but horrified.

"We built the tools of our own imprisonment," he replied.

Bianca could only nod. She had no defense, no way to justify what she now knew to be true.

They climbed higher into the mist-wrapped hills.

By late afternoon, a mining complex appeared between the ridges—weather-worn and eerily quiet. Machinery lay half-buried in dust, and rusted conveyor belts stretched into empty loading bays. Concrete towers loomed above the road like sleeping giants.

Bianca felt a chill—not from the air, but from the sensation of being watched.

Not overtly. Not actively.

But she knew a scope when it settled over someone.

She kept her hands visible.

Benji said nothing.

They had arrived.

And someone—somewhere—was waiting.

Benji pulled the truck into a cored out storage building, parking in what looked like a loading bay, killing the engine. He left his hands on the wheel and sat in silence. Next to them, the recognizable form of a small cargo vehicle sat under a dust-covered tarp.

///Place both hands on the dash and do not move.///

The words in her lens startled Bianca. She scanned the room as she complied. Nothing seemed out of place at first. It simply looked like an abandoned complex to her.

Her geist alerted her before she ever saw it—an oddly shaped shadow on the rafters directly above and in front of the truck. She zoomed in via her lens and cycled through its various modes. Settling on electromagnetic, she identified the shadow's source and froze.

A small mine was placed under the rafter above the cab. Its own digital camouflage made it near impossible to notice. Had she not been taught on the front lines of Concillium, by haggard PanOceanian Fusiliers just trying to keep her alive, she wouldn't have noticed it either. If the mine detonated, both she and Benji would be hit square on by the blast. Any ease Bianca had been feeling evaporated as she stared at the mine.

///Exit the vehicle.///

Benji led the way, getting the same messages, Bianca guessed. She watched him get out and raise his hands. He did not seem calm but resigned. Ready to accept whatever came next. Bianca mirrored him on her side, exiting with her hands raised. Adrenaline was coursing through her veins. She knew she was being watched.

///Step in front of the vehicle, turn around, place your hands and forehead on the hood.///

They both complied. Face and hands pressed into the hood of the transport, Bianca felt hands begin to pat her down. She hadn't heard them approach, no footsteps, no breath, no noise at all. Adrenaline spiked to fear as she imagined turning around to see her orange armored captors. The search was professional but thorough. They emptied her pockets, dropping any contents onto the ground.

Bianca felt a hand around her wrist unclasping her comlog. She began moving to protest and was met with the barrel of a very heavy metal object into her temple before she had even opened her mouth. She got a good look at the Breaker Pistol threatening to fry her brain and decided her protests over the comlog could wait.

Her hands were roughly manacled behind her back, and a dark sack was thrown over her head. As the anxious sweat built up on her brow, she was suddenly very grateful the bag over her head was clean on the inside.

She thought she heard Benji get the same treatment, then she was pulled away. A single hand pulled her along by her elbow. They turned and walked enough times that Bianca was completely disoriented, which was the point, she guessed. After more aimless wandering, Bianca felt rough ground give way to a paved surface which began to descend.

The air chilled as they walked deeper. Two more turns later, Bianca heard a door seal behind her before another opened in front of her. It felt symbolic and life threatening at the same time, like passing through an airlock.

She was blinded when the hood was removed. As she looked into the well-lit chamber, she was surprised to see Benji wasn't with her. She wasn't sure when they had been split up.

"State your name." The voice behind her was as menacing as it was surprising. It was decidedly feminine, she noticed.

"What's going on?"

"State your name."

Bianca closed her eyes and willed her racing heart to slow, even as sweat trickled down her spine. "Bianca Chen."

The trill of a Cube scanner being activated made her jump.

"Welcome to Kuraimori, Miss Chen."

The manacles were removed, and her captor stepped around her into view. She was taller than Bianca with dark, chin length hair held back by the Multispectral Visor sitting on her forehead. Her expression was as hard as teseum and as threatening as the SMG in her hands. A sleek black and grey tech suit hugged her body in a way that would make teenage Bianca blush. As it was, she had a hard time not staring at the stunning woman. "Thank you. I think?"

"More specifically, welcome to what's left of the Jimoshiro Mine. You may refer to me as Song."

"Nice to meet you. Where is Benji?"

"He is gone."

Bianca's heart dropped with the finality of the phrase. Stiff and nauseous, she braced herself against a wall and tried not to wretch.

"Oh, he is not dead, you needn't worry there." Song's left eyebrow rose slightly, a hint of amusement on her otherwise deadpan face as Bianca visibly deflated. "Let me show you around, we will be here for a little while."

23.

The hologram shimmered to life around her, casting pale blue light on the wood floor of the chamber. Su-Yeong walked into the ghost of the past, through the faded remnants of a dead night on Shentang.

The night sky held the soft glow of Yutang above. Shentang's celestial twin reflected sunfire like a distant, second moon. Atmospheric overlays labeled temperature, wind speed, humidity. She ignored them. Her attention was on the phantom soldier pacing just ahead of her, projected in faint blue—Private Zihan.

He was talking to someone. The playback tagged it: Sentry One, routine check-in. The sound of his voice came through her earpiece—bored, distant. Comms chatter rippled through, detached from its source now.

Around her, a boulder-strewn field rolled beneath the projection like a ghost landscape. The listening post—one of several that had gone dark—was a solitary prefab building that glowed faintly, translucent. She passed through one of the receivers as if it were mist.

Zihan continued his patrol. A recorded laugh, a muttered comment to his partner. A private channel opened—non-standard procedure, the overlay noted in red.

Then something changed. The voice on the other end—Li—shifted from playfulness to unease. The words were fragmented: "Do you hear that?" Static. A strangled breath.

Su-Yeong paused the recording with a gesture and walked over to the holographic representation of Zihan. She stood in his footsteps, letting the projection resume. He tried the line again.

///Connection failed.///

Information from his comlog recording displayed across her lens. The system annotated his elevated heart rate and mild tremor.

Zihan moved cautiously now, following Li's beacon. Su-Yeong ghosted behind him in silence, a passenger in his wake. Her own comlog began flagging discrepancies in the playback—sudden packet loss, sensor distortions, subsonic interference. She filed it away.

Then the scene shifted. A sudden snap of noise—weapon fire—followed by wailing comms static. The projection flared, and Zihan's hologram flinched as he threw his earpiece away. Su-Yeong winced.

Even in simulation, the sound was deeply unpleasant—distorted, sharp.

The playback followed him into the building.

She stepped through it just as he did. A soft lamp flickered, revealing the dead—sitting upright—frozen in time, blood rendered as floating particles of data. The comms tech's slit throat gaped wide in cold blue light. The portable receiver blinked red: damaged by a single shot through its casing. More bodies behind the partition—labels overlaying each name.

She'd read the report. She'd seen the stills. But here, inside the moment, it was somehow worse.

Zihan backed out, vomiting. Heart rate: spiking. He ran.

Su-Yeong was pulled along his path at a steady pace, passing through crates, equipment, and wreckage as the projection recreated his desperate sprint toward Li's beacon. The system's ambient audio filtered in—wind first, then something else. Something tonal.

She frowned.

The wind carried more than atmospherics. A musical structure had emerged—recorded at such low volume that the cleanup filters almost scrubbed it out. She toggled audio isolation and let it rise. She heard a hidden, soft melody. It was discordant—like punk music favored by the younger Japanese—dissonant with the scene before her, ethereal.

Zihan approached Li's last known location. Su-Yeong paused again, rotating the view.

The image reconstructed Li's corpse in still blue light—suspended from a boulder by a titanic spear.

///Unidentified Weapon: Composition unknown. Energy residue: active///

The recording resumed and Zihan spun, raising his spectral weapon directly at her. Su-Yeong turned slowly, following his sightline.

She could see it now.

Even as a projection, the figure was terrible. Standing atop the transport like something—a woman—summoned from myth. A familiarity itched in Su-Yeong's mind as the system tried and failed to categorize her: height, build, weapon, even her silhouette refused consistency. The only detail tagged with certainty was the gleam of metal on her arm.

Zihan stood frozen. His vitals bottomed out—subconscious override, physiological lock.

The melody sharpened.

Su-Yeong instinctively stepped back, as if the projection could touch her. Her skin tingled. She checked her readouts—no haptic feedback was enabled. She was just reacting.

Then the spear moved.

A blur of light and noise as it tore itself from the stone, whistling past Zihan. The system overlaid its trajectory. It had sliced his ear open and he didn't notice the blood down his face or the trickle down his leg.

The woman caught the spear and it unfolded, transforming into a wicked scythe.

///Melee weapon: modular. Unknown origin. Pattern match: zero.///

The simulation froze.

Su-Yeong had not paused it.

///Error: Playback interrupted. External signal interference.///

She stepped back. All around her, the hologram began to fragment. Zihan's final scream stretched like corrupted data, his rifle bursts echoing endlessly in a soundless chamber.

Su-Yeong stood still—cold.

She turned her head slowly.

Behind her, the room remained empty.

* * * * *

In and out of consciousness, Takeshi grasped that he was traveling, but otherwise, time had little meaning. Shortly after his rescuers had put him back into the makeshift bed in the back of the van, the engine started. He fought to stay alert as they began to move, but he was fighting a losing battle.

Over time, glimpses of light and sound crept through the darkness, like snatched and stolen secrets. Their journey wound through the coastal woodlands of Kuraimori. Takeshi could hear the cry of sea birds in the distance.

He started to sweat. Feverish tremors ate through the wall of sleep and wracked his aching body. Goro climbed in the back, checking him over. Takeshi could see the afternoon sky outside the window as he did. He reached for the comfort of his sword and came up empty.

"Nothing to be done but sleep, Neko. Just need to ride it out for a little while longer, we're almost there. Bite is a nasty one on a normal dose, especially the first time. They loaded you up so much that I'm surprised you didn't die."

Goro had a surprisingly soft manner for one so large. He was strongly built, a formidable force no doubt. Up close and in the light, Takeshi saw the signs of a hard life written across him. He had scarred knuckles and callused hands. Skin dark from sun exposure covered a bald scalp and a smiling face. Takeshi wasn't sure if Goro's red jacket was more or less weathered than his face.

Takeshi mumbled his thanks as a shivering darkness took him once more.

In a fever dream, the vehicle stopped, and he was hurriedly carried into a building. Deep in his subconscious, he was vaguely aware of vomiting and thrashing violently.

The next time Takeshi woke, he felt like he had been in a head on collision with a battleship. He found himself in a comfortable bed, clean, and wearing a simple robe. The room was beautifully decorated with handcrafted furniture, and a massive landscape portrait dominated the wall. It was Japan, he recognized the mountainous coastline immediately. He also took notice of the distinct lack of windows.

The medical monitor was replaced on his arm and softly blinked green. Water sat on the bedside, waiting with a bottle of pain relievers. He sat up and gratefully took both. Even so, Takeshi felt more clear-headed, if not still exhausted, than he had since his capture.

Voices beyond the wooden door caught his attention.

"—Jon checked in." Goro's voice was soft and distant.

"Good." His rescuer's relief was palpable, even through the wall. A weight leaned into the door, shifting it slightly.

"Kairi is picking him up. He had to go dark to shake off a tail, and he smashed his comlog," Goro continued, matter of factly.

"Slagg me. Glad he's okay."

"Whatever you say, Boss." He heard the soft scuffle of a playful punch and Goro's playful laugh. It was a booming, joyous sound.

The woman gently chuckled as well. She opened the door, and the smile on her face faded into a sterner demeanor. "Awake again, I see."

Takeshi could make out a man in a clean cut black suit standing outside the door with Goro before she stepped into the room and closed it. A fact that instantly put him on guard.

"I am." In the light of day, he got a much clearer picture of her. She was wire taught, not an ounce of fat on her body. She wore a cropped top under her open red jacket. She carried her sheathed wakizashi in her left hand where he couldn't help but notice her missing finger once more. Her tattooed hands and upper chest were visibly covered in unmistakably *irezumi* designs. Laced ink glittered metallically in the light as her tattoos seemed to ripple and move. "You are yakuza."

Her bold-faced laugh caught him by surprise. Deep, from the belly, it lit her face in amusement and joy. Takeshi felt mocked.

"Where do you think you are, pretty boy?" Her laughter eventually died down, and she sat on the edge of the bed. "You are surrounded by them, Neko. Best mind your manners."

He sat silently for a moment. The juxtaposition of her carrying a blade and him not having one ate at him. His world was upside down.

"You are one lucky idiot. Scratch one of your nine lives off."

"Wonderful." He needed to assess the situation and plan his escape. He was still behind enemy lines, one way or another. "What happened?"

"You almost died. You were technically dead for a few seconds. It was a near thing too. Fortunately for you, we have experience with this sort of thing."

Takeshi waited for her to continue but felt his stomach turn. Another close scrape where he survived and someone else didn't. He thought of Taka.

"Luckily, *Oji-san* has a soft spot for—" She trailed off as they both noticed the door opened. Her face dropped.

An older man stood facing them. "I have a soft spot, do I?"

* * * * *

Mizu quickly rose from the bed and bowed deeply. *Kuso*, she had shoved her foot ankle deep into her mouth on this one. She was amazed, and terrified, at how quietly the old yakuza moved.

Yoshihiro moved into the room as his bodyguards closed the door behind him. They were not in the least bit worried for his safety here of all places. The old man was clad in a vibrant blue kimono and hakama. The delicate silk threads danced visibly in the overhead lights, making the sky blue appear to ripple in an unseen wind.

"Welcome to my home." He spoke softly to Neko while Mizu remained bowed. "I am glad we were able to be of service."

"You have my thanks, sir." Neko's voice was closed, guarded.

"You are most welcome. Get up, Mizoku."

"*Hai*." Mizu rose at the command and moved to stand by the door, out of the way. She watched Neko scan the old man over, like a threat analysis subroutine looking for a weakness. Neko not so subtly looked at her blade once more, held behind her nonthreateningly. Yoshihiro noticed too. Mizu tried to ease the tension. "A soft spot for stray cats, *Oji-san*."

"That I do. Which would bring me to you—" Yoshihiro laughed softly. "—Takeshi."

Mizu watched the wild panic climb out of the mask and across Neko's features as he tensed. Her gut twisted as the shake started to rattle her bones.

"Ah, yes." Yoshihiro continued as if not noticing. She knew better. "Your presence on Kuraimori is no longer a secret."

With a flick of the old man's finger, a floating projection of Takeshi Oyama, in full battle plate, and again in a kimono, floated next to a third figure. She could see it now. It was cleverly done, enough to fool the eye or even a casual scan. Subtle changes had been made to his face, skin, and hair. The cosmetic surgery was extensive, but beneath it, there was no mistaking the three floating figures were all the same man.

Yoshihiro flicked a second finger, and the projections moved to the walls. There, they were joined by dozens of amber arrest bulletins. Every city would see the alert. It would be shunted into the vision of every single citizen on the island. Garrisons would no doubt be mobilized and search parties would be going door to door. There was no name, just a picture and description, beside the priority target.

Mizu felt rage—and the shake—building inside of her, and she started forward. "You slagg'n—"

Yoshihiro silenced her with a glare that stilled her soul. Even the shake fled his deathly stare. She halted mid-stride and quickly returned to her place by the wall. She stood silently, trying to cool the anger inside. To her, Takeshi was just another rich samurai wannabe making everyone else suffer.

"So why are you here, Oyama-san?" Yoshihiro's question lingered in the air. Mizu didn't know the full operational details yet. She had already been forced to share what she did know as currency to get the detox Neko needed. They were four days behind their timeline at this stage, and things were getting more complicated by the minute.

"With respect, I cannot tell you that."

He was good, Mizu had to admit. Neko's features were neutral but not stern. He sat calmly on the bed, hands folded neatly into his lap. He would fit right in at trial or in a courtly hall. She guessed his experience leaned more on the latter.

Yoshihiro nodded. "Very well. Then I will have to make a uniformed decision on what to do with you." He looked at Mizu. "Both of you." With a gentle click of the door, he was gone.

Mizu stood silently for a moment, staring at Neko, who stared at the door.

"If you expected some glorious homecoming, you are dumber than I thought." The shake reared to the surface. Mizu fumed. "There is no parade, no marching band. The only song I hear is pain and death."

Neko locked eyes with her. She saw the mask he wore slip just a fraction, and beneath it was pain. "I know."

Mizu was dumbstruck. Speechless, she turned and left him there.

24.

The Oyama estate was a modest thing. Built to cleverly hide the extensive technological workings within, it gave the outward appearance of an Edo period lord's manor. While the times had long since left some Japanese traditions, the allure of the past could be seen painstakingly woven throughout the estate. Recreated shoji made of modern, lightweight materials led into each room. Wooden floors creaked and chirped, not from looseness, but in homage to ancient nightingale flooring used to alert guards of intruders.

To Su-Yeong, the estate was more than just clever design—it was a living testament to a legacy. Something she appreciated more than most. It was precisely why she had chosen this place as her base of operations.

The Oyama family had called this place home once. They were careful stewards of both tradition and the future. Kōichi Oyama was a brilliant warrior whose ideas helped shape the future as well as defend it. A future he never got to see. His eye for detail and craftsmanship was evident in every inch of his family's estates, as well as work as a warrior.

Dressed and armored, though unhelmed, Su-Yeong waited by the front gate with her hands clasped behind her back. An honor guard of four soldiers stood paired on either side of the gate at attention. It was an appropriate display of respect, while not being deferential.

As the orange armored attack craft flew over the valley and into view, Su-Yeong's gut knotted. These were not just reinforcements. Control knew her methods well. Subtly and subterfuge were her tools. She was much like her stealthy personal aircraft, a blade in the night… unseen.

The message had been clipped, short. Her… guest… left no room for discussion when he contacted her directly.

The craft that shrieked its way toward them into view was no stiletto. Nor was it a blade of any sort. The *Lǎohǔ* Assault Craft was a wrecking ball. It was an antiship cannon brought to a gun fight. Heavily armored with orange and black plates and festooned with weaponry, it was designed to bring overwhelming fire superiority to a combat drop. Four extensions branched out from the central fuselage like fins, twisting and moving to stabilize the hammerheaded craft.

Unhelmed, the jetwash tossed her chin-length hair wildly. Her robes thrashed violently in the wind and threatened to tear away from her armor. Yu Jing and Imperial Service pennants whipped in the fierce wind. Su-Yeong refused to bring her hand up to shield her face. She would not be intimidated. It was an impressive sight.

As the blunt-nosed aircraft settled onto its landing skids facing the estate, the pilot killed the engines. The craft clicked and hissed as it cooled ominously. The front facing assault ramp slowly lowered, the prow-mounted armor plates opened. At no time was the impressive amount of firepower tilted away. It would truly be a terrifying sight in the heat of battle. Before the ramp completed its descent, she noticed two combat remotes, in a folded configuration, held in drop cradles beneath the craft. Su-Yeong didn't recognize them but tagged the recording to review later.

Down the ramp ran a dozen warriors. Celestial Guards by their ident tags, visible through her lens. Their armor was of a newer mark than what her detachment wore. They lined up on either side of the ramp and snapped to attention. Behind them strode a viper in orange.

Standing several centimeters above his warriors, their leader descended the ramp. Unhelmed, but clad in brand new power armor, with black ceremonial robes flowing in tails from his back and waist, walked Imperial Agent Zhang Bo. The warrior was a known quantity in the Imperial Service. He was a soldier through and through, down to the close cropped hair on his head. Despite being a noted socialite, he was most known for his martial prowess. A soldier inspired by the unshakable belief in his cause and the righteousness of Yu Jing, Agent Zhang was deeply in the favor of the Imperial House. He also just so happened to outrank Su-Yeong.

"Agent Lin." His voice was a thunderclap of reality crashing down on her carefully laid plans.

"You honor us, sir." Su-Yeong bowed as she spoke, as was befitting his rank and station. Behind her, the guard detachment did the same.

Silently, she cursed her luck.

* * * * *

"Do you know why I am here?" Agent Zhang stood in plain robes of office—black, as was the current style in the capital.

"I believe I do." The second floor study enjoyed an extensive view of the main garden and pond. Beyond was a breathtaking view of the valley, with mountains climbing up to backdrop the picturesque sight. "Takeshi Oyama. Accomplished warrior of the Domaru Butai, traitor to the StateEmpire, and former resident of this very building."

"Indeed. He is on Kuraimori. Your contingent had him in custody." Zhang's eyes gleamed hungrily as he spoke. "And lost him."

"We did." Excuses would serve no purpose at this stage. It was simply the truth. Hsu paid for that mistake with his life. "The Japanese have cleverly shielded his Cube to show us a fiction. We have Hsu's diligence to thank for running the DNA test."

"Diligence that came too late to make the arrest meaningful. So here I am, forced to clean up this mess."

Su-Yeong, also unarmored, was watching the assault shuttle arrive from its second trip and unload its stores. Not a single member of Zhang's entourage wore an armor mark she recognized. "Your armaments are a marvel."

"Indeed. Perhaps if you were more in favor in the capital, you would have been told." Zhang's barb was neither veiled nor contemptuous. He simply stated the facts as he saw them.

"What is that?" Su-Yeong ignored the bait, her curiosity focused on the unfolding constructs below. A soldier in similar, but lighter, armor to Zhang's had arrived in the assault shuttle's second trip. Behind them, a rolling pallet emerged from the craft. It bore a statue cast in the shape of a stylized dragon. It was very similar to the *chiwen* that dotted the imperial palace on Yutang, but not quite the same. Painted in orange and black, the sculpture radiated menace.

"Ah. That would be the new Bayara Palace Guard." He had joined her at the window, watching the process. "Just wait."

Below, the guard approached their charge, and the pallet settled in the courtyard. At their command, the sculpture came to life. Shaking itself awake, the serpent statue scanned their surroundings before following its minder out of sight.

"Marvelous feat of engineering is it not?" Zhang was facing her, probing; clearly he was taking the measure of her.

Su-Yeong turned to face him, face impassive and unreadable. "It is."

The agents stood in silence, eyes locked in challenge. This was her operation. He may hold seniority, imperial favor, and marvelous new technology… but Hansei was hers, as were its secrets.

Clearing his throat to cut the tension, Lieutenant Da entered the room. "I apologize for the interruption, ma'am. Sir." He bowed slightly to Zhang in deference to his closeness to the high court.

"Report, Lieutenant." Su-Yeong had to admit, while his entrance was ill-timed, it did defuse the situation if only for a moment. That said, she refused to break eye contact.

"Another listening post has failed to report in, ma'am."

Zhang broke eye contact first, turning to the officer. "I will investigate it. Send the details to my pilot."

With a bow, Da was gone.

"Why has Oyama returned?" Zhang looked at her once more, a challenge clear across his face.

"That I do not know." She lied.

25.

Mizu wandered the grounds of Yoshihiro's estate aimlessly. As the sun began to set, she found her way to the small fitness room in search of something to take her frustration out on. The gym was blessedly empty. More of a weight room than a dojo, she tossed her jacket over a bench and laid her sword across it; neither belonged on the ground.

She started slowly, moving through strikes and blocks in a few practiced patterns before letting instinct take over. She had little hand to hand training in any formal sense. A hard life had been Mizu's teacher: turf wars and street fights were her sensei.

As she threw punches at the mannequin, strike marks lit up in her lens. Each hit left a red-smeared emoji with crossed eyes on the training dummy as she accelerated: left, right, punch, jab, strike, block, kick. Her geist cheerily mocked the sparring stand as she laid into it. No matter how hard she tried, she couldn't hold onto the image of Neko's face in the emoji's place. She wanted so badly to hate him, to blame him for all the suffering.

Faces flashed before her eyes with each strike: Henzo, Jomu, Nika, Sho, Ei, Shigiro. Dozens of close friends, the only family she had really ever known, were lost. Many of them died right in front of her… And for what? To give up and run. Neko and his kind left hers behind while they ran to safety.

A familiar sense of rhythm overtook her, and she began to clear her mind. She struck harder and harder, breaking skin on her knuckles. She relished the sting. The shake subsided, and a sense of peace came as her pace built; adrenaline spiking without the crushing anxiety of life or death…

Jon was right though. She jumped at the chance to fight back again. She barreled head first into Sparrow's summons, dragging the Hands with her. They all volunteered to fight without hesitation. She couldn't help but wonder if they were just following her. She had told them all the risks and still they answered the call, just like her.

She was dripping with sweat and refused to let off the throttle until her arms could barely move and her legs had deadened from uncounted kicks. Her clothes were soaked by the time she slowed down.

Breathless, chest heaving, she leaned forward, hands on her knees, and she stared at the dummy. The anger was finally gone.

"Impressive."

Mizu spun around angrily to see Yoshihiro standing by the doorway. Anger diffused into embarrassment as she bowed, hoping he had not seen the surprise on her face.

"Get up, Mizoku."

She obeyed and stood tall, defiant.

"Ever the rebellious one." He entered the room and inspected the training dummy, and then her hands. "Sit."

She obeyed as he retrieved a small medical kit from a cabinet.

"Will you let him live?" The question was burning in her mind. Handing Neko over would be a huge boon for his position here on Kuraimori.

"There would be little point in helping him, just to kill him." The yakuza boss's face was impassive but not unkind.

"I've seen you do worse, *Oji-san*."

He knelt down with the first aid kit and began to clean the cuts on Mizu's hands. His touch was surprisingly gentle. "True. I have already been asked about your presence by the Imperial Service, both of you." He held Mizu's hand firmly as she tensed and continued his work.

"What did you say?" Mizu's impatience showed in her voice.

"Always in such a rush." He chided her but continued his work, wrapping her hands. It was an old fashioned treatment, but the message was clear… let it sting for a while. "You are tied to this now, Mizoku. You and the Third Hand."

Mizu's jaw dropped. Yoshihiro had never referred to her crew as anything other than her 'little family.' This was a different side of him.

"Do you know why I stay here, child?"

"No."

"When Kuraimori was abandoned, we had a choice. The StateEmpire approached us before the war was over. Their offer was simple. Stay and keep order, or be hunted across all of its lands forever. So we stayed. Those in this house and beyond stayed to protect our family. We peddle in Bite and Silk because we are commanded to. It is delivered to our door in a jade transport. We are little better than hostages, Mizoku. Much like your Hands, we do what we must to survive. Thanks to the diligence of you and others like you, we keep a steady supply of medicines on hand to help those we can."

"That's where Goro…" Mizu trailed off, speechless. She reevaluated an opinion formed over long, hard years in the space between his words. When she had turned to the bottle, and then to Bite herself, Goro had never told her where he got the detox. When she had thrown herself back into it not once, but twice, he had been there with the cure.

"*Hai*. Goro, Kairi, Jon to his credit. They all came to our door to find you. It would have been a painful death to anyone who tried to stop them..." Yoshihiro finished his work and stood.

Mizu stood as he did, offering the aging man a hand. He no longer looked like the indomitable monster she had built him up as in her mind. He was just like everyone else on this island; trapped and trying to stay alive.

"Now to your question, Mizoku. I have reported your presence here." He held up a hand to forestall her reaction as one of his men came to the door and bowed. Yoshihiro nodded and turned to leave.

Mizu felt the shake scream and rattle inside her. She was trapped, suspended somewhere between fight and flight.

He stopped at the door and turned back. "My hand was forced. One man in my house has sold his soul, not nearly as quietly as he thinks he has. I have made sure he is guarding your guest tonight, Midnight Rider."

Mizu gasped despite herself.

"Yes, Mizoku. You are not the only one who talks to Sparrows." He trailed off for a moment as silence hung between them.

Shock held her firmly in its grasp and stilled her tongue. Yoshihiro never ceased to amaze her. She thought him cruel—given over to the StateEmpire's thrall and grubbing for power. Yet somehow he was still gentle and caring to her…

How wrong she had been. Beneath it all, his honor remained.

"Goodbye, Mizoku-san."

"Goodbye, *Oji-san*."

* * * * *

The crash of bodies through the door snapped Takeshi from the twisted realm of the past and into the present. He sprung out of bed to see Goro's fists rising and falling like pistons, in rapid succession. The yakuza he was pummeling desperately tried to block him and failed miserably. His rescuer, Mizoku the old man had called her, strode in the door behind him with purpose. She looked outwardly confident, in control, but Takeshi saw the wild light behind her eyes.

"The situation has changed, we have to move." Her eyes burned with a fire he hadn't noticed before. She tossed him a bag and turned to Goro's beaten and cowering victim, holding her sheathed sword before her, an obvious threat. "You are a slagg'n traitor and a coward!" She tossed a knife at the floor. It clattered before him. "Choose."

Goro bodily shoved the man to his knees. It took Taskeshi but a moment to realize she was offering him a way out. A way to reclaim his honor. The yakuza caught on too.

He chose poorly. The yakuza lunged at Mizu, snatching up the dagger. The ring of honed steel hung in the air as blood flew from Mizu's blade. The speed of her strike impressed Takeshi. The yakuza crumpled to the floor as his head lolled back, spine barely keeping it attached. Blood quickly soaked the rug as the yakuza's heart pumped on for a fleeting moment in time. Outstretched, Takeshi noticed the etching on her blade: *Akai Te*.

"Coward..." Mizu breathed as she cleaned and sheathed her blade.

Takeshi nodded silently, taking it all in. In a different setting, he could easily see this same scenario reversed. The similarities between them were unnerving.

He opened the bag and found clothes, a knife, a standard issue Yujingyu pistol, and a series of auto-injectors.

He smiled to himself.

Goro kicked the yakuza once more for good measure, then moved to the exit. He flashed a hand signal to Mizoku that Takeshi didn't recognize, then turned to him. "Two minutes."

Takeshi immediately dressed as the two left the room. The clothes were a basic fitness outfit in subdued greens and, thankfully, fit well. He checked the pistol. The Friend/Foe system was already keyed to him. Takeshi continued to reevaluate his opinion of his rescuers. He checked the magazine with the mechanical precision that decades of practice brought. Satisfied, he grabbed the bag and hurried to the others.

At the door, Mizoku offered him another pair of injectors. "Stim—low dose—but I need you on your feet, and a detox. You'll need to take them regularly for a few days, adrenaline makes the symptoms worse, fair warning."

He slammed the offered injectors into his thigh one by one. Takeshi felt the muted rush of combat stims. His vision sharpened as he took in the hallway. His body felt like a coiled spring, ready and waiting. The bone-deep itch that followed was always the worst part. It was then that he noticed neither Goro nor Mizoku had a weapon drawn. She had slung her sword over her back. "What is the situation?"

She flashed a series of hand signs he didn't know—and one very rude one he did—then stopped herself. "*Kuso*, you don't know our signs."

"What?" Takeshi wished for his personal comlog. His geist would have analyzed and translated the hand signals much more quickly than he would be able to. It was uploaded into his armor too, something else he wished for currently.

"Nevermind. We're slagg'n burned. Our ticket out of here is the same cargo we came in on. It's fueled and waiting." She started to move down the hall then stopped herself. She turned to Takeshi, brow furrowed. "Non-lethal only. Am I clear?"

"Understood, Mizoku."

"*Chikusho,* just Mizu."

"Understood." He tucked the pistol back into the bag as he slung it over his shoulder. He had questions, but they would have to wait. For now, Takeshi felt a renewed strength in being in control of his own fate again—or it was the stims. His teeth definitely itched from the stims.

The trio crouched low and crept down a long corridor. The cool air and stone around him brought to mind a subterranean cellar. Similar rooms to his sat open on either side, like suites in a recovery ward—a hidden medical wing in the gangsters' home.

Moving quickly behind them, Takeshi marveled at the coordination between Goro and Mizu. They quickly checked each room as they passed, slicing the corner as they rotated around each opening before moving on; alternating with one always watching ahead. Clearly they had done this before. Takeshi nodded approvingly as he saw two more gangsters tied up and gagged in the last room. As the trio approached the end of the hall, a broad staircase led upward. The space above was a small wood-paneled gallery that seemed to be ground level, confirming his prior cellar theory. It was a narrow space, with sparse furniture and two exits.

Running feet and shouting greeted them as they reached the top of the stairs. Six yakuza, wielding tantos, rounded the bend and didn't hesitate. With a stim-fueled roar in challenge, Takeshi dropped his meager possessions and sprung past Goro to meet their assailants head on.

The first gangster slashed his dagger downward into empty space as Takeshi sidestepped. Building his momentum into a spin, Takeshi moved around the attacker, back to back. With a sharp crack, he landed a fist into the second attacker's temple, dropping him cold, while he continued his spin. The first man yelled as he spun back around, ignoring Goro and Mizu, only to meet Takeshi's heel crashing across his nose as he brought the force of his spin up and kicked the yakuza in the face. He didn't hesitate, didn't slow, never stopping or yielding the advantage.

The third attacker lunged with his blade and Takeshi grabbed his wrist, diverting the blade to his side as he twisted inside his guard. With a swift step forward, Takeshi pushed the gangster off balance and forced him to stumble backward into the remaining three assailants. As they recovered, another came forward with a flying knee, trying to make use of the cramped space. Takeshi ducked under the assault and stood up into the airborne man. With a swift upward push from Takeshi, the hapless man smashed into the ceiling before falling to the floor, unconscious in a shower of plaster.

Takeshi moved into the now recovered yakuza and his remaining comrades like a furious beast. Sharp strikes, kicks, and punches, broke their guards apart. It felt good to let loose again, to do it his way…

In the breath of a moment, Takeshi stepped past the last assailant as they dropped, joining their comrades on the floor—none were conscious. Takeshi nodded approvingly then turned back to his rescuers. They stared at him, grinning.

"You said 'non-lethal.'"

Mizu chucked to herself. "That I did."

Goro broke into a soft, slow clap. "Slagg me, why are we even here, Boss?"

"What are you talking about, Goro? We're indispensable." She checked the pulse of the first yakuza to fall. Satisfied, she nodded to herself. "Let's go."

"Didn't even touch him…" Goro followed behind, laughing quietly.

Takeshi felt the joy of tension released and the liberation of combat-fueled clarity. Goro's praise brought a sense of pride that caught Takeshi off guard.

The unlikely team quickly moved through the rest of the conspicuously empty house before emerging into a small garage. Their cargo van was waiting for them, fueled and ready, just as Mizu claimed. Next to it, a pair of menacing armored trucks sat cold and idle.

Takeshi watched as she quickly circled their van, slapping small devices around its exterior before boarding. Goro hit the bay controls, then hopped into the front with Mizu, and they were off.

The trio accelerated into the night through the open gate, and onto the provincial road ways. Takeshi immediately recognized his surroundings. Familiarity and dread filled him. Next to him, Mizu locked the controls onto auto-drive and flipped open her comlog. He watched her spin through a series of commands before selecting one. The holographic dash console lit up with a cartoon hare bouncing madly. He raised an eyebrow at Mizu, and she winked at him. Glancing back at the dash, he saw the rabbit dissolve away and the console blinked twice—as if rebooting.

///Cybermask Initiated.///

"Will that work?" Takeshi knew of such programs. They were usually limited to the size of a person. He quickly put the pieces together, realizing that was how Mizu had impersonated the Imperial Agent back in his cell—a bold move.

Mizu shared a holoplane with him. "It'll work."

Takeshi watched a wireframe of the van filter away and be replaced by a Yujingyu courier vehicle. The change started from four points around the vehicle—where she had placed the devices.

"Resourceful." Takeshi continued to reevaluate his opinion of her. There was much more to these criminals than he had initially given credit.

Mizu's laughter balanced somewhere between inviting and unhinged.

26.

Su-Yeong heard the interrogation before she reached the cell. The basements had been refurbished at her command and now resembled a gaoler's hall. A far cry removed from their prior use as mundane storage. All three cells were occupied after the night's failure. The yakuza had all too willingly given up the man responsible for letting their targets escape. Conveniently, it was also her mole. A shrewd move, she had to begrudgingly respect.

Agent Zhang had not been so even-tempered about the ordeal when he had arrived onsite. He would have slaughtered the lot of them had she not gently suggested their future usefulness over comms when he reached out for any information she might provide.

She was so close. Zhang's very presence was threatening to upset the delicate operation she had been running from the beginning. By the time she was able to return, the 'interrogation' had already begun.

A pair of Zhang's guards were posted outside the door. Fully armored, they were anonymous behind their helmets. They stoically waited for their commander to finish outside the cell. By the sound of it, she wouldn't call it an interrogation. Heavy, wet impacts could be heard down the hall as Su-Yeong approached.

"Open it."

"No one is allowed in, ma'am." There was no hesitation in the soldier's voice.

Su-Yeong was used to being heeded. Zhang's soldiery would receive no exemption.

She looked at the one who had spoken, then struck the opposite soldier. His silence was rewarded with three lightning quick punches: One to each side of the neck and one to the throat. As he crumpled, the small knife she left in his neck from the final strike could be seen by his bolder comrade. Blood poured down the soldier's chest.

Calmly, Su-Yeong repeated herself—something she was not accustomed to doing. Whatever insanity was happening in the cell had ended, and the silence only reinforced her command. "Open. It."

Fear claimed the standing guard as he scrambled to obey her.

"Your comrade will live. If you hurry, he may still even be able to speak." She glanced contemptuously at the unconscious soldier then stepped past, dismissing them both from her mind.

The door slid open with a slight hiss, retracting into the wall. As it did, a red bar floated across her vision. A visual deterrent, but also a scanner she had included to inform her anytime someone entered or exited the cells. She had designed the upgrades to the estate herself, it was her domain. Such tricks were how she knew this was even happening in the first place.

Inside, suspended from the ceiling was a sack of meat that had once been a yakuza. The room's monitoring system told her what she already knew. Yoshihiro Shubitsu was barely alive. Hovering in her vision, his vitals were low. Neon arrows highlighted the cuts on his skin, but it was easy to see that blunt force trauma had caused much of the damage. Zhang had washed his hands in a priceless porcelain bowl stitched together with gold and was drying them with a silken cloth when she entered.

"Zhang!"

He turned to her sharply, anger held back but only barely. "What do you want, *Agent Lin*?" His tone was threatening and contemptuous.

"Why are you murdering my asset?" Su-Yeong kept her voice level.

"Asset? Your ASSET allowed Oyama to escape… again! Your carefully orchestrated network is proving fangless." Zhang's contempt laced every word.

"I disagree." She held his gaze, unwavering. "Until I receive a mandate from Control, this is still *MY* operation. You have burned this asset." She looked at the yakuza as she spoke. The old man was nearly dead—but still somehow conscious—and defiant as he looked at her through hazy eyes. It was testament to Zhang's understanding of the human body and its limits. Su-Yeong suppressed a shudder of sympathy for the old man. She quickly drew her pistol and shot him anyway. Vitals flatlined, and she dismissed the alert from her vision. It was better this way.

"I was not done with *that*." Zhang breathed venom as she holstered her sidearm.

"He could provide you with nothing useful. He ran a mid-level branch of the yakuza family we forced into cooperation years ago. His name was Yoshihiro Shubitsu. His father was yakuza as well, but died before the Uprising, and he took up the mantle. Is there anything else you would like to know?" Su-Yeong crossed her arms behind her back and locked eyes with the taller warrior. She would not be intimidated by him. She suspected his martial skill and ruthless reputation fought most battles for him. Perhaps more than his cunning… "I, however, have had success in my investigations."

"Very well." Zhang's anger cooled, but only slightly. "Tell me what you have learned."

"Hidden on Kuraimori is a vault: secret projects, weapons schematics, a trove of intelligence. I have narrowed it down to this valley." Su-Yeong was eminently pleased with herself. It was a misdirection, and she knew it—and a risk—but it was also the truth. He would learn of the vault eventually, but his dismantling of her network was unacceptable.

"That is what Oyama is here for?" His jaw worked with anger.

"Yes." Su-Yeong would rather give this hound a different scent to chase.

"You lied to me."

"Yes."

Watching Zhang's shock was more than worth his possible wrath. But it was Su-Yeong's turn to be surprised.

"Impressive." His expression faded, sliding into a quite smug smile.

Su-Yeong briefed Zhang on just enough intelligence to wet his appetite, but not enough to spoil her hard work. He would take the credit—or the shame—from however this ended. She thought it best to keep the best bits for herself.

* * * * *

The armor clicked into place around Su-Yeong's torso with a smooth, final hiss. Environmental seals activated. Her vitals blinked green on the HUD. Good. No wasted motion.

Above her, the holographic screen hovered in the air, its faint blue glow flickering over the interior of the prep chamber. The interrogation feed played out in real time—grainy in places, patched in from overlapping cameras—but detailed enough to show everything that mattered.

She adjusted the tension on her gloves as the surveillance feed shifted focus.

The prisoner sat in silence, alone in the repurposed storage cell. Shackled, but not slouched. Waiting. He hadn't been moved yet. Probably calculating, she knew that look—he wore it like a second face.

He looked older than he had when she first brought him in, but that was a trick of the feed—more shadows than years. Still, there was something different now. A tightness around his mouth. Resolve, maybe. Or exhaustion.

A faint sound came through: footsteps. The cell door creaked open.

Su-Yeong paused her final boot lock and watched as the tall silhouette entered the cell—Zhang. A true believer, the kind who never second guessed themselves because they genuinely believed they *were* justice.

Blood stained his sleeves from the previous interrogation/ execution. He hadn't even cleaned it off. Intentional, no doubt, but it wouldn't work here.

"Predictable."

The prisoner didn't flinch. He just looked down.

Zhang began to speak, reciting the charges like scripture.

"Ryōki Kano. Enlisted in the glorious service of the Invincible Army Intelligence Corp…"

It continued. Names. Bombings. Espionage. A note about the magistrate's daughter. Su-Yeong saw the briefest shift in the prisoner's face—a smirk.

Su-Yeong laughed quietly in her chamber. "Still proud of that one are we?"

Zhang continued. "Even then, you are but a minnow. There is always a bigger fish."

Zhang paced slowly in front of the recording, circling the prisoner who remained silent, still. She knew exactly what he was doing. Pulling in. Building walls inside his own mind. He'd already left the room, in a sense.

Then it came. "Tell me about Takeshi Oyama."

The strike came so suddenly that even Su-Yeong did not see it coming. The prisoner fell back, head bouncing against the wall he sat against and crumpled.

Su-Yeong checked the sensors. He was still conscious, even after a blow like that—impressive. "There's the real you, Zhang."

She wondered why Zhang was hunting Oyama.

She resumed her prep, sliding the weapon into its holster.

In the recording, the prisoner remained calm, controlled. He didn't answer as Zhang struck him two more times.

Zhang withdrew and the door opened again. Two more shadows entered. Chains rattled.

She watched them string him up—wrists pulled above his head, toes just brushing the floor. The weight would tear at his shoulders within minutes. They'd drag it out. Try to break him physically before they tried again verbally.

"Last chance. Tell me about Oyama." Zhang spoke calmly, as if ordering tea.

Nothing.

He gave the signal and a small case was unlatched. Tools placed on a tray, neat and deliberate. Familiar shapes, some too old-fashioned to be efficient—meant for effect.

Su-Yeong closed the final seals on her armor and stood tall, letting the internal systems finish their calibration. The holoplane transitioned to an internal screen, displayed on her lens next to a timer that slowly ticked down toward her mission deployment.

The prisoner screamed—agony breaking through the silence, bringing her focus back to the image of him dangling. Blood began to flow. She didn't blink as she watched.

Minutes later, she killed the feed. Su-Yeong checked her armaments one last time. All systems were operating nominally. Her personal network updated into the armor, copying her personal files, codes, and access keys.

Sealed inside her armor she felt walled off, emotionless. The years spent in the Imperial Service had been a long, slow drain on her humanity. When she donned her robes and armor, she felt protected—emotionally. The yakuza's death didn't bother her. It did bother her how close Zhang was coming to derailing everything she had labored for. Years of meticulous work could be undone if she was not careful. His interference would cost her the mission if she wasn't able to contain his aggression.

She opened a private channel with Lieutenant Da.

"Yes, ma'am."

"There is something I need you to look into for me, Lieutenant."

27.

The night was crisp and brittle—perfect for ghosts. Yasbir moved with silence so complete it mocked the idea of sound. Imperial Agent Lin Su-Yeong had just exited the estate, her Celestial Guard gliding in formation around her like blades in orbit. Their movements were sharp, disciplined, and practiced. Yasbir admired that, but it made no difference. The guards were vigilant only to what they expected. He lived in the space they didn't.

She moved fast, efficiently sweeping through Hansei's hollow streets, crumbled walls, and silent homes that passed in her periphery. Her route seemed erratic to the untrained eye. Yasbir saw the pattern beneath the chaos, the spiraling dance toward the Hansei Civil Services Depot. Always circling, always drawing closer—like a noose.

He tracked her from above, bounding silently from one ruined balcony to the next, never more than a shadow among shadows. He spotted them too—the other shadows moving in the night. Shinobi stalked him and the Imperial agent both—silently threading the city like veins. Yet another complication, but Yasbir couldn't divert to deal with them, not yet.

Yasbir had a different objective tonight. Something far more precise.

As Agent Lin stepped into the depot's administrative building, he paused. She stayed longer than expected. Quantronic echoes shimmered in the air—brief, sharp pulses sensed rather than seen. He marked the spike and waited.

Time passed. Eventually, she emerged and began moving again, the guards tightening formation. Her pace was slower now. Thoughtful. She had found something—he could see it in her gait.

Yasbir didn't follow immediately. He waited, measuring wind and shadow, waiting for the ideal moment to drop into her path—not to confront her, but to be close enough to almost touch her; briefly, invisibly.

He caught up several blocks later as she passed beneath a half-toppled tower in what had once been a government square. Her guards were fanned wide, covering rooftops and alleys. One passed within a meter of him and never even felt the wind shift.

Then came Su-Yeong—close enough to touch. Yasbir tapped the small device on his belt. A chirp inside his sealed helm preceded a progress bar before his eyes, rapidly climbing.

Yasbir moved with her, no louder than the quiet breath before dawn.

One step, then two—he kept close enough to complete the signal. She paused. Her head tilted—some distant input distracting her.

///Download Complete.///

A soft chime in his ear, and Yasbir withdrew.

She didn't flinch. She kept walking.

Yasbir vanished backward into the dark, pulse steady.

Only when they were gone from sight did he permit himself to exhale. The device felt heavier now—more with expectation than in weight.

"I have it." Yasbir sent across a secure channel.

"Well done, friend-of-mine."

Yasbir watched a man-shaped shadow move behind a window. "I have company."

"Proceed as planned."

* * * * *

The tunnel yawned before him like the throat of some ancient beast—reinforced, cold, metallic. Yasbir imagined it was a starship's bones buried beneath a city. He moved without sound, his shadow long against the walls in the low light. He kept tabs on the six shinobi—Koga clan—as they followed him, silent and armed. They peeled out of the shadows like specters made into orange armored flesh. Though they spoke no words, their presence pressed against him like the weight of a closing trap.

Their fieldcraft was nothing like the ancient clans they foreswore—he tracked them easily. Still, he followed the quantronic pulse he detected from Agent Lin Su-Yeong—a faint data smear pulsing like blood on snow. It ended here—in this junction, several stories beneath the city.

Yasbir paused.

The scene before them was a ruin of old blood: shattered turrets, red-and-white remotes crumpled like paper, burned-out cover shields, long-dead Domaru warriors in white armor. Their helmets cracked open. Their blades shattered beside them, but no serviceable weapons remained—or bodies of their assailants. Not one.

Yasbir narrowed his eyes and whispered. "This place saw fire."

He knelt beside a Domaru, brushing two fingers along the plates. Smooth. Scoured by time, not by weather. The dry air here was too preserved. It reeked of memory. A last stand that hadn't mattered.

The signal was here, but Yasbir saw no emitter. No drone, no mine, no sign of life.

Which meant it was bait.

He stood sharply, and the six Koga closed in. Their wide brimmed helms cast ominous shadows in the low light. Hands drifted near hilts. They were done toying with him.

Their formation shifted subtly. Closing in. Not like wolves. Like surgeons. And then—

"You will go no further."

The voice echoed from every direction, vibrating through the reinforced walls, bouncing through their comms. Yasbir felt the static in his teeth.

The Koga froze, seeking the threat—nothing.

"The Koga have betrayed their oaths. You are nothing but pale imitations of what you once were."

Yasbir took a half-step back, knowing what was coming. He was bearing witness to a private war now.

In the silence that followed, the Koga acted—blades drawn, a silent convergence toward the center of the tunnel. Toward empty space.

Then, as if the shadows themselves had held their breath until now, something moved.

A hiss of wind. A single breath.

One Koga stiffened—then his head slid from his shoulders and hit the tunnel floor with a wet crack.

Yasbir didn't even see the blade. Just the absence that followed.

Nakama had arrived.

His camouflage dropped like a curtain parting. One moment nothing—then black armor, red-lined techsuit glowing faintly like banked coals. His three eyed mask was stylized, almost serene, as if at prayer. The katana he held shimmered faintly, its monofilament edge sizzled with fresh blood.

The Koga attacked.

Yasbir didn't move. He couldn't. The air itself turned electric as the Oniwaban waded into the five remaining assassins like a divine wind given flesh.

A katana swung—batted aside by an armored gauntlet. A second blade flashed—sidestepped. A third came from above—ducked under with inhuman speed. His friend moved through them with impossible grace, deflecting, redirecting—killing in motion.

Yasbir watched a pair of long knives strike as one—only for their wielder to cry out, wrist sheared clean and skull cracked open by a rippling counterattack. A whirring chain coiled around Nakama's arm—its wielder holding the sickle at the other end. Nakama leaned into the tug that followed and *used* it to slingshot forward. He slid beneath a sickle swing, severed a leg mid-turn, and rose spinning—his blade cleaving through armor, flesh, and spine.

A flashbang cracked. Another. Yasbir turned away instinctively as his helm's sensors were overloaded, but Nakama wouldn't have stopped moving. He was one with the dark, one with death.

Yasbir recovered to see Nakama move through the last two Koga like a storm. A parry, a kick, a final burst from his sidearm—and silence returned.

Only the dead remained—the dead and Yasbir.

Yasbir looked at his friend and nodded. There was nothing to say.

Nakama simply sheathed his katana with a single click. His face plate slid upward and back, revealing the monk's smiling face. "Will you help me with something, friend-of-mine?"

* * * * *

Su-Yeong angrily answered the summons. She had just started a shower and turned on some music to relax—the fourth overture of her favorite orchestral piece—in her chambers when the message had arrived, interrupting her hard-earned moment of peace.

///Report to my chambers. - Zhang///

In truth, it was nearly morning, and she wasn't going to get much sleep at this point. Not bothering to dress, she threw a robe over her slim form and trudged upstairs.

Su-Yeong knew Zhang was in a foul mood, unable to get the Kempeitai to say anything during his interrogation. She shrewdly pondered how to make his failure her gain as she walked to Zhang's door.

It was open. The robotic Bayara dragon waited by his door and swung toward her menacingly. It swiftly stepped to the side in a half bowed position. Its handler and one of Zhang's Celestial Guard detachment were waiting outside.

Inside, she found Zhang angrily staring at six heads in a box.

28.

Mizu gripped the wheel a little tighter as the mountain roads curved beneath them. Every tight switchback brought back flashes of old nights—rain-slick asphalt, engines howling, neon lights streaking by in the dark—thunder runs. Back when she had a crew who didn't flinch at blood or reckless speeds, when honor was settled in burnt rubber and scraped chrome. Now they were just *bōsōzoku* legends.

She didn't speak as they climbed higher. The past felt too loud already.

The mining access road had long since crumbled at the edges, but she followed Sparrow's data trail to the letter. Goro hummed some half-remembered pop tune in the seat beside her, trying to break the silence. Neko sat stiffly in the back, as if the very idea of being in her vehicle was dishonorable—or maybe it was just her. His posture said military. His aura said noble. She wasn't sure which she wanted to punch more.

"Sooo. Are we going to talk, or are we all just pretending this is a funeral drive?" Leave it to Goro to break the silence.

Mizu smirked. "You want small talk while we're heading into a mountain full of ghosts?"

Goro pointed at her. "See? That. That was almost banter."

"I'm great at banter," she muttered.

"Whatever you say, Boss." He turned toward the back. "Neko? You good back there?"

"I am mission ready," came the reply—crisp, polite, distant.

"*Chikusho!* Come on, you two. It's not like either of you is gonna poison the other." Goro sighed. "Probably."

Neko's eyes met hers in the rearview mirror—intense, measuring.

"I know what you are," he said softly. Not accusing—just stating it, like reading a line from her record.

She didn't flinch. "Then you know I did what I had to do to survive. Same as anyone who's still left breathing. Not that it's any of your slagg'n business."

He held her gaze a moment longer, then looked away without a word.

"Tense," Goro muttered. "I swear, this is like being stuck between a rusty katana and a pipe bomb."

"I am the pipe bomb," Mizu said without missing a beat.

Goro grinned. "See, now *that* was banter."

She couldn't help it—her lips twitched at the corners. Just for a second. In the mirror, Neko's mouth twitched too. So he was human after all.

They reached the end of the drivable path not long after. Mizu ditched the truck in a narrow shaft like planned. Henzo's projectors—bless his ghost—went into her pack. The three continued on foot, flashlights low and narrow. The walls absorbed their sound. There was no echo. Just silence.

The tunnels here were massive. A hovertank could drive through half of them—and she was sure someone once had. Her boots crunched on gravel and old wire casings. The line in her comlog glowed faintly, pulsing forward. Breadcrumbs left by Sparrow in the dark.

Goro stayed close, steady and alert, but relaxed as always. He didn't wear silence like armor the way Neko did. The noble's footfalls were near silent. He carried his pistol like a man who didn't need to look dangerous.

Mizu caught him glancing at her sword—at *Akai Te*.

She didn't say anything. Just met his eyes and gave him a faint, understanding smile.

He looked away.

She exhaled.

"I didn't carry it for a long time," she said, voice low. "Thought it was the only way to survive."

Neko looked at her then. Not harshly. Just surprised.

"You're carrying it again," he said.

"Yeah. Took me a while to remember why it mattered."

A beat of silence. Then, quietly: "Who gave it to you?"

She rested her hand on the hilt. "Someone who knew I'd need it. Even when I didn't."

He gave a slight nod. "I can very much understand that." Neko's face drifted into memory.

She nodded back. It wasn't a truce. But it was something.

They camped in the dark that night—if it even was night. Hard to tell, deep in the guts of the mountain. Goro found an old bench and passed out like it was a five-star hotel. Neko took the first watch. Mizu lay down with her back to the others, one hand always near her blade. She didn't sleep. Just let her breathing slow and her mind drift.

In the stillness, she caught Neko humming something under his breath. A lullaby. It echoed faintly in the cavern.

She pretended not to hear it.

The next day, the air grew colder. Their lights caught dust and thin cables clinging like veins to the ceiling. Some of the tunnels had collapsed long ago. Others had been carved in angles no sane miner would ever use. It was easy to get turned around. But the pulsing green line in her lens never failed.

Sparrow didn't leave things to chance.

Eventually, the path ended.

Mizu slowed and raised a hand to halt the others. In the dim beam of her flashlight, a worn metal wall emerged from the shadows—sealed flush into the rock. A small garage-style door dominated the center. No signs. No guards. Just a single word stenciled in faded kanji across the top:

Maintenance.

She exhaled and let the silence settle.

"Well," Goro said brightly, clapping his hands once. "This place feels friendly."

Neko arched an eyebrow. Mizu let out a dry snort.

"I've broken into worse," she muttered.

"Yeah, and usually with more explosives," Goro said with a wink.

She chuckled, shaking her head. "I still can't believe you survived that generator room job."

"I can't believe you threw the whole charge while I was in the room."

"I said heads up!"

"You said 'boom'!"

That got a laugh out of all three of them. Even Neko let out something halfway between a chuckle and a cough, then looked embarrassed to have made a sound.

Mizu grinned. "Don't get shy now, samurai."

"I am not—" Neko started, then sighed and let it go.

Suddenly, Mizu's lens flickered with new input. Across her vision, neat digital text appeared—no sound, no warning.

///Place your hands and forehead on the wall.///

"...Okay, that's not ominous at all," Goro said.

Mizu stepped forward slowly, her palm brushing the cold steel. The dust clung to her skin. Her heart beat once, heavy.

No going back now.

She placed both hands and rested her forehead against the wall.

Behind her, she heard Goro and Neko follow suit. For a moment, all was still.

* * * * *

Takeshi chaffed at being handcuffed and bagged, but he complied. He had trusted Mizu this far, and she seemed to be expecting this, so he complied willingly. After being led through the bay door, he was surprised to hear a familiar voice.

"State your name." Song's voice was, as always, as sharp as a blade's edge.

"Tak Gi-ung." He smiled beneath the bag over his head. Hearing the familiar voice brought a palpable wave of relief.

"Hello, Neko."

Mizu laughed out loud, muffled through the sack. "A bit past that, aren't we? The whole island knows who you are by now, slagghead."

Mizu's voice was light and playful. Gorro laughed from the belly, it was a warm sound. Song's chuckle was sharp. Takeshi was surprised to see a hint of her smile before it faded once more as his bag and manacles were removed.

The hallway was dimly lit to mark the hour. Bare stone walls gave way to the occasional partition that served to create rooms with a much larger area at the end that had once served as a workshop, keeping mining equipment serviceable. The space smelled of stale lubricant, old chemical spills, and the rich mineral scent of being buried under a mountain.

Song moved on to Mizu and Goro, unbinding them before returning all of their possessions. Takeshi felt a pang of sympathy as Mizu nearly snatched her katana back from Song. Beyond them, Takeshi spotted the source of the fourth voice.

"Tak Gi-ung lived a short life it seems. Oyama-san." Bianca Chen stood at the end of a short hallway against a closed door. Her arms were crossed and a smug smile was plastered on her. She wore simple fatigues, and her dark hair was piled up on top of her head.

"It is a pleasure to meet you again, Miss Chen." Takeshi hoped his surprise was covered well enough as he offered her a slight bow of the head. At this point in the mission, her presence did not truly surprise him.

"The pleasure is all mine. And please, just Bianca." She smiled broadly and returned his bow.

* * * * *

After brief introductions, Mizu followed the rest, mind drifting. There was an uneasy sense of trust among them, but it was by no means complete. Song was, she gathered, used to the clandestine world and trusted no one. Bianca was observant and inquisitive, which made her more likable than Neko was at first. Neko clearly recognized them both but didn't trust them. It was an odd dynamic.

Goro made eye contact and crossed his hands before closing a fist to his right shoulder. *Wary. Danger.* Everything was a statement of fact with hand signs, but Mizu caught the question across his features.

"No. I think we're okay."

"Whatever you say, Boss." They spoke the sentence in unison and both broke out laughing from it.

Shouts of 'Mizu' and 'Boss' preceded familiar figures running down the hall toward them. Slipping past Song, Bianca, and Neko were the younger Hands. Emil, barely seventeen and trying as hard as he might to grow into Goro's shoes. Shen, the tallest of them and wickedly fast with a knife. Lux was Kairi's little sister at thirteen years old. Tot was the shortest, as his nickname would suggest. At twenty-two, he certainly wasn't growing anymore. Foks was always quiet but was a genius with a wrench.

Mizu barely contained the tears seeing her family coming together again. Once Jon and Kairi arrived, her crew would be complete again, if only for a moment. Goro's smile split his face as he fist-bumped Emil and Tot. Shen swooped in and hugged Goro with tears in her eyes, throwing a wink at Mizu. She had suspected the two had gotten close but never asked. Privacy was hard to come by in their lives, what little they had was cherished.

Over Lux's head, she spotted Neko watching. His face was down, not quite sad. Mizu couldn't put a finger on it. He caught her eyes and simply nodded before turning to follow Song again.

29.

"Walk me through it, one more time." Song's stern demeanor seemed to cut right through Jon and Kairi.

Mizu was glad they were okay. They arrived shortly after her, and Jon looked like he had been through hell.

"When I ditched the decoy truck, I thought I was alone. I barely made it a block when I realized I wasn't. By that point, someone was already trying to hack me. I never saw who did it. I managed to ditch my comlog and smash it before the feedback locked me up. If I had to guess, they were trying to Carbonite me, lock me up, and take me alive." Jon shuddered at the thought. He looked down in shame. "After that, I ran when the shooting started. It just came from nowhere. I never saw the shooter. No idea how they didn't hit me."

Mizu knew Jon was the most cautious of the group. His paranoia had kept them alive a lot longer than they would have been without him. Naysmith or not, Jon was a survivor. If someone had gotten the drop on him, it was bad news. She smiled encouragingly at him. "Keep going, Jon."

He nodded back. "Right. I dove into the sewers and backtracked to an old hide near downtown. I managed to snag a spare comlog I had stashed and called Kairi for pickup. I'm glad I had an old hacking deck backup too." He paused, exhausted, but steeled himself. "I'm fully operational, just tired. I was riding on fumes till Kairi snagged me. Slept the whole way here." He offered a weak smile. Mizu saw something deeper there but didn't push it. Her eyes darted down, drawn to the comlog, now that he had pointed it out. It was one of the newer Yujingyu models, but if she knew Jon, it had been thoroughly scrubbed—nothing to worry about.

"Thanks, Jon. Get some rest." Mizu patted her friend on the shoulder. He looked wrecked.

"Briefing in eight hours," Song added, mission-focused.

"Roger, I'll be there." Jon left the room and was greeted by cheers. He was quickly pulled away by the Hands.

"Hope they let him sleep." Kairi seemed lost in thought.

Song looked at Kairi, unreadable. "What?"

Mizu nodded to Kairi, encouraging her to answer.

"The shake's got him." Kairi inhaled deeply and sighed.

Song's voice sharpened. "The what? Explain."

Mizu cut in. "He's slagg'n rattled. It's been a long time since we've been in the thick of it. Give him a break. He'll be ready."

Song stood silently, looking back and forth between them. Mizu felt like she was being analyzed by a predator. The fact that they were alone in a small room didn't help the feeling; like being trapped with a shark. Thankfully, Song nodded and left. Somehow, Mizu wasn't sure if she felt better or not.

Mizu waited a few moments before she turned to Kairi and narrowed her eyes.

"Out with it."

"He's scared, Mizu," Kairi answered, barely holding her gaze. "He didn't want to do this to begin with."

"I know. We all are."

"No—really scared. He was never good with this. He will ride. He would do anything to keep us safe, but just look at him. *Chikusho,* getting jumped scared the hell out of the slagghead. He looked like he'd seen a ghost, just staring at his comlog when I got to him." Kairi looked genuinely worried.

"Let's all keep an eye on him. He's one of us, our responsibility."

"You got it, Boss." Kairi tried to playfully mimic Goro, but her voice was far from certain.

Mizu felt the same.

* * * * *

Takeshi watched the cheering gaggle reunite with their returned comrade from across the open bay space. It was a joyous thing to see. Absent the strictures of code and conduct Takeshi lived by, the raucous group was all over one another: teasing, tackling, hugging, punching, and laughing. It was a riot of affection: chaos. Yet, there was something enduringly honest about their love for one another. It made Takeshi uncomfortable.

The recently arrived Jon, he heard the name shouted several times, was slowly warming and relaxing in the group's embrace. He still looked haunted, like he had never expected to see them again, even as Goro swept him up in a crushing embrace. It was the look of someone who stared death in the face. Someone who blinked. Takeshi chose not to judge him harshly. He had no idea how hard their life had been. It had been far worse—a horror show—than expected since he arrived. Taka had…

Thinking about the Kempeitai stalled Takeshi's thoughts and crushed his chest. He had been so focused on survival that he had not spared a thought for the man who had promised to get him into the country… and get him out. Now he was gone, presumed dead, and Takeshi could not help but blame himself. He wanted Takeshi to be patient and let things play out. He had not listened. Takeshi couldn't even remember actively reacting. His code of honor was so ingrained in him, it felt like watching someone else move in hindsight. It felt surreal.

"I'm not sure who looks more haggard." Bianca offered him a drink. She had approached quietly and was leaning against an abandoned tool cabinet.

Without answering, Takeshi took a swig of stale, recycled water. "He has been through an ordeal by the look of him. They have all survived so much..."

"And you?"

"Pardon?" Takeshi furrowed his brow at the question.

"You two have the same look. You've both been through something profound recently, and neither of you are processing it." The kindness in her eyes surprised Takeshi. Bianca was a war reporter. Warcors were usually as hardened as the soldiers they chased across the battlefield. Yet Bianca seemed to truly care.

"You are not wrong." Takeshi admitted it to himself as much as to her. Memories of imprisonment and torture surged unbidden through his mind, making him wince. He pushed the pain aside, burying it deep to deal with only after this was all finished. "So why are you here, really?"

"Would you believe me if I told you that Yasbir asked me to come?"

"At this point, yes. Yes, I would."

"I'm supposed to be witnessing the rescue of Prince Hasib." Bianca trailed off, clearly withholding the rest.

"You don't entirely seem convinced that is the whole story." Takeshi took another sip of water and passed the canteen back to her.

"Is it ever with him?"

"That is a fair point." Takeshi had only met a Hassassin a few times, but it was never simple when he did, and rarely bloodless.

A cheer went up as Mizu returned, the last of their motley family in tow. The band had already helped themselves to whatever crates or counters they could use for seating. The maintenance bay had plenty of unused surfaces to spare. Further cheering erupted as a bottle of whiskey was produced from a bag.

"Even with all they have been through, they are so full of joy and hope." Bianca seemed lost in thought. "I envy them."

"Me too." Takeshi admitted to himself more than Bianca.

* * * * *

Mizu studied Neko and Bianca as Shen waved them over to the fire. Bianca was still a mystery—why anyone had brought a Warcor into this was beyond her. Maybe Sparrow wanted a record in case they didn't make it out. Or maybe the Warcor was a weapon of a different kind. Mizu didn't trust her, but she wasn't going to fight about it now—not that she trusted easily to begin with.

Neko—somehow—she understood. The weight he carried felt familiar. She had seen that same haunted look in her own reflection, in the long nights buried under neon lights, bottles, and worse—wrapped in the hum of regret. He looked pale now, sweating despite the cold. His hand trembled when he reached to steady himself.

"Neko." Mizu made a small motion with her fingers, miming a slap to her thigh. He blinked, then nodded slightly and produced the injector from his belt. The hiss of the autoinjector was soft, but Mizu still winced. Bite wasn't something you could ever really leave behind—not without it taking something from you on the way out.

They settled into a circle. Goro had passed around some sort of bottle—whatever it was, it smelled like burnt fruit and regret. Mizu caught Shen—sitting with her arm through Goro's—watching Neko, not suspiciously, just thoughtful.

"You're not the first to fight your way out of the dark," Shen said after a moment. "That stuff in your eyes—I've seen it before. Wore it myself, for a long time."

Mizu raised an eyebrow. This was unexpected.

Neko's surprise was genuine. "Looking at you, I would never know."

Shen smiled. "Doesn't mean I started that way."

Bianca leaned forward slightly. "What happened?"

Shen looked into the fire. Her face didn't change much, but something about her seemed older suddenly. She exhaled slowly, like she'd been holding the memory back for years.

"I was twelve when the airstrikes hit our town. An advanced Yujingyu infiltration team triggered the whole thing. Our little farming town wasn't even a target—just in the way." She paused. "My parents were trying to pack up the house when the fire came down. The stream near our house boiled. I still hear the screaming sometimes when it's too quiet."

Even Goro went silent. He held her close.

Mizu didn't say anything. She just stared at Shen. Not because she was surprised—violence wasn't rare and she knew the story too well—but because she had offered it so plainly, like the memory didn't own her anymore.

She respected that—a lot.

Shen continued, voice steady. "I buried what was left of them in the scorched mud. Then I walked east for three days before Henzo's patrol found me. They gave me a blanket, a protein bar, and orders." She smiled faintly. "After the war, I stopped moving long enough to mourn, and it dragged me under—the Bite—I got moving again and haven't really stopped since."

"I am sorry," Neko said quietly. "That is not something a kid should carry."

Shen shook her head. "None of us got to choose what we carried."

Bianca stared at her hands, unusually quiet.

Mizu met Shen's gaze and gave her a slow nod. "Still standing, though."

She nodded back. "So are you."

Laughter broke the heavy silence when Bianca took a swig of the bottle and immediately coughed. "What the hell is this stuff?" she managed, grimacing as she shoved it back at Goro.

"We take what we can get!" Kairi snorted. "Yujingyu whiskey is awful, but it's better than the disaster Goro tried to make that one time."

"Give me a little credit! I was experimenting." Goro grinned. "It got you all good and wasted, didn't it?"

Mizu shook her head, laughing. "It was pure evil. Never again, Goro." She pointed a warning finger at him. "Don't say it!"

Her Hands looked at each other with gleeful mischief, then chimed in unison. "Whatever you say, Boss!"

The chorus of laughter rolled through the circle. Even Jon let out a genuine laugh, his shoulders relaxing for the first time in hours. Mizu caught the change in Neko too—he wasn't smiling exactly, but the tightness in his jaw had eased. His posture loosened. For a noble with a lineage of straight spines and cold honor, it was practically a nap.

She leaned back—hands laced behind her head—as the warmth of the booze touched her face. Strange, how the road to war could sometimes bring moments like this.

Maybe, just maybe, they were going to be okay.

30.

Morning came, and Takeshi felt like hell. Slapping himself with another detox injection, he counted four more doses. He had not consumed much of the whiskey, but Mizu already warned him its effects would be amplified due to the narcotics fighting his system for control.

Hiro appeared at his door wheeling something covered in a tarp. His hair was slicked back, and he wore combat optics—fitted over his eyes like solitary lenses had replaced them. He wore light armor with ivory white panels over a sleek stealth suit. "Morning."

"Good morning, Hiro."

"I thought you would like to know. Taka is alive."

Takeshi felt like a vice in his chest finally released. The subconscious weight of guilt lessened ever so slightly—just enough to breathe again. He sat back down on the cot he had claimed for the night.

"Do we know where?" Takeshi kept to the mission to keep his mind focused.

"You'll never believe this." Hiro let the suspense hang for just a moment, smirking to himself. "He is in the cell right next to our wayward prince—in your old home. Looks like we are making a rescue after all."

To Takeshi, it felt like fate was playing tricks on him. "Fortuitous."

"Indeed. Get dressed. Briefing in thirty." Hiro grinned as he turned and departed, leaving his baggage behind.

Takeshi could hear him moving down the hall, whistling to himself. Hiro's outwardly carefree attitude bothered the stoic warrior if he focused on it. He had to trust Song and Taka's word that he was as good as they said. He shook his head and got up to inspect what Hiro left behind. Under the tarp, he found an armorer's case.

He opened the case and studied the armor inside, a faint, almost imperceptible smile touching his lips. The cold plates lay silently waiting—familiar, steady. It wasn't just protection; it was a reminder of purpose. Quiet and unspoken, the comfort it brought was something he couldn't afford to fully acknowledge—at least, not yet.

The black and grey tech suit he removed first was a part of most current JSA heavy armor sets; it afforded modest protection on its own. Once he stripped and donned the suit, it conformed to his body, mimicking his musculature. Ports waited to interface with armor plates and would provide more accurate control of the suit of heavy powered armor in the case. Piece by piece, Takeshi withdrew the clean armored plates and locked them into place. It was easier with help, but training had taught him how to do it on his own—when the need arose.

As the suit powered, articulated components interlocked, fully sealing him in a skin of reinforced platting. Takeshi was surprised to find his own geist loaded into the factory fresh armor. His vision augmented and overlaid with a screed of data as the virtual intelligence ran a systems check on the suit. A cast of his eyes to the diagnostics his geist displayed showed Takeshi the stealth generator in the backplate was fully operational, and a dark grin forced itself forward. Standard in the Domaru Butai, the generator helped dampen the signature of his powered armor—not a full optical camouflage system like Hiro's suit appeared to have, but helpful nonetheless. Takeshi was thankful it was fully charged—just what he would need to close in and show his foes just how ferocious he could be.

Takeshi had spent many years wearing just such a suit, and donning the sleek near white ivory panels was akin to donning a second skin. Albeit one that amplified his strength, speed, and made him near impervious to harm. The familiar split-toed *tabi* armored boots, the weight of the plate against his shoulders, the padded armorcloth *haidate* over his thighs: All of it together gave him the appearance of the samurai of old. Each and every piece was a comfort. Wearing the familiar armored suit made Takeshi feel more prepared for what was ahead than he had been since he had departed the palace on Earth. The only thing missing was the comforting weight of weaponry. Takeshi thought of his lone, remaining sword back on Earth.

Finally, his angular helmet—stylized lines sweeping back to a slight point—sat on a white sleeveless armor-cloth haori, trimmed in red, waited at the bottom of the crate. On its back was the stylized, almost cartoonish, face of a cat. Takeshi smirked despite himself and donned the garment. He could have it reprogrammed later if he needed to, but now was not the time to sweat such things.

"One cut at a time. One fight. Focus."

Words spoken, mind steeled, Takeshi tucked his helmet under his arm and grabbed his scant kit—including his detox shots that were not compatible with the suit's onboard medical suite. He would need to carry those since they didn't match with his armor's med-suite. As he headed out for the briefing, he was surprised to see Mizu being led, blindfolded, down the hall by one of the young members of her gang.

* * * * *

"Where are we going, Lux?" Mizu disliked being blindfolded, but the jubilation in Lux's voice held back any objection. It was easy to forget that Lux was only thirteen; at thirteen she had already fought, and killed, to stay alive more than most would in a lifetime. Death haunted the teenager's eyes. To kill the joy was more than Mizu could bring herself to do.

"Just trust me!"

"Okay, okay, I trust you."

Lux led her through the warren of tunnels, past what felt familiar. The temperature dropped, meaning they were definitely past the living quarters the group had been using. They stopped, and a door shut behind her. Mizu could hear several others in the room, including Jon and Kairi whispering low, conspiratorially.

"Are you ready?"

Mizu grinned despite herself. Something was up, and Lux was proud of it. That alone was enough to bring a grin to her face. "Lay it on me."

Her blindfold was removed in a flourish. In front of the gathered Hands was the most beautiful thing Mizu had ever seen. Sitting on a maintenance cradle and clad in red was two wheels bookending pure sex appeal.

"TZ Tsurugi–IIs." Song stepped into view, gesturing at the motorcycle. "An upgrade from the old Broadsword models you are familiar with. These are prototypes fresh out of R&D—with improved acceleration, handling, and range from their predecessors. You speed freaks can eek an extra thirty to fifty kph out of them on the top end. Lighter composite plating makes them more nimble at the cost of some durability."

Song rattled off more specs as Mizu paced around the machine. Her geist raced around her vision in celebration, its avatar a tiny motorcycle.

The sleek bike was more aerodynamic than the previous models she had ridden. The blunt nose replaced by cleaner lines; and fat, armored tires gave it a menacing stance, hunched forward like a predator. Locking stations were set on each side, in front of the rider, to accommodate weaponry easily at hand. That alone was a huge upgrade to having to sling them in the past. Its jet black body was hastily sprayed with *san* on each side, flying the colors of the Third Hand.

Mizu connected her comlog to the machine and in-loaded the specs. By the numbers, it was point-for-point improved at every level. A wireframe schematic appeared, sorting through the specifications, one at a time.

It took Foks piping in for Mizu to realize the room had gone quiet. "It's a hell of a machine, Boss. I tweaked a few settings based on how you used to like your bikes and slaved it to your comlog. She's all yours."

Mizu fought back tears as she looked at Song and the rest. "Thank you."

"And I painted it!" Lux cut in. "It was boring…" She trailed off sheepishly as Jon pulled aside a curtain, revealing three more black machines sitting in cradles. They were predators one and all. One additional cradle sat empty at the back of the room.

"It's perfect." For the first time in years, the shake was silent, and Mizu stopped fighting the tears.

* * * * *

Takeshi watched Mizu and her friends from the hall. Her outpouring of emotion over the motorcycles caught him off guard. It seemed such a simple thing to him: equipment or gear more than anything else. To Mizu, it was a cherished moment. Her friends surrounded her as tears poured from her face.

Song approached him as she left the family to have their moment in peace. "I have something for you as well, Neko."

Takeshi tore his eyes from the small *bōsōzoku* gang and followed Song. "They are just motorcycles."

"To us, yes." Song's voice was clipped, caught with emotion. He watched her closely as she led him to another chamber. "To them, motorcycles are their way of life. A way of life they sacrificed in the name of their nation. You know what it is like to lose a part of yourself,

I think."

The tiny room was full of old weapons crates. Several were open, empty, and all were covered in the thin film of dust that permeated the old not-so-abandoned facility. His lens displayed the missing contents of each as his comlog read the recessed shapes and extrapolated from there. Takeshi was surprised at the sheer amount of ordinance the room had once held. Logically, he knew there would be cells operating here on Kuraimori, but to see such a large weapons stash…

All of this was nothing to the wooden box, just over a meter long, set on a bundle of cloth on a narrow workbench at the other end of the room. His geist outlined the box as it drew him in instinctively. He approached, finding himself nervous. As he turned back to ask, Takeshi watched the door shut behind Song as she left him alone.

The wood was a beautiful lacquered cherry: simple, unadorned, but exquisite. Takeshi's hands hovered over the case, hesitating. He knew what was inside by the shape alone.

Steeling himself and letting out the breath he didn't realize he was holding, he opened the box. A handwritten letter, reminiscent of the one he received from Nakama, sat upon a red silk cloth that covered the rest of the contents. He found the elegant calligraphy was not Nakama's.

It is my will that you take these blades and be my hand. Know that you can do no wrong when you act in service to our great nation and your Emperor.

Takeshi found himself frozen, his note in hand. He could not say how long he stood unmoving as he fought back tears.

Beneath the silk, a pair of blades awaited him. Matched katanas, handles wrapped in black and gold, sat sheathed in rich red scabbards. Gold etchings of blossoms blowing in the wind decorated the handcrafted sheaths. At the top of each was displayed the Yoshihara mark once more. The seal stared back at him as he stood transfixed. The closest he had come to such exquisite works was his uncle's. Takeshi would expect no less exquisite craftsmanship from the Emperor's own bladesmiths, but even still, it took his breath away.

Takeshi stopped fighting the tears.

31.

Bianca stood near the back of the room as Song gathered the rest of the team. She was an observer in this. Her part was to tell the story and not be involved tactically.

With their permission, she filmed the goodbyes from the younger gangers when Benji returned to take them away. Bianca had known them less than twenty-four hours but was still grateful they would be safe. Benji promised Mizu to protect them with his life, and Bianca couldn't help but catch a bit of awe in his voice when he spoke to her. Out of the entire rambunctious group of bikers, only a determined Mizu, Jon who seemed more at ease today, Goro who was all smiles, and Kairi watching the rest like a mother hen, remained.

Song, Hiro, and Takeshi/Gi-ung/Neko rounded out what was left of the team.

Now, she watched a tactical projection materialize as Song synced it to everyone's lenses. The Hansei Valley appeared in all its glory across the floor of the room, giving the impression that those in the space were standing on it like giants.

"Alright ladies… and other warriors," Song addressed the group, letting her words hang, as serious as a heart attack. "Consider this briefing life or death, classified from this moment forward. The core mission has not changed, however the disposition and intentions of the enemy have changed since all of this was set in motion. We are also down one."

Bianca watched Neko blanche at that—guilt written across his face like a flashing sign.

"Can't be helped now, but thankfully Taka was taken to the Oyama estates… So consider him to be target number three. No one left behind, understood?" Song waited for a nod from each member of the team.

She caught a tightening of Neko's posture and a frown. He gripped the handle of a sword reflexively, one of a beautiful pair he had equipped for the endeavor.

"Now. Target One is the data vault." Once within, we will gather any and all data that can be salvaged and destroy the rest. Deletion, electromagnetic and incendiary charges, the works. *Nothing* left to be found. Vault team will each be given the necessary charges and data storage. Do not load it onto your personal networks. Understood?" Song pointed at devices arrayed on a nearby cart.

Bianca recognized mines when she saw them. That left several small square packs, each no bigger than her trusty Flash Pulse, to be the storage devices complete with their own carrying pouch.

"I'll copy the data into each person's device and start the encryption cycle. Do *not* attempt to access the device. They'll wipe if tampered with." Song made eye contact with Bianca, lingering before moving on like she was the prime suspect. "Oh, and not just wipe—but also explode."

Song winked at Bianca in a way she found nothing short of threatening. Song was not a woman she wanted to cross. She reminded Bianca of Yasbir in that aspect.

"Targets two—the prince—and three—Taka—are at the Oyama estates. Finally, Sparrow will provide extraction."

That piqued Bianca's attention. "Sparrow?"

"Yes, Miss Chen, Sparrow." The interruption clearly annoyed Song.

"Okay." Bianca bit back further questions. It was a common enough callsign, but it had to be one in the same as her contact.

"In order to get to this point, there are a few things that need to happen." Song gestured, and the projection of the valley zoomed out and highlighted a point on the flatlands to the southeast. "This strip was once a part of the larger Hideyoshi Base complex. After its destruction, a portion of the airfields were rebuilt as a forward operating post for the Yujinyu Special Air Division. From here, all drone reconnaissance and aerial strike operations within a few hundred kilometers or so are launched, maintained, and so on. It is also home to a Feìquán squadron."

At the mention of the small base, images of various drone craft appeared. Larger than the rest were the Feìquán. A central, rounded fuselage was shaped much like a motorcycle while twin thrusters and antigrav pods framed it. An underslung weapon mount was equipped with both lethal and nonlethal options. They only seemed to highlight the Imperial Service's reputation for both taking prisoners and killing them on a whim.

Bianca watched the collected bikers harden as Song turned to them.

"This is your target. You will have Hassassin support. The infiltration team is already in place."

Mizu was all business as Bianca watched her walk through the projection like a giant crushing the landscape, analyzing the terrain and nodding to herself. "Can you enhance this?"

With a wave of her hand, Song did as requested, and the airbase materialized in detail. Bianca read a determination in Mizu's eyes that she couldn't explain. The coiled viper that she had seemed was gone, and now a calm battle commander remained.

"Here." Mizu highlighted a mountain pass, narrow and winding, and eyed her crew. "This is our route. We can run silent most of the way without draining the batteries too badly, then light it up at this bend. That's what, five hundred meters or so in the open, maybe less? Rest of the run is loud and proud."

"Is what?" Neko chimed in, confused.

"Loud and proud, Neko. Call it lightning in the storm. A flash, a bang, then we're gone." Mizu's grin held a feral quality that Bianca couldn't help but feel wary of.

"Understood." Neko nodded, visibly unsure how to take her himself.

"I'll give Yasbir your link so he can coordinate if necessary." Song tapped out a command on her comlog.

"So that's where the duck-butts went." The looks Bianca received ran the gamut from incredulous to utter confusion.

"Sunduqbut, Miss Chen. They are called Sunduqbuts." Song was clearly frustrated by yet another interruption.

Bianca threw up her hands in apology. "Whatever they are called, they were scary as hell."

"Imagine how the Yujingyu will feel," Hiro piped in, grinning maniacally.

"Enough chit-chat!" Song reclaimed the briefing and continued on. She walked through the timing of the strikes and the coordination of the final push.

Try as she might to pay attention, Bianca's mind kept drifting back to Yasbir.

* * * * *

As Bianca, Song, and Hiro spoke quietly, Takeshi triple checked his equipment in silence. The cool rock and dust kept company with his thoughts as he checked over the weaponry Hiro had given out. The comfortable weight of a snub-nosed Contender and a heavy Chain Rifle were nothing compared to the reassuring weight of blades at his side.

With the briefing concluded, they would be setting out soon. The bikers had withdrawn for their own preparations, honoring their own traditions. Takeshi's opinion of them had transformed in a way he had not expected. Mizu had many opportunities to kill or betray him in some fashion. They were a rowdy gang, thugs, rebels… yakuza… and yet he trusted Mizu with his life. Takeshi smiled gently to himself, remembering General Daichi challenging his views. It felt like a life ago, despite it being mere weeks.

His team would be heading out soon, traveling through the mines and into the open sky above. After they raided the data vault, it would be time for the final push. It was a strange sensation, to be going home. Takeshi could already feel the years of phantoms nipping at his heels coming to a head.

Even before the Uprising, he had not been home in years. This mission had forced the realization that even now, years after the loss of his father, Takeshi had still not… dealt with it. When he joined the service, he had thought his father would be proud of him. Yet it had only forced a distance. Uncle Daichi, his mother, even his mentor repeatedly spoke of his father's pride in him.

Family dynamics in the noble lines were as myriad and complicated as anywhere else. For those that walked the warrior's path, life was focused on the blade. Family was supposed to bring only thoughts of duty and honor. In reality, Takeshi had to admit the Oyama clan was as complicated a family as any other.

"Time to go." Hiro interrupted his reverie as he walked toward the exit. He was laden with a Heavy Rocket Launcher and a rucksack, no doubt full of various flavors of death.

Bianca and Song followed as Takeshi fell in line. They journeyed through the bay where Mizu and her crew waited.

"Good luck, and don't forget your dose," Mizu called.

Takeshi smiled and offered a slight bow. "Understood. Good luck to you as well." He paused. "Keep your head down."

Mizu laughed aloud, leading a chorus from the other bikers. "I thought you knew me better by now."

Takeshi wasn't entirely sure if he should be afraid of, or attracted to, her as she grinned manically and winked.

* * * * *

Mizu turned back to her friends as the others left. Takeshi outwardly seemed to genuinely care about their safety. A pleasant shift from his earlier hostility and distrust. Mizu wondered how he would have handled living her life, and she his. She quickly decided neither would have survived long.

It would be a few hours before it was their turn to go. Their brand new Tsurugi–IIs would make the longer journey through the mountains in half the time it would take the other team to slog it on foot. For Mizu, it would be an absolute pleasure to ride again, no matter how far the distance. For now, she would look to her team, and wait.

Goro had pulled the left side cowling off his bike and was inspecting the machine. His comlog had multiple dials up, showing Mizu the beast's impressive stats.

"How's it look?"

"Slagghead engineers actually got something right. These things are works of art! Slim, lightweight, should maneuver like a dream." Goro's excitement was infectious.

"Can't wait." Kairi joined the conversation. "It feels good to do something, anything, that really means something."

"I'm just glad we got the rest out." Jon chimed in from where he was tinkering with comlog—he was spending a lot of time on the new device. The new model must have been more finicky to set up if he was still at it.

"Me too, Jon." Mizu couldn't agree more. It was a weight off all their shoulders that could be felt. "It's just us and the job now. No more strings, no more looking over our shoulders."

Jon frowned. "I just want us to make it out too. Whatever it takes."

"We will." Kairi was full of hope.

Her optimism was infectious, and soon Mizu was smiling in Jon's direction. She threw him a wink and he smiled back, but it was halfhearted, and she knew it. It felt like Jon wanted to believe, but was afraid of what failure would mean for the lifelong friends. Mizu struggled to understand him sometimes, but she knew exactly how he felt right now.

"Has anyone seen that bottle from last night? I think this calls for a drink!" Goro's voice was full of excitement. Mizu saw Jon crack a real smile once the bottle was found with enough left for the four of them to raise a toast.

"Ride, die, ride forever. Loud and proud!"

32.

The slow creep through the pine forest brought a riot of memories to Takeshi. He spent his childhood roaming these woods with friends, in search of mythical creatures. Later years were filled with hunts, and then his training progressed past the dojo and into the wilds. The skills he learned here were invaluable, giving him the foundational fieldcraft that set him above his peers.

Song ghosted through the woods ahead of him while Bianca held the rear. Occasionally he glimpsed Hiro moving on the left flank, a specter between the trees; the rest of the time, he was merely a marker in his lens.

Takeshi kept his armor's vents open, despite wearing his helmet. While he could seal himself in, even surviving in a vacuum, he relished the cool air of the early morning. It was spring now in this part of Shentang, and the forest felt alive, vibrant with life… a far cry from the lonely, lifeless tunnels.

"Hey." Bianca had moved up next to Takeshi in near silence. Takeshi begrudgingly reevaluated his assumptions about her fieldcraft, moving her mostly out of the 'liability' category—mostly. She was keeping up easily and moving with a degree of stealth that was beyond a natural inclination—someone had trained her well.

"Yes, Miss Chen?"

"How does it feel to be back in Hansei?"

"It is the mission."

"Not what I meant."

"Is this the appropriate time for an interview?" Takeshi hoped he hid his annoyance at the line of questioning.

"It's never a good time, Neko. In my line of work, you get used to just asking what you can, when you can."

It was strange to hear her refer to him as Neko. While he had become accustomed to it from the rest of them, it was the first time from Bianca. Looking ahead, Song was nowhere to be seen.

He felt the hit before he heard it. The small caliber shot rang against his shoulder, failing to penetrate. It glanced off and buried itself in a tree behind them. The forest around them erupted.

From ahead and to the left, a barrage of small arms fire shredded the low foliage. Bianca had reacted, but not quick enough. Takeshi shoved her, and she rolled into a depression. He followed her in a heartbeat, placing himself to block the torrent of fire that followed.

He dropped to a knee and brought his Chain Rifle to bear. Takeshi's geist quickly calculated and highlighted the approximate sources of gunfire in his vision. With a squeeze of the trigger, a cone of super-heated, twisted metal shrapnel was launched into the chaos, obliterating a small sapling and silencing one of the attackers.

///Three Shàng Jí. ~~Five~~ two Zanshi. One unknown moving fast. Flanking.///

Song's intel flashed through his vision as Takeshi charged into the gunfire. He felt a twinge of sympathy for the enemy and smiled. He was already looking forward to a bit of a stretch. Intelligence told them the Yujingyu Invincible Army kept several garrisons on Kuraimori and used its mountainous terrain as training grounds. It wasn't uncommon for branches of the StateEmpire's war machine to work together. It was just unfortunate that they happened upon each other.

///Aircraft on approach.///

Hiro's update was more troubling.

Pushing it all from his mind, Takeshi charged forward like a berserker of old. Heedless of the small arms fire pinging off his plate, he emptied his Chain Rifle in an arc before him as three heavily armored soldiers of the Shàng Jí Invincibles met him head on. Their countercharge shifted his focus from their more lightly armored counterparts, but it made them the next to die. Their heavy orange and grey plate was identical—smooth and protective. His lens highlighted their armor's weak points with slashes of neon blue.

Dropping his Chain Rifle and drawing his Emperor-given blades, he activated their cores; one crackled with an electromagnetic discharge while the other built a kinetic charge. As the heavy troopers reached him, he dropped to one knee and slid through the first. His kinetic blade released its fury into the soldier's hip. First the reinforced edge cut through armor like it was nothing, then the kinetic charge released. Like a Double Action round from the barrel of a gun, the blade hammered home with a gravity of its own, pushing itself cleanly through his assailant and out the other side, cutting the legs from the body.

Not wasting his momentum, Takeshi threw a foot forward to arrest his slide and used the forward motion to push into a crouch. He lashed to his left with the second blade, burying it in the Shàng Jí's torso. The E/M charge released, frying the armored suit's systems and locking its occupant in an unnatural standing pose, frozen in place as he died.

Takeshi stood to his full height as the third and final trooper brought his gun to bear and fired, point blank. Takeshi threw himself to the side in a futile attempt to avoid the MULTI Rifle as it unloaded its armor-piercing hate.

Red flashed across the status silhouette in Takeshi's lens before the pain in his arm even registered. Only a single round penetrated, catching the lighter protection of his tech suit between plates of reinforced armor.

Biting his teeth through the pain, Takeshi turned back to his assailant just in time for the rocket to strike the heavy trooper, obliterating him in a ball of fire.

"You're welcome." Hiro laughed jovially over comms.

"You have my gratitude." Takeshi replied calmly, Hiro's laughter grating in his ear. He rose and followed the sound of small arms fire, ready to whet his blade on the next opponent.

* * * * *

Bianca watched Neko fight the Yujingyu from the relative safety of the small gulley she had been tossed into.

"Not my best moment," she mumbled as she maneuvered to a better position, letting her bionic eye record the fight. Neko truly was an artist with a sword, it was humbling to behold. The fights with Joan of Arc and the Military Orders she had recorded were vicious, passionate affairs full of conviction and righteous zeal. Neko was anything but—he was destructively efficient, wasting no energy as he meted out death. He was a cold, brutally calculating reaper of men.

It was breathtaking. That, or she was still recovering from the tumble which deposited her face down ingloriously, Bianca wasn't quite sure.

Just past the unfolding fireball that engulfed the heavily armored Yujingyu, something larger loomed into view. With a predatory grace that seemed incongruous with its size and mechanical nature, a fast moving, orange-plated leopard barreled into Neko, knocking him off his feet and sending him sailing into the air.

Bianca's geist labeled the thunderous cat as a 'Sù-Jiàn, Immediate Action Unit' as it tapped into her archives. It dove into a roll; transforming from its massive feline form into a hulking humanoid machine. The remote transformer extended an arm as it finished its roll in a crouch, lining up its Spitfire with Hiro's last location. The torrent of fire was a terrifying, booming staccato of death. The woods around Hiro's form shredded in a blink, throwing pine dust and splinters up like a cloud.

"No!" Bianca cried out, despite knowing better than to draw attention to herself.

As the air cleared, an image of Hiro was still there, untouched and flipping a very rude hand gesture at the Sù-Jiàn. The fast attack machine rose and walked toward Hiro, firing again and again, more like an automation than the graceful machine it had been moments before. Bullets tore through the holographic decoy until it faded from view. Losing its target, the lethal machine turned its attention toward her.

Bianca's gut tied itself in a knot as she realized her mistake, and she reached for her Flash Pulse. The self-defense weapon would be utterly useless if the robot got a bead on her, but she drew anyway.

A whine and ping emitted from the pistol-shaped device in her outstretched hand as a laser thin line of unseen energy and superfrequency sound shot forth and slammed into the Sù-Jiàn. Bianca had never been a bad shot, but never a marksman. Luck was on her side this time, and the robot recoiled from the stunning shot.

It leapt backward, folding its frame upon itself and abandoned its humanoid combat form. Landing on all fours, tail extended, the massive mechanical cat braced to charge her.

Its motion was arrested by Neko's katana, slicing cleanly through the beast's neck as he appeared at its side. The E/M discharge coursed over the 'cat's' frame as its internal workings fried.

Only in the moment did she register that the background noise of Combi Rifle fire had ceased. A cold, anxious calm came over Bianca as she scanned the forest around her to catch Song limping toward them.

"Combined patrol. Unfortunate, though your blind firing did us some good, Neko. I only had to deal with a few stragglers." Song limped over to the forcibly decommissioned Sù-Jiàn and slapped a D-Charge to its side. "Airborne assets are still inbound. We should get out of here."

"How do you know?" Bianca's innate curiosity took over as they walked away.

Song grinned through gritted teeth, there was blood in her mouth. "A little bird told me." Song snapped an auto-injector into a thigh port of Ryuken armor and winced, but stood a little straighter afterward and discarded the spent cartridge. "Let's move."

Bianca hurried as she kept up with the rest of the group. The silence stretched on eerily; she knew it was only a matter of time before—

She winced as the D-Charge exploded behind them. It was still loud, despite the distance they put between it. She shook her head, wondering if that was only the first of the enemies they would encounter.

33.

The airfield was a sparse affair compared to more major installations nearby, but holographic safety lines and air traffic guides lit up the quantronic space like a nightclub on Bakunin. The land around the airstrip was a barren, empty place. Vegetation had recovered, but it would be years more before it was forested once again.

Drones and the flyers of the Feìquán Imperial Tactical Wing occupied the tarmac with only two maintenance hangars, a two story control tower, and barracks to make up the rest of the walled facility. Yasbir enjoyed the symmetry of these new flying motorcycles being pitted against the reckless aggression of the *bōsōzoku* speeding this way. He had seen what both could do in action, and his bet was on the Japanese.

Yasbir was a calculating warrior, like the rest of his order, reading the patterns of events and influencing them. He would not be here if the risk was not worth the potential reward.

He moved easily through the Yujingyu airfield as he made his way to the control tower, walking in the open as if he belonged there—with an imperious air, moving with the authority of someone who knew they could not be stopped. His Holomask had been running for hours now, and the disguise would need to be reset soon. Until then, no one saw him. They saw the long emerald and gold robes, meticulously maintained beard, and monocled scowl of Dragon Lord Ruan Xian. The real Ruan was on Concilium, and had been since the armistice with the Combined Army. Yasbir had met the man and disliked him greatly. It made the impersonation all the more enjoyable.

The holographic guise was crafted through tiny quantronic projectors woven into his lightly armored jumpsuit. No one would know the difference unless they subjected him to careful scrutiny, which Dragon Lord Ruan would not tolerate.

It was the kind of disguise Yasbir secretly loved. It was a blatant and flagrant disrespect to his foes. It was also something that suited his purpose well as no one would question him, no one would dream of stopping him, lest they earn his ire.

He had already deployed his charges where they could best serve their purpose. Bianca's precious drone was waiting to launch at his command. The Aragoto were moving rapidly into range, and it was up to him to ensure they were welcomed upon their arrival.

"Be somewhere else." Approaching the guard posted at the door, Yasbir sent them away with a lethal stare. His voice was a perfect mimic of the real Ruan.

Inside, the spartan interior was typical of Imperial Service facilities. Yasbir's geist scanned ahead as he moved down the short hallway. Three doors and a stairwell lay ahead of him, and his suit's limited sensors told him everyone in the small facility was upstairs on the observation level.

Removing his pack caused Yasbir's Holomask to flicker, too much intricate movement causing its programming to struggle to keep up. He deactivated it temporarily; thanks to his thorough reconnaissance, he already knew there were no cameras in this level. Yasbir's tan armor was made of a layered suit of synthetic fibers that were proof against most small arms but would provide minimal protection from heavier calibers. Its Bio-Technical Shield was stronger for his own safety; a nick from his own Viral-laced blade would spell disaster—a very agonizingly slow and painful disaster.

From his pack he produced three small mines and placed them around the entrance. Satisfied with his work, Yasbir discarded the pack and proceeded upstairs, reactivating his Holomask with a smirk beneath his enclosed helmet.

* * * * *

Spines stiffened the moment the masked Imperial Agent entered the observation deck. His armored form exuded lethality—ceremonial in shape, functional in purpose—but the silence was what unnerved them. He stood at the back of the room, letting the weight of his very presence fill the narrow space. The nearest drone operator shifted uncomfortably, likely having never met an Imperial Agent in person. He could see it in the way the operator—the name Lai visible in his ident halo—tried not to look at him directly, the way his breath caught.

A ping broke the stillness—Lai's control cradle pulling data from the perimeter. Vehicle, high speed, the approach vector was too clean. He watched Lai's expression shift—Lai recognized the signature.

Operator Lai tapped through his logs like a man hoping to be wrong. He found what he was looking for and hesitated, then forwarded it to the watch commander.

Good, Yasbir wouldn't have to prod.

"Confirm this ident, Operator Lai," the commander said.

"I did, sir. Ident confirmed, it's the same courier from the recent raid."

Time to move.

"Open the gates." The Imperial Agent stepped forward. The sensor tail of his helmet swayed behind him, as if blowing in the wind. His voice was flat and final through the helm's modulator. The commander complied with the blind obedience required of him.

"Everyone," the Imperial Agent said, projecting his voice across the room, "delete this vehicle from your archives, now. Confirm once complete."

A momentary pause of confusion was followed by compliance. Voices, one by one: *"Done." "Confirmed." "Wiped."* They would believe he was cleaning up the trail of something they wanted no part in. They were right, in a sense.

He crossed to Lai's station and turned the cradle to face him. Operator Lai awkwardly tried to bow. Yasbir let him.

Then Yasbir drew a long, single-edged blade. Its shape and make were at odds with Holomasked Yujingyu armor.

The point slid through the fabric of the operator's uniform and into the cavity—between heart and lung—with ease.

No flourish or anger, just lethal purpose.

Lai gasped, wide-eyed. His mouth filled with blood and something darker—biophages blooming from the molecular edge of the blade. He wouldn't feel much after the nerves dissolved. It was clean, efficient—exactly how Yasbir preferred it.

The disguise collapsed. Armor plates recoded their color. Holographic alterations to his size and shape vanished as Yasbir's true form appeared. A second skin of tan and green unfolded across him like a mantis revealing its wings. The agent they had feared was gone. The Hassassin remained.

Now they were truly afraid. The room shifted around him—gasps and panicked flight—but it was too late. They were already dead, Yasbir simply needed to show them.

On the operator's screen, the courier ident blinked out. Four red dots appeared in its place, breaching the open gates fast: hostiles inbound, exactly as planned.

Yasbir spotted another, larger ping on the sensor screen—moving northwest, fast... not as planned.

* * * * *

"Goro, keep it tight back there." Mizu worried he was slipping back too far. Her Cybermask was being pushed far beyond its intended use for this insane stunt. It was thanks to Henzo's tiny emitters mounted on each bike that it was even possible. Mizu silently thanked her long dead friend one more time.

Warnings flashed through her vision as Jon's bike bumped hers.

"Roger." Goro tucked back in, front wheel between hers and Jon's.

"This is insane!" Kairi's voice was thick with thrill.

"Slagg'n brilliant is what it is!" Even Jon was caught up in the rush, his dour mood forgotten.

Their bikes rubbed together. One wrong move and they would all meet a catastrophic end. The shake rattled in her ribs. Mizu was locked on her bike with white knuckles and luck.

They accelerated on the final stretch. It was a huge risk trying to overlap it across all four bikes. They had to tuck in so close that their fairings were rubbing down to the bare composite. Mizu's amplified Cybermask failed as they spaced out to slalom through the barriers at the gate. It was white knuckle tense through the last bend, but with a straight shot to the opening airfield gate, they opened it up and spread out. Her geist began to float in the upper reaches of her vision, its avian form dancing around Bianca's camera drone that launched from one of the rooftops. It slaved to her comlog and chased her on an intercept course.

The wash of nostalgia at first riding again was nothing compared to the gut-wrenching thrill of the shake being satisfied. The coiled beast within her smiled as the wind rushed past, matching her own grin beneath her jet black helmet. *Akai Te* rode on her back with her trusty Boarding Pistol on her hip. A Combi Rifle was maglocked to the bike's weapons stations, and her Light Shotgun sat across her lap waiting to be used.

The Hands' acceleration reached one hundred and twenty kph as they blasted through the gate. The guards only just realized that the bikes were hostile as Mizu shot the first one point blank in the chest as they burned through. Next to her, Kairi sat up on her ride, hands free as she braced her Spitfire and unloaded on the gate house, stitching two Yujingyu with bullet holes. Alarms and gunfire roared in their wake—too slow to catch them.

Goro and Jon blitzed between her and Kairi, then peeled apart. Like an explosive lily, each of them darted away toward their objectives. As Mizu closed on the control tower, she watched a pair of Celestial Guards charge into the building only to be met by a coiling electrical explosion, frying them both in their armor. Behind the explosion came the tan armored form of Yasbir—rifle in hand. Spotting her, he ran along a parallel course as she downshifted and released the throttle. Gears were more of a nostalgic holdover for most speed freaks, being long since outmoded by modern engines, but the bike slowed considerably regardless as its onboard processor understood her intent.

Mizu's breakneck speed wasn't completely arrested by the time the bike came alongside Yasbir. She hit her auto-stabilizer and slowed just enough for him to leap on behind her. She gunned it, turning toward the hangar.

"I thought you said we had fire support?!" she shouted.

"Patience!" Yasbir was out of breath, his voice clear in her helmet. "Look at the buildings."

As he spoke, Mizu watched as a pair of Sunduqbuts' thermo-optic camouflage peeled away as they rose from their hiding places, already firing. How Yasbir had gotten them in the perimeter, Mizu hadn't the first clue.

One machine unloaded a shoulder mounted Spitfire, armor-piercing rounds tearing through drones by the dozens as it closed on the parked Feiquán. Its shotgun swiveled toward a Yujingyu tech who got too close, launching him backward. The second Sunduqbut stood on top of a small maintenance dock, burst firing armor-piercing shots from its Feuerbach at anything that moved.

"That'll slagg'n do!" Mizu shouted in exhilaration and slowed once more.

"Thanks for the ride!" Yasbir dismounted in a graceful roll and darted toward the hangar, quickly moving out of her line of sight.

Mizu slammed on her rear brake, sliding the back wheel around as she cleared the structure, and chose the barracks as her next target. She hit the stabilizer assist on the bike and rose up with her Combi in hand. What she would have given to have that feature on their old rides! She lined up a long shot at the Feìquán pilots scrambling from the building as they fired at the invading Aragoto, but her rifle's Friend/Foe selector held her fire as Jon cut across her line, chasing another target.

"*Chikusho*, Jon!" Holding the trigger, the rifle began spitting three-round bursts at the running soldiers once he was clear.

"Sorry!"

Grateful she couldn't have blasted her friend, Mizu crouched back down on her ride and gunned it into the fray.

Weaving between light poles, she stowed her Combi, drew her sidearm, and aimed her ride at the line of jetbikes before her. Her geist fed tactical data stored in her ride directly into her lens, showing Mizu the weak points of the Yujingyu craft. They didn't need to destroy them, though that was a bonus if they could; but fouling the engine would do.

Mizu slowed as she rode past the line of neatly parked craft and pulled the trigger behind each one. The rapid fire bursts emitted a loud 'brap' that was barely muffled by her helmet, unloading a cloud of shrapnel into the thruster ports. In the corner of her eye, she caught the camera drone chasing her overhead.

"Boss! Left, left, left!" Goro's call came with not a moment to lose.

Mizu reacted without thinking, throwing her steed into a hard left turn as a torrent of shells shredded the space she had just abandoned. "Target?!" The shake reared its fangs.

"Rui Shi." Kairi must have spotted it.

"Painted!" Jon chimed in.

Mizu's comlog pinged a target location. Rui Shi remotes were a problem. With rapid fire assault weapons and advanced optics, the quadrupedal robots moved nearly as fast as they did and could see straight through the mimetic fields their bikes generated. Mizu glanced toward the marker and saw it instantly, highlighted in all their lenses by Jon's Spotlight program. The dual fin shaped antennae rising off the machine's back were unmistakable.

Mizu clamped down on her fear, forcing the shake into its cage, and devised a plan. This wasn't going to be easy, but it was definitely going to be fun.

"Scatter pattern four!"

* * * * *

Yasbir fired around the corner at the remaining Celestial Guards inside the hangar offices. Rounds from his Viral Rifle chewed through their light armor and the flesh beneath, dropping them, but not before one of them clipped him. The force of the blow spun him to the ground, smashing his head into a nearby desk. Silence met him as he collected himself and moved on. Silence reigned inside, even the chaos outside was barely a whisper inside the reinforced building. The armored hangar he had breached was set aside for special purpose craft, like those belonging to Imperial Agents...

Yasbir coldly doubletapped a cowering technician who thought he was hidden behind another desk off to his left and moved inside the main hangar.

Ahead of him was his prize.

The sleek black ray-shaped silhouette of Agent Lin's prototype craft waited, outlined in his lens as a priority target in the otherwise empty hangar. Its stealth drives—new, state-of-the-art, and undetectable—started up as he approached, sensing the ident code he had lifted from Agent Lin. Once he was clear of the combat zone, he would need to work quickly to strip every scrap of data from it he could. Of the heavier assault craft brought by Agent Zhang there was no sign. Troublingly, there was only an empty landing pad and a wire frame silhouette where his lens said it should have been.

Next to it, six more Feìquán transport cradles sat empty.

"Unfortunate." Yasbir stood still for only a moment, calculating the possible damage to their plans for but a moment before running toward the angular black aircraft.

34.

They made it into the outskirts of Hansei when it was on them with all the wrath of a tyrant god. The orange painted, blunt-nosed craft looked like a hammerheaded battering ram in the sky as it flew past, cannons blazing. Thruster vents danced in a ballet of defiance, keeping physics at bay for a craft so heavily armored that it never should have flown.

Bianca's lungs burned as she ran along a row of houses while the roof above and road beside her were forcibly unmade with thunderous cannon fire. Fear and the thin green line in her vision pulled her onward, promising salvation. Song had shared the route, in case they got split up, and Bianca was glad for it.

Neko was ahead of her, his armored form smashing through fences and clearing a path. Hiro had vanished from sight, blending into the shadows and moving parallel to them as he had before. Song lithely darted in and out of the shadows far ahead of Bianca. All of them ran for their lives.

Their airborne executioner turned for another pass, and Bianca watched in terror as two large metallic objects detached from its belly and plummeted toward them. As they began to unfold, magnified by her ocular implant, their frames reminded her of the boxy duck-butts Yasbir had taken with him. Raptor-like with two legs and more rounded than the Hassassin machines, these bore weaponry in their ventral arms. Where the others had mounted weaponry on their shoulders, these orange-painted meteors deployed black skeletal wings. Anti-gravity generators pulsed on the outstretched appendages at the last moment, and their drop was arrested much more quickly than a mortal trooper could have survived.

As they slammed into the earth ahead of Neko, who never slowed his headlong charge, they brought strangely shaped weapons to bear. Her geist labeled the Adhesive Launcher Rifles right as they began to spit balls of semi-solid substance from their barrels. Glue struck the wall of the house next to Bianca as she dove for the comparative safety of the home's interior.

* * * * *

Takeshi powered through the adhesive shots, trusting his armored frame to keep his momentum up. He had heard of the new Jīnyáo drop unit but had yet to see one in action. He thought it looked like a robotic chicken. He fired the last of his Chain Rifle's ammunition—a cone of white hot, shredded, twisted bits of metal—at the robots. They lithely dogged with a pulse of their jets and flew in opposite directions, spacing themselves to his right and left. He chose right.

His frenzied charge into the open could have seemed like a desperate gamut, but to Takeshi, it was a calculated risk. His heavy armor could take the punishment that Bianca and Song could not. He locked his rifle to his backplate and drew a single katana—activating its Electromagnetic field—and his Contender. The short-ranged weapon spat hardened teseum-tipped ammunition at the bot, forcing it to dodge aside once again; but Takeshi hit his mark, putting its left thruster out of commission. Stubby arms stowed the Adhesive Launcher, and the machine opted for the more rapid fire Submachine Gun built into its torso.

Takeshi fired again, Contender shots going wide but forcing the Jīnyáo to shift closer. Its SMG blasted full auto, bullets skipping off his armor as he ignored the suppressive fire. With a defiant roar, Takeshi leapt at the machine and sliced down. His masterwork Yoshihara blade sliced cleanly through its frame—E/M discharge frying its circuits.

Takeshi's momentum sent him crashing into the wreckage and tumbling through the front window of a small shop. Abandoned memorabilia and small trinkets rained down on him as he destroyed shelves in his tumble.

* * * * *

Bianca managed to record Takeshi's impressively destructive leap. She allowed herself a private smirk as he tumbled head over heels through a glass wall and into a shop before turning back to her own immediate survival.

She hid in a small kitchen of an abandoned home. Dust coated everything, but the eerie signs of life were all around her. A pot left on the stove in preparation to cook. A doll left on the floor by a playing child. A blanket draped on a couch as if waiting for its owner to return and bundle themselves once again. Hansei was never resettled after the Uprising. It felt like a ghost town. Bianca wondered what had prompted the family to leave.

Her musings were cut short by a thud on the roof overhead. The whir-click of the remaining remote hunting froze her in place.

Equally terrifying was the hand that closed over her mouth as it reached from behind, clamping down like a vice as something hard was pressed aggressively into her kidney. Torn between surprise and terror at both the sudden presence behind her and the rooftop threat, Bianca couldn't move. She swore she was alone mere seconds ago.

"Be very still, Miss Chen." The whisper was neutral, unidentifiable.

Across the living space, the glass doors of a large cabinet showed her the faintest reflection. Her form was easily identifiable in the reflection, but the orange armored body behind her made her knees weak. That brief glimpse was all she got before agony chased over her in the all too familiar sensation of a PARA-baton activating. Paralysing energies coursed through Bianca, overloading her nervous system and overriding any control of her own limbs. She crumpled to the floor; a sack of twitching, useless meat; aware, but powerless. A black bag was pulled over her head, blocking out light and dousing all hope as the room above her threatened to collapse under the weight of an explosion.

* * * * *

Takeshi scrambled to his feet just in time to track a rocket's flight through a jagged break in the wall. The contrail lanced across his view—no lens overlay needed. He didn't need digital confirmation to know Hiro's shot would land. A heartbeat later, the explosion lit up the street beyond, the shockwave thudding through concrete and dust. Shards rattled from the ceiling above him. One more down. Clean.

But the threat wasn't over.

The real problem groaned through the sky a heartbeat later, a thunderous jetwash slamming low across the rooftops. Takeshi ducked instinctively behind the rubble of his entrance, watching the assault shuttle scream overhead. Its thrusters cast shadows like falling towers. It was a monster. Bigger than anything they should've been facing in this kind of op—and it wasn't alone. If it was still in the air, then so were its passengers.

Hiro knew it too. Takeshi spotted his silhouette break off of the street and disappear down an alleyway, moving fast but careful, like he was threading a needle. His thermooptic camo flickered, then failed completely. Takeshi tracked him, watching as Hiro paused to drop a Decoy behind him. Not running from the fight, but baiting the next one.

From Takeshi's distance, he couldn't hear the click of the mines Hiro placed near the decoy, but he didn't need to. The man was setting traps, building layers of misdirection. Takeshi adjusted his grip on the Contender and sheathed his sword, eyes sweeping the area as Hiro crossed open ground and vanished into a squat three-story building—the only one with enough height to matter.

Takeshi toggled his optics to thermal briefly—the building was active, power still flowing.

Stairs. He'd take the stairs. Even if the lift was functional, Hiro wouldn't trust it.

He lost visual contact for a few seconds. Then Hiro pinged the team channel, a quick pulse that swept the net and flagged the assault craft's projected path. The signal was a beacon. Any half-decent pilot would see it—and the shuttle was creeping back toward the source.

Perfect bait.

Song's voice cut through the comms, sharp and taut: "What are you doing?!"

"Kinda busy, sweetheart," Hiro answered, too calm, too casual.

Takeshi didn't need to see his face to know what he looked like. That smirk was probably glued in place, a shell against the tension of combat. Hiro hid behind jokes where Takeshi just buried it deeper.

"Get back here, mission comes first."

"Don't I know it." A door opened on the third floor. Hiro was close.

More comm chatter. Something about firewalls. Takeshi could hear the lie. Something soft to ease Song's fear. Song knew it. Hiro knew it.

That shuttle was a god's hammer, and it was going to crush them unless someone drove a spike into it now.

"Neko, I need a favor," Hiro said.

Takeshi responded instantly. "Go for Neko."

He didn't ask questions. He'd already moved into position when Hiro forwarded the location—an open courtyard near the building Hiro had just climbed.

"Here, in a minute, I'm going to need you to distract that thing, draw it out."

"Understood."

Takeshi muted his own channel and took a slow breath. The assault shuttle was almost within range. No way his weapons would scratch it, but that wasn't the point. He just needed to make it look real.

His position was tight—a half-collapsed stairwell, high enough to give him a lane of fire, but shadowed and cluttered enough to offer cover. He waited.

Hiro's camo pinged once, then went dark. He was on the roof. No more time. "Status?"

"In position." Takeshi's reply was low, controlled.

"On my signal, spray the thing, then bolt southeast from your position."

Takeshi acknowledged with a click. He was already braced, finger resting lightly on the trigger.

"Don't be a hero." Song's voice—softer this time.

There was a pause, and then Hiro's voice came back, half-laughing, distant and warm: "Go."

Takeshi leapt from his hiding spot and darted into the open, Contender in one hand and Chain Rifle in the other, both with fresh magazines loaded. Warnings flashed across his vision telling him in bold red letters that his Chain Rifle had a point zero-zero-three percent chance of achieving partial penetration of the shuttle's armored shell. His Contender, on the other hand, displayed an optimistic fifteen percent chance of a positive penetration. He squeezed both triggers anyway, unleashing a torrent of fire that did nothing more than irritate the beast.

The assault craft swung about, bringing its arsenal to bear, and more critically, swung its primary thruster complex toward the apartment building on the opposite side of the square.

Takeshi ran.

Armor-weighted strides pounded as he bolted, instincts screaming. He didn't need Hiro to shout a warning—he felt it in the shift of air, imagined the faint click of the launcher priming. One more second in the blast radius and he'd be shrapnel.

Behind him, a hollow thump cracked through the air—Hiro's rocket leaving the launcher. A half-second later, the low whine of thrusters igniting roared behind his heels. Takeshi dove forward—shoulder-first through a thin wall—as the world behind him went white.

Heat washed over him—mingled with the dust and masonry—like a tidal wave of fire.

His lens dimmed the flare automatically, but he still saw the bloom of fire and the shriek of twisting metal as the rocket tore through the enemy dropship. Hiro had picked his mark clean—the linkage between fuselage and thruster. Takeshi didn't need to see the telemetry to know the hit was good. The first explosion belched fire and smoke. Then something ruptured, jetting out light and heat in a blinding arc. A heartbeat later, the whole rear engine went critical.

The dropship pitched like a dying animal.

Takeshi rose from the rubble just in time to watch the final explosion flip the craft backward into the side of a building. Debris rained down. The shockwave slammed through the rooftop and knocked him back a step. He turned just in time to see Hiro's silhouette get tossed like a doll from his rooftop perch.

Then nothing.

A moment passed.

"Hiro!" he called out, already sprinting. "Status?"

"Hiro!" Song hinged between anger and fear.

Static.

"Remind me never to do that again," Hiro groaned, voice strained and half-laughing.

Neko rounded the building and there was Hiro—dangling by one hand from the third-story roof, camo field flickering uselessly, eyes wide.

* * * * *

Takeshi searched the ruined house for as long as he dared. The second Jīnyáo's destruction had compromised the structure beyond repair, and all that was left was a pile of rubble and a bit of wall. The Warcor's disappearance was troubling him deeply… but time was not on their side.

"We have to move, Neko." Song's voice was hushed in his ear piece, as if she feared speaking would bring the enemy upon them.

Destroying the shuttle had given them precious breathing room. Time enough to regroup did not mean they had time to waste. Bianca's comlog had gone completely offline at this point. Now there was no trace of her, nothing.

"Where could she have gone?"

"I'm sorry, Neko, we don't have time for this." Hiro started off east at a slow jog.

"He's right, Neko, we have to go." Song's voice carried more empathy than usual.

Focus, Takeshi. One strike at a time.

Takeshi left the small home behind, Bianca's disappearance weighing on him. He could not shake the idea that they were all going to die—just like they always did.

35.

Mizu threw her bike hard over, slamming it onto its side and sliding under a missile blasting through the space she had just occupied. Her lens displayed the flight path and the minuscule difference in timing that would have ended her mission, and her life. Her geist showed itself once again, a cartoonish cat face sticking a tongue out at the rocket. She would have to get that update someday, but not dying took priority. Mizu hit the auto-stabilizer to kick her ride upright once more and she was accelerating once again.

The Rui Shi had not been alone. A pair of smaller Yáokòng remotes had entered the fray moments behind it. Equipped with missile launchers, they immediately became priority targets for the Aragoto as they rapidly criss-crossed the airstrip, setting up their attack run. The remotes were always a possibility, but since they weren't shooting indirect fire, they must not have a forward observer on the field. Thankfully, Mizu could use that to their advantage.

"Goro, left crab is yours. Jon on me, lock the Rui Shi down. Kairi, on the right. Don't bother shooting till you get in range, focus on dodging."

As one, the bikers tucked in close, reducing their signature, and waited for the bots to shoot. Accelerating hard, Mizu exhaled. Ten.

A pair of missiles torched off toward them.

Eight.

Kairi peeled right at the last second as the lead missile passed between her bike and Jon's. She turned tight back toward her target, foot pegs dragging a cascade of sparks behind her. She used the time it took the machine to reset the launcher to line up her shot and unloaded her Spitfire.

Five.

Goro pushed in high, standing on his bike to present a bigger target. He dropped into the saddle and hung off the side of his bike, narrowly missing being speared by the warhead, before pushing his machine to its limits and firing his Boarding Shotgun point blank.

Three.

Mizu unloaded her Combi Rifle in a futile spray, making as much proverbial noise as possible to shield Jon behind her while he worked. Motorcycles so close they could be one machine, they arrowed toward the Rui Shi's flank as it turned toward Goro's maniacal path.

Two.

"Jon!"

"Done!" He shouted back and peeled off.

Directly ahead of her, the orange machine stood, frozen in place, Carbonited by Jon's hacking the second they got in range, with not a millisecond to spare.

One.

Mizu slammed on her brakes and kicked off the bike when her speed dropped to merely dangerous from near-suicidal. Her bike wobbled, riderless, and it careened past the immobilized bot. Mizu landed in a roll, trusting her reflexes to complete the impetuous maneuver. Springing up at the end of her tumble, *Akai Te* in hand, she buried it in the Rui Shi's optics cluster.

Leaping on to the machine's back, to clear its weapon's line of fire, she placed her Boarding Pistol against a weak joint between armor segments and fired the entire magazine into its central processor. A quick backhanded slash removed the antennae of its back. Link severed with the pilot, unable to function independently and immobilized, it was a useless hunk of reinforced alloys and wiring at this point.

"Status?!" Mizu gasped.

"Target down." Kairi whooped, shouting over comms despite the helmets they all wore keeping ambient noise to a whisper. The urge to shout as adrenaline coursed through them was undeniable. "I'm dry!"

"Boom!" Goro's celebration accompanied the munitions stores of his target cooking off.

"Great job, Jon!"

"Thanks, Boss." Jon sounded thin. She would need to check on him again soon.

"On me, everyone." Mizu hadn't felt this alive in years. The rush of violence and speed was a trickle feed of nitro-fuel directly into her soul. The shake stayed quiet, smiling as it gorged itself on the feast of adrenaline. With a flick of the wrist, her ride righted its course and rolled toward her. "Ghost, what's your status?!"

"Departing. You are in the clear, Rider." Yasbir's voice in her ear was far more smooth than his breathless shouts earlier.

"Eye in the sky staying with me?" Bianca's camera drone was still orbiting above her, its small frame was impressively able to keep up as long as she didn't hit her top speeds. From Mizo's perspective, it felt like the drone and their gleaming new bikes belonged to another world entirely, one that had long since raced ahead and left Kuraimori's people stranded in the years after the Uprising.

"Affirmative, Rider. Notice: Six previously unknown flyers unaccounted for."

"Acknowledged. Happy hunting, Ghost." Mizu cut the channel and isolated her comms as she watched the sleek black craft exit the armored hanger's roof. The Sunduqbuts were in a fighting withdrawal toward the central fuel reserve, as planned, and Yasbir was in the clear. It was time to go.

"Form up, Hands!" Mizu grabbed her Combi Rifle from her bike, reloaded it with her last mag, and tossed it at Kairi. "Let's roll!"

She mounted up and saw the Sunduqbuts turn their weapons on the fuel depot. A pair of helpless technicians burst from cover, running away as the machines dumped their ammunition reserves into the volatile storage.

Mizu locked her front brake and gunned the throttle, swinging her rear tire around. Once aligned with the gate they came in, she released the throttle and let the shake choke on the breakneck acceleration as she raced her friends to the exit.

Behind her, fuel cells began to explode.

The dash away from the airstrip was pure adrenaline as Mizu wound through the hills, more at ease than she had been in years. Jon led the way with Goro and Kairi behind Mizu, though all of them could have ridden it blindfolded. These roads were familiar, home. Blasted by Yujingyu artillery fire during the Uprising, there were very few trees left until they reached the mountains. Until then, they were running in the open, exposed.

"Mizu." Jon had opened a private channel. His voice tremored, uncertain.

"Hey." The smile on her face faded. "You okay, Jon?"

"I'm fine. I just…" Jon sighed aloud. "I keep wondering, why are we doing this?"

"What do you mean?" Mizu scanned over at her lifelong friend. His Combi Rifle was visible from her angle. All its magazines were still latched in their places on the fairing. Her lens displayed an ammo count above each one in green—all full. Jon hadn't fired his Combi at all. He carried a shotgun, like she did. Being up close must have bothered him more than she thought.

The road raced by as they wound their way north, toward Hansei. The Hands were running silent, on batteries only, to keep their signatures small. Goro and Kairi wove through the hills—tight behind her—displayed in the corner of her lens with Bianca's drone keeping up behind, slaved to her comlog.

"I just… We had a chance to say no."

"Where is this—"

"We can still leave, Mizu. All of us. We can just fade away."

Mizu took a deep breath as she leaned with her bike, hugging a turn. "We're in this, Jon."

Jon's laugh sounded like a desperate thing dredged up from despair. It tugged at the shake buried deep within her.

"You're scared, aren't you, Jon? *Kuso*, we all are but…"

"Scared? Of course I'm slagg'n scared!" Jon's admission sounded manic. "You leapt right back in, Mizu, no hesitation. You can't resist the rush, *chikusho*! It's a slagg'n addiction for you, and you dragged us all right back in with you. You broke last time, how many years did it take us to get you clean?! How many had to die?!"

The venom in his voice was like a gunshot to the gut. He knew her better than most. Jon knew how to hurt her. The worst part was he was right, he always was. She had dragged her friends into this suicide run without a second thought, ready to jump back into the cause. Was it for *giri*, or for a fix? She couldn't honestly answer that.

"We can't keep saving you from yourself." Jon was soft, broken.

Mizu reeled at how fast he'd turned on her—one moment a comrade in the fire, the next a stranger with a blade pressed to her ribs. The sudden shift left her off balance, unsure if the ground between them had ever been solid at all.

The silence chewed at her gut. Mizu's heart somehow ached and raged simultaneously. Jon's words were smothering her. Like a grenade in her chest, he tore her apart. Inside, the shake laughed and mocked her pain.

"*Chikusho!* I'm tagged!" Jon shouted on open comms as his location lit up like fireworks and his presence was broadcast across the net. "No, no, no… not now! Slagg me, incoming!" Jon gunned his ride as their sensors lit up. Fast movers were bearing down on them.

"Slagg me!" Mizu echoed as three fully operational Feìquán jet bikes rose over a hill to their right on an intercept course. Mizu scanned their surroundings but couldn't find the hacker that had painted Jon.

"Left!" Concern laced Kairi's voice as she pointed at three more jetbikes rapidly closing in the distance while leaning low on her ride.

"Slagg it, on me." Voice cold and steeled, Jon kicked his motor on and took the lead. His bike roared as he pulled further ahead of the team as they twisted through the hills.

In a straight line, Mizu was certain they would outpace the Yujingyu. Since the Hands were forced to maneuver along the surface, they handed the advantage right back to their pursuers, who could fly straight at them. Mizu slashed a quick 'follow' with her left hand. She flipped her motor over and let it roar as she tucked in behind Jon, Goro and Kairi hot on their tails. She hoped their greater maneuverability would see them through.

Jon led them at suicidal speeds down the winding highway as the Feìquán caught them. Small arms fire lit up the road around them, E/M Carbines trying to disable the nimbler Aragoto bikes. By luck alone, the Hands wove their way toward the mountains.

Without warning them, Jon leaned hard right, turning off onto a smaller arterial path with no sign. Mizu pulsed her ride's scanners ahead, quickly spotting the genius of Jon's plan.

"Thunder Run!" The shake roared inside her. Mizu clung to her bike for dear life as the shake drove her onward.

Jon blasted through a flimsy barricade warning motorists to stay out of the mining area, spraying shattered plastic shards in the air. The lead Feìquán was tucked low, too low, and ate the spray of shrapnel at high speeds. Instinct took over as the pilot jinked to dodge the detritus, only to slam into a light pole, shearing a stabilizer off. The unrecoverable jetbike flipped end over end, tossing its rider before landing on them in a fireball.

"Slagg!" Urgency laced Jon's voice.

The five remaining Feìquán didn't hesitate and stayed behind their prey.

"*Kuso*, they're going to follow!" Goro warned them all, sliding into the rearmost slot, protective of Kairi as the jetbikes kept up a steady rate of fire.

Mizu followed Jon, screaming past long abandoned excavating equipment, ducking under a conveyor belt and throttling toward the mine entrance in silence. The ground blurred past as the gang poured into the tunnel at over one hundred kph.

Mizu's lens amplified the darkness as her bike looked ahead, sharpening and outlining the walls or any obstacles. Her bike mapped the tunnels in an instant, plotting the 'safest' route out. Luckily, it happened to be straight into Hansei. Mizu thought they just might make their rendezvous, with a bit of luck.

The first Yujingyu pilot miscalculated and slammed into the entrance wall, a cloud of dust and fire rising from his impact. Mizu still saw four on her scanners, suicidally following them. Bianca's drone fell behind, not maneuverable enough to take the tunnels at high speeds.

Her conversation with Jon had rattled the shake loose from its cage, and so she did the only thing she could do. Mizu fed the addiction. Grin splitting her face, she ignored the warnings flashing in her helmet and throttled past Jon. He waved at her, letting off the throttle, yelling something she didn't hear. She didn't care. Speed was her fuel, her salvation. The white knuckle grasp on life while death chomped on her heels.

"Stop!" Jon called. "No!"

Goro and Kairi shot past Jon as well, following her lead. Warnings flashed across her vision as the motorcycle's sensors screamed at the danger ahead, but the shake had the throttle now. She was just a passenger, laughing in her helmet. Mizu tore around the bend, wheels inching up the sidewall of the tunnel as momentum gave her wings. Beyond the reach of her headlight, the tunnel changed. Her lens outlined abandoned mining equipment in the dark and trucks that should not have been there.

Lines of bright green light sprung into existence just ahead of her. Warnings continued to flash across her vision, but Mizu was gone and the shake didn't bother to read.

Mizu clocked her speed hovering just below one hundred and twenty kph—just before everything came to a halting stop. An electromagnetic grid. Time slowed, but she still wasn't able to curse. Her motorcycle died in an instant. Its autostabilizing functions had kept her ballistic run survivable, and without them, her Tsurugi–II was just a two hundred kilogram weight with wheels that was off balance and out of control.

The E/M current coursed through Mizu's body, riding her nerves like she rode the curves of the mountains. Unable to control her own limbs, she spasmed, sending the bike's wobble into a tumble, and Mizu was launched from her ride. She hit the cavern wall, bouncing off like a pebble as her bike flipped behind her, tumbling end over end. Deep in her mind, she felt the bones break.

"No! Mizu—" Jon's panic cut off as her comms died.

Time resumed its normal march. Her bike, a blur, spun. Crash—a Yujingu truck, then an explosion—a blinding blue fireball.

Another crash. Her body this time. She didn't feel her limbs. She saw them, flailing like a ragdoll. She was powerless.

More crashing—had to be Goro and Kairi—followed by the gut-wrenching scream of twisting metal.

Another snap. Her leg. She felt that. She was too numb to scream. A ledge raced toward her, backlit by another explosion.

The darkness beyond swallowed her.

36.

"*Kuso.*"

Takeshi caught the concern lacing Song's voice. She had stopped ahead of him long enough for him to catch up to where she crouched in the shadows. She spun a quantronic dial before her with urgency. Takeshi knelt, guarding the way they had come with his Chain Rifle. A Chain Rifle that he was preciously low on ammunition for.

"The Aragoto have gone dark. I've still got a ping from Bianca's drone though."

Takeshi looked at her, frowning beneath his helmet. "How close are we?"

"No, we can't. The mission comes first. I've just sent them all the help I can." Song's brow furrowed as her head shook in frustration. She called Hiro. "Find the entrance?"

"Sure did. Marking it now."

Takeshi received the marker across their shared tactical link, and his geist loaded it in his vision. They were close.

Song's statement didn't shock him. Their mission was critical. The StateEmpire could not get their hands on the vault—he'd seen the files—it was simply not an option. Japan's heart and soul would crumble if they failed.

Takeshi had seen so many comrades die in battle that he had stopped counting. Somehow he kept coming out alive despite impossible odds each time. He thought about them all. The younger ones who were escaping even now and those in harm's way. They were a strong group, stronger than he had given them credit for. Most of all, he thought about Mizu. Her fire and determination had seen him through to be where he is now. Even when he was helpless.

Takeshi pulled out a detox dose from his pouches and dosed himself—utilizing an external med-port in his armor. If they had fit, he would have loaded the doses into his onboard medsuite. He could see Mizu's smile, talking to him like a child. In many ways, he was a child in her world, and she in his.

"Ready to move?" Song interrupted his reverie.

"Affirmative." Mourning the dead would have to wait. Takeshi glanced at Song and wondered if she was next.

* * * * *

They stalked the tunnels in silence, respecting the catacombs for what they were. Long dead magnetic rail lines stretched in both directions like guideposts in the distance. There was very little dust or detritus accumulated in the shaft, and Takeshi felt like he was robbing a tomb. Granted, it was a tomb an assault shuttle could fly through it. Power still coursed through the network, leaving it partially illuminated but with no holographic signposts or guides to follow beyond the markers the team made for themselves.

They came upon a forgotten rail car. Hiro beckoned Takeshi forward. "What do you make of this?"

The car was settled on its parking skids and unpowered. Outfitted for both passengers and cargo, the interior was dark and empty, save for the bodies. Six of them, laid out and stripped bare. Pieces of orange armor plates were tossed in the corner, many of which were sliced clean through as if carved away.

As Hiro climbed on top of the car to keep an eye out, Takeshi and Song inspected the bodies. All were missing their heads, feet, and hands. Most disturbing of all was the peeled back skin on their necks. In the exposed meat sat their Cube docks—tiny wired circuits with a socket no larger than his fingernail. Theirs sat empty, taken.

Someone had taken the time to carve away the heads, hands, and feet of the deceased and taken their Cubes. It felt like some ancient curse designed to punish them in the afterlife.

Takeshi shuddered, suppressing a gag. This was not the treatment of an honorable foe, by an honorable adversary. It smacked of ritual… of punishment. He recognized the small autumn bellflower tattooed on each body in different places.

"Koga." Takeshi recognized the clean cut on a scrap of armor Song was inspecting. His voice was tense and guarded. "Are there other assets in the field?"

Song dropped the scrap of armor and locked eyes with Takeshi, deadpan and emotionless. "*Hai.*"

A cascade of conflicting emotions wretched through his mind: trust and honor warred with secrets and operational security. Just when he was beginning to feel at ease with his comrades and his role in this mission, it all came crashing back like a wave of unease. Takeshi said nothing and turned away, leaving Song with the tortured souls of the dead.

They continued in silence. Following the tunnels with Song at the lead, Takeshi fell in behind her, keeping a distrustful eye on her. Hiro roamed behind them now, guarding the rear. Takeshi couldn't shake the feeling that *he* was being watched.

* * * * *

Their stealthy advance paid off when Song called a halt and snuck ahead. She shared her vision across their link. In one eye, Takeshi saw the corridor beside him, while in the other he saw a battlefield. Scattered and destroyed combat remotes lined a series of deployable barricades. The older Yujingyu remotes were painted in the white and red of JSA and bore familiar heraldry. Takeshi held his breath as he watched on in silence.

Song's perspective panned over a squad of soldiers armored in the same make he wore. Warriors of the Domaru Butai. Their white and red armor could have placed them anywhere within the wider JSA military, but the unit markings were unmistakable.

"I'm coming up." His tone left no room to discuss.

Song said nothing but clicked her comm twice to acknowledge him.

Takeshi entered the tunnel junction slowly, inspecting each of the deceased warriors as he did. Their bodies were decayed and unidentifiable, but the armor had withstood the years just as it was designed to do. Etched in a navy blue, along the left pauldron and right breast of each suit, was the mark of the elite First Defense Corps. Each soldier's personal heraldry was etched upon their plate, a calling card, unique and instantly recognizable. Takeshi knew these men.

All those years of disciplined composure came crumbling down in an instant. Things left unsaid wracked through his soul as he frantically searched the dead for him.

Takeshi felt as if his heart stopped. He couldn't breathe.

The First was the home guard of Kuraimori, close to the Emperor while not being of his house. They shouldn't have been here. They died, to a man, in Kume.

He tore his helmet off, eyes wide, gasping.

Song watched him in silence.

"You knew!" The accusation echoed through the tunnel. The rage burned inside.

Song stood her ground in the face of his fury. "Yes, and you were briefed." She paused. "We are not your enemy, Takeshi-san."

"You did not tell me what unit it was." His hands shook.

He had always prided himself on control. Ice cold discipline was a hallmark of the *bushi* life. To Takeshi, it was everything. The urge to strike her down was unbearable. He was breaking and he knew it: Bianca, Mizu and her friends, all his comrades… his father.

His hand tightened on the grip of his sheathed blade.

The world shattered around Takeshi. It took him far too long to realize it was not a metaphor as automatic fire tore the junction apart. Caught in a crossfire and assaulted from multiple directions, Takeshi stood in a maelstrom of death. Beside him, Song shouted as she drew her Submachine Gun and fought. It was a strange detached sensation when he heard nothing of what she said. A rocket streamed past their position as Hiro joined the fray. The heat of the explosion blossomed beside him.

Time stopped.

Takeshi turned and stepped forward as a round grazed his cheek, seeing the pack of madmen charging him with desperation in their eyes. He met the Kuang Shi with blade in hand. The blade was the only constant he knew, the only certainty in life.

One fight at a time. Focus. One cut.

The *Kensei's* words came like a detached memory as he met the suicide troops.

One cut. A head flew away as the body stumbled past him, bomb pack detonating behind him.

One cut. The man lost both of arms as the E/M charge of his blade shorted out a detonator.

One cut. Chain Rifle fire skipped off his chest, cutting his face as another Kuang Shi died. He kicked the body away before the bomb strapped to its neck blew.

Time finally caught up to Takeshi as he slammed into the suicide troopers' handler sword first—a Celestial Guard who he tossed over his shoulder. The Yujingyu was dead before he hit the ground. No longer moving out of pace with time, Takeshi joined the fray.

Their small team was cornered. Orange-clad troopers closed in around them as Takeshi drew his Contender and fell back toward the wall. The fight was collapsing around them.

A sudden pain lanced through his side. A round caught him—deep enough to slow him, not deep enough to stop him. Not yet. Blood warmed the inside of his armor and made each breath feel like chewing glass. His armor raced to mend his injured form, flooding his body with Serum and nanites.

Song was ahead, reloading with the precision of habit. Behind her lay the dead—fallen Domaru sprawled across the floor like broken flags. She ducked behind the barricade again, eyes flicking toward the blank wall. He knew the order she'd been given. They all did.

If they couldn't hold the vault… He didn't want to think it.

Movement in his peripheral vision—not an enemy. A flicker—an origami sparrow drifting just above Song's head, just where Neko would see it too. Digital. Camouflaged to his lens signature. She didn't think he could see it. She was wrong.

Neko said nothing.

She muttered something under her breath. He didn't catch the words, didn't need to. She spun up her comlog, fingers flicking through familiar routines. Then a spike in his lens—subtle, but there. A thread of system interference. Song was reaching into his suit.

She was using a backdoor. Why didn't she just tell him?

He felt the link as it snapped into place. Not a request. A command. His biomonitor synced to her system—heart rate, vitals, access. He didn't react, continuing to fire at the advancing Yu Jing. Did she think he didn't notice?

A guard broke cover ahead—clean line of fire. Song dropped him in one smooth burst. They were pushing too hard, too fast. Fanatics or fools. Either way, it was working.

A rocket streaked Takeshi's head, detonating amongst their attackers. Hiro slid in beside her—low and fast—dropping his launcher. "I'm out!"

Song tossed him her SMG without a word. He rose to a knee and opened fire, giving Takeshi the cover he needed. Even with it, his legs felt too slow, his armor too heavy. The weight of the wound was slowly outpacing his armor's ability to keep up. A smear of blood trailed behind him as he moved.

"Neko! Get down!"

He adjusted course, slid behind a stack of crates just before the next burst chewed through the space he'd been in.

Safe. For now.

Song's attention flicked back to her comlog. Neko could feel the systems inside his suit respond—something deeper than telemetry. She triggered some hidden protocol. One she must have planted before he ever stepped into the armor.

Data streamed from his suit—his genetic code, encoded, and sent forward. In his lens, he saw it cascade: a double helix rendered in energy, fractals of light trailing to the sealed wall. It responded. The outer casing cracked with a sound like splitting stone.

///Vault access confirmed.///

The wall behind them began to peel away. Plate by plate, the metal wall of the tunnel junction pulled in on itself, retracting to reveal a door. Baffle plates ringed the circular door, masking its presence from his lens even as he watched it open. A thin, horizontal line marked the seal. Smooth armored alloy plates chipped and dinged as they blocked the torrent of small arms fire that was getting louder.

There had been nothing there. Moments before, they were fighting a desperate last stand against a featureless tunnel, but now... His side ached. Even small arms fire got lucky, he thought as he assessed the damage. He was bleeding between the plates. His onboard biomonitoring systems were going haywire, so he had no idea how bad it was.

He glanced around the cover he crouched behind long enough to see they were surrounded before ducking back to avoid his unarmored head from being pulped by incoming fire, grimacing in pain. Orange armored warriors had them boxed in. His helmet lay discarded meters away—in the open—next to his discarded Chain Rifle. His Contender was low on ammo, and Takeshi was lucky to have not been hit more seriously yet.

"The door!" Song drew his attention back behind him. The seal was moving. It had rotated ninety degrees and was sliding open, behind it a featureless antechamber waited with a second seal beyond.

Hiro met Song's glance then looked at Takeshi with a nod—he looked like he was ready to die. They moved. He primed a mine and slapped it against the barricade they'd just left. Good angle. Good coverage. Friend-or-foe filters calibrated.

Hiro drew a D-Charge next and gave Song a look Takeshi didn't need translated.

"Prep it," Song said. Her voice was iron now. "Just in case."

Then to him: "Neko, vault!"

Hiro was already moving.

Song drew her sidearm and fired at a charging Yujingyu. The high-tech Breaker Pistol overloaded the power armor's circuits and immobilized the soldier while killing him: frozen in place as a statue of a vainglorious end.

"Go!"

Takeshi stood; he felt something snag, but he didn't have time to consider what it was as he sprayed his Contender indiscriminately. The Yujingyu had pulled back and were beyond the reach of his blades, so he sheathed it and brought an armored gauntlet up to cover his face.

He moved quickly, boldly shielding Song and Hiro as they darted to the vault's entrance.

A stillness came over the scene. Behind him, the Yujingyu had stopped firing as they reached the entrance. Takeshi stood in the open, exposed in the entrance as Song and Hiro hugged the thin scraps of cover on either side of the door. A second, identical seal waited a scant few meters away.

"Oyama!" The shout echoed through the chamber, amplified by the speaker's helmet.

Takeshi turned, following his geist's clues to the now outlined soldier. Clad in a newer design of armor he did not recognize, the shouting warrior had black smartcloth streamers coming from his orange plate. The unmistakable seal of a Crane-ranked Imperial Agent was clearly feasible, spun in silver-white. His helmet was pristine orange, save for a silver line slashed diagonally from chin to left ear.

"Oyama! Face me!" The agent strode forward confidently, his power armored form exuding authority. Behind him, a squad of Wú Míng advanced, weapons at the ready. Two bore heavy machine guns in their arms.

Reinforcements arrived—too many, too fast. Not a counterpush. Not a bluff. This was the endgame.

He didn't need to check the feeds to know what it meant.

Beside him, Hiro wore that reckless grin—the one he always flashed right before doing something heroic and stupid. Song noticed too. Her eyes flicked his way, sharp as ever.

"Don't even think about it," she snapped.

Neko didn't move. He didn't need to. His stance said everything.

She turned to him next. "Neko." His name came out low, edged with warning.

He met her gaze but didn't argue. A flick of her hand summoned the command glyph into the air. Song tapped it without a word—eyes on Takeshi. The vault shuddered to life.

Takeshi watched the warrior as he advanced with lethal grace. He shifted a foot back and placed a hand on his blade. The challenge was clear, and he would not be found wanting. Even in the era of galactic struggles and alien races, there was a certain honor amongst warriors.

Takeshi stood just inside the threshold and waited. He had seen too many desperate last stands over the years. Perhaps this would be his last.

What song will you sing at the end?

Nakama's words echoed through his mind as he waited. The Yujingyu warrior advanced, drawing his dueling blade, challenging.

"Neko!"

He heard Song shout in a distant corner of his brain. The door began to move in front of him as the vault began to close them in.

Takeshi made up his mind. He always knew this was how he would die.

His geist screamed in alarm before he took a single step forward, and warnings flashed across his vision as it was overwhelmed. A hacking program attack pierced his armor with ease, as if his defenses weren't even there, and his bulky frame locked up, frozen in place. Eyes wide, Takeshi struggled to move in vain.

"No!" The Imperial Agent roared in defiance at the twist of fate as the doors crept closer. He would never close the distance in time.

Takeshi watched, frozen and exposed, as the Yujingyu warrior sheathed his blade in a single—a practiced motion—and tore a Heavy Machine Gun from the grips of one of his warriors.

A breeze rippled past him—too big to be a bullet. The angle was wrong.

"No!" The Imperial Agent's repeated roar was drowned out as the weapon began to spit hate down the tunnel.

Takeshi stood, unable to move as the vault slowly sealed him in. Like a tide of horrific, stinging insects, bullets swarmed him through the gap. In a detached place, he noted how they pierced the reinforced layers of his armor with ease. Less than a meter of space remained open as the HMG cycled up to its maximum rate of fire and the spray of rounds tore at him, only a few found their mark—it would be enough.

System warnings overwhelmed his vision as the pain finally caught up to his armor's attempts to suppress it. Immobile and caught in the open, he was helpless.

He never thought he would die like this… unable to resist.

"Shit!" Song's voice was distant and thin.

The collision came from his right, and he felt the world teeter off balance. He opened his eyes one last time as he toppled like a statue—still frozen. Hiro landed atop him, and somewhere in his fading consciousness, he saw that Hiro was bleeding.

///Life signs: critical. Seek medical attention immediately.///

Takeshi Oyama closed his eyes and waited to die.

* * * * *

"And you are certain of this?"

"Yes, ma'am." Lieutenant Da's voice was unwavering in her ear.

Su-Yeong smiled as she removed her helm. This was a pleasant turn of events indeed.

"Where is he now?" She knew exactly where he was. This valley was hers. Every drone, every hidden camera, every helmet cam, every iota of data in this valley was hers. Even Zhang's forces were not immune to her web. She broke their encryption with ease the day they arrived and burrowed her tendrils deep into their private net.

"In the tunnels beneath the civil services complex," Lieutenant Da reported.

"And his team?"

"Spread out. Some are with him, others have been confirmed in the mine tunnels to the south."

"Your doing?"

"No, ma'am. Agent Zhang took—" Da seemed to search for the right words. He wouldn't want to impugn an Imperial Agent's name—Su-Yeong knew he wanted to.

"I'm waiting."

"Agent Zhang took initiative on the decoy driver lead. He seems to have spun a trap out of it, though I don't know the details, ma'am. He cut me out of the investigation."

The operation in the tunnels was a surprise, but not wholly unmanageable. It would all be dealt with very soon anyway.

"Summon Zhang. Immediately."

"Summon him?" Da's voice was uncertain.

"You heard me, Lieutenant." Su-Yeong cut the line before he could hear her laughter.

37.

Bianca woke up in a cell. It was cold, windowless, and quiet—but not empty. Bianca blinked once, activating her lens overlay. The room lit up in soft monochrome, the outlines of cinderblock walls and old rusted chains resolving with clinical precision. No sound. No guards. Just her breathing and the soft pulse of her vitals in the corner of her lens.

She scanned the space, already cataloging possible weapons—loose bolt, wall anchor, maybe a pipe fragment half-buried in grime—when the figure caught her attention.

He was crumpled in the middle of the floor, unmoving. Heat signature barely there. Human, but barely. Blood soaked through his shirt and dried in a pool beneath him, dark and sticky against the concrete. His limbs were twisted in angles that made her stomach clench. One eye swollen shut. The other was missing entirely.

She didn't scream, but her breath caught.

He breathed.

She startled so badly, she nearly tripped over him.

"Oh my God, you're alive?!" she breathed, dropping to her hands and knees. The man was a ruin. Blood crusted his face, and one of his eyes—gouged clean out—left a hollow that made her stomach lurch. His limbs were bent wrong. Hands and feet swollen, purpling.

And still… he moved. The sheer will—and fortitude—astonished Bianca.

Bianca's hands hovered over him, unsure where to touch without hurting him more. His one eye fluttered open, clouded with pain but trying to focus. When he saw her, something like recognition softened his broken face.

"...Chen," he rasped.

"You… you know me?" Her voice cracked. "Never mind, just call me Bianca. Better yet, don't speak." She glanced around the cell, as if help might be hiding in the cracks, knowing full well there was nothing.

"How long?" His voice was barely a breath.

"I just woke up. I've only been here a few hours." She still had no clue why her captors hadn't taken her comlog. "No idea how long you've been lying here like this." Her gaze ran over his body again, more clinical this time. Her lens didn't tell her anything she couldn't tell on her own. "It doesn't look like it was pleasant."

"Wasn't." He winced as he tried to sit up.

"Don't—wait, here." She moved to his side, careful not to jostle his limbs, and eased him upright against the wall. He sagged there, breathing shallow.

"Who are you?" she asked.

"Taka."

The name hit her like a slap. "Wait. Taka, as in Song and Hiro, Taka?"

He let out a rough, strangled sound that might've been a laugh. "The one and only." A weak smile ghosted his lips.

Bianca sat back on her hip, staring at him. "They said you were alive. I'm going to add *barely* to the description."

"Glad to know I was missed," he coughed, and it turned violent fast—wet and rattling. She moved closer, unsure if she should brace him or back away.

Then he gestured with his chin toward her hip. "What's that?"

She looked down and frowned. A small Yujingyu orange belt pouch. She hadn't noticed it earlier. Her fingers went to it instinctively.

"I… I don't know. It's not mine." She looked back at him.

Taka grinned, and she recoiled a little. There was something feral in that grin—broken teeth, swollen jaw. "Open it," he said, turning his head toward the wall. Then he shouted, or tried to—his voice barely carried. "Hey, Hasib!"

Bianca stiffened.

A voice, muffled but unmistakably human, called back from beyond the wall. "You're alive!"

The sound cracked something open in her chest. Bianca nearly cried.

Taka laughed again, weak and raw. "We are getting out of here."

* * * * *

Imperial Agent Zhang Bo, Crane Rank, stormed into Su-Yeong's study, raging before he entered the room.

"I am not some worthless cur to be summoned by the likes of you!"

"And yet, you came." Su-Yeong smiled from where she sat. She knew she was poking the beast, a very deadly beast. She too was dangerous, but that meant little in Zhang's mind, she suspected. He had no idea what she was truly capable of.

Zhang was fully armed and armored, carrying an ivory Domaru helmet like a prize in his right hand—while his own helm was mag-locked to his side—and gripping the dueling blade at his hip with the other. His whole body exuded threat. Cold hard fury sat heavily on his features.

"What did you just say to me?!"

"You heard me, Zhang. I know exactly who you are." Su-Yeong rose from her armchair and walked to the window. She kept her voice light, reading from a quantronic window hung in her vision. "Agent Zhang Bo. Served with excellence in the Invincible Army, fifty-fifth regiment, for four years until you were inextricably transferred to the Imperial Service Academy. A sudden and unlikely advancement had it not been for the bribes your family paid to have you transferred into a position of power… closer to home. Still, you rose to the prestigious Crane Rank in no time at all. You are an incredible swordsman, skilled… no, gifted… in a dozen fighting styles, you are a decent shot, thought nothing to brag about…" She let that last bit hang mockingly.

Looking out the window, Su-Yeong relished her commanding view of the valley. It was coming to an end, all things did eventually. She saw him in the reflection, fuming.

"... and lastly, you are currently on extended leave, pending a full evaluation from Control."

Zhang's eyes roared defiantly, but he wisely kept his mouth shut.

"It would seem your superiors believe your near-death experience on Earth, at the hands of Takeshi Oyama, left quite an impression on you." She turned to face him, menace and threat clear. "Did I miss anything?"

He was shaking. Su-Yeong had Da station a squad of her guard outside the room, only a closed door and a hint of threat from Zhang separated her from them.

She waited. He looked as if he would crush something in a rage or draw his blade to strike her down. He looked as if either would suit him just fine.

He could try anyway. She'd preloaded a Carbonite program, just in case. Su-Yeong didn't need to kill him, not yet anyway. He might still be useful.

"Oh, dear me, I did forget something..." She mocked him now, openly. "It seems there has been an inaccurate report as to the distribution of your equipment. I'm sure Control would be quite upset to learn of the resources you have squandered in an unauthorized crusade."

Zhang cried out in anger, gripping the stolen helmet in both hands and crushing it between two armored gauntlets. He petulantly hurled it across the room where it crashed through the side door, revealing Lieutenant Da and his men—weapons raised.

"Are you done?" Su-Yeong waited for the warrior to calm himself. The reality of his situation settled onto Zhang's face. His jaw worked in silence, eyes wide, manic.

"Why, Zhang?" She genuinely did want to know. Several minutes passed. "Why?"

Through gritted teeth, Zhang finally gave an answer. "I have never lost a duel."

"Until now."

"I have still not lost." Defiance lit his eyes.

"I see." Su-Yeong softened her features. "And you wish for a resolution."

"Correct."

"And you are willing to risk everything, even bringing disgrace upon your family, to do so."

"My actions are my own."

"How naive." She returned to her chair, crossing her legs casually while he stood rigid and on guard. "But forgivable. Possibly."

Su-Yeong watched it happen. The slow dawn of realization. He was in her web now, and he knew it.

38.

Row upon row of bushi *stood in perfect formation. Years of rigorous training had brought them to this singularly pivotal moment in their lives, and not one would be found wanting. Takeshi Oyama stood amongst the front row—honored for his achievement. His silken haori, embroidered with the Oyama family crest, was proudly displayed over the bone white armor of the Domaru Butai.*

Six hundred students began alongside Takeshi, but now only two hundred and seventeen remained. Some were held back, continuing their training to achieve passable marks, while five of his contemporaries were pulled from the training grounds mysteriously, whispers of the Shikami program following in their wakes. One hundred and eight had been dismissed, leaving forever shamed.

Excelling in every task, two intense years had crawled by at the time, but now felt like a blink of an eye. He stood front and center as the top of his class and therefore closer to the Emperor.

He beamed with pride as he spotted Kensei *Hayachi, who had awarded him an honor chord to wear across his chest. The golden braid was the* Kensei's *personal seal of excellence, and he had awarded it only one other time in his life.*

Takeshi could see the Emperor upon the dais, elevated above the gathered soldiers and their families. He looked resplendent in a golden kimono, shining in the high sun. Cherry blossoms blew in Kuraimori's spring air. One by one, his classmates were called forward. Each deeply bowed to the Emperor and knelt in the training sands before Him.

'Uncle' Daichi stood amongst his fellow Hatamoto, armed and armored as always, but no less formal. A golden cord was visibly strung across his white armor as he scanned the crowd, eyes ever vigilant as he protected the Emperor of Japan. Takeshi locked eyes with the honored general and saw him smile with pride. It was everything Takeshi had worked for, had dreamed of: this moment.

He scanned the stands, spotting his mother dressed in newer fashion, but no less elegant for it. Beside her an empty seat... His heart ached.

"Takeshi Oyama."

"Neko."

His name was read from the roll, and Takeshi marched forward...

... into the explosion as artillery fire rained down around him. The jungle canopy shredded and burned as the JSA fireteam held their ground. Yet another frenzied push came from the red-skinned alien Morats.

"Ready!" Takeshi rallied his comrades, and steeled himself for battle. "With me!"

He surged out of the markshift trench as his comrades followed him. Sword held high, he met the first warrior with a downward stroke. The Dāturazi lunged at him with its alien sword. The rectangular blade darted forward, spearing toward his midsection...

...Uncle Daichi's thrust preceded a rain of strikes. Takeshi backpedaled in the sands, stepping over the ring that marked the edge of the training pit. He tripped over the stone lip and stumbled backward, landing unceremoniously on his backside.

"Ow!"

Daichi laughed softly and offered him a hand. "Rise, Takeshi-san. We all get beaten from time to time. Sometimes getting back up and doing it again is all we can do."

Takeshi accepted the hand, rising and brushing himself off.

"Let's take a break, I think your father is leaving."

Takshi bowed to his uncle and quickly made his way inside to say goodbye to his father. He raced to the garage, only to see tail lights. Takeshi was crushed. His mood tumbled into despair.

"Why?"

Disappointed, he returned to the sparring ring...

"NEKO!"

... and sliced the antipode's head off. The wolf-like creatures were ever a problem on Dawn, and today was no different. The head rolled across the forest road as its packmates closed in...

... and smiled. Takeshi did not see his father smile often. Sitting here, in the family garden, he looked up at his father. Kōichi Oyama looked like a giant to Takeshi's ten-year-old eyes. His father was regal, every bit the noble warrior: grizzled, stern, wise... haunted.

Takeshi promised himself he would make his father proud.

"NEKO!"

* * * * *

Takeshi screamed as he was torn raging into consciousness by the crushing, burning pain in his chest as it knit itself back together. The oh, so familiar sensation of Silk-laden nanites screaming through his system was oddly as grounding as it was painful. His breath was ragged, and sweat poured down his face. His arms and legs were heavy, his body weighed down by deactivated armor as he tried to scramble to his feet.

"Stop! Stop! *Chikuso*, hold still." Song sat atop his trembling frame, bodily holding him in place. A feat she could not have accomplished had his armor been active. "Neko! Takeshi!"

His name had a grounding effect, opening his mind to the here and now, holding back the dark recesses of unresolved nightmares. His body rebelled, shaking inside his armor, and he started to vomit. Song rolled him on his side to keep him from choking.

"That's better. Easy." Song spoke in soothing tones, something he never would have expected from her.

"Hey," Hiro's voice was soft, painful and distant. "We almost lost you there."

Takeshi heard Hiro force a laugh that quickly devolved into a wet cough. He joined the chorus, coughing up bile before nodding his gratitude as Song wiped his face.

"Not today it would seem." His voice was unsteady and hoarse.

He found himself in a strange room. Takeshi had been dragged into the chamber, if the smears of blood stretching from his position to the entrance were any indication. The closed, and hopefully sealed, round door was identical to the one they had entered. Sensor baffles lined the stone walls as the chamber stretched on. Close at hand, automated turrets pointed toward the entrance, powered down—though not from lack of power, as row upon row of databanks sat further in the hidden chamber. Additional portals were visible, sealed in the distance. Dim overhead lights illuminated the chamber.

"Another life down, yeah, Neko? You weren't quite flatlined, but don't do that again." Song stood, pausing to look back at him. "Consider that an order."

"Understood." Takeshi reactivated his armored tech-suit, which booted his armor piece by piece. Systems came back online, displaying the damage in his lens and showing Takeshi just how far he had gone toward the edge of death… Powered, his armor once again was a second skin, bolstering his strength. He still shook in his armored shell. Nausea fought for control of his stomach.

He sat up under his own power and saw Hiro. The wily operator sat against one of the turrets, in a small pool of crimson, clutching his abdomen. He shot a pained smirk at Takeshi. "It's not as bad as it looks."

"It looks…" Takeshi could not find the words.

"Eyes front, Neko. Mission first."

Nodding was the only reply he could bring himself to give.

"I've stabilized him—I think. Neither of us are doctors, but we are used to patching each other up in bad spots. I found a medikit," Song gestured to a long dead body, one of several, at the edge of his vision, "but he only had the basics."

"I'm good to go—wounds are all closed. Just give me a few." Hiro forced a smile. "You two go on ahead. I'll cover the door."

Takeshi weakly rose to his hands and knees, armor doing most of the work. He coughed up blood. The now familiar sense of Bite withdrawal ate at his mind, and he reached for the pouch containing his detox.

It was torn and loosely hanging from his belt.

Panic threatened to overwhelm him as he rose upright and looked about, searching. Hiro and Song both saw his face.

"We know. Lost them in the fight." Song offered a soft smile, more caring and tender than her usual razor sharp demeanor. She activated a dial at her wrist, bringing a window up in Takeshi's vision.

He saw himself, crouching for cover during the fight. He watched in silence as the pouch caught and tore as he rushed toward his comrades and the opening vault. He dismissed the window.

"Well, we know where they are, so that is something." Hiro's voice was pained.

"Understood." It was all he could bring himself to say.

"Let's look around." Song offered Takeshi a hand.

Takeshi took the offered aid and grunted as he rose to his feet. Before he followed Song, Takeshi handed the Contender to Hiro, whose eyebrows shot up as he accepted the weapon. He joined Song, and together they moved further into the vault. Row upon row of quantronic servers and processors stood in silence, faint lights blinking along them. A thin trail of discoloration led further ahead on the smooth metal floor. His lens analyzed the trail and identified it as blood, evaporated long ago, but the discoloration remained.

As they walked past, Song shared the information coming into her comlog with his: armor patterns, weapons schematics, experimental remotes and TAG designs, and so much, much more. "There were a lot of programs that were abandoned during the withdrawal from Kuraimori. *Saisei*, *Ten No Bushi*, *Kakushita Katana,* and Aibōt just to name a few. We will take anything we can retrieve before we wipe it."

They moved past four maintenance racks holding unpainted combat remotes. The only coloration, past their plain grey armored exteriors, was a series of hazard stripes that reminded him of an aerospace shuttle. The strange bots sat with their legs retracted, held aloft by the rack itself. The narrow mast above the sensor cluster and boxy main body gave the machines a look reminiscent of a horned beetle.

Takeshi was baffled by the prototypes and amount of sensitive intelligence left behind. As a child, all of this was under his feet over the years and he never knew, never had an inkling: more secrets.

"You put a back door into my suit's subroutines." Takeshi's voice was flat as the memory came back to him. No accusation in his tone—just fact. "You should not have used it."

She didn't answer right away. "You were injured. We were outnumbered. I needed access—"

"You did not trust me."

"Neko, that's not—"

"You wrote yourself into my armor before I ever put it on." His gaze met hers, unreadable. "You didn't think I would find out?"

Song stepped closer. "It is protocol—operational fail-safes. In case something happened to you—"

"You mean if I disobeyed you."

Silence.

"You should have told me." He leaned against the wall and looked down at his gauntlet, as if it was the same interface she'd hijacked. "I felt it when it activated. You were too busy opening the door to notice I was bleeding out."

"I saved our lives."

"You gambled with mine."

That landed. Her mouth opened, then shut again. The excuses didn't come this time.

"Then you bricked my armor."

Takeshi pushed off the wall, slower than usual. The pain was manageable. The hollow feeling behind his ribs was not.

"Next time," he said without turning, "just tell me I am expendable."

Song didn't follow. Didn't speak.

Takeshi kept walking, the numbness settling in where the anger should have been. A trail of discolored tiles pulled him to a small alcove between two computing stacks.

At the end of the row, a still powered console waited expectantly. His lens magnified the monitor, and he saw that it was waiting for a final command to initiate a *Last Oblivion Protocol*—ominous.

A meter shy of the console, a skeleton wearing white armor and an achingly familiar blue haori lay sprawled, as if crawling to the end of the row, fighting to reach the console. Takeshi stared, breathing heavily and fighting vertigo. Nausea that had been lingering in his gut overwhelmed him once more, but his stomach had nothing left to give as it wretched.

///Kōichi Oyama: Colonel: Executive Officer: First Home Guard.///

Takeshi did not need the name in his lens to know who lay before him. The markings on the pauldron, the battle-worn haori, the empty scabbards… Takeshi braced himself, slowing his collapse only a little. He half fell—leaned against a server row next to his father's final resting place.

"I'll give you a minute." Song left him to his grief.

Takeshi sat and stared at the armored corpse. Time slipped by. The room swam.

He waved his left gauntlet over his father's armor. His geist read his intent and linked with the deceased Domaru's comlog—searching for a *jisei*. Not every warrior had the luxury of time for a death poem, but sometimes—

///I stand in moonlight
Knowing what is left unsaid.
Beneath stars I tread
Dawn will come without sorrow
A Son will rise to meet it.///

Years.

Years of not knowing his father's ultimate fate had festered in the lingering wound of their relationship. His thin emotional scar was torn wide open by the verses. He had hoped in vain that his father would arrive on Earth one day—a part of a prisoner swap or by some heroic escape. All those hopes had held back the pain, the truth—the tears.

Takeshi wept.

He sat there wounded, adrift in the withdrawal haze of an insidious Yujingyu poison, and felt it all: pain, loss, regret, sorrow. His inability to die while all those lives were lost around him, yet he kept on *living*.

The tear in his family was unspoken but ever present. Takeshi prided himself in living up to the mythicized samurai legend. He lived as if he was *bushi* personified, but that did not mean he did not feel.

Beneath his armored shell lay an ocean of feeling. Chest heaving, Takeshi let it go. No more walls kept in the pain. No dam to keep it at bay.

He wept until his tears ran dry.

"Tears are the eyes' way of speaking when the heart is too full for words, Takeshi-sama."

The soft voice startled Takeshi. He turned to the source—drawing his pistol—finding a dark silhouette barely perceptible in the shadows. Three dots of light—optics lenses—began to glow on the shadow's helmet. The figure stepped forward, and Takeshi clumsily rose to a knee, hand moving to his blade.

Takeshi had seen shinobi on the battlefield before, both as allies and adversaries. The largest of the shinobi clans were hushed whispers amongst the elite houses and the military's upper echelons. Most were little better than mercenaries in his eyes, selling their services to the highest bidder, while some served the nation of Japan and its military often and with distinction.

What he was, was not that. Oniwaban were rumors of a myth, long forgotten—the Emperor's personal hand in the shadows.

"Peace, student-of-my-friend. Peace."

He knew that voice. "Nakama?"

"Takeshi-sama."

The Oniwaban's sleek helmet peeled away, articulating piece by piece to some silent command. Nakama's face was sad. He looked from Takeshi to the fallen warrior beside him.

"Nakama? How?" Takeshi slumped back, barely in control of his own body.

"What matters, Takeshi-sama, is that I am here." He crouched down—silent as the night—arm outstretched. In Nakama's black gloved hand were all three of Takeshi's remaining detox injections.

*****

They stood together at the final door, deep in the silent heart of the vault. The corridor behind them was littered with wreckage, corpses, and burnt-out turrets—mute testimony to the gauntlet they'd survived. This door was different. Smooth. Seamless. Ancient in its elegance. It offered nothing and dared everything.

Nakama, his helmet sealed once more, stood with them. The Oniwaban moved like a phantom, and though he said little, his presence loomed. He helped treat their remaining wounds with practiced precision. Takeshi felt his armor's med-suite dulling the ache in his ribs, even as the bruises beneath reminded him had been bleeding somewhere inside.

He stood in silence, fists clenched. His father's haori was bundled and tied at his hip—not as a weapon, but as a vow. No one had commented on it. He didn't expect them to.

"So..." Hiro said, eyeing the door like it might blink. "End of the line?"

Song's smirk was thin and humorless. "Not yet." Her eyes stayed on the seal, calculating. Distant.

There was something different in her tone—uncertain—and Takeshi didn't miss it.

Takeshi stepped forward, watching her face as she studied the door. "This is it, then."

She didn't respond. Her eyes were locked on the seal, but she wasn't seeing it. Not really. The expression she wore wasn't fear or defiance—it was resignation. Something had already been decided. The pieces clicked into place.

"You and Hiro," Takeshi said quietly. "You never planned to walk away, did you?"

Her jaw tensed, just a fraction. Still, she didn't look at him. "Some missions don't come with round trip tickets."

"Hiro knows?"

She exhaled through her nose. "Of course he does."

He took a step closer, but not too close. "You can still change that."

Finally, she turned to look at him. There was no fire in her eyes—just a strange calm. "You sound so sure."

Takeshi did not know what to say to that. He wanted to argue. To reach for something—duty, hope, even spite—but she wasn't inviting it. Whatever choices they'd made, they'd made them long before this vault.

She looked away again. "Just make it count, Neko. The mission is all that matters now."

"No." He shook his head. "It is not all that matters."

There was a silence—heavy. Not the kind between friends, but the kind that falls before steel is drawn. Song's face hardened once more.

Hiro stepped forward, his voice dry. "Okay, so we're all tired, full of holes, and teetering on a deep psychological cliff. Can we hold off the drama until after we open the death door?"

No one laughed. But the tension cooled just enough to breathe.

Nakama nodded to Hiro and moved forward without a word, raising his gloved hand to the door. The sigil of the Imperial House shimmered into being, rotating slowly as the vault's ancient mechanisms stirred awake: clicks, whirs, a deep magnetic hum.

Three bright red, layered seals unfurled in the space between Nakama and the wall, then dissolved.

The door slid apart, revealing a small chamber—barely the size of a small closet. Inside, suspended in a gravity field above a pedestal, spun a single object.

A simple disk, unadorned except for the faint, glowing crest of Greater Independent Japan.

It was a hollow frame, inside of which floated a tiny data core—a Cube.

Takeshi stepped forward, breath caught in his throat. He did not know what he expected—but it had not been this. Cold. Small. Fragile.

Nakama knelt, bowing low to the object. When he rose, it was with solemn reverence.

"Is that—" Hiro began.

"*Hai,*" Nakama said. "It is a copy of the Emperor's Cube."

The weight of the words settled over them like ash.

Nakama's hands moved quickly, producing a small device from seemingly nowhere and inserting the Cube. The empty frame dropped with a soft clink onto the pedestal, forgotten. Red lights, a spiral of holographic information, quickly appeared in Takeshi's lens and spiraled down—deleting information.

Takeshi stepped beside him, voice iron. "You are destroying it?"

Nakama nodded. "A fail safe, during the Uprising—one of a few. This was the last."

Takeshi nodded when the device went dark. "It is done then?"

The Oniwaban's masked face turned to Takeshi. "It is done."

39.

Pain. It was all the universe was.

Mizu woke to pain.

Not sharp, but total. Pressure filling every nerve, bone, and breath. For a long moment, she couldn't move. She couldn't even remember how. She was just a shape in the dark, strung together by agony and the rhythm of her pulse hammering in her ears.

Darkness held her like a grave, suffocating and complete.

Her mouth was dry. Every breath scraped down her throat like gravel. Mizu tried to swallow and nearly choked. Her helmet was still on mostly, one side caved inward against her cheekbone, the other shorn away. She tasted blood where her teeth had bitten her tongue.

The dark had weight. She couldn't see her hands. Couldn't tell if her eyes were open.

She blinked, but nothing changed.

Mizu came back piece by piece. A weight behind her eyes. A numbness in her jaw. Cold, sticky wetness down her body. She didn't know if it was blood or just the way the dark clung to everything in here.

She became aware of her leg next. It was twisted at a wrong angle and felt heavy. Every time her heart beat, it sent a spike of nausea twisting up her spine. Her fingers twitched toward it by instinct, but her arm barely responded. Her left shoulder felt loose, dislocated and numb.

The memory came slowly, like it had to crawl the same road her body had.

Green light.

Jon shouting at her.

The hum of E/M fields.

Then.... nothing but velocity, stone, and the sound of her body breaking.

A breath left her lips. Half a laugh that became a whimper.

Mizu wasn't dead—not yet. The pain proved that.

A cracked rib shifted when she tried to roll, and the world spun out from under her. She froze, breathing through her teeth until the dizziness passed.

She noted the familiar weight of her blade was gone.

Mizu groped about and her hand found only gravel. No way to know how far she'd been thrown, how far she had fallen. No way to know if the others made it.

Others. There were others. Kairi and Goro and Jon.

She got her helmet off and pressed her forehead to the cold earth. It was the only thing that didn't hurt.

For now, that was enough. The tremors started in her fingers first: not fear, just effort.

She grit her teeth, locked her jaw against the scream building in her throat, and dragged her right arm forward. Gravel tore at her gloves. Her ribs ground against themselves. Her broken leg screamed behind her with every inch, but Mizu didn't stop. Couldn't.

The bike was gone. So was everything except forward.

One elbow at a time. Forward.

The tunnel sloped up slightly ahead of her, slick with runoff and scattered stone. Every millimeter of progress was paid for with grit and blood and breath she couldn't afford to lose. Her comlog was off, but the shape of the space around her told her she wasn't in a tunnel like the one they had traveled. She was somewhere deeper, maybe a maintenance shaft or side channel. Somewhere with no signposts, no lights.

Just her and the rough drag of her body against stone.

Time thinned, minutes bled into each other, warped by pain and the tunnel's endless dark. She wasn't sure she was moving anymore. Her arms felt like rubber. Her mind slipped sideways into half memories, half hallucination. Henzo's voice came and went. A fragment of a melody she didn't know she remembered. The pressing feeling of a crowded bar. Sharing a drink with a stranger.

Then a breath of air. It was different, cooler.

She froze. There was a breeze. Faint, stale, but moving across her cheek. She wasn't buried, not entirely.

Mizu dug her fingers into the stone and kept crawling. Her pistol was gone. Her scabbard drug behind her by its torn straps, empty.

"Reset." She managed to croak the word. Her booting comlog blinked lines of code in her lens as it came slowly back to life.

Somewhere ahead, a groan answered her. It was a sound she couldn't mistake, a human sound. Weak and ragged, but alive.

Mizu pushed herself forward, every movement a battle. Her arm trembled, her leg screamed, but the sound pulled her on like a lifeline.

Her lens sharpened, focused as her comlog sprang back to life. Her avatar wore a mining helmet and stumbled around.

Then she saw them.

Outlined in her lens, Goro leaned against a jagged wall, pale and sweating, his left arm held tight against his side. Kairi laid close by, eyes closed, breathing shallow but steady. A darker shade of black stained her midsection. They looked like she felt.

She tried to call out. A gasp was all that came out.

"Mizu..." Kairi's voice was a cracked whisper, but it held enough strength to break through the fog drowning her.

She swallowed the surge of relief and pain and forced herself forward, half crawling toward them. Goro's eyes flicked open as she came closer, and a faint, tired smile ghosted across his face.

"We didn't think you'd make it," he said.

"Neither did I," she answered, voice raw.

They settled together, three broken souls pressed against the cold stone, each clutching whatever scraps of strength remained. For a moment, there was no fear. Only the quiet company of survival.

They sat, silence stretching. The darkness between them felt heavy, like it had weight of its own. Goro shifted to brace himself better against the wall, teeth clenched as his ribs protested. Mizu leaned her head back. The rock was cool against her skull.

Kairi was the first to speak, asking the question on everyone's mind. "Where's Jon?"

The question floated there, small and sharp. Mizu didn't answer right away. She replayed it: his hand waving her back, the green light blooming ahead, his voice crackling in her helmet just before the crash. She didn't even hear what he'd said.

"We were alone when his comlog got foxed." Mizu's heart broke at the realization. Minutes passed in silence.

"Did he…" Goro choked, not finishing the thought.

"He led us into that," Kairi said at last. "Peeled off right before the E/M field lit up." Her voice cracked. Her face was unreadable in the dark.

"*Chukuso*." Goro rubbed at the blood crusting his temple, voice small. "Maybe… maybe he didn't see it. Maybe he thought we could push through."

Kairi shook her head, but the words caught in her throat. "Then why peel off? Why lead us in?" She sounded like she was trying to convince herself more than anyone else.

Mizu stared into the darkness, heart twisting. “What—What if he was forced? What if someone got to him first?” Even as she said it, the words felt hollow.

Goro’s voice was desperate. “He wouldn’t just… turn. Not Jon. Right?”

“I—” Kairi choked, unable to finish.

The silence that followed was heavier than any answer. The pain in her heart overtook the agony in Mizu’s battered body. It smothered something deep inside her. “We can’t deal with this now.”

Silence, long and heavy, smothered them. Mizu’s shoulders heaved for tears that would not come.”

Kairi looked toward the tunnel, her voice low and soft. “Are they still out there?”

“I don’t know,” Mizu finally said. “Some chased us in. Then there were the trucks.”

“Trucks…” Goro’s brow furrowed. “Haven’t heard much since we fell.”

They let that hang for a moment. It didn’t feel like safety, just a pause.

“We need to move,” Kairi said eventually, quiet but certain. “We stay still, we die down here.”

“Leg’s broken,” Mizu said. “Goro’s wrecked. You’re bleeding. We’re going nowhere fast.”

“I didn’t say fast,” Kairi whispered. “Just forward.”

That word again. Mizu clenched her jaw and nodded, barely visible in the dark. She reached out, found Kairi’s hand, and gave it the smallest squeeze.

“Alright,” she said. “Forward.”

Goro rallied enough strength to fashion a splint for her leg out of the ragged straps of her jacket and her empty scabbard. Mizu gritted her teeth through the pain as he cinched the straps down, blacking out briefly. Tears mingled with the dirt and blood on her face.

They climbed to their feet, leaning on each other, and started moving. Their lenses outlined a rough approximation of the rock walls, and they started forward.

* * * * *

Goro tapped Mizu's shoulder and pointed. A jagged bite in the shaft wall, just wide enough to stand on, led into a faint spiral carved long ago into the rock. It looked like some sort of old access route or worker's ledge, meant for inspections perhaps. Most of it was choked with rubble, but it went up. Wound its way like a scar around the edge of the pit.

Mizu didn't speak. Her lips were white with pain. But she nodded.

It was Kairi who moved first, testing the ledge with her weight. Gravel scattered down the drop, disappearing into the dark. She waited—counted seconds. Nothing gave way. Then she took the first step. Another. Slow, leaning into the wall, one hand trailing the stone for balance.

Mizu went next, her arm slung over Goro's shoulders. Her broken leg barely brushed the ledge, dragging behind her like agonizing dead weight. Every step was a negotiation between collapse and forward motion.

They climbed in silence, broken only by the sound of breath and grit sliding underfoot. The ledge narrowed halfway up. One part had crumbled into a gap barely wider than a boot. She watched as Kairi crossed it first, back flat to the wall, fingers clawing at old bolt holes for support. Goro followed, guiding Mizu like a wounded pack animal, keeping her upright with a hand on her ribs.

Jon crept in her mind. Their conversations, his laugh, his last words… She forced it down. Survival came first. Forward.

She slipped once, her foot catching a loose stone, her knee buckling. Goro caught her, locking his good arm around her waist. She didn't thank him, she couldn't speak through the pain. Just grunted and kept going.

Every meter stretched into eternity. By the time they neared the top, all three were soaked in sweat, bruised, shaking with fatigue. The last stretch was half-buried in debris. Kairi kicked through it with her boots, clearing a gap wide enough for them to scramble through one by one, but sending an echoing cascade of rocks into the black.

They all froze, waiting. Voices echoed in the distance.

They continued slowly, teeth clenched, lips bloodied—guarded and bleeding. They emerged into a narrow opening to a larger tunnel. Mizu's chest rose and fell like a broken engine, but she was smiling, just barely.

"That sucked." Goro nearly collapsed, Kairi catching him at the last minute.

Mizu half stood, leaning against the wall and staring into the dark ahead of them. At least the shake was silent. "Let's keep moving."

And so they did: slow, battered, together.

Forward.

* * * * *

The path from the vent curled up into a narrow service corridor—half-collapsed, roof bowed, railings twisted. The mine had been abandoned for years, but now the dust was disturbed. Scuffed. Tracked.

They kept going, moving slow. Every sound echoed—boots on grit, broken breath, the occasional quiet grunt when someone slipped or twisted wrong.

Kairi stopped, and Mizu nearly walked into her back before she saw.

The corridor widened ahead—split into a small staging chamber, maybe once used for equipment checks or cargo intake: old lockers, dented carts. The air stank of ozone and blood. Four bodies lay dead, hauntingly illuminated by the tac-lights mounted on their rifles.

Yu Jing armor showed the Imperial Service insignia. All dead.

One with a clean puncture through the chest plate, straight into the heart. Another was missing most of his face, while the other two lay in varying states of dismemberment.

Kairi crouched beside the nearest. "Still warm."

Goro moved to cover the hall behind them, his hand trembling slightly on the knife he salvaged from a dead man's belt. "This wasn't a firefight."

"No," Mizu said, voice flat with pain. "It was art."

"Jon's not here," Kairi whispered.

She limped forward, eyes scanning the scene with old instincts. None of the soldiers had gotten a shot off. No scattered shots in the walls. No scorch marks. Just clean kills—fast, efficient, brutal.

"One blade," she muttered. "Maybe two, they never saw it coming."

Kairi stood slowly. "Who the hell…"

A shrill scream echoed deeper in the gloom.

Mizu tapped her comlog and brought up her hacking programs. She couldn't focus on the words for too long or her eyes started to glaze. Thankfully, years of living on the edge of survival meant stripping Friend/Foe protocols was something she could do with her eyes closed. "Grab some pistols."

* * * * *

The tunnels yawned open into a freight chamber long since abandoned. The space stretched wide and jagged, its ceiling partially collapsed. Chunks of broken stone littered the rails, which curled upward in places like the twisted ribs of some buried titan. Dust clung to everything. Here and there, the old emergency lights flickered—frail, sputtering pulses of pale blue that gave just enough illumination to make the shapes in the gloom unsettling.

Goro froze at the threshold, one fist raised in warning.

Figures moved in the half-light—Celestial Guards. Very much alive. One dragged a wounded comrade into cover while another barked frantic orders, his voice cracked with fear.

And there—just behind them—was the silhouette: Jon, pistol in hand.

He moved with the soldiers, but not like them. Nervous. Twitchy. Sweating in the cold.

Mizu's breath caught.

"Move!" Kairi rasped, pulling Mizu behind a half-buried excavator, her voice cracked and raw. They were all running on fumes, but it was too late: shouts, then gunfire.

A volley of Combi Rifle shots screamed across the chamber. Metal tore away from the excavator in bursts of white-hot sparks. One round slammed into Mizu's thigh and dropped her like a stone. Pain bloomed in her skull, white and sharp, but she clenched her jaw and smothered the agony behind a screaming wall of fury.

She twisted, blood soaking through her pants, and raised her pistol with both trembling hands. She fired once, twice—at the silhouette slipping toward a side tunnel. The second round caught him in the side. He shot back blindly. Mizu shot him again. He staggered, grunted, and vanished into the shadows.

She didn't feel satisfaction—just the cold ache.

Kairi flanked right, letting off suppressive bursts that screamed overhead and forced two of the Celestial Guards to duck behind a half-collapsed storage crate. Goro braced himself against the excavator, teeth clenched, and returned fire. One of the Guards collapsed with a strangled shout.

Mizu tried to rise, screamed silently, then dragged herself forward with one hand and hissed through her teeth. Blood trailed behind her.

"Jon!"

Guilt tried to worm its way in, but pain and fury kept it at bay. She'd done what she had to do.

The firefight ground on—desperate, erratic, messy. Two of the guards rushed toward an emergency shaft. Goro clipped one in the shoulder. The other hurled a grenade—too far, too wild—and it exploded against a distant wall with a flat, useless whump.

Then the growl came: low, mechanical, bestial.

The tunnels trembled as darkness thundered.

A shrieking roar of an engine peeled through the chaos as the Tsurugi–II came into view—red, running dark in predator-silence until the last second. Dust and gravel exploded behind it as it ripped through the far tunnel and into the chamber like death itself. The rider wore a gleaming red helmet and a matte-black bodysuit, the outline unmistakable—the metal arm familiar.

She had come. She was a myth, a whispered *bōsōzoku* legend—the Kuroshi Rider. Mizu's eyes bulged. Could it have been hallucinations from the pain? She fought to believe what she was seeing: the Kuroshi Rider wasn't *real*. Yet… here she was. They called her Red—less a name than a warning, spoken in the same breath as blood and death.

She didn't slow. Her bike pivoted hard, tires fishtailing, rear end drifting out in a perfect, controlled skid as a polearm unfolded from her back. The shaft extended into a cruel crescent blade with a snap-hiss like a guillotine's breath.

One of the guards turned, shouting, trying to raise his rifle—too slow.

Red's scythe sang through him. Blood spattered against the wall in a thick, crimson arc as his torso separated cleanly from his hips. His rifle clattered to the floor before his knees did.

Another turned to fire.

The bike launched upward—a quick rise over a collapsed section of the floor—and struck him mid-chest. The man vanished beneath the wheels, crushed and silent. Red never slowed.

The remaining two ran. One screamed, panicked. The Kuroshi Rider gave chase, blade dragging low enough to spark as it kissed stone.

"*Chikusho*. Red's real." Kairi breathed, the words trembling like she'd just seen a ghost crawl out of a nightmare.

Mizu coughed and spit blood, dragging herself up on one arm. Her leg was fire, but her heart still burned hotter.

A faint buzzing—like tinnitus filtering into her awareness—brought Mizu's awareness to the space above her. Bianca's small drone was there, recording everything.

"Useless slagg'n piece of—" Goro noticed it too.

"Jon?" Mizu's voice was a whisper.

"I saw him, I think," Goro muttered, reloading behind cover and pointing. "Took off that way when…"

Kairi's face was pale, jaw locked. "You shot him?"

"I did." Mizu didn't know if it was pride or grief that made her say it. She tasted both.

Kairi nodded. Mizu saw her struggle with words before moving off to search ahead.

A soft whirring came as Bianca's drone approached and began scanning Mizu's injuries, its small light casting her bloody face in harsh relief.

Kairi called out from ahead. "Blood trail! This way!"

Mizu spotted it in the gloom. A thin line of crimson dots stretched toward a fractured corridor, smeared with frantic boot prints.

"Jon," she said again, this time a curse, not a question.

With Goro's help, she got to her feet, leaning on him heavily. Kairi moved like a ghost just ahead of them, already tracing the trail toward whatever came next.

Mizu didn't feel fear.

She felt hollow.

She had aimed center mass.

She hadn't missed.

They found a destroyed Feìquán first. The jetbike was explosively severed in two, split from the bottom up, along with its rider.

And then they found *him*.

Jon.

Curled near a collapsed vent shaft, clutching his blood-soaked waist. A gut shot—painful, fatal. His breath a series of sharp, panicked gasps. He looked up, eyes wide, full of animal fear and pain. "No, no, no… don't, Mizu, I…"

Mizu stopped out of arms reach, leaning heavily on Goro, head swimming. She felt numb—dead.

"Coward!" Kairi roared as she stepped up beside Mizu.

"I didn't know they'd—They said they'd only take Oyama and the others, not us! We would walk free! Here." Jon tossed his gun at her feet. "All we have to do is—"

"You tried to sell us for your own skin," Goro said, spitting. "They just didn't give you the full price."

"Not us! Them. I tried to warn you!"

"How long?" Mizu's question hit them all like a trench hammer.

Jon was silent for a long time. Tears of pain—physical and emotional—rolled down his face, trailing dirt in streaks.

"Two years." Jon couldn't look them in the eyes. His admission was as much a killing stroke as the bullets in his gut.

Mizu felt something die inside her. A thousand cuts of agonizing loss tore through her.

"Traitor." Soft and sorrowful, Kairi had lost her fire.

Jon looked at Mizu, pleading.

"We can't keep saving you from yourself, Jon." Mizu's voice was flat. She felt numb using his own words against him, but the fresh tears told her otherwise.

Behind them, a motorcycle rumbled closer, idling in the dark—judgment.

Jon cowered, whimpering as he bled. "Please, help me. I'm bleeding."

Mizu stared at him for a long time, trying to find her friend in his eyes. She didn't see him. Only his fears. "We all bleed, Jon. You just chose to do it alone."

They walked away, leaving his desperate, raving screams behind them in the dark.

40.

The vault hummed with nervous energy. They had a plan. An insane plan, but a plan. Behind them, Hiro ran a final check on the automated turrets, coaxing them back to life. Ahead, the door to Hell.

Takeshi stood near the wall, refastening the armor plates over the hasty repairs to the tech suit underneath. His wounds itched. Every movement was deliberate, controlled. Not rushed—he knew what came next.

"You were right," Song broke the seal of silence.

Takeshi did not turn to face her. "About which part?"

"The part where I didn't trust you."

He said nothing. The quiet between them was louder than gunfire.

She stepped closer. "It was about contingencies—mission insurance. It was about control. I thought if I had access to your systems, I could protect us better. I could get into the vault faster. Maybe even protect you in the process."

"You did not," he said flatly. "You put my life at risk."

"I know." She stared at him—direct, unapologetic. "And I'd still make the same call if it meant completing the mission."

Takeshi finally turned toward her—she looked *small*—his expression hard behind the tension in his jaw.

She hesitated under his stare, just briefly. "But I should've trusted you before I put a hand on your leash."

That gave him pause.

She continued, quieter this time. "You didn't need a handler. You needed an ally. I see that now. I should've seen it before."

For a long moment, Takeshi said nothing. Then, quietly: "Are you going to yank that leash again before we breach?"

"No," she said. A sly grin grew, overshadowing her own exhaustion. "Not unless you give me a reason."

"Fair."

Song smiled thinly, helmet under her arm. "Probably still going to die."

"One cut at a time. There is always a chance. Succeed or fail, our fate is in our hands."

A moment passed between them. Not forgiveness. Not warmth. Just understanding.

Then Hiro's voice crackled over the link: "Clock's ticking, kids."

Takeshi stepped forward. "Let us finish this."

* * * * *

Takeshi stood beside the threshold, weapon ready. He was calm, prepared. They had devised a plan that gave them a fighting chance to make it out. Once the doors opened, Nakama would initiate the Last Oblivion Protocol, and the countdown would begin. Song explained what would happen next. Dormant viruses would load onto each server, wiping them clean before E/M charges would detonate inside each row, obliterating any remaining scrap of information. Finally, industrial-grade D-Charges would collapse the chamber. They had two minutes to make it far enough.

All that would remain of the hidden Hansei vault would be on the data storages that each of them carried, protected by the bearer, rapidly cycling encryptions, and small explosive cores.

"Ready?" Song waited for them each to check in before unsealing the chamber.

The vault doors slowly retracted, weapons fire poured in the expanding opening. Revitalized automated defense turrets answered the barrage with HMG fire of their own. It was deafening. The roar of small arms fire into the vault slowed as screams filtered over the heavy staccato of the turrets.

The turrets ran dry. Takeshi counted to five—just long enough to let the surviving Yujingyu poke their heads out of cover. He and Hiro both stepped into the open, their stolen Heavy Machine Guns dragging ammunition belts behind. These were heavy emplacements. Stouter versions of the familiar HMG weapon system, making them clumsy to wield.

Takeshi depressed the jury-rigged trigger. His heavy Domaru armor had a much easier time bearing the makeshift weapon system than Hiro did. Hiro advanced beside him, firing in short bursts. Past the outer door, hastily erected barricades hid dozens of Yujingyu soldiers—more than enough to overwhelm the injured team in the end.

Takeshi's weapon clicked rapidly, its belt spent before he reached the outer seal. He dropped the HMG and ducked to the side, hiding in the slim cover of the threshold as Hiro did the same, his weapon dropped, ammo not quite expended but out of time.

A trio of missiles blitzed past them from inside the vault, obliterating the first set of barricades with ease and scattering corpses into the air.

Takeshi ducked low, peeling around the corner—diving to the side to avoid the few stray shots that still peppered the vault. Ahead of him, three rows of barricades remained. Heavily armored Wú Míng and more lightly clad Celestial Guard began to poke their heads around their cover as three more missiles came streaking from the vault.

With the last pre-planned missile barrage fired, Takeshi drew a blade along with his Contender and charged forward. He leapt the first barricade before the return fire resumed, his berserk charge putting him in arms reach of two Wú Míng.

One cut. One fight.

A downward chop buried his blade in the first soldier's neck, blossoming his head open like a two-petaled flower. He twisted aside as the second brought a Boarding Shotgun up and fired. Takeshi was not there—he blasted empty space.

Takeshi pulled past him and dispatched the trooper with a backhanded swipe, simultaneously spraying the next barricade with his Contender. Ultra-hard teseum-tipped shells tore through the portable barrier and shredded the Celestial Guard behind it.

Hiro slid in next to him—feet first—snatched up a dropped Grenade Launcher and jammed a hacking spike into its interface. The single use tool fried the weapon's programming and installed its own.

Takeshi charged laterally as weapons fire began pouring in from the remaining barricades. He threw himself toward a trio warriors, twisting parallel with the ground and barreling them down with his armored weight.

Behind them, short bursts of HMG began to spray out of the vault ahead of an unpainted remote. As its horned sensor mast emerged, he knew Song would be behind it, directing its actions remotely. The experimental Aibōt was no marksman, but its weight of fire mattered more right now.

The Aibōt shredded three soldiers before they adjusted to the new threat.

Takeshi lobbed an E/M grenade over the barricades ahead of him then ducked for cover. He looked back to Hiro's position and watched the operative blindly fire grenades, sending them skipping off the wall and careening into their foes.

Takeshi used the brief lull to survey the battleground. "Just go straight!" Song yelled from behind, running out of the vault behind the remotes.

Forward.

It was a wild plan, spearheading into the foe, but they had little alternative. Takeshi liked it.

A second Aibōt emerged from the vault, Missile Launcher lending its wrath to the chaos. A third came close behind. Its Flash Pulse was the only weapon Song was able to get active. It would be less effective, but Takeshi wasn't going to turn it down.

Hiro finished his barrage and discarded the heavier weapon. Bullets stormed down the tunnel, forcing Hiro to drop prone as he took two rounds in the chest plate. "I'm okay!"

Takeshi tossed him a discarded Yujingyu SMG for him to strip for ammo. Their own weapons were Yujingyu models so the ammo was compatible. Hiro reloaded Song's borrowed SMG with the pilfered magazine and drew his pistol.

With a nod, they both leapt forward. Takeshi charged the more heavily armored Wú Míng on the right and Hiro the lightly armored Celestial Guard on the left.

He pushed everything else from his mind.

One Cut. One fight at a time. Focus.

Takeshi rammed his armored bulk into the barricade ahead of him. His heavy impact lifted the portable shield, moving it back more than a meter as his legs pistoned, driving him on. The maneuver knocked the troopers sheltering behind it off balance. One stood up. Takeshi rewarded his courage with a Contender burst to the chest.

Takeshi stowed the Contender and vaulted the barricade. He hacked clean through a MULTI Rifle brought up in a desperate block and buried the blade into the chest of the soldier wielding it. The built up kinetic energy released, forcing the blade further into the dying soldier's chest.

The third Wú Míng died before Takeshi ever touched him, shredded by the HMG Aibōt.

Around him, death sang its ugly tune in the last gasp of the hopeless. Weapons fire flew back and forth as each side announced its righteousness. Takeshi was calm. His heart beat slowly, evenly. He noted the Crane Agent's absence, but he had more pressing matters at hand.

Battle was his art. This was his symphony.

Takeshi moved forward, into the next row of soldiers, and struck them down, one cut at a time.

* * * * *

The first explosions that reached him were less intense than Takeshi had expected, almost underwhelming. The vault closed behind Song when she exited, so the E/M charges were a muffled, tinny sound.

The D-Charges were something else entirely.

The entire junction collapsed behind them as they pushed forward. Troopers trying to sweep in and flank were crushed in the rolling wave of fire and stone. Dust rolled past him in tandem with the concussive bow wave, obscuring the final line of surviving Yujingyu troopers.

Even bracing for it, he was knocked unceremoniously off his feet. Dust swirled everywhere, obscuring everything. Takeshi closed his eyes against the swirling dust and waited. His ears still rang from the blasts, and he couldn't rely on them either.

All three Aibōts marched clear of the dust cloud. The airborne dirt had painted them a motley red brown. Song moved with them, pistol drawn and using their bulk to shelter her—resolved to live, he hoped. Hiro came in last, nearly laughing at death. Nakama was nowhere to be seen.

They made it this far. One more fight. One more cut.

Together they quickly dispatched the stragglers and regrouped—miraculously unharmed—to plan their path forward. It was time to go home.

* * * * *

Crouched in an abandoned building, Takeshi looked out toward their objective. It was difficult to think of it as his 'home.' The last time he set foot inside those walls was long before the Uprising. While his father remained on Kuraimori, duty-bound and stoic, his mother was on Earth when the war began. A stroke of luck in the end. Now the white walls and gardens displayed the Jade banner of the StateEmpire.

Takeshi let the anger simmer just below the surface, focusing it in his mind.

"Everyone ready?" Hiro triple checked his Heavy Rocket Launcher—recovered and reloaded from the stores of the dead.

Their already small force had dwindled significantly since the start of the operation. The Aibōts waited—powered down to reduce their signatures—a few hundred meters away. Song and Hiro sat quietly together watching as he stared at it—home. It felt so distant, yet intimate.

Inside the white painted walls, three structures stood, all familiar. The main house, his father's dojo, and mother's study. The two smaller buildings framed gardens that Takeshi was surprised to see maintained. At the back of it all, rising taller than the rest, was his home. Its two-story frame appeared no worse for wear from its time in Yujingyu hands. Somewhere in the house he once called home, a Haqqislamite prince awaited rescue along with Taka.

The estate was set on a small, leveled hill and pushed up against the mountainside. It would be an uphill sprint across open ground. Suicide.

One cut. Focus.

A grin slowly spread across Takeshi's face. He turned back to his comrades. "I have an idea."

41.

A barrage of heavy munitions pummeled the side wall of the once-Oyama estate turned Yujingyu camp. Even as they struck, Takeshi sprinted up the hill—recovered Chain Rifle in hand—his legs pounding beneath him, closing the distance as quickly as he could. Stims burned in his veins, urging him on. He reached the summit and crashed through the masonry. Arm up to protect his head—his helmet had been nowhere to be found—his enhanced frame burst through the weakened wall, showering masonry into the back of his mother's studio. The gap between the side building and wall was their entry point—this was their beach head, and he was its anchor.

To their credit, the Celestial Guards inside the grounds responded quickly to the assault, and Takeshi was dodging fire as soon as his armored body cleared the wall. He brought his Chain Rifle to bear and sprayed a cone of superheated shrapnel at his assailants. They dove for cover, giving him enough time to do the same.

He came to a knee next to the building and was caught by surprise as an unfamiliar draconic statue turned its head. Takeshi barely had enough time to throw himself back as it swiped at him, claws crackling with energy. It reminded him of the *chiwen* statues that lined the grand palace on Yutang, the seat of the StateEmpire. The statue's four eyes lit an ominous green as it shook off the dust of Takeshi's entrance, like a dog shaking away water. Casting off debris, the black and orange paint showed through and melted away the pretense of sculpture.

The serpentine construction wasted no time and charged, moving more like a viper with legs than a machine. Lashing out quickly then darting away, the lithe machine tested his defenses. Takeshi blocked the reinforced tail and claws, strike after strike with his Chain Rifle, unable to draw his blade fast enough. Deep gouges rendered his rifle quickly beyond repair.

His backpedaling was punished by an explosive discharge of crackling electricity when he triggered a hidden mine. A surge of lethal energies pulsed through him, threatening to cook him inside out. Thankfully, Takeshi's armored shell grounded him, shunting the shock into the earth; quite painful, but not deadly.

As the next darting strike came from overhead, he hurled his rifle at a nearby Yujingyu and caught the mechanical tail in both hands at the last second. Its bladed point shook just out of reach of his face, held back by both hands in a desperate struggle. Takeshi braced against the machine as it leaned into him. He slid backward.

The mechanical dragon shifted forward, lashing a clawed foot, forcing Takeshi to release the tail and backpedal once more. A second electric explosion rocked him, another hidden mine showering his body with energy. Rather than letting the charge dissipate, he stepped forward, into the dragon.

One strike.

Takeshi drew his weapon. The electromagnetic blade surged with barely contained power, and he struck his foe—draw to strike, a single slash. Suddenly, the living statue was his conduit, and the pent up electricity discharged through his blade and into the construct. It spasmed, thrashing violently as the blow overloaded its systems. Its workings locked up, freezing the machine in a tableau of agony.

* * * * *

Su-Yeong stood in her study, watching the chaos unfold, helmet tucked under one arm. She looked on silently as horned remotes assaulted her walls with sustained barrages. Her forces, and Zhang's, responded admirably, but were focused outward when the right most wall was breached. Their response time was impressive, but the damage was done.

Zhang paced behind her, fuming. He recovered the ruined Domaru helmet and clutched it like a talisman of violence. His fury off-balanced him. She liked that.

"Well?"

"Well what?!" He rounded on her, hands clenched—like claws.

"What do you recommend, Agent Zhang?" Su-Yeong smiled. Her toothy grin ate down his defenses. "You are the more experienced battlefield commander. Subterfuge is my art. Warfare is yours."

He was dumbstruck.

She had unmanned him and taken control of his forces, and now she was asking for his advice. All his years of courtly play and power grabs were nothing compared to her, and she knew it. He did not know how to respond. It showed.

"Come now, Agent Zhang. Surely you wish to take the credit for coming to my aid." She paused, letting his jaw work in anger once more. "Or you can take the blame, your choice."

The threat was not necessary and she knew it—he would do as he was told. He was a hound straining at his leash, begging to hunt. Another barrage of indirect missile fire blasted away a weapons emplacement as if to punctuate her remarks, framing her argument in fireworks as the emplacement's magazine lit off.

"Release combat authority to me." His voice was more of a growl than anything human.

Su-Yeong turned, shielding her movement from his vision as a hand crept toward her sidearm. She looked to the side as a holoplane appeared before her. Su-Yeong tapped the command she had prepared for just this occasion and broadcasted on open comms. "I am releasing combat authority to Agent Zhang for the duration of this engagement."

She turned back to address Zhang, but he was already out the door.

Su-Yeong smiled.

* * * * *

Bianca sat against the stone wall, listening to the chaos outside. Taka was sound asleep, recovering, despite the noise. She held the mysterious pouch in her hands, inspecting it over and over. The auto-injector was of Haqqislamite make. It looked golden in the low light, the Serum within had glistened with Silken nanites, like stars suspended in honey. It was the sort of thing she would expect to find in an emergency medical kit on a starship lifepod, not on Shentang.

She had reset Taka's broken digits, following his instructions, then stabbed him with the injector after he passed out from the pain halfway through the ordeal. Bianca was a reporter, not a paramedic, so she opted to trust his word on this.

She sat in silence. Bianca had never been a prisoner before and was not enjoying the experience, though she did admit this was likely an atypical one. It still felt like waiting for the end, but hoping for salvation.

Her lens displayed minimal information at the moment. The window where she would usually see her drone's footage remained blank, as it had since she arrived and Yasbir took it from her. Bianca never thought losing it would incite the loss she was feeling. The drone had followed her through the years, capturing everything and providing her a bird's-eye view of so many battlefields.

When the feed returned, Bianca was confused, believing it a Yujingyu trick. She expanded the view to her entire field of vision. The familiar sense of vertigo when interfacing with the drone was a welcome sensation. What she saw gave her no further clarity.

It was dark, like a tunnel, light at the end rapidly approaching.

The cell door opened, pulling her back to the moment at hand. She dismissed the window and paled. A lithe Imperial Agent stood in the doorway holding a large shotgun casually in one hand and her helmet in the other. A pistol and combat dagger sat threateningly on her hip. Short hair framed her face in black.

"It is time." Her eyes were cold and threatening even as she smiled.

Bianca kicked Taka awake. He grimly stared at the newcomer, immediately alert.

She stood there, silent and menacing. Bianca was certain she was about to die.

"About time." Taka rose and caught the shotgun when it flew through the air.

Bianca's jaw dropped open, bewildered. A muttering 'what?' was all she managed to get out before the newcomer turned back to Taka.

"Reinforcements will be here soon, couldn't stop the call. Zhang will have called even more, I'm sure. There is a garrison close enough to prove troublesome." Her voice was calm, collected. No more troubled than if she were merely checking the weather.

"Slagg me." Taka nodded to the Imperial Agent as if it was just another Tuesday. He inspected his newly acquired firearm, checking the chamber with military precision. "Hey, Sparrow, got any presents for her?" He gestured to Bianca.

The woman's eyes softened, joining the smile on her face as she approached and presented Bianca's Flash Pulse back to her. "It is good to finally meet you—face to face—Miss Chen. Please see to the prince." And she was gone.

"Sparrow..." Bianca whispered.

Bianca walked with renewed purpose. There was only one other cell. The distant alarms felt muted here. Taka had already overridden the lock sequence, and it slid open with a hiss of recycled air and privilege.

Inside, the air was warm. Perfumed. Almost humid. She wrinkled her nose.

Plush carpeting greeted her feet. Soft ambient music filtered through hidden speakers. A faux teakwood desk stood in one corner, opposite a chaise lounge beneath a hanging light display that mimicked a sunset over Bourak. The cell was a lie—a simulation of freedom. A velvet cage.

Prince Hasib was sprawled languidly on the chaise in elegant lounge wear, a steaming cup of something floral and expensive in one hand. His hair was immaculate.

He looked up with vague interest—until he saw her face.

"Bianca!" He sat straighter.

Bianca stepped into the room without invitation. The door closed behind her, sealing them in. She didn't say a word.

Hasib fidgeted.

"You've come to release me then? About time—" He trailed off, uncertain.

Bianca walked a slow circle around the room, surveying every luxury without a trace of reaction. "How very… comfortable," she said at last.

"I am a diplomatic detainee," Hasib said, lifting his chin. "The laws are very clear."

"You've got silk sheets."

"Basic human dignity."

Bianca stopped in front of him. Her voice dropped just above a whisper. "Do you know how many men and women died protecting you, Hasib?"

The prince stiffened. "I—"

She leaned in, eyes locked on him.

"Yasbir is with us," she said, softly.

Hasib paled.

Bianca didn't have to say more.

He knew the name, all too well. Yasbir, the specter at the edge of his family's shadow.

Hasib's breath caught. His mouth opened. Closed.

"Good," she said, turning toward the door. "Let's go."

* * * * *

Takeshi left the *chiwen*-shaped bot behind and broke into a sprint across the central garden, gravel crunching under his boots. The breath was ripped from his lungs in a brutal shock as something slammed him to the ground. His ribs burned; the taste of copper filled his mouth. He forced himself up just enough to scan for the shooter—there, on the roof to his right, a Yujingyu framed in the glare and the black maw of a MULTI Marksman Rifle locked on him. The rifle barked again, the round hissing past his ear. He hurled himself into a roll, grit grinding into his palms, and scrambled toward the nearest cover—a sun-bleached stone barely big enough to fold himself behind. Two more rounds smacked into it with bone-jarring cracks, sending flecks of rock stinging his face.

He had nothing for a fight at this range—no clean shot, no way to close the distance. His new blades might as well have been scraps of steel. Takeshi risked a glance upward—and caught the split-second flare of a warhead before the world above him detonated. The rooftop vanished in a bloom of fire and shattered concrete, the Yujingyu reduced to a smear in the inferno. Shockwaves punched through his cover, showering him in grit and smoking debris.

"My thanks," he growled into the comm, heart still hammering.

"Any time!" Hiro's voice crackled back, obnoxiously cheerful, like they were not both dancing on the edge of death.

Takeshi used the lull to his advantage and took in his surroundings. The garden, trampled and bullet ridden though it was, was so familiar. He knew this place intimately. The main home rose above him, two stories of history and emotion. He was born here. So many emotions clawed at the back of his awareness beneath the adrenaline rush of combat and the itching stims: joy, sorrow, contentment, loss, happiness.

Most of all, Takeshi felt pride. Not in this home, but in himself; in his family, in his father. Kōichi Oyama served his Emperor—and his people—to his last breath. He set an example that Takeshi could only hope to live up to.

Thunder echoed through the valley, shattering the moment. The blue sky spoke with the ferocity of a hurricane gale, but it was wrong—

focused. In the lingering stillness that followed, Takeshi searched for what he knew was coming next. It started with a low growl, muffled by the distance, but growing louder.

By the time he caught sight of the drop craft, the sound had already risen into a banshee's wail. The war machine didn't fly so much as rip the air apart in its descent. Sleek and angular, the assault shuttle's outstretched wings bristled with vectored jets that flexed and twisted to guide its violent plunge. Along its armored spine ran a massive Hyper Rapid Magnetic Cannon, the oversized weapon's dark length like a promise of annihilation. Takeshi had ridden inside transports like this on Paradiso, and he knew what waited within: a quick reaction force, armored and ruthless, ready to crush any spark of resistance the moment their boots struck the ground.

Takeshi stood, steeling himself as he looked across the Hansei Valley at the approaching doom. "*Kuso.*"

42.

Takeshi stood firm, trusting Yujingyu doctrine to not have changed much in the years since the Uprising. First would come the Liú Xīng. Even as he thought it, the shuttle twisted skyward, pushing away from its roof-skimming path and gaining altitude for the jump pack equipped troopers. The heavy infantry would wait their turn for the second pass.

Takeshi watched, holding his blade skyward—high guard—in challenge and standing in the open. He wanted them to come to him. He needed Song and Hiro free to complete the mission. Answering his challenge, four dots kicked out of the shuttle as it tore past the battered estate. Missiles rose up from the streets below as a co-opted Aibōt challenged the assault craft.

All four Liú Xīng struck the ground just out of arms reach, their jump packs wailing. Their explosive landings were as deafening as they were deadly. Their armor was the standard fare of Yujingyu orange, accented with green chest plates and pauldrons. Triple vectored jump packs hung heavily on their backs, supported by built-in stabilizers.

Takeshi braced as the competing jump packs buffeted him from all sides. He brought his armor-cloth haori up to shield his exposed face, blinding him as well. Their downdrafts were so intense that heat warnings flashed across his lens. Takeshi felt like he was being boiled alive in his armor.

He was rewarded for surviving the draft with the familiar boom of a large shotgun blasting into his back. At this range, there was no way they could have missed. The force of the blow knocked him off his feet; warnings flared across his vision, and his armor groaned in protest as he flew forward. The roar of four jump-jets announced the drop troops leaning into their greatest strength, movement.

Tucking into a shoulder roll, Takeshi used his sudden momentum to reposition, coming to his feet and drawing his second blade. One Liú Xīng landed on the roof of his home with a spiral of holoplanes appearing around his arm, two kept close by, and a third rocketed overhead, attempting to flank.

One fight. One cut. Focus.

Lunging back, he dodged a burst from a Spitfire and twisted to face the flanker as he landed, blade lashing out. At full extension, all he could do was clip the jump trooper's weapon arm, but it was enough. E/M discharge coursed through the soldier, seizing up his armor.

Takeshi kept moving and cut through the immobilized soldier's gorget in the process. Arterial spray blossomed. He dodged right, missing a second Spitfire blast—by millimeters. Takeshi sprinted toward the entrance of the dojo, hoping to take away their maneuverability and reset the fight. He crashed through the entrance, shredding its thin *shoji*-framed entrance with ease.

Song piped over coms. "Neko, I'm going af—"

She was gone. Takeshi's vision cleared: vitals, communications, armor status, battlefield outline, tac-link, all of it—gone. It was not the first time he had been isolated by an enemy hacker, but it was never a good thing. He cycled the armor's systems, hoping to reset.

Jump pack on full burn, a shotgun-wielding Liú Xīng plowed into him and kept going, impact knocking the blade from his right hand. The heat of his jets lit the dojo ablaze as they barreled into the back wall. Takeshi turned in time to raise his left arm between them, using the Yujingyu's momentum to bury his other blade to the hilt.

Takeshi hit with a bone jarring crunch and saw stars. The familiar sensation of a bone dislocating rattled up his right shoulder. His hand spasmed, and Takeshi lost his grip on the second blade. Jets disengaged, the drop-trooper dropped dead, only to be replaced by another, pointing a Spitfire at Takeshi from the entrance.

* * * * *

Sparrow moved swiftly up the basement stairs, Taka behind her, the weight of what was about to happen already anchoring her heart. She didn't falter. Not now. The door to the comms room hissed open, revealing a mess of cables and makeshift command rigs. What used to be a guest lounge had been consumed by war: floating holopanes flickering with tactical feeds, sweat-slicked techs issuing rapid reports, the hum of chaos held just barely in check.

At the center of it all stood Lieutenant Da—steady, competent, predictably alert.

"Ma'am!" he called, eyes widening as she stepped in, sword drawn. "We—"

Recognition bloomed in his features at the sight of Taka behind her. His instincts didn't fail him. Loyal to the end, Da moved without hesitation—shielding her with his body, drawing his sidearm to face the threat coming from behind her.

Da was a good man, loyal, brave—too brave.

She caught his wrist before he could fire and—without hesitation—drew her knife and drove it through his back.

There was a breath—a stillness—as Da stiffened, then collapsed against her. She lowered him gently, feeling the warmth of his blood soaking into her sleeve. He would've died for her. Instead, he died because of her. No time for mourning. That was a luxury they couldn't afford—not now.

Behind her, Taka's shotgun thundered. Each blast echoed with fury, sorrow, and a pain he must have locked deep inside. She didn't look. She didn't need to. The storm he unleashed was his own. She felt it in the room's vibration, in the way dust lifted with each report. She gave him that space—to grieve and vent his pain the only way he could.

By the time the final Yujingyu hit the floor, Sparrow was already working.

She raised her arm and began swiping the air above her forearm, fingers dancing through projected code. Her focus narrowed, her mind slipping into the quiet hum of execution. She launched the virus and watched it bloom across the servers like ink in water—consuming, replicating, destroying. The command feeds glitched. Backup protocols screamed. Then came silence—a blank slate.

They were ghosts again.

Taka was gone. She glanced once over her shoulder, catching only the fading outline of his withdrawal from the room.

Footsteps echoed behind her as she stepped over Da's body and turned toward the stairwell. Bianca and Hasib were there—huddled just out of sight. Their eyes locked with hers for a beat too long.

No time to explain.

"Let's go," Taka barked as he emerged from the gloom, face ruined, grinning through it like a devil out of a story.

"You look awful," came a voice Sparrow hadn't expected to hear.

Song.

Sparrow froze, heart stuttering once. Then she turned.

"*Kuso*, you look like shit," Song said, one brow arched, but her tone held something gentler than the words. "It's good to see you." Her gaze flicked to Taka—softer—then to the others. "Good to see you, Bianca. Your Majesty."

Sparrow allowed herself one breath. Just one breath to mourn Su-Yeong and Da. Then she started walking again.

* * * * *

From a hidden perch among trees, Yasbir watched chaos unfold through the valley below. He didn't need much to understand the fight—just the language of motion and fire. A heavy assault shuttle came in hard over the valley, thrusters roaring as it banked too low, too fast. It was suicide, or precision—maybe both. Further reinforcements rolled in from the south: two light transports.

He tracked the flare of countermeasures spilling from the shuttle like sparks from a dying firework: flares, chaff, bursts of microwaves that distorted the surrounding air. Someone down there had teeth. The shuttle twisted through them like a knife.

Missile trails chased it like angry ghosts. Yasbir followed one—caught the brief shimmer of its origin. A rooftop silhouette. Too far for detail, but the size and movement screamed combat remote—maybe a Yaókòng? No, the shape was wrong—something new.

He adjusted his magnification just as the Yujingyu assault shuttle pulled into a sharp, banking hover. A second later, a gout of flame and dust erupted from its nose. Hyper Rapid Magnetic Cannon fire was brutal, unforgiving. Buildings between it and the rooftop remote shredded instantly—an entire floor collapsed under the weight of its spite.

"Overkill," Yasbir muttered.

A wash of dust choked the skyline. Even from this distance, Yasbir could feel the shockwave in his ribs. He flicked through vision modes—infrared, E/M, silhouette scan—but the shuttle pilot moved first. The shuttle surged through the haze, strafing the skyline.

A lone figure—black and white armor, wide stance—stood like a ghost against the destruction. Heavy Rocket Launcher in hand. Yasbir's breath caught. The shuttle let loose again—this time, the nose-mounted HMG. Yasbir could almost hear it from here: the churning purr of death.

The figure didn't flinch.

Instead, it raised one hand. Not in surrender, but in insult. A clear gesture, unmistakable even from kilometers away.

And then it vanished—a decoy.

"Clever."

The shuttle swung wide, preparing another pass. Yasbir noted the shimmer of another launch, another rocket cutting the air. The shuttle twisted, firing blindly—but effectively. Another rooftop. Another collapse. A small figure tumbled like a broken doll, a smear of red marking the spot.

Yasbir lowered his head. "May Allah protect you." He captured the location and sent it on in a tight, encrypted comms burst.

The Japanese were making a lot of noise.

And whatever was evolving down there wasn't clean. It was a war zone.

He clicked his tongue and tapped a quick message into his comlog.

No reply.

This wasn't his fight. Not yet. He still had to wait and protect his prize, hidden in the woods behind him.

The Yu Jing reinforcements crept closer and closer.

* * * * *

Takeshi came to a knee, right arm hanging useless, in the burning dojo. He held his first sword in this place. The weapons racks had all been removed, along with his mother's paintings. Her artwork had made this space feel alive, without it, it felt sterile—on fire, but sterile.

He stared at the jump troop, helpless. One blade lay on the floor near the Spitfire trooper, the other sticking up vertically from the green chest plate of the trooper he had buried it in. He was helpless.

The trooper fired. He dove left, snatching his weapon from the dead and crying out in agony as his dislocated arm struck the floor. The Spitfire spoke for only a moment before being cut off. The Liú Xīng's arms fell to the side, weapons clattering to the floor as he stared down at the sword that burst from his neck.

The soldier toppled, revealing a second Yujingyu. Sealed inside smooth orange power armor, with black banners of office streaming from his back and pauldrons, stood the Crane Agent from the tunnels, Spitfire on his back, sword in one hand, and a crushed Domaru helm in the other. The agent's helmet bore a single silver line, painted like a scar across his faceplate.

"Oyama." He tossed the ruined Domaru helm at Takeshi's feet.

Takeshi saw his ruined helm for what it was—a challenge—and came to a knee. He brought his blade up in a one-handed guard, his other arm still limp at his side. "And you are?"

43.

The building burned around them as Takeshi came to his feet. The Crane Agent had him dead-to-rights, but he just stood there. Smoke billowed out of the damaged structure. Takeshi had no idea what was happening, but he certainly wasn't going to turn down the moment to breathe.

The agent stooped down, reaching into the low flames permeating the floor, and picked up his dropped Yoshihiro blade. He held it gingerly, looking it over: examining the blade, the crest on its hilt. Takeshi swore the masked warrior was… admiring the blade. He watched in utter shock as the Yujingyu agent tossed it across the floor. It rattled through the flames, sliding past the wreckage of his helmet to a stop within arm's reach.

"Prepare yourself. Traitor."

The word 'traitor' growled through Takeshi's soul. Fury threatened to overtake him. "You know nothing!" he shot back, chest heaving.

"I know all I need to know, Oyama."

"Then you're a fool."

"Or just the one who will kill you."

"Who are you?!" Takeshi thought of many more colorful things to say at that moment. He thought Mizu would have been proud of him, if she were here.

"I am Zhang Bo, and I will be your end."

Adrenaline dumps and fatigue had slowly built in Takeshi. Multiple intense fights had battered his still-recovering body. The emotional wounds were open and raw: finding his father; being captured; losing Mizu, Taka, and Bianca.

The ache in his chest was building slowly. He didn't know what it was. The Bite, coming back to haunt him? His body shutting down? Mizu spoke of the shake like a demon over her shoulder, waiting to claim her. He wondered if her demon had chosen him as its next victim. Takeshi looked down, eyes on the katana at his feet.

The realization struck him like a hammer blow. He was laughing.

A low chuckle built into a booming, honest laugh. His face split with a smile. He couldn't remember the last time he laughed like this. It felt good. It felt real. Like an alien sensation from deep within, Takeshi Oyama felt joy.

Takeshi sheathed the blade in his hand and turned to the wall. With a grunt that barely broke through the laughter, he slammed his shoulder against a beam. Agony spiked as the bone locked back into its place. He dosed himself with detox, just to be sure he was not hallucinating.

"Zhang who?" Still he laughed. He felt absurd. The structure around him was so damaged that the fire suppression systems refused to cooperate. The whole thing would not burn, but it was enough that heat warnings continued to ping on his lens. He stared at Zhang, the smoke threatening to pull tears from his eyes, as a malicious grin spread.

"I am Zhang Bo! You mock me?!" He raged, shaking with fury while Takeshi shook with laughter.

The Crane Agent was a dark mirror held up for Takeshi to see—what he could become.

"Do you hear yourself? You just killed your own man! Has the Imperial Service gone so drunk on power that you think yourself invincible?" Takeshi stooped down and took up his katana. His undersuit was protection enough against the heated metal, but he could feel its warmth. "I have no idea who you are. Zhang? I am…"

"You will fight me again, Oyama, and I will kill you. We will finish what we started."

"No, you won't."

"What did you say?!" His mirror agent raged and stalked forward, black cloth of his armor billowing in the heat but not burning.

"I am Neko, and you don't have enough lifetimes to kill me."

Zhang launched forward on the offensive. Takeshi countered, keeping his katana low, gripped in both hands, twisting with the strike to protect his exposed head. Zhang reacted quickly, altering his path and thrusting high. Both blades missed by a hair's breadth.

Zhang lashed out again. His blade was long and thin, a dueling weapon that burned at a memory in Takeshi's mind. He batted it aside with an armored gauntlet.

They passed each other, each pivoting to see who could strike first. Takeshi was faster. His pivot became a roundhouse kick that connected with Zhang's back. The Imperial Agent was launched forward, face first to the floor. He planted an orange arm, catching his momentum and tumbling back onto his feet. He turned back to Takeshi, and the two collided once more.

* * * * *

The clash of blades drew Bianca's attention. She and a sniveling Hasib had taken shelter in the main house on Sparrow's instructions. Taka covered them from the rear entrance. They waited while the operative donned her helmet and darted out the back of the house with Song in tow. She could see into the burning structure from her position and capitalized on the comparative lull of the moment to watch the confrontation. Neko and a second Imperial Agent traded blows that could shatter bone. The agent was nimble, darting and stabbing while Neko was grounded and stoic. The difference in training and style was stark, almost poetic.

Despite her years running through battlefields alongside some of the Human Sphere's greatest heroes, Bianca was no swordswoman herself. She could keep up with their movements but had no idea what went into them. They might as well be superhuman in her eyes, like two mythic heroes battling right before her.

She recorded everything.

Instinct had her pulling at the connection to her drone. Glancing at its window in her lens brought its point of view front and center. Inexplicably, the small drone was heading right for her. Two Yujingyu transports raced ahead of it.

"Double shit. We have a problem!" Bianca slapped Taka's shoulder.

Hasib groaned in fear. "Yasbir isn't here, is he?" The prince kept looking over his shoulder.

"Worse than that?" Taka pointed skyward. The weapon-festooned dropship was on fast approach. Judging by its speed, it would get here before the transports. "*Chikusho*, we have another problem!"

Taka dove from the window as it shattered. A heavily armored trooper crashed through it, orange armor broken up by a green chest plate and heavy jump pack on his back. The soldier barreled through the window, rifle first, knocking into Taka and sending his weapon scattering.

Bianca darted for the stairs, following Hasib as the prince ran blindly for his life. Taking cover while Hasib ran upstairs, Bianca charged her Flash Pulse, took aim, and fired at the Yujingyu trooper. She hit her mark, but the trooper ignored its stunning effects. He twisted from Taka, bringing a terrifying MULTI Rifle to bear on her.

Taka dove across the rifle—bodily deflecting the Yujingyu's aim—and was tossed aside like a doll for his trouble. The trooper turned back to her, judging her Flash Pulse to be the bigger threat over an unarmed man.

Bianca prayed she had enough time for one more shot and charged her Flash Pulse as the rifle came to bear once more. Taka's distraction bought her precious seconds, and she fired first by a heartbeat. The banister beside her exploded in a shower of splinters, peppering her face with shards of flying wood and knocking her to the ground.

The trooper staggered. Arms out as if blinded, even in his suit of armor and with the visor down, he was stunned. It was all the delay Taka needed. Bianca watched him smash a chair across the Yujingyu's head with both hands. The chair shattered, but Taka did not relent. She thought he must have wells of courage kilometers deep as he leapt upon the power armored trooper, splintered chair legs still in hand.

Taka wrapped his legs around the trooper, and Bianca watched his arms piston over and over, pummeling the shattered chair legs into the warrior's visor. Taka roared as he mauled his foe.

An armored hand flashed up and hurled him to the side. The warrior's visor was bent in, ruined, and he wretched it off. Face bloodied, he stared Bianca down and brought his rifle to bear in one hand, wiping his eyes with the other. She was dead.

A thunderclap ripped through the ruins of the house, echoing like a cannon. Bianca flinched, expecting pain—but found none. She looked down at her chest. Still intact.

The Yujingyu trooper in front of her twitched once, then collapsed like a puppet with its strings cut. His head was simply gone—neck a mangled stump. Blood painted the walls. Chunks of skull and brain clung to the ceiling like obscene decorations.

Taka stood just behind him, smoking shotgun in hand.

He was absolutely soaked—face, coat, hair. Unbothered.

Bianca stared at him, wide-eyed. "Remind me never to make you angry."

Taka tilted his head, still grinning, red dripping from his jaw. "What? This is me calm."

Bianca swallowed and pointed at the wreckage of a body at her feet. "That was your version of calm?"

He winked. "You should see me on a bad day."

She didn't laugh.

Taka slung the shotgun over his shoulder and offered her a gore-slicked hand. "C'mon. We're not done redecorating."

Bianca hesitated, then took it.

There were worse monsters to have on your side.

* * * * *

Takeshi planted his boot firmly in Zhang's chest and launched the pretentious warrior out of the burning dojo. He flew through the remnants of the entryway and plowed into the gardens.

Cherry trees, once carefully cherished by his mother, now burned as the background to their fight. It was once a vibrant and lively place. The flowers and rock formations were still there, now trampled by armored feet. Its desecration stoked Takeshi's ire.

He charged out of the burning structure, blade clashing with Zhang's. There was something familiar about the grace in the way the Yujingyu moved—like he had fought this fight before. It tugged at his mind as blades flew.

One fight. Focus.

Takeshi parried a series of focused strikes, each aiming for a weak joint in his armor, and was forced to backpedal, yielding the momentum. It was Takeshi's turn to receive a boot to the chest, but he saw it coming. Anchored firmly, he stepped into the blow, defusing Zhang's momentum, and Takeshi lashed out with a fist, forcing Zhang to bend his outstretched leg or shatter his knee. Zhang crumpled, off balance, and his momentum forced him to tumble into Takeshi.

The warriors fell into a series of punches and kicks as they grappled. Each lost their blades in the process. Takeshi pinned Zhang's arm, threatening to break it. The agent responded with a fingertip strike to the neck. Takeshi choked, hands instinctively releasing the Yujingyu and guarding his neck. Zhang rolled away and recovered his sword.

When Takeshi recovered, he saw Zhang, standing out of reach with his blade in hand. He looked down at Takeshi's blade on the ground and back again.

"Traitor."

Awareness flooded Takeshi as the pieces fell into place: the island. Watching and rewatching the fight to learn his opponent's moves drilled a familiarity with the unique style into his consciousness he had not yet realized. It was a calling card, more distinctive than a fingerprint. The silver slash across his helm mirrored the strike Takeshi landed in their rainsoaked fight. That voice…

Only the armor was different—newer, more agile. It only enhanced Zhang's fighting.

Traitor.

The word echoed over and over in Takeshi's mind.

Traitor.

Zhang's power armored foot rose above his masterwork blade—a painful symmetry.

Zhang's foot hovered above Takeshi's blade like the executioner's axe. The Yujingyu didn't need to say anything else—he already had. That one word echoed louder than gunfire.

Traitor.

Takeshi tensed, ready to dive forward, to snatch the blade, to fight and die trying. But the moment never came.

A gunship screamed overhead.

The assault transport howled low over the roofline, its belly disgorging Shàng Jí like falling thunder. Reinforced deployment cables hissed then disengaged. Boots crashed to earth. In seconds, a full squad of gleaming Shàng Jí heavy infantry locked down the ridge with precision and power.

Takeshi staggered back to his feet just as Zhang took a step away, blade still in hand, watching as the Yu Jing soldiers fanned out. Their commander moved with the confidence of someone who had never once doubted his orders.

They moved in, weapons pointing at Takeshi, whose eyes narrowed.

"Not like this," he whispered. But they couldn't hear him.

"Enemy front!" one of the soldiers shouted. "Friendly! Friendly!"

Takeshi barely had time to raise his hands before the HMG opened up. Armor-piercing rounds tore into the ground around him, kicking up clouds of dirt and stone. He dove, rolled, scrambled—but they weren't aiming to kill, just keep him pinned. Like he was a rabid dog.

"NO!" Zhang's voice cracked like lightning. Then came the impossible. Zhang turned, Spitfire already in hand, and opened fire—not on Takeshi, but on the Shàng Jí.

Takeshi's breath caught as the lead heavy infantrymen collapsed in a heap. The others scrambled, yelling for orders. They did not understand what was happening.

Neither did Takeshi.

He lay on the ground, frozen, watching through the haze as Zhang unloaded into his own allies with cold fury.

That kind of firepower would not normally engage friendlies. Yu Jing firewalls locked you out—until they did not. Imperial Agents played by different rules.

Takeshi looked from the fallen soldier to the Crane Agent, and something inside him turned. This was not order. This was not unity.

This was chaos masquerading as control.

One by one, the Shàng Jí broke. Not in retreat—just in shock. Their commander stood frozen—weapon lowered—staring at Zhang like a man who did not understand the world anymore.

Takeshi slowly stood, every muscle taut.

His blade still laid where it had fallen, covered in blood and dirt—just like him.

He stepped toward it.

No one stopped him.

Not even Zhang.

44.

Takeshi was bleeding from three places—shoulder, hip, gut—and the alerts screamed red across his visor. Pain stabbed with every breath. His armor's medi-system deployed coagulants and pressure fields in a losing battle to stabilize him. Reinforcements crested the ridge—a pair of armored trucks. He was done.

Takeshi had seen executions before. Cold, calculated—orders given and followed. But not like this. Not mid-operation. Not in the middle of a live battlefield. Zhang was a madman. He'd disengaged his Friend/Foe safeties, something Takeshi did not even think was possible. The Spitfire still howled in his hands.

Takeshi forced himself to upright, gritting against the raw fire in his gut. Zhang faced him now, lowering his rifle—then tossing it aside like it was meaningless.

"You really are insane," Takeshi growled, half in awe, half in disgust.

Zhang said nothing.

A moment passed. The air between them was charged with violence, static, with unfinished history.

And then a voice cracked in his ear, warped by signal bleed but unmistakable.

"Hey, Neko! Looks like you could use a hand."

Takeshi froze.

No.

No, that was not possible. He was hallucinating—had to be. Blood loss was messing with his head. That voice was burned into his memory, not his comms.

"Slagghead knows how to leave a girl hanging," came the laugh, bright and real, over the commlink.

"Mizu?" he rasped.

"Loud and proud."

Takeshi spun, scanning for her—nothing but chaos. The Shàng Jí heavies repositioned. Zhang stood motionless. Smoke curled from the building and trees burning around him. Enemies everywhere—and still, that voice.

And then it happened.

Up the rise came a pair of trucks, barreling toward the drop team. One of them was new—too sleek, too fast. Its engine did not growl—it screamed.

The Shàng Jí—their lieutenant by his armor markings—turned, slow to react, dazed from betrayal. The truck did not stop. It did not swerve. It charged straight into him.

Or so it should have.

The body of the vehicle peeled apart like liquid steel. It swallowed him.

Takeshi saw it—watched it. He saw the man's body vanish inside the vortex of armored plating, holographic shimmer, and the roiling mass that did not truly exist. He blinked, and the Shàng Jí's head hit the ground five meters away from his legs.

He was not hallucinating.

She was here. And she was not alone.

* * * * *

Mizu's eyeballs burned. Not from the wind—though she was bareheaded—that was the easy part. It was the Serum. Two full shots of mil-grade stim yanked from a Yujingyu medikit twisted through her blood like wire. The first had fused bone. The second had flayed her from the inside out. She didn't scream.

She rode.

She was on Jon's stolen motorcycle, it had a cracked fuel cell and dented left stabilizer. It rattled when she leaned too hard and bucked like a pissed-off horse when she pushed the throttle past safe—fitting, painful. Every bump in the road reminded her of him—and how he'd left them.

She didn't have time to mourn the betrayal. Not yet.

Goro and Kairi were in the armored truck behind her, moving fast and low. Kairi was still hurting, half her ribs caved in, but she stayed sharp. Goro had dosed too, barely slowed. The truck roared like it wanted blood—maybe it did.

That's all Mizu needed.

She gunned it.

Tires screamed as she tore around the debris, pain and adrenaline in a cocktail that left her teeth grinding. Takeshi stood bleeding—barely upright. Shoulders dipped, armor slashed. But alive.

Her heart cracked seeing him like that—the noble warrior broken. He was like her—brought low.

Her hands stayed steady.

"Hey, Neko!" she shouted over comms, the connection ragged from interference. "Look like you could use a hand!"

She saw him flinch. Disbelief. Hope.

"Slagghead knows how to leave a girl hanging," she laughed.

Red soared past her, the Kuroshi Rider's black armor gleaming like oil and fire. She was a flash and roar of *bōsōzoku* and fury—a living, defiant piece of history coming to haunt the invaders. Her massive scythe spun in a perfect arc, carving through a retreating Shàng Jí like its heavy armor was simple cloth.

The illusion rippled and failed as she passed, breaking the Cybermask hard—Henzo's emitters shattered.

"Mizu?" Takeshi hoped.

They were exposed—no more ghosts, just vengeance.

"Loud and proud," she added, voice hard now.

The Crane Agent loomed as she flew by—her Combi Rifle blasting fury and pain. His blade rose to charge at Takeshi.

Goro never flinched. The truck veered sharply, armored flank catching the Crane's side with a bone-jarring crunch. The Imperial Agent was gone, hurled through the air like a kicked can—disappearing into a half-collapsed building. Dust exploded. Support beams folded.

That bastard would live—probably.

But it bought Neko a heartbeat to breathe.

Behind her, the truck swerved back into the road. Kairi popped the top hatch and brought her rifle to bear. Goro was a shadow behind the wheel. Silent. Focused. They were both burnt by loss, just like her.

Mizu leaned low on Jon's cycle, eyes narrowing as she clocked the last three Shàng Jí—scattered, panicked, leaderless, and running for the streets beyond. Not on her watch.

Mizu throttled forward, closing the distance.

Red peeled off left.

Kairi opened fire from above.

Goro spoke with the roar of the truck's engine.

And Mizu—Mizu bared her teeth, the wind screaming around

her, motorcycle snarling like it wanted revenge as bad as she did.

* * * * *

Takeshi rose, recovered blade in hand. He saw the biker with blue hair and immediately recognized Mizu. "She's alive."

His own words shocked him. It was something he rarely heard himself say. So many years of last stands had blinded him to the joy of… survival. Bringing anyone home was as good as myth for Takeshi.

From the wreckage, Zhang emerged, limping through the haze. His robes were shredded, his armor dented and powdered white from debris. Blood trickled between the plates, carving crimson lines through the grime. He worked one arm—testing an injury perhaps—but the other still gripped his blade.

He looked like something risen from a tomb—relentless, inevitable.

Zhang stopped five meters from Takeshi. Not charging. Not speaking. Just watching.

Some twisted sense of honor? Maybe. Or maybe he wanted Takeshi to feel the weight of what was coming. Either way, it bought Takeshi precious seconds to steady his stance, to quiet the alarms screaming across his lens.

Inhaling deeply, Takeshi stilled his rampaging heart. If he fought unbalanced, he would lose.

Takeshi's mother's trees blazed behind Zhang in a row.

"Neko!" Bianca called to him from the house, half carrying a beaten but alive Taka with the help of Prince Hasib. They were alive too! Bloodsoaked and missing an eye, Taka mouthed something that Takeshi's geist read across his lens.

///Kill that bastard.///

Zhang fumed at the interruption, drew his sidearm, and sprayed rounds at the survivors. They dove for cover.

Breathing ragged, shoulder on fire, Takeshi raised his weapon.

"You want me! Here I am!"

* * * * *

A shrill roar cut through the chaos. Bianca's eyes snapped toward the sound—too low-pitched for incoming aircraft. It wasn't another gunship.

It was a motorcycle—terrifyingly fast.

She caught only a glimpse at first—red frame, blue hair, and a familiar blur of motion clinging to it. A glint of chrome.

Mizu.

"Holy shit," Bianca breathed.

She gunned the bike out the courtyard entrance with a screech, vanishing around the far corner in pursuit of something. The warpath was etched in every muscle of her body, every subtle lean of the frame. She was going after the retreating Yujingyu. Whoever had run, they weren't going to make it far.

Bianca blinked, heart still racing, as her attention snapped back to Neko.

* * * * *

The assault shuttle roared overhead, its profile wide and ugly against the sky—exactly what Sparrow needed.

She—and Song—were already in position, kneeling in the clearing with rifles barking into the trees. To any eye above, they were Imperial Agents under siege. Desperate. Vulnerable.

Sparrow didn't flinch as the shuttle dropped toward them. She counted the seconds between the weapon burst and the thrumming descent of the armored beast. Timing was everything. Make it too clean, and it looked staged.

The shuttle slammed down with the grace of a falling brick, its HMG hammering blindly into the foliage beyond. The pilot thought he was a hero. Cute.

The moment the landing ramp touched earth, Sparrow bolted. Song moved with her, perfectly in sync, rifle lowered now, posture urgent but not panicked. Just enough wear on the act to be convincing. They vaulted up the ramp and into the belly of the shuttle, and before the wind had even settled behind them, the bird was climbing again.

Sparrow gave it three seconds, listening to the whine of acceleration. Then she moved to the blast door and banged once—sharp and deliberate.

The lock disengaged with a hiss.

"Welcome aboard, Agent. How may I be of—"

Two quick shots. Center mass. The pilot and his copilot slumped forward, limbs twitching once before going still. Autopilot functions took over immediately.

Song's Cybermask shimmered and fell away—revealing ice cold focus. They dumped the bodies out the back.

Sparrow slid into the still-warm pilot's seat and got to work. The firewall wasn't bad—two layers, maybe three—but she sliced through them like silk. Her fingers knew the rhythm, the muscle memory of old break-ins and stolen craft guiding her. Her perfectly legitimate Imperial Service ident gave her the Friend/Foe override they desperately needed.

"They've got automated distress calls now?!" Song said from the copilot seat, reading the data scrolling across her lens.

"Unfortunately," Sparrow muttered, eyes never leaving the console. She angled the shuttle hard—disengaging the autopilot—pulling it away from its return-to-base course and swinging it back toward Hansei. "Can you kill the transponder?"

"Working on it!"

The controls felt sluggish—like flying a freight ship through a swamp—but Sparrow adjusted. She would miss her old craft—the way it had responded like an extension of her own instincts. This one? This one growled and stomped like it hated being airborne. But it was armored and armed, and that would have to do.

She pinged the valley once with active scans, holding her breath. One blip. Then six. Then more.

"Shit," she whispered. "That's an armored column."

No time to play it safe. She nosed the shuttle down, fingers dancing across the stick, dragging the beast into a low, predatory glide.

"Hit that control for me," she said, pointing without looking.

Song didn't question. She tapped the holo switch, and the HMG controls lit up on Sparrow's lens. Both weapons slaved to her control.

Their stolen shuttle crested a hill, and Sparrow grinned.

"Time to return the favor."

With an ionized shriek, the HRMC came to life, and Sparrow bore down on the tanks like a falcon diving on prey.

45.

Mizu sat on her bike and surveyed the scene. The remaining Yujingyu heavies had consolidated in one place after collecting their dead. While that meant they were easier to spot, it also meant assaulting a hastily fortified position with overlapping fields of fire—shooting at everything that moved. Her Combi—Jon's Combi—hadn't scratched their armor.

The building was a single story set into a row of other homes. That gave her crew no good options.

"What's the plan, Boss?" Goro's voice piped over comms.

"Honestly, I have no idea."

A second bike slid into place next to her silently. The Kuroshi Rider sat up and looked at Mizu. Her wicked polearm was in a folded configuration and latched to her back. It was definitely a she, that much Mizu could tell. Red's left arm was entirely synthetic, its working spreading up over her shoulder and back. Familiarity clawed in the back of her mind.

"Any ideas?"

Red looked back at her, tinted visor revealing nothing while her hands spoke. *Assault. Smoke. Two-pronged.*

Mizu had given up being surprised at this point and slashed *Affirmative*. "Follow Red's lead."

Red kicked her motor on and gunned it. As soon as she banked into the street, a mounted Smoke Grenade Launcher began to fire. Mizu watched Red rapidly fire seven smoke canisters downrange and caught on to what she was doing. They wouldn't be able to see through the smoke—but neither could the Yujingyu. The front of the building was a visual deadzone, that left the back—

Mizu hit the ignition and peeled out, turning to flank through the alley.

Her hunch paid off as she heard more than saw two Shàng Jí crash through the back door of the building—chasing the sound of her bike—taking defensive positions. She throttled over hard, bouncing off the alley wall, and gave chase. She drew her Light Shotgun and held it close as she rapidly closed.

The Shàng Jí saw her. One turned to fire while the other flipped his wrist. Mizu saw the holographic sigils—hacker. Shots skipped off her bike's composite armor.

She sat up as she rode, trusting the wounded bike to keep her steady, and suddenly she was between them. Shotgun in one hand and comlog opening her hacking programs in the other.

This was bliss.

Mizu's laughter was feral.

She fired both simultaneously. The lighter shotgun—shoved in the neck seal of the first warrior, launched his headless corpse backward. Mizu watched the hacker seize and twitch violently in her mirror as her Trinity struck home, the program fried his brain from inside the helmet. The close range didn't matter for hacking, but the thrill of tapping his helmet as she blasted by—now that was something she could be proud of.

There was no shake, no rush of fear and addiction.

Mizu was free.

A third trooper crashed into view, firing as she ripped his friends. The shot holed her tire, and Mizu scrambled to keep her bike balanced as she thundered down the alley, out of control. The blown tire was reinforced, but that meant little to Armor-Piercing ammo. The bike shuttered and skipped as she fought to slow, bouncing off the alley wall, knocking her off balance.

This time she bailed at a much slower speed than she had in the tunnels—thankfully. She hit hard, shoulder-first, and rolled behind a stack of forgotten garbage bins.

The heavy trooper came after her, combat knife drawn, closing in with merciless intent.

Mizu looked for her weapons, but they were all out of reach. She stood, crouched low, ready to take him on with her bare hands if necessary.

A side street opening separated them.

As the trooper stepped into it, a Yujingyu armored truck barreled into him, smashing him into the wall. The sound was sickening. Mizu flinched, then exhaled when she saw Kairi and Goro rattled but alive inside the vehicle. Rapidly dissolving impact foam covered their forms as they disembarked.

The soldier somehow still moved, dragging himself from the twisted wreckage.

"Kuso," Mizu breathed.

She watched Goro and Kairi level their weapons and fire shot after shot, faces cold as steel, until their enemy stopped moving.

"Three down," Mizu gasped. "Three more to go. Where's Red?"

In the next moment, a window exploded outward in a flash of sparks. A fourth Shàng Jí was flung through it like a ragdoll, hitting the ground in a heap—his armor smoking. Red followed out the window a heartbeat later, her polearm arcing in a savage sweep that sent a fifth soldier's head and helmet tumbling into the street.

"Five," Mizu muttered. She limped to her feet—pain flaring in her hip and shoulder—and recovered her Combi.

The last Shàng Jí burst from the building, firing wildly at Red, who dove and rolled to cover. He was in full retreat—panicking.

That was a mistake.

Kairi popped the back of the truck and tossed Mizu a Panzerfaust they had salvaged from one of the other trucks. Mizu swung it up, aimed at the soldier, and fired without hesitation. The final soldier vanished in a cloud of shrapnel, smoke, and fire.

"Six."

The street fell silent.

Mizu leaned on the bumper to keep herself upright, and her shoulders started shaking. It was infectious. The three Hands cracked up, half from relief, half from shock, the kind of laugh that only came after you stared death down and spit in its face.

It wasn't joy exactly. But it was life. And it felt good.

Red turned toward Mizu and signed something quickly.

Mizu blinked. "That means *get in the damn truck*, right?"

Red gave a short nod and jogged over. Kairi and Goro were already climbing back into the cab. Mizu, limping, looked back once at the bodies in the alley—smoking armor, blood on the walls.

She climbed into the truck, flopping into the back seat.

"Let's go," she said. "There's nothing left for us here."

Goro peeled out before the doors even closed. The tires screamed as they roared off to the others—toward whatever mess came next. Red stood on the back step, one hand on the frame, the other gripping her scythe like a war flag.

Mizu rested her head back against the cabin wall, Combi across her lap.

This time, no shake. No nightmares clawing at the edge.

* * * * *

Bianca's back was pressed to a cracked wall, her breathing shallow, heart drumming loud in her ears. Prince Hasib cowered beside her, bumbling and useless. Taka covered their rear while Song and Sparrow were nowhere to be seen. Rubble shifted near her boots, and the air was thick with smoke and the tang of scorched metal. But it was the sound of steel on steel that kept her rooted—drawn, even. She turned toward it, eyes wide.

Neko—Takeshi—was a storm of motion in the courtyard. His coat was torn, blood soaking through at least three points along his side and shoulder, but he barely seemed to feel it. He moved like a force of nature, sword held in a brutal two-handed grip, every strike driven by a quiet, terrifying resolve. His blade crashed against his foe's, ringing out like a funeral bell.

The Yujingyu warrior danced around him with a deadly grace, his polished orange armor gleaming even through the smoke, helmet flashing like the carapace of a poisonous insect. He was fast—blindingly fast—darting in and out, trying to find a weakness. To Bianca, it looked like a hornet battering against stone. And Takeshi was the stone, immovable and cold—inevitable.

They clashed again, blades shrieking. Sparks flew. Neko caught the agent's wrist and twisted, forcing a retreat. He didn't let up. Bianca watched him press forward like a hammer on an anvil, each strike driving the Crane back, his wounded body ignoring pain through sheer will. One step. Another. Then—

A sharp sidestep. Takeshi let the agent slide past him, then surged forward and drove a knee into the warrior's side. The impact was audible. The Crane stumbled. Neko slammed into him with his shoulder a heartbeat later, sending the armored figure crashing to the ground.

Bianca nearly cheered, her knuckles white on her pistol grip. He was winning.

But the Crane rolled with the fall, fluid and furious, springing back to his feet like a coiled spring. He came on again, silent and deadly.

The Crane Agent had recovered fully now, weapon raised once more. The dance was about to begin again. Bianca wanted to scream for

Takeshi to fall back, to rest, to survive—but she knew better. This was his moment.

And she had never been more terrified. She recorded it all.

* * * * *

Takeshi stood firm as Zhang leapt back to his feet, dust trailing from his armor, joints hissing like steam valves under pressure. The Yujingyu was ferocious and unrelenting, a force given human shape. Their first duel flashed through Takeshi's mind like a reflexive nightmare—the blinding pain, the near loss of his hand. He could still feel the phantom snap of bone and tendon, the way the blade kissed wrist.

Now, it didn't haunt him. It focused him.

Zhang lunged, aiming a precise cut at Takeshi's ribs, but Takeshi twisted aside and slipped in close, slamming a fist into the Crane Agent's faceplate. Metal rang like a cracked bell. Then another hit—*bam*—and another—*bam*! Takeshi's reinforced gauntlet crushed into Zhang's visor until it splintered, spiderweb cracks dancing across the polarized surface. Alert pings screamed in Takeshi's optics, warning of pressure damage to his own gauntlet, but he didn't stop until Zhang reeled backward, stunned.

The Yujingyu staggered, then tore his helmet free with a snarl. His face was a ruin—nose broken, cheek torn open, one eye red with blood. Yet even bloodied, he looked more alive than before. Eyes burning with hatred, teeth bared in a snarl, Zhang roared and charged.

Takeshi braced for impact.

Zhang's blade came in fast, a blur of trained violence—sweeping slashes meant to test and batter Takeshi's guard. He parried low, caught the next on his shoulder plate, and ducked the third entirely, feeling the wind of it pass his ear. Zhang's rhythm changed constantly—one moment calculated, the next wild.

But Takeshi didn't yield.

He grounded his stance, letting Zhang crash against him like waves on rock. He blocked a rising slash with his forearm, wincing as the blade glanced off and scored his armor. Another came in tight toward his neck. Takeshi ducked, rolled his shoulder, and caught Zhang in the ribs with a short elbow that drove the air from his lungs.

Still Zhang came on.

Another exchange—steel rang on steel, blows broke against armor. Takeshi slipped a hook under Zhang's guard, but the Crane Agent countered with a brutal knee to his thigh. Takeshi stumbled. Pain flared. His injuries were beginning to sing now, each one a note in the rising chorus of fatigue.

Zhang smelled it. Pressed his advantage.

The blade whipped toward Takeshi's knee—he barely turned in time. Another feint high, then a boot to the gut. Takeshi staggered, breath stolen. His vision blinked for half a second.

He grit his teeth. No.

With a cry, he drove forward, pistoning into Zhang with raw force, nearly lifting the man off the ground. They tumbled into the burning husk of a tree, staggered apart, then circled again like predators testing each other's limits.

Takeshi breathed hard, sweat dripping into his eyes. Blood trickled from his side. His leg was sluggish, his strikes not as sharp.

Zhang grinned—blood staining his teeth. "You're slowing."

"So are you," Takeshi growled.

Zhang struck again and again. He was ferocious, determined. What would drive a man to such heights?

Takeshi pushed such thoughts from his mind and focused on the fight.

One cut.

Zhang stepped in and thrust. Takeshi blocked and pressed forward with a slash across his armor.

Focus.

It all felt familiar, the song of blades between them. The ring of reinforced steel echoed through the air. Takeshi could hear the rain. Thunder crackled in his mind as they fought on the island once more.

Takeshi took stock of his injuries, the compromised portions of his armor. There was no silent resignation for him this time, only the same grim smile that crept across his face. He smiled at death but did not welcome its song, not today.

The pause in combat hung like an unearthly silence as his comrades gathered around, watching. With unspoken consent, Takeshi and Zhang collided once more and fought to survive. Strike after strike they warred across the ruins of his mother's garden. Two masters, each searching for an advantage.

Blades flashed. Two warriors striking relentlessly. A dozen moves flowed flawlessly from each warrior's mind to his heart to his blade as they met amidst the ruins of his home.

Seeing a fatal opening in Zhang's guard, Takeshi struck. It was a perfect killing strike. Left foot forward, balanced across both hips, blade extended to meet the horizon. A flawless rising cut. Perfection. A lifetime of precision, practice, and skill arced his blade at his opponent's neck—but he was not there.

Just like before—on the island—Zhang sidestepped the strike. Takeshi watched the Yujingyu's blade descend once more, darting for his wrist. It was a flawless move, perfection. There was no way he could twist and block with his sword in time.

When you have to fight, fight to win.

Taka's voice echoed through his mind, and Takeshi finally understood what he meant. Takeshi released his blade, letting it fall to the ground.

One cut at a time.

He grabbed Zhang's chestplate with one hand and clamped down on his sword hand—under the guard—with the other. Zhang's perfect balance was ruined—on one foot for the strike—giving Takeshi all the advantage he needed.

He stepped in, suddenly intimately close. Zhang lost all leverage, blade skipping off Takeshi's armored shoulder. Zhang tried to break the embrace, but Takeshi's grip was a vice on his soul.

Takeshi roared as he drove his forehead into Zhang's nose.

There was blood.

More and more blood blossomed from Zhang's face.

Pain lanced through Takeshi's head. His vision blurred, but he did not let go.

Twice more he used his own skull and smashed Zhang's face into bloody ruin. Both warriors stumbled as they parted.

One cut.

Takeshi drew his second blade and stepped forward—a perfect strike.

Flawless.

His E/M katana cleaved through Zhang's armored frame and tore open his chest. The masterwork blade passed easily through armor, flesh, and ribs. Zhang spasmed as his nervous system overloaded with electromagnetic feedback while the charred contents of his chest leaked through sundered plate.

Takeshi stumbled.

The world swam.

Blood poured from his head in sheets.

He smiled and the ground rushed up.

46.

They were still reeling when the armored assault shuttle cut through the smoke, descending hard into the clearing.

Bianca's jaw slackened. "No way—"

Song's voice crackled in their ears. "Get on, now!"

Bianca could see Song in the shuttle's open door and didn't wait for further explanation. None of them did. Prince Hasib was the first to scramble aboard, panicked.

She ran to where Neko lay prone—slick with blood and barely responsive—and with help from Mizu and the strange woman in the crimson helmet, they half-dragged, half-carried him toward the waiting shuttle. He mumbled something slurred, incoherent. One eye was swollen shut. The other barely tracked the movement of his rescuers.

"Easy, Neko," Bianca whispered, brushing blood from his cheek. "You're not done yet."

Together, they hefted him aboard. Mizu's crew followed, minus one. The loss hung in the air, unspoken. With them came a woman no one recognized—but everyone avoided questioning. The red helmet, the aura of death around her—Bianca had heard the stories. The Kuroshi Rider. Some said she was a ghost, a curse, vengeance given form.

And yet here she was, helping to fasten Neko into a combat harness without a word.

As they latched the last strap, Sparrow's warning echoed from the pilot seat. "Hang on!"

The shuttle roared back into the sky, inertia throwing them toward the deck. Bianca barely made it into a jumpseat as the shuttle screamed westward, engines burning hot.

Taka grabbed Song's arm. "Where's Hiro?"

Song's eyes drifted to the ground, and she shook her head before returning to the flight deck.

"Shit," Taka muttered. He glanced at Mizu while taking a seat. "And you must be the Aragoto. You look like hell."

Mizu snorted—challenging. "You're missing half a face. Are you sure that's a fight you want to pick?"

Bianca glanced between them and shook her head. They all looked terrible—soaked in blood, dirt, exhaustion. But somehow, Taka managed a broken-tooth grin.

"You should see the other guy."

Goro burst into laughter, breaking the tension.

The shuttle banked hard, killing the levity. A deep mechanical growl echoed through the hull—then the Hyper-Rapid Magnetic Cannon lit up. The view outside flared with explosions. Taka tapped a control and pulled up a tac-feed on a holoplane, showing Bianca the devastation below. JSA gear left behind—bikes, remotes, anything and everything—each target zeroed and erased from the landscape.

"Overkill?" Bianca asked quietly.

"Insurance," Taka said, eyes cold.

"Wait… who's flying this thing?" Mizu's voice was sharp, head swiveling toward the cockpit.

"That would be our one and only Sparrow," Taka answered, smirking as if that explained everything. "Sparrow! Come say hi!"

The shuttle leveled off. A moment later, the cockpit hatch hissed open once more, and a tall, narrow figure emerged—wearing the bloodstained armor of a Pheasant Rank Imperial Agent.

Mizu's eyes widened. "You?!"

Sparrow gave a polite nod. "*Hai.*"

Before more could be said, Song called out. "We have incoming!"

Sparrow turned to look down at Neko—barely conscious, chest heaving shallowly against the harness. "Strap him tighter. You don't want him to go flying."

They moved as one, securing every strap. Bianca held his hand just long enough to feel the weak squeeze of fingers in return. Still fighting.

As she dropped back into her seat, Sparrow returned to the cockpit without ceremony, voice cool as ice. "Brace yourselves."

Their shuttle dove again—into fire, into danger—but with all of them finally together. Almost all.

Alive. For now.

* * * * *

Yasbir waited patiently as silence fell over the valley like a burial shroud. Faint trails of smoke curled upward in the dying light, heat haze shimmering over scorched earth below. From his vantage—where he and Nakama had once shared tea between kill orders and silence—he had watched the battle unfold, a slow unraveling of desperation and precision.

Now, it was done. Prince Hasib was away, safe for now. And Yasbir's true prize was secured in the forest behind him. He was, as ever, in the margins, the quiet shadow waiting for the proper moment to reemerge.

It was not his place to interfere. Not yet.

Footsteps approached—quiet, measured. As expected, Nakama arrived.

What Yasbir had not expected was that the Oniwaban carried the body of another warrior across his shoulders. The form was limp, armor shredded, and blood caked Nakama's form from carrying him. He reached the edge of the small glade, knelt, and lowered the man with care—as if handling something sacred.

Yasbir's gaze sharpened as he recognized the Ryuken from the mission files. "That one looks horrible."

"Hiro is not dead yet," Nakama said evenly. "I would not carry a corpse, friend-of-mine."

Yasbir crouched beside the wounded man. Pale. Slick with blood. Eyes fluttering with shallow breath. "Hmm. You're certain he's not dead?"

"He said I was 'insufferably late' before he blacked out."

Yasbir allowed a smile. "Then I'll see what I can do."

The two assassins moved through the trees together, slipping between root and fern, old instinct guiding their steps. A half-buried cave mouth stood ahead—no more than a natural hollow rimmed with overgrowth. Yasbir knelt, brushed aside a camouflage tarp, and keyed a thin device at the base of the outcropping.

The rock shimmered, vanishing.

A sleek, matte-black shuttle blinked into view, folding out of active stealth protocols. No markings. No emissions. No trace of its presence in any public registry. The kind of ship that didn't fly as much as *vanish.*

Nakama raised an eyebrow. "Subtle."

"You see why I wanted it, yes?" Yasbir said. "Help me lift him."

Together they carried Hiro inside. The interior was tight—built for function, not comfort. Yasbir activated the onboard auto-doc, scanning Hiro. Bio-readouts flared to life in red and orange. Internal bleeding. Cracked ribs. Blood pressure collapsing.

"He needs stabilizers. Coagulant mesh. And about three weeks of sleep." Yasbir rolled up his sleeves, his tone clinical. "I'll start with the first two."

Nakama watched as his friend worked—precise fingers moving deftly in time with the articulated arms that unfolded from the bulkhead. For all the Hassassin's misdirection and flair in the field, here, in the quiet hum of the shuttle, he moved like a physician.

"Can you fly this craft?" Yasbir asked, not looking up.

"Yes," Nakama said.

"Then you'll need to. I won't leave his care to an auto-system."

"Thank you, friend-of-mine." Nakama nodded once and slipped into the pilot's seat.

"We'll need to go low, and we'll need to go quiet." Yasbir turned away from the Oniwaban and focused on his task.

"I will thread the wind."

The shuttle lifted like a ghost, the camouflage cloak folding once more around its skin as it vanished into the sky.

47.

///...wish to convey our gratitude. This courageous act by the men and women of the Japanese Secessionist Army have returned our honored Prince...///

Bianca read the press release and rolled her eyes. It was the typical non-committal public statement she expected out of the Funduq Sultinate. They were backed into a corner when she released her story on Maya.

Between Yasbir and her agent, she had plenty of encouragement to release the piece. She definitely would never be able to go back to Yujingyu space, but that suited her just fine. There were enough stories, enough planets—it was a pretty big Sphere after all, and only getting bigger.

She closed the screen. The stars were out tonight. It was an odd sensation to be completely relaxed, it made this island all the more special in her mind. She'd never been to Japan before now, but she was grateful to be here.

She sipped her drink and refilled her companion's.

Since the moment Sparrow took off Su-Yeong's mask, she had been changed. Gone was the menace. Gone was the disdain for others. Sparrow's eyes were welcoming and warm.

Bianca felt safe with Sparrow. It was not something she was used to or had expected.

Steam rose around them in their secluded hot spring retreat high in the mountains of Japan. It was a much needed vacation for them both, and a chance to finally meet without the looming threat of death. One thing led to another. Whether it was just burning through pent up energy or something else, it became something quite memorable. Bianca knew it was coming to an end.

"So, where will the famous Warcor Bianca Chen go next?"

Bianca thought for a moment. "Actually, I have no idea. My agent is begging me to get to Concillium again. Something about a Combined-Concullium reconstruction effort but it sounds..."

"Boring?"

"Yep." Bianca laughed. She wasn't made for the quiet life.

"What about you?"

"Actually, I will be leaving tomorrow." Sparrow rose from the spring, her naked body silhouetted in the full moonlight as she toweled off.

Bianca had to admit she was beautiful without all the Yujingyu armor and blood around her, and she sighed. If only… "Somewhere special?"

"All good things end in time, Bianca." Sparrow smiled.

"Fair enough."

Sparrow wasn't made for a quiet life, but neither was she.

"I will tell you this bit for free." Sparrow knelt and cupped Bianca's chin, kissing her one last time. "Listen for the name Shinju, Miss Chen. It will be important very soon."

Bianca watched Sparrow leave. She made a note to look up Shinju later, but for now, it was just her and the stars.

* * * * *

Mizu let the road tell her how to ride as she wound through the star-lit highway. It was a beautiful night. The wind whipped by her, gliding over her coat and helmet. Behind her, Goro tucked into her draft, while the rest followed their lead. In the bend, she could see Kairi bringing up the rear, like a mother hen watching her flock.

It had taken some doing, some help from Song and Neko both, but they all rode beautiful new motorcycles. It was nothing compared to the thunderous machines they had just ridden into battle, but it was freedom. The younger crew all caught on quickly. Riding the highways of Japan was definitely not the same as riding for your life under fire, but they all treated it just as seriously and listened to what they were taught.

Mizu thought back to the offer she received from Oban command. Training the next generation of Aragoto had its appeal. She would be younger than some recruits, but already rumors were spreading about her Hands and what they accomplished. It had been all over the net since Bianca's story got out.

That was a problem for tomorrow; tonight was for her Hands.

She saw the lights before the bar came into view. Mizu slowed early, guiding the pack into the lot as non-threateningly as possible. This wasn't her turf, the last thing they needed was a confrontation the first night out. She led the way, parking and dismounting ahead of her Hands as they glided in next to her. Tot could barely reach the ground, but he managed not to drop his ride when he parked.

So far so good.

Eyes locked onto them the second they rolled in. Colorful jackets on colorful characters craned their necks to see who was coming in. Half a dozen hardened riders stood and approached them immediately. Goro squared up next to her without hesitation. He stood a head taller than most of them.

The Hands' new red jackets were freshly embroidered with their precious *San* on the back. Mizu, Goro, and Kairi also bore the colors of the Kuraimori Guard, Aragoto Regiment on one sleeve.

One last thing set them apart—something priceless to Mizu. Strapped across their backs were beautiful, new katanas—gifted to them by Neko and his family.

The rough looking riders scanned them up and done, eyes searching for strength, for weakness—searching for a challenge.

"You have something to say, slagghead?" Mizu stepped up to the leader. The next heartbeat seemed to drag on for eternity.

"Kuraimori Aragoto?" He nodded his stubbly chin at the patch proudly displayed on her jacket.

She nodded back.

"Seen you on the news."

Mizu expected this. It was now or never. "And?"

"I want to buy you a drink." His smile was crooked and ugly, but it was real. So was the cheer that rose from the crowd. "That was some slagg'n incredible riding."

The crowd roared.

The Hands were quickly ushered inside and drinks thrust into their hands. Most of them looked dumbfounded, being too young to have experienced this on Kuraimori before the war.

The bar felt just like the Steel Saké inside. Memorabilia spread across the walls, commemorating heroes and idiots, crews come and gone.

The bartender waved her over.

"Shakeout." He slid a shot in front of her and pointed. "The Queen sends her regards."

Following his gaze, Mizu saw her. Across the room, seated in a dim corner, was a red-haired woman with a metal arm holding a shot glass high.

"Loud and proud," Mizu whispered, raised her glass, and smiled.

* * * * *

Takeshi walked alone in the garden. It was a beautiful night and the full moon was high. It felt good to be back in Japan, if only for a little while. Things had calmed down since the pageantry of their return. He smiled, thinking about how angry Mizu had been when the Imperial house staff met them in orbit and insisted she wear a kimono for the ceremony. Surprisingly, Mizu won that fight, but only after he had intervened. Such displays were something Takeshi was used to, but the rest of them shied away quickly.

Song was ecstatic when they learned Hiro had survived. The pair vanished before planetfall. Nakama and Sparrow were gone long before that. Their faces—and Yasbir's—were scrubbed from Bianca's footage, despite her protests.

In the end, it had been Bianca, Taka, and Mizu who joined him to meet the Emperor. Taka somehow made his Kempeitai uniform utterly terrifying with an eye patch—an intentional choice on his part.

Tonight, Takeshi enjoyed the moonlight and the solitude, finding himself in the gardens looking up at Mount Gassan once again.

"Takeshi-sama."

He had not heard Nakama approach, not that that particular fact surprised him at this point. Takeshi did not find him any less threatening out of his combat gear. The Oniwaban wore simple monk robes once again and Takeshi wondered how he had ever seemed so forgettable.

"Good evening, Nakama. To what do I owe the pleasure?"

"It is a beautiful night. Need I a reason to visit beyond that?"

"It is indeed." Takeshi let it go.

"You look good in your father's haori."

Takeshi smiled. He had the garment restored upon his return home and wore it often, especially on nights like this.

"Have you enjoyed your leave?"

"I have." Takeshi nodded and closed his eyes. The wind breathing through the trees was the most peaceful sound he knew. It reminded him of the mountains of Kuraimori. He thought of walking through the woods with his father as a child. Takeshi smiled and opened his eyes.

Nakama eyed the swords at Takeshi's waist. "They are exquisite."

Takeshi gripped the hilt. "Indeed they are. I have never held their equal."

"Blades are often named by warriors or smiths for their qualities, or for their deeds. My master wonders if you have named the blades he has given you."

There it was. The reason.

"I have. I think you will approve. *Shi no Uta*." Takeshi smiled.

"Beautiful." Nakama's voice was a fading whisper beside him.

Takeshi took in the night sky and all its promise, letting the moment linger. "It is indeed: Death Song."

Shi no Uta

Death Song

Author's Note

Hey there, thanks so much for reading! Death Song has been quite the ride for me—full of long days and late nights, caffeine and dubstep fueled writing sessions, and a whole lot of fun. I hope you enjoyed following the characters and the twists as much as I enjoyed creating them.

This is the part where I'm supposed to thank a ton of people, right? This all started because I opened my damn mouth to a fellow nerd at an Adepticon panel. That nerd wound up being Brandon Rospond, my editor. One thing led to another and here we are—admittedly it took me a while to get out of my own way. Thank you Brandon for believing in me.

My darling wife, who put up with my insufferable artistic insecurities, is the real champion here. Thank you my love.

There is also Chris "What's your ARO?" McClure who got me into the game of Infinity. Then of course Kittenmarines, Deboe, and Bloodthorn—I promise they are real people and not at all made up in the slightest. They dealt with me constantly shotgunning ideas at them, horrific drafts, and speed run beta reading sessions. Thank you, gents. We will round out my cheerleading section with a pirate named Vinny, my brother north of the wall, a weirdo named Savant, Max from Corvus Belli, and my mother (of course). Hi Mah!

Also, also… I wanted to be as respectful to Japanese culture and their beautiful language as possible. Thank you Masato-san for making sure I didn't make too much of a fool of myself.

In all seriousness, I like to say I'm a storyteller at heart. Stories are what bring us together. They inspire and entertain us. Stories teach us who we are. A lot of this story comes from things that fascinated me—world-building, action (who doesn't love ninjas?), or the messy emotions (and traumas) that drive people. I hope you found something in Neko, Mizu, and the rest that felt real or got you thinking. They are as dear to me as the totally real humans I listed before.

If you want to chat about the book or have questions, feel free to reach out. I'm always excited to hear from readers. Thanks again for tagging along on this adventure. Hope you find something in these pages that sticks with you.

-Gabriel Miller

INFINITY
DOWNFALL
MARK BARBER
INFINITY

TEAM ZED:
SHELL GAME
CRAIG GALLANT
INFINITY

CHRONICLES OF THE HUMAN SPHERE
AIRAGHARDT
JOHN LEIBEE

CHRONICLES OF THE HUMAN SPHERE
BY FIRE AND SWORD
MARK BARBER

INFINITY - THE GAME

Infinity is a miniatures game by Corvus Belli simulating special operations and skirmishes in a high technology sci-fi universe; an exciting and action-packed near-future where secret missions, black ops, and covert actions determine the destiny of Humankind.

Infinity boasts innovative and dynamic rules that keep both players engaged and participating throughout the entire game sequence.

With that philosophy, Essentials was born, the basic line of products that guides the player step by step through the fundamental elements and mechanics of the game: weapons, attacks, rolls, troops, skills and much more.

In addition, it includes a series of explanatory videos to make learning more intuitive and practical.

In the Human Sphere you can inhabit different human and alien factions fighting each other for power.

Choose yours and bring it to the battlefield - the game Infinity!